The *New York Times* b̲e̲s̲t̲s̲e̲l̲l̲i̲n̲g̲ of *Otherwise Engaged* and *The Mys̲t̲e̲r̲y̲...* of intrigue and murder Victorian London.

The Kern Secretarial Agency provides reliable professional services to its wealthy clientele, and Anne Clifton was one of the finest young women in Ursula Kern's employ. But Miss Clifton has met an untimely end—and Ursula is convinced it was not due to natural causes.

Bent on justice, Ursula hatches a plan: take Anne's place as stenographer to the reclusive poet Valerie, Lady Fulbrook. There are dark rumors about Lord Fulbrook, and his gloomy mansion in Mapstone Square seems the logical starting point for an undercover investigation.

Archaeologist and adventurer Slater Roxton thinks Mrs. Kern is off her head to meddle in such dangerous business. But if this mysterious widowed beauty insists on stirring the pot, Slater intends to remain close by as they venture into the darker side of polite society and a den of iniquity called the Olympus Club. Together they must reveal the identity of a killer—and to achieve their goal, they may need to reveal their deepest secrets to each other as well . . .

"Quick's fans will not be disappointed in her latest combination of detective story and sexy romance, a pleasing page-turner."
—*Kirkus Reviews*

"With sassy wit, a mystical touch and delectable sensuality, Quick sweeps readers into another delightful, humor-drenched escapade that is sure to leave fans smiling and satisfied."
—*Library Journal*

"The details of the story's setting in Victorian London are impeccable, and the hero and heroine are honorable, daring and sharply intelligent. The secondary characters aren't just flimsy foils, either; they add charm and humor to the tale, and the mystery plot is cleverly detailed, forming a most satisfactory labyrinth of clues."
—*BookPage.com*

Titles by Jayne Ann Krentz writing as Jayne Castle

GARDEN

OF LIES

AMANDA QUICK

JOVE
New York

A JOVE BOOK
Published by Berkley
An imprint of Penguin Random House LLC
375 Hudson Street, New York, New York 10014

Copyright © 2015 by Jayne Ann Krentz
Excerpt from 'Til Death Do Us Part by Amanda Quick copyright © 2015 by Jayne Ann Krentz
Penguin Random House supports copyright. Copyright fuels creativity, encourages
diverse voices, promotes free speech, and creates a vibrant culture. Thank you for buying
an authorized edition of this book and for complying with copyright laws by not
reproducing, scanning, or distributing any part of it in any form without permission.
You are supporting writers and allowing Penguin Random House to continue to
publish books for every reader.

A JOVE BOOK and BERKLEY are registered trademarks and the B colophon
is a trademark of Penguin Random House LLC.

ISBN: 9780515156065

G. P. Putnam's Sons hardcover edition / April 2015
Jove mass-market edition / April 2016

Printed in the United States of America
3   5   7   9   11   12   10   8   6   4

Cover photographs: Victorian manor © Perspectives / Getty Images; maze © dieKleinert /
Alamy; close-up of antique typewriter © Tetra Images / Getty Images

GARDEN
OF LIES

PROLOGUE

~~~~~

Slater Roxton was examining the strangely luminous paintings on the wall of the ornate burial
chamber when the tomb trap was triggered.

Impending destruction was telegraphed in an ominous rumble and the aching groan of ancient machinery locked deep in the stone. His first thought
was that the volcano that loomed over Fever Island
was erupting. But one by one, massive sections of the
ceiling of the passageway that led to the entrance of
the temple complex slid open. Boulders rained down.

Brice Torrence's voice echoed from the far end of
the corridor near the entrance.

*"Slater, get out of there. Hurry. Something terrible is
happening."*

Slater was already moving. He did not waste time
collecting the lanterns, his sketches or the camera.
He ran to the doorway of the chamber but when he

looked into the long, twisting stone corridor that led to the entrance he saw at once that it was too late to escape.

More sections of the corridor ceiling slid open as he watched. Countless tons of the terrible hail crashed into the passage. The stones piled up rapidly, filling the tunnel. He knew that if he tried to make a dash to safety he would be crushed beneath the falling rocks. He had no choice but to turn back and retreat deeper into the unexplored maze of the tomb caverns.

He rushed across the chamber, grabbed the lanterns and headed into the nearest adjoining passage. The corridor twisted away into dense, unexplored night but no boulders rained down from above.

He ran a short distance into the passage and stopped, aware that if he went deeper he would soon get lost. He and Brice had not even begun to chart the complex of burial caves carved into the base of the volcano.

He hunkered down against one wall, bracing himself. The glary light of the lantern illuminated an eerie painting, a scene depicting an ancient, catastrophic eruption of a volcano. Destruction rained down on an elegant city built of white marble. It was, Slater thought, far too close to what was happening at that moment.

Clouds of dust wafted down the tunnel. He covered his mouth and nose with his shirt.

There was nothing for it but to wait for the thundering to stop. Dread swirled like acid through his veins. At any moment the ceiling of the cavern in which he was sheltering might give way, burying him in the rubble. At least it would all be over in seconds, he thought. He was not sure he wanted to contemplate his immediate future if he did survive. For whatever time he had left he would be trapped in a brilliantly engineered maze.

The storm of rock and stone seemed to go on forever. But eventually the temple caves fell silent. It was another eternity before the dust finally settled.

Warily, he got to his feet. He stood still for a moment, listening to the shattering silence, waiting for his pulse to calm. After a while he went to look out into the vaulted chamber in which he had been standing when the rock trap released its deadly cargo. Small stones littered the floor of the room but it appeared that they had bounced and rolled into the chamber from the massive heap that now sealed the passage that led back to the entrance.

He had survived, which meant that he was now entombed alive.

He began to calculate his odds in a surprisingly academic fashion. He concluded that he was still too shaken to absorb the enormity of his predicament.

There was no reason for Brice and the rest of the expedition team to believe that he had survived; nothing they could do to save him, even if they had some hope. Fever Island was an uninhabited chunk of volcanic rock covered in unexplored jungle. It was situated a few thousand miles from civilization.

The only resources available were limited to the supplies and equipment on board the ship anchored in the island's small, natural harbor. There was no way to acquire the machinery and the manpower required to remove the vast quantity of rock that clogged the temple entrance.

Brice would consult with the ship's captain, Slater thought. They would conclude that he was dead and they would pray that it was true because there was nothing they could do to save him.

He put out one of the lanterns to conserve the fuel. Holding aloft the second lantern, he started walking into the maze. There were, he decided, only two possibilities. The first—and most likely—was that he would wander in the temple complex until he died. He could only hope that death would come before the never-ending darkness drove him mad.

The second possibility—extremely remote—was that he might blunder into a passage that would take him outside into the sunlight. But even if he was so fortunate, it was unlikely that he would be able to find his way back to the ship before it sailed. They had been running low on supplies when they finally found the damned island after being thrown off course by a violent storm. The captain was convinced that another tempest was on the way. He would want to start the return trip to London as soon as possible. He had to think of his crew and the other men on the expedition.

Slater knew that if he managed to escape the maze he would find himself stranded on an island that was not a regular port of call for any known vessel. It could be years before another ship arrived, if ever.

He walked on into the night-bound caverns, his only guide the temple paintings left behind by the artists of an ancient civilization that had long ago been buried beneath rivers of molten lava.

He did not know exactly when he began to understand the meaning of the paintings, if, indeed, he actually did perceive the intent of the stories. He reminded himself that there was a very good possibility that he was already slipping into madness. The eternal darkness and the mesmerizing artwork were disorienting. A man in his situation could easily begin to hallucinate.

But eventually he thought he detected three distinct legends. He stopped when it dawned on him that each tale was a different path into the maze. One series of paintings depicted a tale of war. The second was a story of vengeance.

In the end he chose the third legend.

He never knew how long he walked or how far. At times he stopped, exhausted, and sank into a slumber that was splintered with images from the wall paintings that were his only guide. Occasionally he stumbled across small underground streams. He stopped to drink deeply from them. He tried to make the cheese and bread in his pack last but eventually they were gone.

He kept walking because there was nothing else to do. To stop would be an act of total surrender.

In the end, when he staggered out of the caverns into a stone circle illuminated with daylight, he almost continued walking because he was certain that he was hallucinating.

Sunlight.

Some part of his mind registered the reality of what he was seeing.

In disbelief he looked up and saw that the hot, tropical sunshine was slanting through an opening in the rocks. A series of steep stone steps had been cut into the rock. A long black cord dangled from the opening.

Calling on the last of his reserves, he grasped the rope and tested it to make certain it would hold his weight. When he was satisfied that it was secure he started up the ancient staircase, using the rope as a handrail.

He reached the opening, scrambled out of the temple caves and collapsed on the stone floor of an open-air temple. He had been so long in the shadows that he had to close his eyes against the brilliant sunlight.

Somewhere nearby a gong boomed. The sound echoed endlessly through the jungle.

He was not alone on the island.

A YEAR LATER another ship dropped anchor in the small harbor. Slater was on board when it sailed. But he was not the same man that he had been when he arrived on Fever Island.

Over the course of the next several years he became a legend in certain circles. When he finally returned to London he discovered the great curse that befalls all legends: There is no place to call home.

ONE

~

"I can't believe Anne is gone." Matty Bingham blotted her eyes with a handkerchief. "She was always so spirited. So charming. So full of life."

"Yes, she was." Ursula Kern tightened her grip on the umbrella and watched the gravediggers dump great clods of earth on the coffin. "She was a woman of the modern age."

"And an excellent secretary." Matty tucked her handkerchief into her satchel. "A credit to the agency."

Matty was in her mid-thirties, a spinster without family or connections. Like the other women who came to work at the Kern Secretarial Agency, she had abandoned any hope of marriage and a family of her own. Like Anne and the others, she had seized the promise that Ursula offered—a respectable career as a professional secretary, a field that was finally opening up to women.

The day was appropriately funereal in tone—a depressing shade of gray with a steady drizzle of rain. Ursula and Matty were the only mourners present at the graveside. Anne had died alone. No family had come forward to claim the body. Ursula had paid for the funeral. It was, she thought, not just her responsibility as Anne's employer and sole heir, but also a final act of friendship.

A great emptiness welled up inside her. Anne Clifton had been her closest friend for the past two years. They had bonded over the things they had in common—a lack of family and haunting pasts that they had very carefully buried.

Anne might have possessed a few faults—some of the other secretaries at the agency had considered her a fast woman—but Ursula knew there had always been a distinct twist of admiration in the remarks. Anne's bold determination to carve her own path in life against all odds made her the very model of the Modern Woman.

When the coffin vanished beneath the growing mound of dirt, Ursula and Matty turned and walked back across the cemetery.

"It was kind of you to pay for Anne's funeral," Matty said.

Ursula went through the wrought-iron gates. "It was the least I could do."

"I will miss her."

"So will I," Ursula said.

Who will pay for my funeral when the time comes? she wondered.

"Anne did not seem like the type to take her own life," Matty said.

"No, she did not."

URSULA DINED IN SOLITUDE, as she usually did. When the meal was concluded she went into her small, cozy study.

The housekeeper bustled into the room to light the fire.

"Thank you, Mrs. Dunstan," Ursula said.

"You're certain you're all right, then?" Mrs. Dunstan asked gently. "I know you considered Miss Clifton a friend. Hard to lose a connection of that sort. Lost a few friends, myself, over the years."

"I'm quite all right," Ursula said. "I'm just going to sort through Miss Clifton's things and make an inventory. Then I'll go to bed."

"Very well, then."

Mrs. Dunstan went quietly out into the hall and closed the door. Ursula waited a moment and then she poured herself a stiff shot of brandy. The fiery spirits took off some of the chill she had been feeling since Anne's death.

After a while she crossed the room to the trunk that held Anne's things.

One by one she removed the items that had aroused in her a deep sense of unease—an empty perfume bottle, a small velvet bag containing a few pieces of jewelry, Anne's stenography notebook and two packets of seeds. Taken individually, each was easily explained. But as a group they raised disturbing questions.

Three days earlier, when Anne's housekeeper had discovered the body of her employer, she had immediately sent for Ursula. There had been no one else to summon. Initially, Ursula had been unable to accept the notion that Anne had either died of natural causes or taken her own life. She had called in the police. They had immediately concluded that there was no sign of foul play.

But Anne had left a note. Ursula had found it crumpled on the floor beside the body. To most people the marks made in pencil would have looked like random scribbles. Anne, however, was a skilled stenographer who had been trained in the Pitman method. As was the case with many professional secretaries, she had gone on to develop her own personal version of coded writing.

The note was a message, and Ursula knew it had been intended for her. Anne had been well aware that no one else could decipher her unique stenography.

Behind water closet.

Ursula sat down at her desk and drank a little more brandy while she contemplated the items. After a while, she pushed the empty perfume bottle aside. She had found it on Anne's little writing desk, not with the other things. It was unlike Anne not to have mentioned the purchase of new perfume but aside from that there did not appear to be anything mysterious about it.

The notebook, the jewelry pouch and the seeds, however, were a very different matter. Why had Anne hidden all three items behind the water closet?

After a while she opened the stenography notebook and began to read. Transcribing Anne's cryptic shorthand was slow going but two hours later she knew that she had been wrong about one thing that afternoon. Paying for the funeral was not to be her last act of friendship.

There was one more thing she could do for Anne—find her killer.

TWO

~~~~

Slater Roxton regarded Ursula through the lenses of his wire-rimmed spectacles. "What the devil do you mean, you won't be available for the next few weeks, Mrs. Kern? We have an arrangement."

"My apologies, sir, but a pressing matter has come up," Ursula said. "I must devote my full attention to it."

A disturbing hush fell on the library. Ursula mentally fortified herself. She had been acquainted with Slater for less than a fortnight and had worked with him on only two occasions but she felt she had an intuitive understanding of the man. He was proving to be a difficult client.

He had very nearly perfected the art of not signaling his mood or his thoughts but she was increasingly alert to a few subtle cues. The deep silence and the unblinking gaze with which he was watching her did not bode well. She sat very straight in her chair, doing her best not to let him know that his unwavering regard was sending small chills down her spine.

Evidently concluding that she was not responding as he had anticipated to his stern disapproval, he escalated the level of tension by rising slowly from his chair and flattening his powerful hands on the polished surface of his mahogany desk.

There was a deceptively graceful quality about the way he moved that gave him a fascinating aura of quiet, self-contained power. The dark, unemotional manner characterized everything about him, from his calm, nearly uninflected speech to his unreadable green-and-gold eyes.

His choice of attire reinforced the impression of shadows and ice. In the short time she had known him she had never seen him in anything other than head-to-toe black—black linen shirt and black tie, black satin waistcoat, black trousers and a black coat. Even the frames of his spectacles were made of some matte black metal—not gold- or silver-plated wire.

He was not wearing the severely tailored coat at the moment. It was hanging on a hook near the door. After greeting her a short time ago, Slater had removed it in preparation for working on the artifacts.

She knew she had no right to critique the man on the basis of his wardrobe. She, too, was dressed in her customary black. In the past two years she had come to think of her mourning attire—from her widow's veil and stylish black gown to her black stacked-heel, ankle-high button boots—as both uniform and camouflage.

It flashed across her mind that she and Slater made quite a somber pair. Anyone who happened to walk into the library would think they were both sunk deep into unrelenting grief. The truth of the matter was that she was in hiding. Not for the first time, she wondered what Slater's motives were for going about in black. His father had died two months ago. It was the event that had brought Slater home to London after several years of living abroad. He was now in command of the Roxton family fortune. But she was quite certain that the black clothes were indicative of a long-standing sartorial habit—not a sign of mourning.

If even half of what the press had printed regarding Slater Roxton was true, she reflected, perhaps he had his reasons for wearing black. It was, after all, the color of mystery, and Slater was nothing if not a great mystery to Society.

She watched him with a deep wariness that was spiked with curiosity and what she knew was a reckless sense of fascination. She had anticipated that giving notice, especially in such a summary fashion, would not be met with patience and understanding. Clients frequently proved difficult to manage but she had never encountered one quite like Slater. The very concept of managing Slater Roxton staggered the mind. It had been clear to her at the start of their association that he was a force of nature and a law unto himself. That was, of course, what made him so interesting, she thought.

"I have just explained that something unforeseen has arisen," she said. She was careful to keep her voice crisp and professional, aware that Slater would pounce on anything that hinted at uncertainty or weakness. "I regret the necessity of terminating our business relationship. However—"

"Then why are you terminating our arrangement?"

"The matter is of a personal nature," she said.

He frowned. "Are you ill?"

"No, of course not. I enjoy excellent health. I was about to say that I hope it will be possible for me to return at a later date to finish the cataloging work."

"Do you, indeed? And what makes you think I won't replace you? There are other secretaries in London."

"That is your choice, of course. I must remind you that I did warn you at the outset that I have other commitments in regard to my business which might from time to time interfere with our working arrangements. You agreed to those terms."

"I was assured that, in addition to a great many other excellent qualities, you were quite dependable, Mrs. Kern. You can't just walk in here and quit on the spot like this."

Ursula twitched the skirts of her black gown so that they draped in neat, elegant folds around her ankles while she considered her options. The atmosphere in the library was rapidly becoming tense, as if some invisible electricity generator was charging the air. It was always like this when she found herself in close proximity to Slater. But today the disturbing, rather exciting energy had a distinctly dangerous edge.

In the short time she had known him she had

never seen him lose his temper. He had never gone to the other extreme, either. She had yet to see him laugh. True, he had dredged up the occasional, very brief smile and there had been a certain warmth in his usually cold eyes from time to time. But she got the feeling that he was more surprised than she was when he allowed such emotions to surface.

"I do apologize, Mr. Roxton," she said, not for the first time. "I assure you I have no choice. Time is of the essence."

"I feel I deserve more of an explanation. What is this pressing matter that requires you to break our contract?"

"It regards one of my employees."

"You feel obligated to look into the personal problems of your employees?"

"Well, yes, in a nutshell, that is more or less the situation."

Slater came out from behind the desk, lounged against the front of it and folded his arms.

His sharply etched features had an ascetic, unforgiving quality. On occasion it was easy to envision him as an avenging angel. At other times she thought he made a very good Lucifer.

"The least you can do is explain yourself, Mrs. Kern," he said. "You owe me that much, I think."

She did not owe him anything, she thought. She had taken pains to make her terms of employment clear right from the start. As the proprietor of the Kern Secretarial Agency she rarely took assignments, herself, these days. Her business was growing rapidly. The result was that for the past few months she had been busy in the office, training new secretaries and interviewing potential clients. She had accepted the position with Slater as a favor to his mother, Lilly Lafontaine, a celebrated actress who had retired to write melodramas.

She had not expected to find the mysterious Mr. Roxton so riveting.

"Very well, sir," she said, "the short version is that I have decided to take another client."

Slater went very still.

"I see," he said. "You are not happy in your work here with me?"

There was a grim note in his voice. She realized with a start that he was taking her departure personally. Even more shocking, she got the impression that he was not particularly surprised that she was leaving his employ, rather he seemed stoically resigned, as if he had foreseen some inevitable doom.

"On the contrary, sir," she said quickly. "I find your cataloging project quite interesting."

"Am I not paying you enough?" Something that might have been relief flickered in his eyes. "If so, I am open to renegotiating your fee."

"I assure you, it is not a matter of money."

"If you are not unhappy in your work and if the pay is satisfactory, why are you leaving me for another client?" he asked.

This time he sounded genuinely perplexed.

She caught her breath and suddenly felt oddly flushed. It was almost as if he were playing the part of a jilted lover, she thought. But of course that was not at all the case. Theirs was a client-employer relationship.

This is why you rarely accept male clients, she reminded herself. There was a certain danger involved. But finding herself attracted to one of her customers was not the sort of risk she had envisioned when she established the policy. Her chief concern had been the knowledge that men sometimes posed a risk to the sterling reputations of her secretaries. In the case of Slater Roxton, she had made an exception and now she would pay a price.

All in all, it was probably best that the association was ended before she lost her head and, possibly, her heart.

"As to my reasons for leaving—" she began.

"Who is this new client?" Slater said, cutting her off.

"Very well, sir, I will explain the circumstances that require me to terminate my employment with you but you may have a few quibbles."

"Try me."

She tensed at the whisper of command in his tone.

"I really do not want to get into an extended argument, sir—especially in light of the fact that I hope to return to this position in the near future."

"You have already made it clear that you expect me to wait upon your convenience."

She waved one black-gloved hand to indicate the

jumble of antiquities that cluttered the library. "These artifacts have been sitting here for years. Surely they can wait a bit longer to be cataloged."

"How much longer?" he asked a little too evenly.

She cleared her throat. "Well, as to that, I'm afraid I cannot be specific, at least not yet. Perhaps in a few days I will have some notion of how long my other assignment will last."

"I have no intention of arguing with you, Mrs. Kern, but I would like to know the identity of the client you feel is more important than me." He broke off, looking uncharacteristically irritated. "I meant to say, what sort of secretarial work do you feel is more critical than cataloging my artifacts? Is your new client a banker? The owner of a large business, perhaps? A lawyer or a lady in Polite Society who finds herself in need of your services?"

"A few days ago I was summoned to the house of a woman named Anne Clifton. Anne worked for me for two years. She became more than an employee. I considered her a friend. We had some things in common."

"I notice you are speaking in the past tense."

"Anne was found dead in her study. I sent for the police but the detective who was kind enough to visit the scene declared that in his opinion Anne's death was from natural causes. He thinks her heart failed or that she suffered a stroke."

Slater did not move. He watched her as though she had just announced that she could fly. Clearly her response was not the answer he had expected but he recovered with remarkable speed.

"I'm sorry to hear of Miss Clifton's death," he said. He paused, eyes narrowing faintly. "What made you summon the police?"

"I believe Anne may have been murdered."

Slater looked at her, saying nothing for a time. Eventually he removed his spectacles and began to polish them with a pristine white handkerchief.

"Huh," he said.

Ursula debated another moment. The truth of the matter was that she wanted very much to discuss her plan with someone who would not only understand, but possibly provide some useful advice—someone who could keep a confidence. Her intuition told her that Slater Roxton was good at keeping secrets. Furthermore, in the past few days it had become blazingly clear that he possessed an extremely logical mind. Some would say he took that particular trait to the extreme.

"What I am about to tell you must be held in strictest confidence, do you understand?" she said.

His dark brows came together in a forbidding line. She knew she had offended him.

"Rest assured I am quite capable of keeping my mouth shut, Mrs. Kern."

Each word was coated in a thin layer of ice.

She adjusted her gloves and then clasped her hands firmly together in her lap. She took an additional moment to collect her thoughts. She had not told anyone else, not even her assistant, Matty, what she intended to do.

"I have reason to suspect that Anne Clifton was

murdered," she repeated. "I intend to take her place in the household of her client to see if I can find some clues that will point to the killer."

For the first time since she had made his acquaintance, Slater appeared to be caught off guard. For a few seconds he stared at her, clearly stunned.

"What?" he said finally.

"You heard me, sir. The police do not see fit to investigate Anne's death. As there is no one else available, I intend to take on the task."

Slater finally managed to pull himself together.

"That's sheer madness," he said very quietly.

So much for hoping that he would understand. She got to her feet and reached up to pull the black netting down from the brim of her little velvet hat. She started toward the door.

"I would remind you of your promise to keep my secret," she said. "Now, if you don't mind, I really must be going. I will send word as soon as I have resolved the situation regarding Anne's death. Perhaps you will consider hiring me again to assist you."

"Stop right there, Mrs. Kern. Do not take another step until I have worked my way through this . . . this tangled knot of chaos that you have just tossed at my feet."

She paused, one hand on the doorknob, and turned around to confront him. "*Tangled knot of chaos? A foreign expression, perhaps?*"

"I'm sure you know full well what I meant."

"There is nothing to be worked through. The only reason I confided my intentions to you was that I hoped that you might be able to offer some advice or assistance. Yours is an eminently rational, logical mind, sir. But I see now that it was foolish of me to expect any understanding of my plan, let alone some assistance."

"Primarily because what you intend is not a rational, logical plan," he shot back. "It bears no resemblance to a coherent strategy."

"Nonsense, I have given the problem a great deal of thought."

"I don't think so. If you had, you would realize that what you are proposing is a reckless, possibly dangerous, and, no doubt, utterly futile, endeavor."

She had known that he might not be enthusiastic about her decision to investigate Anne's murder but she had expected him to understand why she had to take action. So much for thinking that she and Slater had formed a connection based on mutual respect.

Now, why did that realization depress her spirits? He was a client, not a potential lover.

She managed a chilly smile. "Please don't hold back, sir. Feel free to express your true opinions of my plan. But you will have to do so to yourself. I don't intend to be your audience."

She started to open the door but he was suddenly there, closing it very firmly.

"A moment, if you please, Mrs. Kern. I am not finished with this conversation."

THREE

Victory. Perhaps.

Relief spiked with a flicker of hope shot through Ursula. She raised her brows at the cold steel in Slater's words.

"You have made it clear that you do not approve of what I intend to do," she said. "What more is there to discuss?"

He eyed her for a long, steady moment and then he seemed to remember that he was holding his spectacles in one hand. Very deliberately he put them on—and she was suddenly quite certain that he did not need them. He wore them for the same reason she wore a widow's veil, as a shield against the prying gaze of Society.

"What makes you so sure that your secretary was murdered?" he finally asked.

At least he was asking questions now, she thought. That was progress.

"There are a number of reasons," she said.

"I'm listening."

"I'm quite certain that Anne did not take her own life. There was no evidence of cyanide or any other poison in the vicinity."

"Poisons can be subtle in their outward effects."

"Yes, I know, but even so, Anne was not the least bit depressed. She had recently moved into a nice little house that she was looking forward to purchasing. She had bought new furniture and a new gown. She seemed very happy in her work with a client of long standing and she was making an excellent salary. In addition, Anne hinted that she was occasionally receiving handsome gratuities from her client. In short, Anne was not suffering from any financial problems."

Slater regarded her with a thoughtful expression and then he walked back across the room. Once again he leaned against his desk and folded his arms. His eyes burned a little behind the lenses of his spectacles.

"I have been told that those who lose friends and loved ones to suicide often say they never saw any advance indications of the victim's intentions," he said.

Ursula turned to face him. "That may be true. All I can tell you is that in recent weeks Anne was in excellent spirits. She was so cheerful, in fact, that I had begun to wonder if she was involved in a romantic relationship."

"That could be your explanation," Slater said. "A star-crossed love affair."

"I admit I had begun to wonder if, perhaps, Anne had made the mistake of becoming intimately involved with a man who was connected to her client's household. I have rules against that sort of thing, of course, and I do my best to protect my secretaries. Forming a romantic liaison with a client or someone connected to the client is always an extremely reckless thing to do. It never ends well."

"I see," Slater said, his tone very neutral now.

"The thing is, Anne was a woman of the world. It's quite possible that she ignored the rules. The client's husband is a wealthy, powerful man, and wealthy, powerful men are often careless when it comes to their affairs."

Slater said nothing. He just looked at her.

She remembered somewhat belatedly that Slater Roxton was a wealthy, powerful man.

"The thing is," she continued hurriedly, "Anne was quite capable of protecting herself in such matters. She might enjoy a discreet dalliance but she would never be so foolish as to fall in love with a man she knew could never return her affections."

Slater gave that some thought. "You say that Anne was doing rather well financially."

"She was comfortably established with some funds put aside for retirement and a bit of jewelry."

"Did she leave her possessions and the retirement money to someone?"

Ursula winced. "I was Anne's sole heir."

"I see." Slater exhaled slowly. "Well, there goes that theory of the crime. I can't imagine that you would be undertaking an investigation that might lead to your arrest."

"Thank you for that bit of logic. I assure you, I had no reason to want her dead. She was one of my best secretaries—an asset to my agency in every conceivable way. In addition, we were friends. She was the first person who agreed to work for my agency when I went into business two years ago."

"You say you do not suspect suicide. What makes you think that Miss Clifton might have been murdered?"

"I found a short note next to the body."

"A farewell note?" Slater asked. His voice gentled with a surprising sympathy.

"No, at least not in the way you mean. She wrote the note with a pencil. I think she was trying to point me toward her killer."

A great intensity infused Slater. "She wrote the note in pencil? She did not use a pen?"

He did understand, she thought.

"Exactly my point, sir," she said. "I do not think that she had time to use a pen. That would have required opening the ink bottle, filling the pen and laying out a sheet of paper in the proper way. A note explaining one's suicide would be a deliberate act, don't you think? An experienced secretary would have used pen and paper. The fact that she only scribbled a few words in pencil tells me that she was in a great rush. No, Mr. Roxton. Anne did not leave a farewell note. She tried to leave a message—for me."

"This note was addressed to you?"

"Well, no, but it was written in her own shorthand. She knew I was probably the only person who would be able to read it."

"What did the note tell you?"

"It was in her unique stenographer's script. It directed me to the location of the notebook and her little collection of jewelry. Oh, and there were two packets of seeds there, as well. I can't imagine for the life of me why she hid the seeds. It is another mystery."

"Where, exactly, did she conceal all those items?" Slater asked.

"Behind the convenience. Didn't I mention that? Sorry."

Slater looked quite blank. "The convenience?"

Ursula cleared her throat. "The water closet, Mr. Roxton."

"Right. The convenience. My apologies. I've spent most of the past few years out of the country. I'm a bit rusty when it comes to polite euphemisms."

"I understand."

"Regarding this note Miss Clifton left—it's obvious why she would conceal her jewelry. You said you don't know why she concealed the seeds. But what of the notebook? Any thoughts on why she would hide it?"

"An excellent question," Ursula said, warming to her theme. "I spent most of last night trying to transcribe several pages but the process did not shed any light on the problem. It's all poetry, you see."

"Anne Clifton wrote poetry?"

"No, her client did. Lady Fulbrook is a wealthy but

extremely reclusive woman. She employed Anne to take dictation and transcribe the poems on a type-writer. Anne said that Lady Fulbrook is recovering from a case of shattered nerves and that the doctor prescribed writing poetry as a form of therapy."

Slater was briefly distracted. "What sort of poetry?"

Ursula felt the heat rising in her cheeks. She assumed a professional tone.

"The poems appear to be devoted to the themes of love."

"Love." Slater sounded as if he were unfamiliar with the word.

Ursula waved one gloved hand in a vague way. "Endless longing, the travails of lovers who are separated by fate or circumstances beyond their control. Transcendent waves of passion. The usual sort of thing."

"Transcendent waves of passion," Slater repeated.

Again he spoke as if the concept were utterly foreign to him.

She was quite certain she caught a flash of amusement in his eyes. She tightened her grip on her satchel and told herself that she would not allow him to draw her into an argument about the merits of love poetry.

"Although the themes are obvious, there are some odd elements in the poems—numbers and words that don't seem to suit the meter. That's why I'm not sure if I'm transcribing the dictation properly," she said. "As I explained, over time a skilled secretary's stenography becomes a very personal code."

"But you can decipher Miss Clifton's code?"

"I am attempting to do so. But I'm not sure what

good it will do." Ursula sighed. "It's poetry, after all. What can it tell me about the reason for Anne's murder?"

"The first question you must ask is, why did Miss Clifton go to the trouble of concealing her notebook?"

"I know, but I cannot imagine a reasonable answer."

"The answer is always concealed within the question," Slater said.

"What on earth is that supposed to mean?"

"Never mind. You suspect that Anne Clifton might have become involved in a liaison with the client's husband, don't you?"

"With Lord Fulbrook, yes, it has crossed my mind."

Slater was starting to take an interest in the situation, Ursula thought. A great sense of relief came over her. Perhaps she would not be alone in this inquiry.

"Any idea why Fulbrook would go to the trouble of murdering Miss Clifton? Not to be callous about such matters, but high-ranking gentlemen frequently discard mistresses. There is rarely any need for them to resort to violence."

Ursula realized she had a death grip on the handle of the satchel.

"I am aware of that, Mr. Roxton," she said through her teeth. "Which makes Anne's death all the more suspicious."

"What of Lady Fulbrook? If she was jealous of her husband's attentions to Anne Clifton—"

Ursula shook her head. "No, I'm quite sure that is

not the case. According to Anne, Lady Fulbrook is
very unhappy in her marriage. I was given the impression that she is also quite timid. Evidently she
goes about in fear of her husband, who has a violent
temper. It is difficult to envision such a woman com-
mitting murder in a fit of jealousy."

"Jealousy is a wildfire of an emotion. Very unpredictable."

In that moment Ursula was certain that Slater
viewed all strong emotions, in particular those associated with passion, as wildfires to be contained and
controlled at all costs.

She straightened her shoulders. "There is another
factor to consider. Anne told me that Lady Fulbrook
never leaves her house. That is not just because of her
poor nerves. Evidently her husband does not allow
her to go out unless he, personally, escorts her."

"So, we're back to Lord Fulbrook as our main suspect. Do you think Anne had an affair with him?"

"I think it's possible," Ursula said. "If that was the
case, I doubt very much that she was passionately in
love with him. I don't think Anne would have trusted
any man with her heart. But she had her financial
future to consider."

"She might have found his money interesting."

Ursula sighed. "That is a rather blunt way of putting it, sir, but the answer is, yes. Perhaps she became
too demanding. Or perhaps she said or did something to set off Fulbrook's temper."

"If that was the case, he would have been likely to

attack her physically, probably in a fit of rage. You
said there was no evidence that she was assaulted."

"No. None."

There was another short silence. After a time Slater
stirred.

"You do realize that if you set out to prove that
Fulbrook killed Anne Clifton you might very likely
put your own life in danger," Slater said.

"I just want to know the truth."

"There is still the strong likelihood that she suffered a heart attack or a stroke," Slater said.

"I know. If my inquiries lead nowhere I will accept
that conclusion."

"What else can you tell me about Anne Clifton?"

"Well, among other things she was a very modern
woman."

"I believe that *modern* is another euphemism, is it
not?"

Anger flashed through Ursula. "Anne was a
woman of high spirits. She was charming, bold, daring, and she was determined to enjoy life to the hilt.
In short, sir, if she had been a man, people would
have admired her."

"You admired her."

"Yes, I did," Ursula said. She composed herself.
"She was my friend as well as an employee."

"I see. Go on."

"There is not much more to say. I believe that
someone in the Fulbrook household, probably Lord
Fulbrook, is responsible for Anne's death. I intend to

find out if my suspicions are correct. And now, if you will excuse me, I must be on my way. I assured Lady Fulbrook that I would send a new secretary to her at the earliest possible moment. I need to get things in order at the agency before I take up my duties."

Slater frowned. "Lady Fulbrook?"

"Anne's client. I just explained—"

"Yes, I know what you said. Damnation, you intend to take Miss Clifton's place as Lady Fulbrook's secretary."

"I start tomorrow afternoon. I assured Lady Fulbrook that the transition would be seamless and that I would arrive at her house in Mapstone Square promptly at one-thirty, just as Anne did."

Slater walked across the carpet and came to a halt directly in front of Ursula.

"If you are correct in your suspicions," he said, "what you are planning is potentially dangerous."

His soft tone rattled her nerves. Instinctively she took a step back, trying to put a little more distance between them. He was no longer simply annoyed or reluctantly curious. He was, in his own subtle way, angry. *At me*, she thought, bemused.

"Don't worry, Mr. Roxton," she said hastily. "I'm sure you can find another secretary to help you catalog your collection. I will be happy to send you someone else from my agency to fill in while I'm gone."

"I am not concerned with finding another secretary, Mrs. Kern. I am concerned about your safety."

"Oh, I see."

He was not furious because she was abandoning his cataloging project, she thought. He was simply alarmed that she might be taking a risk. It had been so long since anyone had been worried about her welfare that she was flummoxed for a moment. The realization warmed her somewhere deep inside. She smiled.

"It is very thoughtful of you to be concerned," she said. "Truly, I do appreciate it. But rest assured that I will take precautions."

Ominous shadows appeared in his eyes. "Such as?"

Her fragile sense of gratitude evaporated in a heartbeat.

"I assure you I can take care of myself," she said coldly. "I have been doing just that for some time now. I regret that I tried to explain my plan to you. That was clearly a mistake. I can only hope that you will honor my confidence. If you fail to do so, you may, indeed, put me in some jeopardy."

He looked as if she had just slapped his face very hard. Equal measures of astonishment and outrage flashed in his eyes.

"Do you really think that I would deliberately do anything that would place you in danger?" he asked softly.

She was instantly consumed with remorse.

"No, of course not," she said. "I would never have spoken to you of my intentions if I believed that to be the case. But I admit I had hoped you might be able to provide some helpful advice."

"My advice is to give up this wild scheme."

"Right." She closed her hand around the door-knob. "Thank you for your ever so helpful counsel. Good day, Mr. Roxton."

"Damn it, Ursula, don't you dare walk out on me."

It was, she realized, the first time he had ever used her given name. It was depressing to know that it was anger, not affection, that had caused him to slip into the small intimacy.

She yanked the door open before he could stop her. She whisked up her skirts and went out into the hall, certain that he would not humiliate himself in front of the servants by chasing after her.

She was proved correct. Slater stopped in the door-way and watched her but he did not pursue her—not physically, at least. Nevertheless, when she arrived in the front hall she was oddly breathless.

Webster, the butler, opened the door for her.

"Leaving early, Mrs. Kern?" he asked. "I believe Mrs. Webster was making up a tea tray for you and Mr. Roxton."

He sounded quite heartbroken.

In the course of the two cataloging sessions it had become obvious that the Roxton household was un-usual in many respects, including the staff. They had all been hired by Slater's mother. As far as Ursula could determine, Lilly Lafontaine recruited heavily from the unemployed, currently between engage-ments, or retired ranks of the theatrical world.

Webster was a lean, wiry man with a skeletal face. With his shaved head, a black eye patch covering one blue eye and a jagged scar that marked his left cheek, he looked more like a pirate than a professional butler.

Ursula had discovered that the accident that had forced him into retirement had occurred onstage. She did not know all of the details but evidently he had been the victim of a fake sword that had failed to collapse properly.

She was also well aware that with his forbidding appearance, the number of employers who would have hired him—let alone elevate him to the status of butler—was vanishingly small. She had recognized him on their first meeting as a kindred spirit—an individual who had succeeded in reinventing himself. The knowledge had not only made her like him immediately, it had predisposed her to look favorably upon his employer.

Rapid footsteps sounded in the hall. Mrs. Webster appeared, a heavily laden tea tray in her hands.

"Mrs. Kern, are you leaving so soon? You mustn't go. You haven't had tea. Cataloging Mr. Roxton's relics is such dry and dusty work."

In her own way, Mrs. Webster was as unexpected as her spouse. She was very likely in her mid-forties but she had been gifted with the elegant bones and the fine figure of a woman who would be striking long into old age. It had come as no surprise to discover that she, too, had once earned her living as an actress. She entered a room carrying a tea tray with more of a flourish than most upper-class ladies could summon to make an entrance into a ballroom.

Like her husband, Mrs. Webster was always on-stage. At the moment she was doing an excellent imitation of a Juliet who has just discovered that Romeo is dead.

"I hope to return at a more convenient time, Mrs. Webster," Ursula said, aware that Slater was listening to the conversation. "It's just that something has come up of a personal nature."

"Are you ill?" Mrs. Webster demanded, hand clutching at her throat. "I know a very good doctor. He saved Mr. Webster's life."

"I assure you I'm in excellent health," Ursula said. "I hate to rush off but I'm afraid I really must go."

Webster reluctantly opened the door.

"Until Wednesday, then," Mrs. Webster said, hopeful to the end.

Ursula pulled the black netting of her widow's veil down over her face and escaped out onto the front step before Mrs. Webster could add *Parting is such sweet sorrow.* She decided not to tell the Websters that she would not be returning on Wednesday or, possibly, ever again, judging by the expression on Slater's face.

The carriage that Slater had insisted on arranging for the twice-weekly sessions was waiting in the street.

The coachman jumped down from the box, opened the door and lowered the steps. His name was Griffith and he was a mountain of a man with a powerful, muscular build. His black hair was tied back at the nape of his neck with a leather thong. Ursula had learned that in his previous career he had worked as a stagehand with a traveling theater company.

"You're leaving early today, Mrs. Kern," he observed. "Everything all right? You're not coming down with a fever, are you?"

This was getting to be ridiculous, Ursula thought. It seemed that everyone connected to the Roxton household had begun to take an alarming interest in her health. She was certainly not accustomed to such close scrutiny, nor did she want to encourage it.

"I'm in excellent health, thank you, Griffith," she said. "Please take me back to my office."

"Yes, ma'am."

Griffith handed her up into the cab with obvious reluctance. She collected her skirts and sat down on the elegantly cushioned seat.

Griffith closed the door. He exchanged dark glances with Mr. and Mrs. Webster before he vaulted up onto the box and loosened the reins. Ursula got the distinct feeling that she would be the subject of some low-voiced conversations later in the kitchen.

She had understood from the outset that Roxton's servants were fiercely loyal to their employer but it was unsettling to realize that they took such acute interest in her. In the two years that had passed since the scandal that had destroyed what she thought of as her *other life* she had successfully reinvented herself. She could not afford to let anyone look too deeply into her past.

FOUR

He stood at the window in the front hall and watched until the carriage vanished into the fog. Everything inside him went cold. He was losing her. *You never possessed her. She was not yours to lose.*

But logic did nothing to push back the endless night that threatened to coalesce at the edge of his senses. It was always there, lying in wait. The time spent in the temple caves of Fever Island had taken its toll. The year in the monastery had taught him self-discipline and the dangers of strong passions. For the most part he had learned to harness the forces of his temperament. The Principles of the Three Ways had provided him with a sense of structure and control that suited his nature. He had found what some would describe as a calling, and he had pursued it relentlessly, driven by a quest for answers to a question he still did not understand.

He thought he had made his peace with the darkness. With the exception of the occasional cathartic flash of violence, he had assumed the role of observer. Even during the rare moments of sexual release some part of him was always standing back, watching.

But Ursula had interfered with the carefully constructed and exquisitely balanced order of his world. She made him want more. And desire was the most dangerous force of all.

Webster cleared his throat in a disapproving manner. "Will there be anything else, sir?"

"No, thank you," Slater said.

He turned away from the view of the street, went back into the library and closed the door. He stood alone listening to the empty silence for a time, thinking about his first impressions of Ursula Kern. She had been wearing black from head to toe but the very darkness of her attire had only served to heighten the rich, burnished copper of her auburn hair.

He would never forget the moment when she had raised the veil of her dashing little widow's hat to reveal an intelligent face made riveting by fiercely brilliant hazel eyes, a strong will and a forceful character.

He had known at once that she was a woman of spirit. He had savored the knowledge in ways he could not begin to describe—*like a damned moth to her flame,* he thought. He sensed that she was a woman who understood the importance of secrets. A part of him hoped that such a woman might come to understand and accept a man who also kept them.

The press speculated wildly about what he had been doing during the past few years. Some claimed that he had studied ancient mysteries in foreign lands and learned strange, exotic secrets. There were rumors that he had discovered astonishing treasures. Other reports insisted that the experience on Fever Island had rendered him unhinged—possibly quite mad.

The general consensus both in the newspapers and in Society was that he had returned to London with the goal of exacting vengeance.

Not all of the rumors about him were false.

FIVE

～

Matty Bingham was at her desk, transcribing dictation on the latest model of the Fenton Modern Typewriter. Ursula stood out in the hall for a moment, watching through the window set into the door. Matty was one of the first secretaries hired and trained by the newly founded Kern agency two years earlier. She had, in fact, walked through the door only a week after Anne Clifton, desperate and determined. Matty had soon displayed a talent for organization and finances that had proved invaluable. Although she still occasionally took private clients, she had become Ursula's second-in-command.

This afternoon her curly brown hair was pinned in a tight bundle on top of her head. The style emphasized her fine brown eyes. Attired in a crisp tailor-made dress with a prim white bodice and a maroon skirt, she was the ideal image of the professional secretary. Her posture in the chair was elegant, her back and shoulders very straight. The movement of her hands on the keys was graceful, almost hypnotic to watch. She looked as if she were playing a piano. That was, of course, an important reason why the new field of secretarial work—one of the very few respectable professions open to women—was viewed as a suitable female occupation.

Those who pontificated on such matters in the press were keen to point out that typewriting was a fine job for women because females could perform their tasks without compromising their femininity.

Ursula privately suspected that the real reason women were welcomed into the secretarial field had more to do with the fact that most of them were so grateful to be allowed to make a respectable living that they were willing to tolerate lower pay than a man would demand. She had made certain that the secretaries of the Kern Secretarial Agency were the exception to that rule.

Kern secretaries were not only highly skilled in stenography, typewriting and organizational techniques, they were very expensive. The women who worked for the agency were paid incomes that allowed them to afford good lodgings and fashionable clothes. The high wages made it possible for them to put aside money for their retirement years. Their steady incomes sometimes lured suitors, as well. In the past two years, three Kern secretaries, including

Matty, had received offers of marriage. One woman had accepted. Matty and her colleague had turned down the proposals, preferring the freedom that came with their new profession.

The Kern agency advertised that their elite secretaries operated the very latest and most technologically advanced typing machines. Ursula and her employees had all agreed that that device was the Fenton Modern Typewriter.

Ursula opened the door and went into the office. Matty looked up in surprise.

"You're back early," she said. Concern tightened her brows. "Are you feeling unwell?"

"Why does everyone insist upon inquiring after my health this afternoon?" Ursula yanked the hatpins out of her hat. "Do I appear sickly?"

Matty's concern immediately transitioned to fascinated horror. "Something dreadful happened at the Roxton mansion, didn't it? Are you all right?"

Ursula dropped the hat and veil onto a side table. "I'm fine, Matty."

"No, you're not fine. Mr. Roxton said or did something to outrage your delicate sensibilities, didn't he?"

Ursula sank into her desk chair and gave Matty a repressive look.

"To be clear," she said evenly, "Mr. Roxton committed no outrages upon my person and he did not offend my delicate sensibilities. Professional secretaries cannot afford to possess delicate sensibilities. That way lies disaster."

"We are respectable females. Of course we have delicate sensibilities."

"No, Matty, what professional secretaries must possess in abundance are the qualities of intelligence, common sense and a willingness to do whatever is required to extricate one's person from potentially outrageous situations before they become outrageous. There are no knights in shining armor hanging about waiting to rescue us. We must deal with the world on our own. Which is, of course, why I make certain that all of my secretaries wear hats with large, sturdy hatpins."

"Yes, I know." Matty brushed the hatpin requirement aside. "Well, if you were not offended, why are you in such a fierce mood? You look as if you could cheerfully throttle someone."

"Do not tempt me."

"Something did happen at the Roxton mansion. I knew it. I warned you about that man, did I not?"

"On any number of occasions."

"You can't expect him to behave like a well-bred, well-mannered gentleman. They say he was entombed alive for weeks on that island."

"His mother informed me that it was more in the neighborhood of a few days."

"It doesn't matter, the point is he was buried alive. After he escaped the temple tombs he was stranded on that island for a full year. That would be enough to shatter anyone's nerves or drive him mad."

"Mr. Roxton is not mad, Matty." Ursula reflected briefly. "A trifle eccentric, perhaps, but I'm quite sure he isn't mad. I think it's safe to say there's nothing wrong with his nerves, either."

"The latest issue of the *Flying Intelligencer* reports that Roxton practices exotic sexual rites upon unsuspecting females," Matty announced.

Ursula stared at her, genuinely shocked for the first time. "Good heavens. I must admit I hadn't heard that particular tidbit."

"Evidently Roxton is in the habit of kidnapping innocent, respectable ladies right off the street. He takes them to a secret chamber where he performs the rituals."

"Is that so? Have there been a number of complaints from the victims of these exotic sexual rituals?"

"Well, no." Matty looked disappointed. "The victims never remember exactly what happens during the ceremonies because he hypnotizes them to make them forget."

"I suspect they can't remember the exotic sexual rites because those rites never occurred in the first place. Really, Matty, you know you can't believe everything you read in the papers."

Matty was a great fan of the sensation press. In the wake of Roxton's return to London two months ago, the papers and the penny dreadfuls had wasted a great quantity of ink discussing the rumors of his so-called "entombment" and speculating on what he had done during the years following his rescue from Fever Island.

Matty had read every word printed about the mysterious Slater Roxton. She had never met him but she considered herself an expert on the man. She was clearly disappointed by Roxton's failure to perform exotic lovemaking rituals on her employer.

"What of the years after he escaped from the island?" Matty asked. "No telling what he got up to during that time."

"He did not disappear after he was rescued from the island," Ursula said. "His mother assured me that Mr. Roxton returned to London at least twice a year to visit with his parents."

"Yes, well, he certainly kept his visits quiet, didn't he?"

"I doubt that it was difficult. There was no reason for anyone to pay any attention to his comings and goings until recently. The only reason the press is agog now is because his father died and left the family fortune in Mr. Roxton's hands."

Matty assumed an all-knowing air. "They say he has returned to exact vengeance."

"That may be Society's opinion but that view was shaped by the sensation press. I doubt very much if it is true."

"Consider his position—he is the long-lost bastard son of a wealthy lord and a famous actress. Upon his father's death Mr. Roxton discovers that he will not inherit the estate and he will never be able to take up the title because of his illegitimate birth. And just to rub salt into his wounds, his father's will charged him with the duties and responsibilities of managing the inheritance for his two *legitimate* half brothers and his father's widow. The injustice of that situation would be enough to make any man seek revenge."

Ursula drummed her fingers on the desktop. "I saw no signs that Mr. Roxton is worried about his own financial future," Ursula said. "His mother does not appear concerned, either. I got the strong impression that Mr. Roxton's father took excellent care of Lilly. More to the point, I don't think that Slater Roxton has been idle during the past few years. His mother indicated that he has done rather well for himself. Something about investments, according to Lilly. Evidently he has a head for business. Furthermore, she assured me that her son is not unbalanced."

"Well, she is his mother, after all. What would you expect her to say?" Matty paused for emphasis. "And while we're on the subject of revenge—"

"We are not discussing the subject of vengeance." Ursula slapped the blotter with the palm of her hand. "Don't you have something that needs to be typed?"

Matty ignored that. "Don't forget the little matter of the Jeweled Bird. Everyone knows that while Mr. Roxton was languishing on Fever Island, his business partner, Lord Torrence, sailed home with the fabulous treasure that was discovered in the temple caves."

Ursula grimaced. "Lord Torrence along with everyone else believed Mr. Roxton was dead."

"Well," Matty said, lowering her voice to a conspiratorial whisper, "there is speculation that Lord Torrence tried to murder Mr. Roxton on Fever Island.

They say he triggered the trap that entombed Roxton so that he could keep the Jeweled Bird for himself."

For the first time since the conversation with Matty had started, a chill slithered down Ursula's spine. The press was notoriously unreliable but there was some truth in the old adage *Where there is smoke, there is fire*. The spectacular Jeweled Bird had caught the public's attention when Lord Torrence had allowed it to be exhibited for a time in a museum. People, herself included, had stood in line for hours to view it. The fact that one of the discoverers had died in the tombs on Fever Island had only added to the sense of fascination. When the fabulous statue was reported stolen shortly after it was returned to Torrence's private collection, there had been another sensation in the press. The Bird had faded into the mists of legend.

Ursula did not think that Slater was particularly concerned about money or the title, either, for that matter. But a man who had been entombed and returned from the grave only to learn that the fantastic artifact he had helped discover had disappeared into the illegal antiquities trade—such a man might harbor thoughts of vengeance. It might also convince him that the terrible accident on Fever Island had not been an accident, after all. One thing was certain, Ursula thought—if Slater set out to exact vengeance, his victim was unlikely to escape.

A great many tales and legends swirled around the mysterious Mr. Roxton. She would not be surprised to learn that a few of them were true.

She leaned forward to flip the pages in her appointment calendar. "I believe we have an interview with a new secretary this afternoon. Oh, yes, there it is. Miss Taylor will arrive at three."

"I can deal with it," Matty said.

"Are you sure?"

Matty smiled, a gentle, understanding smile. "I know Anne's death has been hard on you. There's no need for you to interview the secretary who will replace her. For heaven's sake, the funeral was only yesterday. You need a little time to get past the shock of it all."

"I'm going to miss her," Ursula said. "And not just because she was a great asset to this business."

"I—we, all of the secretaries here at the Kern agency—know that you and Anne were good friends."

"She possessed so many of the qualities I feel I lack. She was fun to be around. Clever. Vivacious. Full of enthusiasm for life. I admired her daring and her boldness. She was a woman ahead of her time in so many things."

"Mmm." Matty picked up the stack of pages she had finished typing and squared the bottom edge against the blotter with a few brisk taps.

"What?" Ursula asked.

"Nothing. It's not important. The poor woman is dead."

"Matty, are you aware of something about Anne that I should know?"

"Oh, no, truly," Matty said quickly. "It's just that, well—"

"Well, what? Matty, I am not in the mood for this."

Matty gave a small sigh. "It's just that some might say that Anne was inclined to be a little too daring and a bit too bold for her own good. She could be reckless, Ursula. You know that as well as I do."

"Her spirited temperament was one of her charms, wasn't it? She was the woman we all yearned to be—the Modern Woman."

"Perhaps." Matty smiled reminiscently and then abruptly wrinkled her nose. "Except for the cigarettes. I never could understand her taste for those things."

"Neither could I," Ursula admitted.

"Do you know, yesterday, when we stood there at the graveside, I thought that Anne must have died from a heart attack or a stroke," Matty said.

"What makes you so certain?"

"We all knew her well enough to be quite certain that she would never kill herself because of a man."

SIX

He came awake on a tide of oppressive dread so strong he had difficulty catching his breath. For a few heartbeats he was back in the burial caves, trying to follow the trail of the third legend. The lantern was dying. He knew it would not last much longer. With every step he was increasingly certain that he had chosen the wrong path. He was doomed to wander the caverns of night until he dropped dead or went mad.

He sat up quickly on the edge of the bed, rubbed his face with both hands and then got to his feet. He turned up a gas lamp and checked the time. It was nearly four o'clock in the morning. He tried to focus. He knew that the dream was his mind's way of telling him that he needed to rethink some of his logic.

He needed to walk the labyrinth.

He pulled on a pair of trousers, took his dressing

gown off the wall hook and picked up the key ring
he kept beside his bed. He left the bedroom and went
downstairs. Opening a door off the kitchen, he descended a set of stone steps into the basement.

The vaulted chambers beneath the ground floor
of the house were very old. Much of the masonry
work was medieval in origin but there were other
sections that dated from the days when the Romans
had controlled Britain. It was easy enough to distin-
guish the two eras if one paid attention. The Roman
construction work was orderly and refined—the
bricks well made, uniformly shaped and aligned
with great precision. In comparison, the masonry of
later generations was nothing short of sloppy. Nevertheless, it had all stood the test of time. He wondered if modern construction would hold up as well
centuries from now.

At the foot of the underground steps he picked
up a lantern and lit it. He continued down a low-
ceilinged stone corridor and stopped in front of a
thick wooden door.

Selecting a key on the iron ring, he opened the
door, moved into the chamber and set the lamp on
the small table near the door.

The glary light illuminated the pattern of blue tiles
set into the stone floor. The tile path formed an intricate, convoluted pattern that eventually led to the
center. Some would have said that it looked like a
maze. But a maze, with its many pathways that ended
in dead ends, was designed as a puzzle, created to
confuse and bewilder. His labyrinth had only a sin-

gle entrance and one true path that eventually brought the seeker to the center of the complicated design.

The very act of walking the labyrinth was a form of meditation requiring concentration and focus. The exercise helped him to see patterns hidden in chaos.

Here in this chamber there were no stone walls and no paintings lining the path so he created the illusion in his mind. He tightened his concentration until he could see only the ribbon of tiles beneath his feet.

When he was ready he walked the path through the invisible caverns of his mind. He could hear the whispers of the old dread that had threatened to rob him of his sanity. The unnerving voices were always there, waiting for him, when he began the journey. It did no good to try to suppress them. Instead, as he had been taught, he acknowledged them from the perspective of a disinterested onlooker and returned his focus to the pattern.

Time did not matter when he walked the labyrinth. If he tried to hurry the meditative process he would not see the pattern. It was only when he ceased to care about finding the answer that it would come to him.

He concentrated on each tile, noting how it was connected to the one that had gone before and the one that came after. With each step he went deeper into his thoughts, deeper into the complex pattern.

And then he was there in the very heart of the labyrinth. He opened his mind and saw a truth that he had known from the start—Ursula Kern might be on the verge of putting herself in harm's way.

He contemplated another glittering shard of knowledge—allowing Ursula Kern into his life came with a degree of risk. She had the power to alter the balance of his carefully constructed world. The truly harrowing part was that the prospect of taking the risk thrilled him.

The words of the Master of the Labyrinth whispered through his mind. "There are many paths to many answers. Some paths must be walked alone but other journeys cannot begin unless one has a companion of the heart."

He picked up the lantern and let himself out of the chamber. He paused to lock the door and then he went up the stone steps.

There was something to the gossip about exotic rituals in the basement of his mansion. Not all of the rumors about him were wrong.

SEVEN

~~~

Lilly Lafontaine banged the delicate china cup into the saucer with so much force, Slater was mildly surprised that both the cup and the saucer survived the impact.

"I cannot believe what you just told me," Lilly announced. "What on earth did you do to my Mrs. Kern that caused her to terminate her employment with you?"

Slater winced. He was on the far side of the drawing room, standing near one of the tall Palladian windows but Lilly's voice had been trained for the theater. It was rich, resonant and inclined toward melodramatic undertones even when she whispered. When she was annoyed—as she was now—she could infuse her words with enough power to reach the cheap seats in the last row of any theater in London.

Lilly's drawing room complemented her strong

voice. It was decorated in a lavish, ornate style that put Slater in mind of a stage set or a very expensive bordello, depending on one's taste in interior design. Heavy crimson velvet draperies were tied back with thick gold tassels. The background color of the patterned carpet matched the red drapes. The graceful settee and the gilded chairs were covered in red velvet and satin.

A portrait of Lilly, done at the height of her career as one of the most celebrated actresses in London, hung above an elaborately sculpted marble mantel. She had been a raven-haired beauty in her younger days—her fine-boned features enhanced with mischievous eyes and a glowing personality that had evidently attracted everyone in her orbit, male and female alike.

There had been a time when most of the wealthy, distinguished gentlemen in town had vied for an invitation to Lilly's exclusive salons. Edward Roxton, heir to a fortune and a title, had been among that crowd of men.

Edward had been married when the liaison with Lilly had begun. Ten years ago the first Lady Roxton had died, leaving Edward without a legitimate heir to the title and the fortune. Although everyone knew that he would do his duty by the family name, there had never been any question of him besmirching the distinguished Roxton lineage by marrying an actress. In the eyes of the Polite World it would have been tantamount to wedding a courtesan. He had, instead, married a young woman of impeccable breeding. The second Lady Roxton had fulfilled her marital obligations, providing Edward with an heir and a spare—Slater's two legitimate half brothers.

As the sole offspring of the decades-long love affair that had existed between Lilly and Edward, Slater had been born with an entrée into two very different worlds. His mother's extensive connections in the theater and the less-than-respectable classes of society known among the elite as the demimonde ensured him a welcome in that sphere.

The fact that his father had always acknowledged him and had provided him with both an upper-class education and a sizable inheritance had been enough to guarantee that he would be received in most upper-class circles. True, the inheritance had been cut off for a time, but that situation had changed dramatically upon the death of Edward Roxton. In his new position as the sole trustee of the Roxton fortune, Slater knew that most of Polite Society was happy to welcome him into its drawing rooms and ballrooms.

But it was his complete lack of regard for the opinion of the Polite World combined with the mystery of his long absence from London that rendered him fascinating to those who inhabited the more rarified reaches of the social universe.

"Kindly lower your voice," he said. "You know I am a great admirer of your talents but I have had enough theatrics from my household staff to last me a lifetime. Mrs. Webster is going about her duties as if someone in the family just died. I'm surprised she isn't hanging crepe in the drawing room. Mr. Webster and Griffith are acting as if they suspect me of having committed a grave crime."

Lilly brushed all that aside with a grand wave of one beringed hand but she did moderate her voice.

"What reason did my Mrs. Kern give you for leaving her post?" she asked.

Slater drank some of his coffee while he considered how to answer the question. He had been expecting it. During the course of the twenty-minute journey from his house to Lilly's elegant little town house, he had considered any number of answers. None that did not include the truth seemed sufficient, however. And he was not about to reveal Ursula's intentions to investigate her friend's murder—not until he obtained her consent.

"She is not your Mrs. Kern," he pointed out. "In fact, I have the impression that Ursula Kern does not belong to anyone except herself. She is a very independent-minded female."

"Which explains why I like her so much, of course," Lilly said. "I interviewed any number of secretaries before I heard about the Kern agency. I knew as soon as I met her that I wanted her and no one else to take down my plays and transcribe them on a typewriter. As the proprietor of the agency, she accepts very few private clients, herself, you know. I thought she would be perfect for you and she did me the great favor of agreeing to take you on."

Slater raised his brows. "Please do not tell me that you were matchmaking."

"Don't be absurd," Lilly said. "I know how you feel about that sort of thing."

The denial sounded firm but the cool, quick response was a bit too smooth, Slater decided. His mother had almost certainly tried to do some matchmaking. He decided this was not the time to tell her that, for once, she might have succeeded, at least in part. The sweet, hot ache of desire that gripped him the first time Ursula walked through his door had shaken him to his core. But he had seen the wariness in her eyes and had told himself that he would have to take things slowly and cautiously.

Now, it seemed, he had destroyed his original strategy by engaging in a quarrel with the very woman he had hoped to seduce. But if surviving Fever Island had taught him anything, it had made him very, very good at not giving up on an objective.

After Ursula had walked out yesterday he had spent what was left of the afternoon concocting a new plan. It wasn't much as strategy went and he had learned the hard way that very few plans worked as intended, but any plan was preferable to none at all.

"Mrs. Kern explained that one of her secretaries was found dead recently, a probable suicide," he said. He preferred to stick with the truth in so far as it was possible. It meant that one had to keep fewer balls in the air at any given time. "Evidently she feels obliged to assume the secretary's duties with a long-standing client until other arrangements can be made."

"Why doesn't Ursula simply send one of her other

secretaries to the client?" Lilly asked. "Why does she have to be the one to take over the dead woman's responsibilities?"

"You will have to ask her that question if you want an answer." Slater set his cup and saucer on a small table. "All I can tell you is that she informed me she had to terminate our arrangement until further notice."

"I'm not sure I believe you," Lilly said. "I think you do have some notion of why Ursula felt it necessary to leave your employ, but you are keeping it from me. Are you certain you didn't do or say anything that made her feel . . . uneasy in your company? I know you would never deliberately set out to offend a lady but you have spent very little time here in London in the past few years. I'm sorry to say your manners have become somewhat rusty."

"I think that if Mrs. Kern objected to my manners, she would have mentioned it quite early on," he said.

"Not necessarily. She may have attempted to grow accustomed to your eccentricities but in the end concluded she could not."

Slater went still.

"What the devil do you mean about my eccentricities?" he asked.

"You know very well what I mean. If you don't, I suggest you consult the latest edition of the *Flying Intelligencer* or one of the penny dreadfuls that features you. Ever since you returned to London two months ago, the press has run wild with rumors about your eccentric nature and odd behaviors."

"Those damned gutter rags know nothing about me."

"Mmm, perhaps not. But that does not stop them from speculating." Lilly's tone turned thoughtful. "I wonder if it is the rumors regarding your knowledge of exotic lovemaking techniques that alarmed Mrs. Kern?"

"Is that supposed to be a joke, Lilly?"

"No, it is not. I am quite serious. Mrs. Kern is a widow so she is certainly aware of what goes on between a man and a woman in a bedroom. But I have the impression that her marriage was short-lived. Her husband died in an accident less than two years after the marriage."

"What sort of accident?"

"I believe he fell down a staircase and broke his neck."

"What is your point, Lilly?"

"I'm simply trying to warn you that any female of limited experience might be shocked at the notion of, shall we say, adventurous lovemaking."

Slater groaned. "I cannot believe we are discussing this subject. I don't think Mrs. Kern walked out on me because of the gossip about me. She is a businesswoman. She was concerned about leaving a client in the lurch."

"The client must be quite important."

"Lady Fulbrook."

Lilly's eyes widened a little and then immediately narrowed. "Of Mapstone Square?"

"Yes. Why? Are you acquainted with Lady Fulbrook?"

"Well, of course I don't have a personal acquaintance with her, Slater. Women in her world never
associate with the women of my world."

"I realize that but you always seem to know a great
deal about what is going on in upper-class circles."

Lilly raised her delicately drawn brows. "I am
familiar with the goings-on of a different generation
of the Polite World—your father's generation. Lady
Fulbrook is much younger. She was married in her
first season. That would have been four or five years
ago at most. Created quite a stir when she was introduced into Society, I understand. She is a stunningly
beautiful woman, by all accounts. But she does not
go about much these days."

"Why not?"

Lilly gave an elegant shrug. "I have no idea. I am
under the impression that she has become something
of a recluse. I can make inquiries if you like."

"I would appreciate it."

Lilly gave him a long, inquiring look.

"Why?" she asked.

"Let's just say I'm curious about the client who
succeeded in taking my place."

"I see."

Lilly's expression was not a good sign, Slater
thought. She appeared much too intrigued. He
searched for a distraction.

"About Mrs. Kern," he said, schooling his tone to
one of mild interest.

"What about her?"

"When did she lose her husband?"

Lilly considered that for a moment. "Do you know, I'm not entirely certain. But I have the impression it was at least four years ago. Mrs. Kern mentioned at one point that she worked as a paid companion for a time before she opened the secretarial agency."

Slater gripped the windowsill. "Yet she still goes about in deep mourning."

Lilly smiled faintly. "Very fashionable mourning."

"Do you think she cared so deeply about her dead husband?"

"No," Lilly said with conviction. "I think she goes about in black because she believes it assures potential clients that she is a very serious businesswoman."

He thought about that. "Perhaps you are correct. She is, after all, quite riveting. She would not want her female clients to worry that the men in the household might notice her."

"Riveting?" Lilly repeated very casually.

He looked out the window and saw Ursula with her hair of low-burning flames and her eyes filled with mysteries.

"Riveting," he repeated softly.

Lilly smiled and reached for the pot. "More coffee?"

EIGHT

"My nerves are quite delicate, Mrs. Kern." Valerie, Lady Fulbrook, clasped her hands on top of her desk. "I have difficulty sleeping. At unpredictable times and for no apparent reason, I am suddenly overcome with anxiety and dread. I am easily tossed into the depths of despondence by matters that, to those who possess sturdier nerves, would seem the merest of trifles. But I have discovered that writing my little poems provides me with significant relief. I was fortunate to find a small publisher in New York that has been kind enough to take some of my efforts for its magazine."

"That would be the *Paladin Literary Quarterly*?" Ursula asked. "I found the address in Anne's files."

"Yes. Paladin doesn't pay, you understand, except in free copies of the *Quarterly*. But I am not writing to make an income. It is therapy."

"I understand," Ursula said. "I'm glad that you have found the services of the Kern Secretarial Agency helpful."

They were alone in Valerie's small, private study. A short time ago a dour-faced maid had brought in a tea tray, poured two cups and departed. She had moved like a ghost throughout the process, making almost no noise.

There was, Ursula noticed, a curiously oppressive hush about the entire household. It was as though the inhabitants were waiting for someone to die.

Ursula had been to the Fulbrook mansion once before when Valerie had sent a message to the agency saying that she wished to hire a secretary. Ursula always insisted upon meeting new clients personally. She took the precaution for two reasons. First, and foremost, it sent a clear message that the agency was an elite establishment and it expected clients to treat the professional secretaries with respect. The second reason she insisted on an initial face-to-face meeting was so that she could gain an impression of the client.

This afternoon Ursula concluded that her initial impressions had been accurate. Valerie was a beautiful but fragile flower that could easily be crushed underfoot. Her blond hair was pinned into a chignon that emphasized her pale skin and fine-boned features. She was small and thin but elegantly, gracefully proportioned—a dainty fairy princess. She appeared composed but there was a bleak desperation in her blue eyes. Her voice suited her appearance, weak and faint, as though the slightest breeze would blow it away.

Valerie was a woman who, in the right gown and endowed with an air of confidence, could have been capable of lighting up a ballroom. But it was clear that she had retreated almost entirely from life.

"I do not pretend that my poetry has any claims to literary merit," Valerie said. "But my doctor tells me it is doing wonders for my nerves."

"I am happy to be able to assist you in the endeavor," Ursula said.

"As I explained when I first engaged a secretary from your agency, I would write the poems myself but I find that I gain a much clearer impression of how they will appear in print if I read them in typewritten form. Also, I fear that I become quite anxious when I try to write down a final version of my own poems. I cannot stop myself from going over them again and again. I get quite frustrated and depressed. But for some reason when I dictate them, the words come more freely."

Ursula had stayed awake late into the night contemplating two things—the fact that she might never see Slater again and a way to introduce the subject of Anne Clifton when she met with Lady Fulbrook. There was no answer to the problem of Slater Roxton, but when it came to the matter of the investigation she concluded that a few straightforward questions might not seem suspicious.

"I realize it must have come as a shock to learn that Miss Clifton had passed," she said gently. "You were accustomed to working with her, after all, and had no doubt established a certain routine."

"Yes, Anne—Miss Clifton—was an excellent secretary." Valerie sighed. "I will miss her. You say the police believe she took her own life?"

"Yes. Those of us who knew her at the agency were astonished by that news but evidently there is little doubt about the facts."

"I see." Valerie shook her head. "How sad. Anne was not only a flawless stenographer and typist. Our working relationship was such that, toward the end, she was actually quite helpful to me. When I had difficulty with my poems, we would discuss the overarching theme. Often the perfect word or turn of phrase became clear to me."

"I doubt that I will be as helpful in that regard," Ursula said. "But I will do my best."

Valerie glanced out the window with the air of a prisoner peering through the bars of a cell.

"You will be surprised to hear this, Mrs. Kern, but these past few months, Anne was the closest thing I had to a friend. I never leave the house now, you see. I looked forward to my twice-weekly appointments with Anne. She was my lifeline to the outside world. I feel her loss quite keenly."

"I understand."

There was a moment of silence and then Valerie rose from her chair with a dignified but weary air.

"Shall we begin?" she said. "I think best in my conservatory. That is where I receive my inspiration. I trust you will not mind if we work there?"

"Of course not." Ursula collected the satchel containing her notebook and pencils and got to her feet.

Valerie led the way toward the door of the study. "I frequently employ images and themes taken from nature."

"I see."

At the end of the cavernous hall, another silent, somber-faced maid opened the door. Ursula followed Valerie outside and across a stone terrace. They walked toward a magnificent iron-and-glass conservatory that loomed in the foggy afternoon light.

When they reached the door Valerie took out a key.

"The conservatory is my realm, Mrs. Kern," she said. "It is the one place where I find peace of mind. The poem I am currently working on is titled 'On a Small Death in the Garden.'"

It was, Ursula concluded, going to be a very long and rather depressing afternoon.

NINE

~~~~~~~

She escaped the gloom-filled Fulbrook mansion promptly at three. *Escape* was not too strong a word, Ursula told herself. There was an ominous sensation about the household that was difficult to put into words. No wonder Anne had often referred to the mansion as a mausoleum.

She went quickly down the steps into the heavy fog. Preoccupied with mulling over her first impressions of the Fulbrook household and its inhabitants, she did not notice the sleek black carriage waiting on the other side of the street until Griffith raised his gloved hand to get her attention.

"No need to hail a cab, Mrs. Kern," he called across the width of the quiet street. "We'll see you home."

Startled, she came to a halt. "What on earth?"

But the door of the carriage had already opened. Slater, dressed in a high-collared greatcoat and boots, got out. He crossed the street toward Ursula. Light glinted on the lenses of his spectacles, making it impossible to read his eyes.

"I see your new client allowed you to leave on time," he said. "Excellent. I was concerned we might be obliged to wait upon Lady Fulbrook's convenience."

He took Ursula's arm, his strong, leather-gloved fingers tightening around her elbow. It was the first time he had touched her in a deliberate manner. She was caught off guard by the jolt of intense physical awareness that shivered through her.

He did not grip her tightly but she sensed the power in his hand. Perhaps it was just the relief of being free of the Fulbrook household, at least for now, that stirred her senses. But she suspected the real reason she was suddenly a little light-headed with excitement was the knowledge that Slater had come for her today.

The spark of pleasure faded when common sense and logic poured icy water on the tiny flame. It was, she knew, highly unlikely that Slater was here simply to escort her back to the office. In the short time that she had been acquainted with him she had learned that, despite appearances, there always seemed to be something else—possibly something quite dangerous— going on underneath the surface.

She dug in her heels, literally, refusing to move toward the carriage. Slater was forced to stop, too.

"What are you doing here, sir?" she asked. "And pray do not tell me that you felt obliged to protect me from the necessity of traveling by public cab. I have been climbing in and out of cabs for years all by myself with excellent success."

"Could we perhaps discuss this matter when we are both inside the carriage? There is no need to stand out here in the street in full view of whoever is watching us from inside the Fulbrook household."

"Good heavens. Someone's watching us?"

Automatically she started to glance back over her shoulder.

"Best not to let anyone know that we are aware that we are being observed," he said. "Also, it would probably be a good idea not to make it look as though I am kidnapping you. It would, perhaps, be useful to give the impression that we are very good friends."

She hesitated, wondering if he had spent so much time out of the country that he did not know that the phrase *very good friends* was a euphemism that was often employed to describe an illicit relationship. She studied his hard, unreadable face and concluded that he knew exactly what he was implying. She was quite certain that Slater always knew precisely what he was doing.

Whatever the case, the last thing she wanted to do was cause Lady Fulbrook or anyone else inside the mansion to wonder if she was engaging in a public quarrel in the street.

"Very well, sir," she said. "But I will want an explanation."

"Of course."

Slater steered her across the street to the carriage. Griffith greeted her as enthusiastically as if she had just returned from a long voyage.

"A pleasure to see you again, Mrs. Kern," he said.

"And you, as well, Griffith."

Ursula collected her skirts, went up the steps of the vehicle and sat down inside. Slater followed her into the shadows of the interior. Griffith stored the steps and closed the door. He vaulted up onto the box, moving with an amazing agility for a man of such enormous size, and shook out the reins. The carriage rolled down the street.

Ursula looked out the window. She thought she saw a curtain shift in one of the windows of the Fulbrook mansion. A chill went through her.

"It seems you were right, Mr. Roxton," she said. "I believe someone may have been watching my departure."

"It's possible that the observer was motivated by simple curiosity," Slater said. "But given your suspicions, we must assume the worst."

She looked at him through her veil. "*We* must assume the worst?"

"I have decided to assist you in your investigation."

"Why?" she shot back. "The last time we spoke you made it perfectly plain that you were opposed to my plan."

"It has become obvious that there is no point trying to talk you out of the scheme so I have concluded that the most reasonable course of action is to do what I can to help you find the answers you seek—always assuming there are answers to be had."

"Assuming that, yes." She drummed her gloved fingers on the seat. "I would appreciate some advice and, perhaps, even your assistance but first I want to know why you changed your mind."

"I thought I explained. I changed my mind because I realized you would not change yours."

"Why not simply let me conduct the investigation on my own? Why do you feel obliged to help me?"

An unexpected smile came and went at the corner of Slater's mouth. "You sound suspicious of me, Mrs. Kern."

"I do not think you are giving me the whole story, sir. Why this sudden interest in my problems?"

Slater glanced out the window. He appeared to be reflecting on his answer. When he turned back to face her she saw cool determination in his eyes.

"Let's just say that after some consideration I concluded that I find your project intriguing," he said.

"I see."

She had gotten her answer but she was not sure what to make of it. She was not even certain why she was vaguely disappointed in his reason for assisting her. But she had to admit that the logic was sound. It seemed plausible that a man of his nature would be drawn to something as unusual as a private murder investigation. He had, after all, spent the past few years wandering the world. Obviously he had been looking for something, although she very much doubted that he knew what he hoped to find.

"How did your first appointment with Lady Fulbrook go?" Slater asked.

She shuddered. "The house is quite grand but it is incredibly dark and gloomy inside. I cannot decide if the atmosphere is so bleak because the lady of the house is depressed or if it is the atmosphere of the place that is responsible for Lady Fulbrook's sad mood. Her only solace, evidently, is her conservatory."

"You said she employed Miss Clifton to take down her poetry in shorthand and type up the results?"

"Yes. Lady Fulbrook has attracted the attention of the publisher of a small literary quarterly in New York. The title of the poem that she is working on now will give you a fair indication of her mood. 'On a Small Death in the Garden.'"

"It does not sound like the sort of thing that would lift the spirits," Slater said. "But poets are supposed to be a moody, depressed lot. It's a tradition, I think. Is Lady Fulbrook any good at writing poetry?"

"You know how it is with literature and other works of art—the beauty of the finished piece is always in the eye of the beholder. Speaking personally, I am not attracted to depressing poetry, just as I am not attracted to books or plays with unhappy endings."

At that, he actually smiled. It was, she concluded, an annoyingly superior smile.

"You prefer fantastical endings rather than those which illustrate reality," Slater said.

"In my view there are cheerful endings and sad

endings but they are all fantastical by definition—
otherwise they would not be classified as fiction."

That surprised a short, rusty laugh from him. He
seemed as surprised as she was by his reaction.

"Very well," he said. "You established that Lady
Fulbrook writes melodramatic poems. Was that all
you accomplished today?"

"It was only my first day in the post. I did not
expect to discover all the answers in one afternoon.
And by what right do you presume to criticize? You
are only just now joining the investigation."

"You are correct, of course. I did not mean to be
critical. I was merely trying to gather the facts so that
we may form some sort of plan."

"I have a plan," she said crisply. "And I think we
had best establish one very important fact right now
before my investigation proceeds any further. I am
in charge of this project, Mr. Roxton. I would appreciate your insights and observations because I respect
your intellectual abilities and your extensive experience in finding lost cities and temples and such. However, I will make the decisions. Are we quite clear
about that?"

He looked at her for a long moment, as though she
had spoken in another language. She had no clue to
his thoughts but she suspected that he was about to
tell her he could not possibly assist her on her terms.
Well, what had she expected him to say? He was a
man who was clearly accustomed to giving orders,
not taking them.

She sat, tense and unaccountably anxious, and

waited for him to declare that a truly equal partnership between the two of them would be quite impossible.

"You respect my intellectual abilities and my extensive experience in finding lost cities and the like?" he said.

She frowned. "Yes, of course."

"Then you will admit that I have something useful to contribute to the project."

"Certainly. That is why I mentioned my plan to you in the first place. What are you getting at, sir?"

"I'm not sure. I think I am trying to accustom myself to the notion of being admired for my intelligence." He paused. "And my extensive experience in finding lost things."

Her patience evaporated. "Well, what the devil did you expect me to admire about your person, sir?"

He nodded somberly. "Excellent question. What did I expect? I don't think I can answer that at the moment so let us move on to the terms of our arrangement, Mrs. Kern."

For some reason, the word *arrangement* stopped her cold. For the second time in the span of only a few minutes she suspected that he was employing a euphemism to imply an intimate liaison between the two of them—a liaison that most certainly did not exist.

"I'm afraid I'm not following you, sir," she said.

She was acutely aware that her voice sounded uncharacteristically breathless. This was ridiculous, she thought. She must not allow him to rattle her in this fashion.

"I cannot guarantee that I will dutifully carry out every order you choose to issue," he said, "but I can promise that ours will be an association of equals. As for situations in which there is some disagreement involved, we will discuss the issue thoroughly when possible before either of us makes a decision. Will that satisfy you?"

She pulled herself together with an effort of will. "The phrase *when possible* leaves a great deal of vagueness in the *arrangement*, don't you think?"

"There may be situations where I shall be forced to make a decision before I have an opportunity to consult with you. I feel it is only fair that I have some room to maneuver—some freedom to exercise my own intuition and judgment."

"Hmm." She gave him a cool smile. "And I must have a similar degree of latitude, of course, as I am the one who will be spending a few hours each week in the Fulbrook household. Obviously I will not be able to simply excuse myself for a few moments to consult with you before I take advantage of the odd opportunity that might present itself."

His jaw tightened. "Just a moment—"

She smiled, quite satisfied. "I accept your terms, sir. Now, precisely how do you intend to contribute to my investigation?"

Slater was no longer looking quite so assured. His eyes were a little tight at the corners.

"I hope to contribute to *our* investigation by taking a close look at the Fulbrook family," Slater said very deliberately. "You did say you are convinced that if

Anne Clifton was the victim of foul play, there must be a connection to the household, correct?"

"That is my theory, yes." She brightened. "What do you know of the Fulbrook family?"

"Very little. But my mother was acquainted with Lord Fulbrook's father. He moved in the same circles as my father."

"I understand." Enthusiasm ignited Ursula's senses. "We could ask Lilly for her observations on the deceased Lord Fulbrook. She may well know something about the son and the family in general."

"She will demand an explanation for our curiosity," Slater warned.

"Yes, of course. But I feel quite certain that we can trust Lilly. Do you think she will be willing to assist us?"

"This is Lilly Lafontaine we are talking about. She will be thrilled to get the part."

"The part?"

"Pardon me," Slater said. "I meant that she will be thrilled to be involved in a murder investigation. It will appeal to her sense of drama. But when this is over you had better be prepared to see aspects of the venture appear in one of her plays."

Ursula winced. "I suspect you are correct. Well, I suppose so long as she disguises the identities of those involved it will be all right."

"After all," Slater said, "who would believe a tale about a secretary and an archaeologist attempting to solve a murder?"

"Indeed."

"That reminds me."

"Of what?"

"Lilly invited us to dine with her tomorrow evening. It will give you the perfect opportunity to question her about the Fulbrook family."

"How kind of her." Ursula smiled, her spirits lifting rapidly. "You're right, it would be very useful to obtain some information from her. I confess that at the moment I have no idea where I am going with this investigation."

"Where *we* are going with this investigation."

She ignored the correction. "Thank you, Mr. Roxton. I appreciate your assistance in this matter."

"I think that, under the circumstances, you really should call me Slater."

She felt the heat rise in her cheeks. She hoped the veil concealed her blush.

"Yes, of course," she said briskly. "Thank you . . . Slater."

There was a short pause. Belatedly it dawned on her that he was waiting for her to say something.

"Please call me Ursula," she added.

"Thank you, Ursula." He inclined his head. "I shall call for you at seven-thirty tomorrow evening. Is that agreeable?"

She thought about that for a few uncertain seconds. When one considered the matter closely it was obvious that being alone in the carriage with Slater at night would be no different from being alone with him now, during the day. But for some reason the prospect unnerved her a little. She reminded herself that theirs was a partnership.

She smiled, satisfied with her logic. "I will be waiting."

It was, she thought, a great pity that every gown in her wardrobe with the exception of her house dresses was black.

TEN

Shortly before midnight Slater sat in the shadows of a hansom and watched the front door of the exclusive gentlemen's club. The cab's lights were turned down low so as not to draw attention. In the fog the streetlamps that marked the steps that led up to the front door of the club were no more than luminous spheres of ghostly energy.

He could have gone up the steps and been admitted to the club. He was a member, thanks to his father's status and power, but he had not exercised his privileges since his return to London. It was Brice Torrence's favorite retreat. It seemed best that he and Torrence did not find themselves in the same room. Brice evidently felt the same way. Whether by luck or by design, in the two months since Slater had returned to London he and Brice had managed to avoid chance encounters.

The only reason he was here tonight, waiting in the mist-bound shadows, was because the club happened to be one of Fulbrook's favorite haunts.

The hansom squeaked a bit when Griffith shifted his weight on the driver's perch above and behind the cab. He spoke through the opening in the top.

"His lordship's been in there a good long while now."

"Are you bored, Griffith?"

"When you told me that you wanted to play detective tonight I thought it would be a bit more exciting."

"So did I," Slater admitted. "Blame Fulbrook. It appears he lives a rather conventional life."

"Do you really think he might have murdered Mrs. Kern's secretary?"

"I have no idea. But Mrs. Kern won't be convinced that her employee was not murdered until we find the truth. At the moment she suspects that the killer might be connected to the Fulbrook household so I thought it might be useful to gain some idea of Fulbrook's habits."

"He'll probably follow the same pattern as the rest of his sort. Spend a few hours at his club playing cards and drinking and then go off to visit his mistress or a whorehouse. It'll be dawn before he goes home, which means we won't get any sleep tonight."

"It might be useful to discover the address of his mistress or his favorite brothel, assuming he has one or the other."

"They all do," Griffith said with world-weary wisdom. "They marry a respectable lady for her family connections or her fortune or both and get themselves an heir. But there's always a mistress on the side."

That was, Slater thought, an excellent summary of his father's lifestyle. Edward Roxton had married twice before he succeeded in fulfilling his responsibilities to the family name and the title but throughout the decades he had never given up the liaison with Lilly. As far as Slater could tell, his parents had, in their own fashion, been devoted to each other. He had no idea how his father's first wife had felt about the situation. He had never met the woman, although, as a boy, he had seen her occasionally from a distance. Like other ladies of her station, she had pretended to be unaware of her husband's other life. For his part, Edward had gone out of his way to keep Lilly and Slater in a separate sphere.

Edward's second wife, however, was a very different matter. Judith had been remarkably clear-headed about the marriage. She'd had her own reasons for wedding a man several decades older than herself. It had been a business bargain for both parties and each had fulfilled the terms of the agreement.

Slater watched the door of the club open. An elegantly dressed man emerged from the front hall and paused at the top of the steps. For a moment his aquiline profile was visible in the glary light.

"There's Fulbrook," Slater said. "Prepare to follow him, and make damned sure he doesn't notice us."

"He won't pay any attention to us," Griffith said. "It's just one more cab in a fogbound night. Doubt if he'll even look back. Why would he? Not like any of his associates will care that he's off to visit a woman."

"Nevertheless, I think it best to be cautious. Fulbrook will know that I have not frequented this club since my return to London. If he were to see me in the vicinity tonight, he might think it odd, especially after having made it obvious that I have taken a personal interest in his wife's new secretary—always assuming he is aware of Mrs. Kern."

"You think he knows that we collected Mrs. Kern from the Fulbrook residence earlier today?" Griffith asked.

"Someone watched Mrs. Kern leave the house," Slater said.

Fulbrook came to a halt at the bottom of the steps and contemplated the row of cabs waiting in the street. He did not select the first in line. Instead he chose a hansom seemingly at random and went up the narrow steps. He disappeared into the deep shadows of the small cab.

"Bloody hell," Griffith grumbled. He shook the reins, rousing the horse into a light trot. "I wasn't expecting that. Most take the cab at the front of the line."

"Most men of Fulbrook's station prefer their own carriages."

"A hansom is faster."

"And so much more anonymous," Slater said. "Interesting."

They followed Fulbrook's cab into the thickening fog. As they progressed through the streets the neighborhood changed. The houses and parks grew larger and more imposing.

"If he's got a mistress in this neighborhood he's keeping her in fine style," Griffith remarked.

"I doubt very much that he's got a woman stashed in one of these big houses," Slater said. "More likely he's headed to the home of a friend."

"Damned late and a far way to travel just to have a brandy with a friend," Griffith said.

"Depends on the friend."

Fulbrook's hansom came to a halt in front of a grand mansion. It was impossible to see much of the big house or the gardens because of the high brick wall that enclosed the grounds. Iron gates barred the drive.

A man with a shielded lantern appeared from the shadows of a small shelter adjacent to the gate. He angled the light into the close confines of the Fulbrook cab. A few words were exchanged. Evidently satisfied, the guard opened the gates and waved the hansom through.

"This is close enough, Griffith," Slater said. "I do not think the guard will pay any attention to us if we remain where we are and keep the lamps turned down. I'd prefer not to attract his attention."

Griffith brought the vehicle to a halt.

Fulbrook's hansom disappeared through the gate. The guard allowed another carriage to depart and then he closed the gates. He had to open them again when a new vehicle arrived.

"There is a great deal of coming and going," Slater

said. "Fulbrook's friend appears to be entertaining tonight." He jumped down from the cab. "I'm going to take a look around."

"D'ye think that's wise?" Griffith asked uneasily.

"I believe it's what detectives do," Slater said.

"It's also the sort of thing that burglars do and they tend to get arrested."

"It's only incompetent housebreakers who get arrested, Griffith."

Slater removed his spectacles and folded them neatly into the pocket of his coat. His eyesight was excellent. The eyeglasses were nothing more than a veil—not unlike the one that Ursula wore. People saw the spectacles—they did not see the eyes. In the years since Fever Island he had found the small disguise very useful in his work. For some strange reason people tended to discount the possibility that a man wearing spectacles might prove dangerous.

He faded into the shadows, simultaneously chagrined and amused to discover that he felt the old dark thrill of the hunt heating his blood. He had Ursula to thank for this, he thought.

He made his way along the narrow lane that bordered one side of the towering garden wall, turned the corner and found the rear gate. It was locked but there was no guard and no streetlamp.

He studied the view of the gardens through the wrought-iron bars of the gate. Most of the thick foliage lay shrouded in deep shadows and fog but the entrance to a hedge maze was lit with brightly colored lanterns. As Slater watched, an elegantly dressed couple disappeared into the green puzzle. The man's drunken laughter was hoarse with anticipation.

The ground floor of the big house was brightly illuminated. There were lights at the edges of the windows of the upper floors but the drapes were pulled closed.

Slater stood quietly for a time listening. Low voices drifted out of the shadows. A woman laughed flirtatiously. A man murmured in what he no doubt believed to be a seductive tone but his words were slurred. Another couple vanished into the maze.

Slater stepped back and studied the gate at the places where it was hinged to the brick wall. The intricate wrought ironwork was intended to keep intruders out but it also provided a number of convenient footholds. The trick would be scaling the gate without being seen. But none of the couples who occasionally materialized in and out of the mist appeared to be paying attention to the gate. In any event the fog was thickening so quickly that it was increasingly unlikely that someone would even be able to see the wall or the gate unless he or she were quite close.

He took hold of one of the iron bars and vaulted upward. He got the toe of one boot on another decorative bit of iron and reached for the next handhold.

Climbing the gate proved simple enough, much easier than climbing out of the labyrinth caves. There were no shouts of alarm. When he arrived at the top of the wall he reversed the technique, dropping almost soundlessly to the ground.

He pulled up the high collar of his coat to conceal

his profile and adjusted the brim of his low-crowned hat so that it shielded his eyes. His black scarf could be converted into a mask for the lower portion of his face if needed but in the fog-infused shadows of the gardens he was quite certain he would not have to use it.

He moved quietly across the grounds, keeping to the deep cover cast by tall, fancifully trimmed greenery. It took him a moment to realize that the hedges were all clipped to form erotic green statues.

Moonlight and the colorful lanterns illuminated the fog with an eerie radiance that rendered the couples he passed into ghostly silhouettes. On the far side of the grounds the great house glowed in the mist, a forbidding castle in a dark fairy tale.

He took care to stay out of the way of guests strolling the gardens but as he drew closer to the mansion it became increasingly difficult to remain unseen. Not that any of the male guests appeared to be focused on anyone other than their female companions, all of whom were remarkably attractive and extremely well endowed.

It soon became obvious that only the men were inebriated. The women laughed and teased and flirted in a practiced manner.

He knew acting when he saw it, Slater thought. The women were all professional courtesans—very expensive-looking courtesans, to be sure. Their gowns were elegant and in the latest fashion.

When he passed near the maze he heard giggles and drunken laughter inside. There were other noises as well—the primal grunts and hoarse groans of men caught up in the throes of lust. The interior of the maze sounded like the upper floors of a bordello.

Slater continued toward the house, stopping a few yards from the lantern-lit terrace. The French doors of a dimly lit ballroom stood open to the night. Inside couples danced and flirted in the disorienting light cast by lanterns encased in shades that were incised with various cutouts. The lamps dangled from wires in the ceiling, shifting, bobbing and rotating in a way that created ever-changing patterns of light and shadow over the crowd.

Slater considered his options. The guests and their courtesans were all attired in a fashionable, formal manner. He had dressed for an evening of discreet observation, not a soiree. He could not risk entering the ballroom. The coat and cap would draw immediate attention. Even if he were to remove them the risk remained. He had spent most of the past ten years away from London and he had not gone out into Society since his return but there were still some who might recognize him even in a darkened room.

On a night when so many guests were being entertained in such a lavish manner there were sure to be a large number of servants bustling about in the vicinity of the kitchen. The rear doors and the tradesmen's entrance would be open to allow the cool night air into a room that was bound to be overheated with cooking fires.

He made his way along the side of the house that faced the gardens, heading toward the far end where he assumed the kitchens would be located.

Within a few yards he found himself in a section that was obviously not intended for the guests. There were no pretty lanterns in the vicinity but there was enough light from the windows and the moonlight-infused fog to allow him to forge a path through the foliage.

He was nearly at his goal when he heard a woman on the other side of a hedge. She was hoarse with anger and a rising tide of panic but she did not raise her voice. Her accent was that of a respectable lady trying desperately to maintain her composure.

"You're hurting me, sir. Please let me go. There are rules."

"The rules don't apply to the guests. You're a whore and what's more, you're my whore, at least for tonight. I certainly paid enough for you."

The man's voice was thickened with drink. Rage seethed just beneath the surface.

"If you don't leave me alone, I'll scream," the woman warned.

But she kept her tone low and something in it told Slater that she did not dare to shout for help.

"You stupid bitch," the man snarled. "You know as well as I do that if you start yelling you'll find yourself on the street. You'll be taking your customers up against the wall in some filthy alley before you know it. Or maybe you'll end up in the river like your friend a couple of weeks back, eh?"

The observation was punctuated by a bark of harsh laughter.

"Wouldn't you care for another dance?" the woman asked, trying to sound flirtatious.

"I've had enough of dancing. Shut up. We're going to get into my carriage and you will do exactly what I tell you."

"I'm not going anywhere with you. I can't. None of the women from the Pavilion can leave the grounds. You know that, sir. The rules—"

"Don't quote the damn rules to me. You may look and sound like a lady but we both know you're just a cheap whore."

"I'm going back into the ballroom," the woman declared with shaky conviction. "*No*, you can't force me to leave the . . . *mmph*."

Slater was quite certain that the man had slapped a hand over the woman's mouth.

"I'll teach you to defy me," the drunken man raged.

Slater moved out from behind the cover of a hedge and saw the pair. They were dark shadows in the fog. The man was struggling to control the woman. He had an arm around her throat, choking her. She fought desperately but it was clear she was overpowered.

Neither of the two noticed him until he gripped the assailant's shoulder.

"Let her go," Slater said quietly.

The attacker was so startled he released the woman and whirled around. He stared into the glary light, trying to see Slater's face but that was not possible. Slater was careful to keep his back to the light, leaving his features in deep shadow.

"Leave us," the attacker hissed. "She's mine. Go find yourself another whore. I've got plans for this one."

"She's not interested in your plans," Slater said.

"You can't have her." The man peered at him, trying to see more clearly in the dim light. "Are you one of the bloody guards? If so, you can take yourself off immediately. This does not concern you."

"I'm afraid you are mistaken."

The assailant swung one fist in a wild, awkward fashion. Slater easily ducked the blow and came back with a short, hard punch to the gut. He followed it with a quick chopping blow against the side of the man's head.

The drunkard collapsed, unconscious, on the lawn.

Slater looked at the woman. She watched him warily.

"Thank you," she said. She sounded grateful but very cautious. "He wanted me to violate the rules. He was trying to take me away in a private carriage. We are not supposed to leave the grounds with any of the guests, as I'm sure you are aware. Mrs. Wyatt is very firm on that point."

Slater nodded and walked to look down at the unconscious man.

"Who is he?"

"His name is Hurst," the woman said. She hesitated. "You're not one of the guests, are you?"

"No."

"I didn't think so."

"Because I'm not dressed appropriately?"

"That and the fact that you're not acting as if you've drunk any of the ambrosia this evening. Who are you?"

"A curious spectator."

"Curiosity can be dangerous here at the Olympus Club."

"Is that what they call this place?" Slater asked.

"You didn't know that?"

"I do now. May I ask your name?"

The woman hesitated. "I suppose you have a right to it after what you just did for me. You may call me Evangeline."

He smiled a little. Everyone kept secrets, he thought. A professional courtesan would almost certainly have a few.

"I assume that Evangeline is your stage name?" he asked.

"Yes," she said, silently defying him to demand more.

"It is a pretty name," he said. "Was Hurst drunk on that ambrosia you mentioned?"

"Of course," she said. She waved one gloved hand to indicate the vast gardens. "They all are. The guests enjoy the drug in various forms. It is added to the liquor. Sometimes they smoke it in the form of cigars. The Olympus is the only place in London where it is served, you see. For the most part the ambrosia invigorates the men to the point where all they can think about is finding a female—willing or unwilling. If they take a sufficient quantity they usually enjoy wondrous visions and a great sense of pleasure. But sometimes the hallucinations can be quite intense and frightening." She glanced at the unmoving man on the ground. "And occasionally the drug affects men the way it did Hurst tonight."

"The ambrosia makes some of the men violent?"

"Yes." Evangeline peered at Slater, trying to see him against the glare of the light behind him. "You likely saved me from a beating or worse." There was a shudder in her voice. "Hurst was behaving very oddly. He is normally a quiet little man but tonight he flew into a rage. Perhaps he took too much of the drug. Some of the other Nymphs have reported similar reactions when their guests overindulged." She paused. "I should not be speaking with you like this. We are only allowed to talk to men who have been introduced to us by Mrs. Wyatt."

"I understand. Thank you for answering a few of my questions."

"Thank you for saving me from Hurst." Evangeline made a face. "I really don't know what got into him tonight. There are rumors that the management of the club has brought in a stronger version of the ambrosia recently."

She turned to walk back toward the ballroom.

"One more question before you go," Slater said softly.

She paused and looked at him over her shoulder. "Very well, but please be quick about it."

"Your friend, the one who wound up in the river—"

Evangeline went very still. "Nicole. They said she took her own life."

"But you don't believe that, do you? What do you think happened?"

"We're all quite certain that she broke the rules and left the grounds with a man who went mad after he took too much of the drug."

"You think her guest murdered her?"

"I cannot say, sir. But as I told you, everyone knows that some of the guests can take odd turns when they're enjoying the drug. That's why there are rules and guards. But as you saw tonight, the bloody guards are never around when you need them."

"What exactly is this ambrosia? Some version of opium?"

"I cannot say, sir. The Nymphs are forbidden to drink it."

Once again Evangeline collected her satin skirts and turned to leave.

"Are you concerned that Hurst will make trouble for you when he awakens?" Slater asked.

Evangeline's light laughter whispered in the fog. "It's unlikely he'll remember much of what happened, sir, not given the large dose of the drug that he evidently took. But if he does, I expect that it is you who will have left an impression on him."

She hurried away and soon disappeared behind the hedge.

ELEVEN

⁓

There was another mention of a perfume shop.

Ursula contemplated the lines she had attempted to transcribe from Anne's notebook. She reminded herself that poetry could be complicated and nuanced, not to mention downright oblique. Some poems were notoriously incomprehensible. And then there was the fact that Valerie was not a professional author. She was using the medium of poetry to soothe her shattered nerves.

Nevertheless, most of the verses in the notebook made sense once they were transcribed. The lines that she had just written down on a separate sheet of paper, however, did not. They looked, instead, very much like an address.

It was possible that Anne had grown bored with the dreary poems Valerie had dictated and had jotted down some private notes—reminders of appointments, perhaps, or, in this instance, the address of a perfume shop that someone had mentioned. It would certainly not have been out of character for Anne to shop for fragrances and fancy soap.

Ursula reflected briefly on the empty perfume bottle she had found on Anne's writing desk. Curious, she flipped back and forth through the notebook. The reference to the perfume shop appeared early on in the notebook, about three weeks after Anne had begun working for Valerie. It had been slipped in between lines of poetry.

. . . The longing in my heart is that of the flower
    for the sun,
Rosemont's Perfumes and Soaps. No. 5 Stiggs
    Lane
Yet tis the night I welcome for in my dreams to
    you I run . . .

Anne had never mentioned the purchase of perfume to her office colleagues and that was unlike her. She had always been very eager to display any new acquisition. A week or so before her death she had received a lovely silver chatelaine from a grateful client—a delicate aide-mémoire. It featured a tiny silver notebook and pencil attached with silver chains. Anne had worn it virtually every day to the office. Everyone had admired it.

If Anne had purchased some perfume or received it as a gift, surely she would have mentioned it.

Ursula reached for her pencil. A faint, muffled

thud on the front steps stopped her cold. The fine hairs on the nape of her neck stirred.

She glanced at the clock. It was nearly midnight. No one would call at such an hour.

Metal clanged lightly on metal, the small noise was distinctive, though barely audible. Ursula shot to her feet, an unnerving chill splintering through her. Someone had just pushed an object through the letter box.

She went to the window and eased the curtain aside. The fogbound street was very quiet. There were no vehicles but a dark silhouette was briefly visible in the glare of the streetlamp. The figure was that of a man enveloped in a coat and a low-crowned hat. He was rushing away from her front door. As she watched he vanished quickly into the night.

There was no noise from Mrs. Dunstan's room. But, then, it would take a gunshot or the Crack of Doom to awaken her after she took her bedtime dose of her own special laudanum concoction.

You are letting your imagination run away with reason and common sense, Ursula thought. But she knew she would not be able to sleep if she did not go downstairs to make certain that all was secure in the front hall.

The gas lamps were turned down very low but they cast enough light to enable her to make her way. She saw the small package on the black-and-white tiles before she reached the bottom step. The icy sensation grew stronger, threatening to overwhelm her.

Someone had, indeed, shoved a package through the brass letter box—at midnight.

The dread that had been gathering in the atmosphere around her struck with storm-like intensity. It took an astonishing amount of determination just to continue down the stairs.

She picked up the package. The contents felt light and flexible. Papers, she concluded, or a notebook.

She carried the package into her study, set it on her desk and turned up a lamp. Taking a pair of shears out of a drawer she cut the string that bound the parcel and slowly peeled away the brown paper.

She fully expected that whatever she found inside would come as a shock but a strange stoicism gripped her when she saw the little magazine. It was a penny dreadful. The black-and-white illustration on the cover featured a woman in a suggestively draped nightgown, her hair down around her shoulders. She was sitting in a tumbled bed, clutching the sheets to her bosom. The artist had made certain that a great deal of bare leg was visible.

The woman in the illustration was not alone in the bedroom. There was a man with her. He was in his shirtsleeves, his tie and the collar of his shirt undone. His formal evening coat was draped over the back of a boudoir chair.

The woman and the man gazed in stunned shock at the bedroom door, where a well-dressed, obviously scandalized lady stood in the opening. She had a gun in one gloved hand.

The title of the small magazine proclaimed the contents:

THE PICTON DIVORCE CASE

**An Accurate Record of the Testimony of
Mrs. Euphemia Grant and Others. Adultery!
Scandal! Attempted Murder!**

Ursula opened the magazine with shaking fingers. A handwritten note slipped out and fluttered to the top of the desk.

*You have been discovered. Silence may be
purchased. Await instructions.*

Ursula sank slowly down onto the chair. She had always feared that the day would come when someone would uncover her true identity. She had known that if that happened her newly invented life would fall apart and she would once again confront disaster. She had put aside a fair amount of money to prepare for such an eventuality. She'd had some notion of purchasing a ticket to Australia or America to start over yet again, if necessary.

But as she read the note a second time, it was anger, not fear, that stormed through her. She had made plans to leave the country if her past was exposed. But she had not anticipated the possibility that someone would attempt to blackmail her.

She needed a new plan.

TWELVE

~

"That's an amazing machine," Griffith said.

The expression on his face was one of intense fascination, perhaps even awe. Slater understood the reaction. He was impressed, himself. Although he had seen typewriters—in recent years they had begun to appear in offices around the world—he had never come across one as advanced in design as the machine Matty Bingham was demonstrating.

"It's my latest model," Harold Fenton said. He beamed with pride. "It has a great many new and improved features. But it requires an operator of Miss Bingham's exceptional talents in order to obtain the best results."

"She's certainly very skillful," Griffith said. He gazed at Matty's flying fingers, clearly entranced. "It's like watching a lady play the piano."

Matty appeared to be unaware of his interest. She

maintained her professional air but her cheeks were
flushed a deep pink. Griffith was right, Slater thought.
Matty's fingers moved on the keys for all the world
as though she were playing a musical instrument.
Her hands were elegant and graceful.

Slater took out his pocket watch to check the time.
He and Griffith had arrived at the offices of the Kern
Secretarial Agency a short while ago and found only
Matty Bingham and Fenton.

Fenton was a little gnome of a man. Judging by
his rumpled, ink-and-oil-stained coat, he had come
straight from his workshop. He was going bald. What
scraggly gray hair he had left had not been touched
by a barber in a very long time. Behind the lenses of
his spectacles, his gray eyes glittered with passion
for his creation.

"Mrs. Kern and I have established a professional
association," Fenton said. "I advertise that my typewriters are tested here at the Kern agency. That information
attracts the very best class of buyer, you see, because of
the reputation of Mrs. Kern's business. My goal is to
put a Fenton Modern in every office in the country."

He whipped out a card. Slater took it and glanced
at the wording.

FENTON MODERN TYPEWRITING MACHINES.
Tested by the expert typists at the Kern
Secretarial Agency.

Matty stopped typing and smiled. "Every time
Mr. Fenton makes an improvement in his machines,

he brings one around for us to test." She patted the new Fenton Modern on her desk in an affectionate manner. "This is the finest one yet, Mr. Fenton. I do believe you have outdone yourself. None of the keys or type bars jammed. I did not have to slow down or pause at any point."

Griffith leaned over Matty's shoulder to get a closer look at the keyboard. His brows scrunched together. "Why are the keys arranged in such an odd fashion? Q, W, E, R, T, Y come first. Shouldn't it be A, B, C, D, E?"

Fenton snorted. "Sadly, after the success of the Remington typewriting machines, everyone has grown accustomed to this keyboard design. Damned shame but that's what you get when a manufacturer of firearms turns its attention to other products."

Slater looked at him. "A trigger?"

"No, mass production." Fenton looked deeply pained. "So many Remingtons out there now with the QWERTY keyboard that it's become the standard, as far as the public is concerned. I've given up trying to persuade people to change over to another arrangement of the keys. None of my competitors have been successful with new designs, either. But that's not to say that there isn't room for improvement in the machines."

"Mr. Fenton is constantly increasing the efficiency and striking speed," Matty explained. "So many typewriters jam when one works too quickly. I've even heard that's the real reason the keyboard is designed in this odd manner—to slow down the typist so that the keys and type bars won't get tangled up with each other."

Fenton brightened. "I'm actually working on a device that will get rid of the basket arrangement for the type bars altogether. All the letters and numbers will be on a ball that rotates, you see. It is quite revolutionary—"

He broke off as the office door opened. Slater turned and saw Ursula. He knew at once, even before she removed her hat and veil, that something had happened. Her shoulders were rigid. Her eyes were cold and grim. It was obvious that she had not slept well.

When she saw him, he could have sworn he caught a flash of near panic on her face. But it disappeared almost instantly behind an aura of cool reserve.

"Good morning, everyone," she said. She stripped off her gloves and set them aside. "We don't usually have so many visitors at this hour of the day. I see you have brought us a new model, Mr. Fenton."

"Much improved," Fenton assured her.

"The action is extremely smooth," Matty said.

Fenton glowed.

Ursula nodded at Griffith and then looked at Slater with an air of challenge.

"What brings you here today, Mr. Roxton?" she asked.

They were back to Mr. Roxton. Something had most certainly happened during the night, he thought. He wondered how long it would take her to get around to telling him what had upset her.

"I am hoping I can persuade you to accompany

me to an exhibition of some antiquities at a museum this morning," he said. "I wish to do some research in preparation for our cataloging project."

She looked first startled and then wary. "I'm afraid I have work to do today."

"I believe your other client, Lady Fulbrook, will not be requiring your services until tomorrow. You may consider the visit to the museum a professional outing. I plan to make some notes which I will dictate to you. You'll need your stenography notebook."

She stared at him for a couple of seconds as if she were about to argue, but when he slanted a meaningful glance at Matty, understanding dawned in her eyes. Matty knew nothing about the investigation.

"Very well." Ursula took a breath, as though marshaling her forces. "In that case, let us be off. I'm sure Matty can deal with whatever comes up in the office today."

"Yes, of course," Matty said eagerly. "There's nothing unusual on the calendar today. I'll be fine. Oh, and by the way, I hired Miss Taylor. She will start training tomorrow."

Ursula nodded once, a crisp little acknowledgment of the new hire.

"Excellent."

Slater glanced at Griffith, who was still hovering very close to Matty.

"Griffith," he said. "If you don't mind?"

Griffith straightened quickly. "Right, then. A pleasure to meet you, Miss Bingham. Thank you so much for the demonstration."

Matty smiled. Her cheeks turned a little more pink and her eyes were very bright.

"You're very welcome, Mr. Griffith."

It was, Slater reflected, very likely the first time that Griffith had been addressed as *Mr.* Griffith. He appeared dazzled by the honor. He stood in the middle of the room, gazing at Matty, evidently struck dumb.

Amused, Slater cleared his throat. "*Mr.* Griffith, if you don't mind—"

Griffith pulled himself together. "Right, sir, the carriage."

He tipped his cap to Matty and headed toward the door. Matty's gaze lingered on him until he disappeared into the hall.

Ursula retrieved her hat and gloves. Slater took her arm. She stiffened briefly but she did not pull away. He had been right about the tension radiating from her. He could feel it now that he was touching her, a small electrical current shivering throughout her body.

He started to steer her toward the door.

"Ursula, wait," Matty said. Her chair scraped as she got to her feet. "You forgot your satchel. You'll need your notebook and pencils if you are to assist Mr. Roxton today."

Ursula stopped. "Yes, of course, thank you, Matty."

Smiling, Matty collected the satchel from Ursula's desk. She winked when she handed it to Ursula.

"Enjoy the museum," she said with a knowing look at Slater. "I'm sure the antiquities will be fascinating."

Ursula looked quite blank. Slater steered her out into the hall. He waited until they were seated in the carriage and headed toward the museum before he spoke.

"Am I mistaken, or were Miss Bingham and Griffith looking at each other as if they were both interested in something a good deal more personal than the new typewriter?" he asked.

Ursula was momentarily bewildered. "What are you talking about?"

"Never mind," he said. He searched for another neutral topic and abandoned the effort. He had never been much good at idle conversation. The experience on Fever Island and the career that he had pursued afterward had not improved his social skills. "What the devil is wrong with you, Ursula?"

"People keep asking me that. I am perfectly fit." She gripped the handle of her satchel very tightly. "Why don't you tell me the real reason you asked me to accompany you to the museum?"

"As a matter of fact, there are two reasons," he said. "The first is that I wished to talk to you in private. I have some news."

That got her attention. She watched him intently through her veil. "You have discovered something about Anne's death?"

"I cannot say, not yet. But I have learned something about Fulbrook which may or may not prove useful."

"As it happens, I started transcribing some of Anne's notes last night and I, too, discovered something but it is rather baffling. Before we exchange details, you had better tell me the second reason we are off to visit a museum at such an early hour."

"I thought touring the new exhibition of antiquities together would enhance the impression that our association is personal, not just professional."

She absorbed that. "I see. Why do you think that is wise?"

"Because based on what I learned last night it's possible this investigation may take a dangerous turn. If anyone is watching you, I want that person to be well aware that you have a friend who would be in a position to cause a great deal of trouble should anything happen to you."

She stared at him. "You're serious."

"Very. Damn it, Ursula, what the devil did you discover last night that has rattled your nerves? I did not think there was anything that could do that."

She tightened her gloved hands on the satchel positioned on her lap. "I came across a reference to a perfume shop in Anne's notebook. There was an address. It struck me as odd."

He waited. It was the truth, he concluded. But not all of it. When she did not add anything else, he tried another question.

"Was Anne Clifton fond of perfumes?" he asked.

"Oh, yes. That is not the point. It was just strange to find the address written down in the same notebook as Lady Fulbrook's poems. Tell me, what is your news?"

She was changing the subject a little too quickly, he decided. But this was not the time to press her. The carriage clattered to a halt in front of the museum. Slater reached for the door handle.

"I'm afraid my news falls into the same category as yours—odd and unusual but perhaps no more enlightening," he said. "I will explain once we are inside."

THIRTEEN

~~~~~

I t's a fake, you know," Slater said.

Ursula contemplated the statue of Venus. The nude goddess was portrayed in a graceful crouch, her head turned to look back over her right shoulder. There was a suggestion of surprise on her face, as though she had been startled by an intruder just as she was about to bathe. The sculptor had certainly gone out of his way to emphasize the lush, ripe contours of the female form. The sensuality of the figure was unmistakable, bordering on the erotic.

It was still early in the day. The gallery featuring the Pyne Collection of antiquities was only lightly crowded. Ursula was suddenly very conscious of the fact that she was viewing the nude Venus in the company of the most fascinating man she had ever met. She was grateful for the veil that concealed her flushed cheeks.

"No," she said. She made an effort to sound as if

her interest were purely academic in nature. She was not about to let him see that she was flustered. "I did not know it was a fake. How can you tell?"

"The modeling of the hair is clumsy and the expression on the face is insipid," Slater said, clearly impatient with spelling out the details of his analysis. He sounded very academic. "The proportions of the breasts and hips are exaggerated. It's the sort of figure one would expect to see decorating the hallway of an exclusive bordello."

"I see." Ursula turned away from the Venus. "Well, I expect the Romans had their own houses of prostitution to furnish."

"Certainly. But they usually installed a better grade of statuary. I can tell you that under no circumstances would they have decorated one of their establishments with this particular figure."

"What makes you so sure of that?"

"Because it has all the hallmarks of one of Peacock's statues."

Ursula blinked. "Who is Peacock?"

"Belvedere Peacock. He's been producing what he is pleased to call *faithful artistic reproductions* for years. He has managed to pass his pieces off to some of the most noted collectors in the country. I shall have to drop by his workshop and congratulate him on having one of his statues on exhibit in this museum. Quite an accomplishment."

Ursula moved a few steps away to inspect a handsome brass and wood chariot. The little card declared the piece to be Etruscan.

"Will you say anything to the museum staff about the Venus?" she asked.

"Of course not," Slater said. He came to stand beside her. "I only deliver an opinion on such things when I am asked to consult. In this case, no one has requested my opinion of the Venus." He studied the chariot for a moment and shook his head. "In any event, the task of identifying all the fakes and fraudulent pieces currently residing in museums and private collections would consume far too much of my time. The mania for collecting antiquities has produced a brisk trade in *faithful artistic reproductions*."

Ursula raised her brows. "Are you going to tell me that this chariot is not Etruscan?"

Slater glanced dismissively at the chariot. "Looks like Albani's work. He has a shop in Rome."

Ursula smiled, briefly amused.

"I do believe that there is something to be said for keeping one's opinions to oneself," she said. "I would have taken considerably more enjoyment from this exhibition if you had not informed me that most of the pieces are fakes."

Slater gave her a sharp, impatient look. "I didn't bring you here to study the artifacts."

"Right." She moved on to a large urn painted with a number of male and female figures engaged in what appeared to be complicated gymnastic poses. "You said you had matters to discuss."

Slater joined her in front of the urn. "The first is that I followed Fulbrook to a private club last night. The Olympus."

"What of it? Most high-ranking men belong to a number of clubs."

"This one is rather unusual in that there were several women present."

"Good heavens." Ursula turned quickly. "How very modern. I have never heard of a gentlemen's club that admits ladies."

"I don't think the Olympus deserves any credit for advancing the cause of women's rights. The females looked as fashionable and as expensively dressed as ladies at a Society ball but they were all employees of an exclusive brothel known as the Pavilion of Pleasure. The proprietor is a certain Mrs. Wyatt."

"Oh, I see." She hesitated, well aware that she should not follow up with the first question that came to mind. But she was unable to resist. "You are acquainted with this brothel and the madam in charge?"

"No. But I intend to make further inquiries."

"Why?"

She had not intended to put an edge on the question but it came out in a singularly demanding manner. As if she had any right to ask him why he wanted to make further inquiries into an exclusive brothel, she thought. Really, it was none of her concern. Many men patronized brothels. It should come as no surprise to discover that Slater was among that number.

"Because we are investigating Fulbrook," he said, as if she were not terribly bright. "His membership in the Olympus Club may be important."

"What makes you say that?" she asked.

"While I was on the grounds of the club last night

I had occasion to speak to one of the women who works for the brothel. She calls herself Evangeline."

Ursula glanced at him very quickly. "What do you mean she *calls* herself Evangeline?"

"I doubt that's her real name. She's a professional courtesan, Ursula. By definition, she is playing a role."

"Yes, of course, I see what you mean."

Just as I am playing a role, she thought. *I am not the woman you believe me to be.* Would Slater care if he knew the truth about her? There was no way to be certain how he would take the news of her past. Most gentlemen would be scandalized, of course. But Slater was different. Nevertheless, to tell him the full story would be to risk the total destruction of their fragile relationship.

She reminded herself that she had a plan to take care of the problem that had arisen during the night.

"Evangeline told me that the club dispenses a drug they call ambrosia to its members. It affects different people in different ways," Slater continued. "It induces pleasurable fantasies and visions in most of the men but some turn violent under the influence. She said that the newest version of the drug seems to be more powerful. She is convinced that recently one of the women from the Pavilion was murdered by a club man who was using the ambrosia."

"Good heavens."

"The women of the Pavilion were told that their colleague—Nicole—jumped off a bridge but they don't believe it."

Ursula considered that for a moment. "That is interesting but what does it have to do with Anne's death?"

"Perhaps nothing. But Fulbrook is a member of the Olympus Club. Presumably he uses the drug. At least one woman who earned her living providing sexual favors for the members of the club is dead in recent weeks. Anne worked in the Fulbrook household and now she is dead. Those facts may be links in a pattern."

"Anne certainly was not beaten to death. There were no marks on her body. I checked. If she was murdered it was most likely by poison. Perhaps the drug can kill in large doses?"

"It's possible. Do you think that Fulbrook might have lured her into working as one of the courtesans at the club?"

"No," Ursula said. "Absolutely not."

"I mean no disrespect to your friend, but you did say that she possessed a rather adventurous temperament. You indicated that she might have been involved in a romantic liaison."

"Exactly—a liaison," Ursula said. "She was not working as a prostitute."

"How can you be so sure?"

Ursula moved one hand to sweep the issue aside. "Among other things, she lacked the wardrobe for that sort of career."

That stopped Slater cold.

"Huh," he said. "Never considered that aspect of the situation."

"No doubt because you are a man. You said the woman you met last night—Evangeline—and the other prostitutes on the grounds of the club were dressed as fashionable ladies at a ball."

"Right. I'm no judge of fashion but it was obvious that Evangeline's gown was expensive. She also had some long gold earrings set with crystals."

"I can assure you that Anne did not own any ball gowns, expensive or otherwise. She possessed some jewelry but it wasn't the sort a woman would wear to a soiree. Her pieces were of a more practical nature—the kind of items a woman can wear to go out shopping or to tea with friends. There is a pretty little watch that could be pinned to a coat. A cameo. A locket. Her most expensive piece was a lovely chatelaine with a little silver notebook and pencil attached. A former client gave it to her. She loved that piece. But none of her jewelry was suited to a ballroom and neither were any of her gowns. Trust me when I tell you that if she had owned any items that fashionable or expensive she would have been unable to resist showing them to the rest of us at the office."

"You're sure?"

"Positive," Ursula said.

"Nevertheless, it strikes me as more than a coincidence that two women who are at least remotely linked to either Fulbrook or his club are dead. I think we should arrange to speak with Mrs. Wyatt, the proprietor of the brothel."

"If she is making a great deal of money supplying prostitutes to the men who belong to the Olympus

Club it is unlikely she will discuss her business affairs with us."

"I'm hoping Lilly can persuade Mrs. Wyatt to talk to us."

"Your mother is acquainted with her?"

"My mother's connections reach far and wide," Slater said.

Ursula smiled at the wry twist on his words.

"Yes, I did get that impression when I took dictation from her," she said. "She was certainly one of the most interesting clients I've had."

Slater started to make another comment but he stopped abruptly. Ursula realized that he had gone quietly alert, his attention snagged by something or someone at the far end of the hall.

When she turned to follow his gaze she saw a well-dressed, distinguished-looking gentleman and an attractive lady in a yellow-and-blue gown. The man was tall, blond and athletically built. He carried himself with the sort of languid self-possession that came naturally to one who descended from several generations of wealth and status. The lady appeared to come from the same world. The two were examining the sensually rendered Venus.

"Time for us to leave," Slater said.

It was a command, not a suggestion. Nor did he wait for a response. Instead, he gripped Ursula's elbow and headed toward the rear entrance of the gallery. She did not resist.

"Something amiss?" she asked softly.

"Someone, not something."

"I take it we are fleeing the exhibition because of the gentleman and the lady who just arrived?" she asked.

"We are not fleeing, damn it."

But Slater immediately slowed his pace. She knew he had not liked the implication that he was running away from the newcomers.

"Well, then?" she prompted. "Why are we rushing off? Do we have a pressing appointment?"

"Take it from me, it's best that Torrence and I do not find ourselves in the same room together," Slater growled.

"So that is Lord Torrence, your partner on the Fever Island expedition?"

"And his wife, Lady Torrence."

"I understand now why you wish to leave," Ursula said. "If the gossipmongers and the press discover that you and Torrence were both seen in the same gallery together there would no doubt be some wild speculation."

"Precisely."

"But what is the point of trying to avoid Lord Torrence? There are bound to be future encounters between the two of you. The Polite World is a very small town in most respects. I suggest that you simply act as if there is nothing out of the ordinary occurring."

"Thank you for the advice," Slater said. He sounded as if his jaw were clenched tight. "But as it happens I don't give a damn about Torrence or the gossips. It is you I am attempting to protect."

"Me?" She was dumbfounded. "But I am not in-volved in your dispute with Torrence."

"That may not prevent Torrence from attempting to find a way to use you to strike at me."

This time she was genuinely shocked. "Surely that nonsense about the bad blood between the two of you is just so much fodder for the press and the penny dreadfuls."

"Not all of it. For what it's worth, it's a one-sided feud. He is the one who has avoided me since my return, Ursula."

"Hmm."

"What the devil is that supposed to mean?"

"Never mind. Just a fleeting thought. None of my concern, really."

"Let's get out of here."

Slater whisked her along the gallery, past urns, statues and assorted bits and pieces of Roman armor. They very nearly made good their escape. But just as they were about to go through the door a very large, very rotund figure appeared directly in their path.

"Roxton." The round man's jovial voice boomed the length of the gallery and bounced off the walls. "Come to examine my collection, eh? I am honored, sir. Deeply honored. I'd heard that Torrence planned to put in an appearance but I must say it's a surprise to see you here. I was told that you don't get out much these days. Absolutely delighted that you made an exception for my little exhibition. I trust you will introduce me to your companion?"

They were caught, Ursula thought. Heads were

turning. There was no escaping the scene. She could tell Slater knew he was trapped. He brought her to a halt.

"Mrs. Kern, allow me to present Lord Pyne, the generous collector who donated these antiquities to the museum," Slater said in cold, formal tones.

"Lord Pyne," Ursula murmured.

"Mrs. Kern, a pleasure to make your acquaintance." Pyne bowed over Ursula's gloved hand. Then he straightened abruptly. "Who's that admiring my Venus? I do believe it's Torrence and his charming wife. Well, well, well. Roxton and Torrence. Two of the most esteemed antiquities experts in England have come to inspect my artifacts. I am deeply gratified."

"It is a very interesting collection," Slater said. He tightened his grip on Ursula's arm. "But I'm afraid Mrs. Kern and I must be off. We have a pressing engagement."

"Of course, of course. But first you must give me your opinion on the Venus." Pyne raised his voice, although that was not necessary. "I should like your views, as well, Torrence."

"The figure is quite . . . robust," Slater said.

Torrence and his wife took a few steps toward where Slater and Ursula stood with Pyne.

"Your Venus certainly draws the eye," Torrence allowed. He avoided looking at Slater.

"And the ladies?" Pyne chuckled. "I would be remiss if I did not ask for your opinions."

"I know very little about antiquities," Lady Torrence said in a strained voice. "That is my husband's area of expertise."

She managed a demure smile but she was watching Slater with eyes that were wide with an expression that bordered on horror.

"Mrs. Kern?" Pyne prompted. "What do you think of my Venus?"

"She is obviously the star attraction in your fascinating collection, sir," Ursula said. "And now, if you don't mind, Mr. Roxton is correct. We do have another appointment."

"I would not dream of delaying you," Pyne said. "Run along, both of you. And I thank you, again, Roxton, for coming here to view my collection this morning. Your positive opinion, combined with Torrence's, will ensure that these antiquities will attract any number of visitors. Indeed, I expect your visit and your comments will be in the morning papers. Next thing I know, the Pyne Collection will be famous around the world."

"I have no doubt of that," Slater said.

Evidently concluding that there was no longer any point trying to evade Torrence and his wife, he took the frontal assault approach to the problem. Instead of trying to escape via the rear door, he tightened his grip on Ursula's elbow and guided her back toward the main entrance of the gallery.

The path took them directly past Torrence and the terrified Lady Torrence. Ursula gave the woman what she hoped was a polite, reassuring smile but that only seemed to further alarm Lady Torrence. She clutched her husband's arm.

Torrence watched Slater the way a man might watch a tiger, as if he were waiting for the beast to spring.

Slater took the initiative, nodding curtly but never slowing his pace.

Torrence's jaw tightened and his eyes clenched at the corners. He acknowledged the greeting with an equally brusque inclination of his head. Ursula felt Slater hesitate almost imperceptibly. She got the impression that he was contemplating the possibility of turning back to confront Torrence. Determinedly, she kept going, forcing him to keep up with her.

"Damn," Slater said. But he said it so that only she could hear.

Ursula did not halt until they were safely outside on the street.

"That was a trifle awkward," she said after a moment of acute silence. "I think Lady Torrence was actually afraid that you and her husband would come to blows right there in the middle of the museum."

"Why would I engage in a fight with Torrence?"

"Well, according to some sources, there is a possibility that your former partner and supposed friend deliberately triggered the trap that nearly killed you in those temple caves. Following the disaster, Torrence sailed home to London with the fabulous treasure the two of you discovered—a treasure which has since disappeared, I might add. Some would say that sort of thing is sufficient to engender a deep dislike and distrust between two men."

Slater glanced at her, amused. Sunlight glinted on the lenses of his spectacles. "What sources are you citing, Mrs. Kern?"

"Just the usual. The gutter press."

"I thought so. I'm afraid they are somewhat misinformed."

She smiled. "I'm shocked. The press? Misinformed?"

"Not all of the facts are wrong. But one thing is clear—Torrence hates me for having survived Fever Island," Slater exhaled heavily. "I have no idea why, but there is no escaping that conclusion."

"Oh, no," Ursula said quickly. "That wasn't hate that I detected in him or in his wife, either."

"What, then?"

"Fear."

"That makes no sense."

"It does if he thinks you blame him for what happened on Fever Island. I realize it is none of my business but would you care to tell me exactly what did occur?"

"Considering that the story of our encounter with Lord and Lady Torrence will no doubt be the chief topic of conversation at breakfast all over London tomorrow morning, you have a right to some answers."

FOURTEEN

M rs. Kern, what a pleasure it is to welcome you again." Webster's scar crinkled the side of his face when he beamed at Ursula. "Mrs. Webster will be delighted, as well. I shall inform her immediately."

"Thank you, Webster," Ursula said, touched by the warm greeting.

Slater looked hard at Webster. "It's not as if Mrs. Kern has just returned from a voyage around the world. She was here only a couple days ago, if you will recall."

"Yes, of course, sir," Webster said. "It's just that the staff had been afraid that she would not be returning soon. This is a delightful surprise."

Hurried footsteps sounded in the hall. Mrs. Webster came onstage.

"Mrs. Kern, you're back," she exclaimed as though she was the heroine in a play who had just discovered that a long-lost relation was alive after all. "How wonderful to see you again."

"Thank you, Mrs. Webster," Ursula said. She smiled. "I'm afraid I won't be staying long—"

She stopped abruptly because Slater's powerful hand closed around her elbow. He hauled her off in the direction of the library.

"Mrs. Kern and I have work to do," he announced over his shoulder. "Kindly see that we are not disturbed."

Mrs. Webster gave him a steely look. "You'll be wanting a tea tray."

Slater groaned. "Fine. Bring us a tea tray, make sure there is coffee on it, and then see to it that we have some privacy."

Mrs. Webster relaxed into an approving smile. "Of course, sir. I'll just be a moment."

Slater drew Ursula down the hall and into the library. He closed the door and turned around.

"The Websters have missed you," he said.

"They are a very nice couple." Ursula tucked the veil up onto the brim of her rakish little hat. "And somewhat unusual."

"My mother offered to hire my staff two months ago because I had absolutely no idea how to go about the process, nor did I want to be bothered with learning how to do it properly."

"Of course you didn't," Ursula said. "I'm quite certain that hiring the household staff is not something that a gentleman is taught. That is the work of the lady of the house."

His expression became unusually grim, even for him, she thought. He walked behind his desk chair and gripped the back with both hands.

"There are times when living in this household with a staff composed of failed actors and other assorted theater people is like living in the middle of a melodrama," he said. "The actors are especially unreliable. They quit on the spot if they get a hint of a bit part in a play. Then, when the play folds after two nights, they're back, asking for their posts. But it is not as if I've got much choice in the matter. I can hardly toss them onto the street."

"Why not?" Ursula asked calmly.

The question clearly stopped him for a moment.

"Well, among other things, it would be very difficult to find more traditional, more professional replacements," he said finally. He exhaled slowly. "Very few well-trained people in service would tolerate what the press and the gossips are pleased to call my eccentricities."

"Mmm. Perhaps. But I don't think that is the only reason why you do not let the Websters and the others go."

"No?" His brows rose. "I can't think of a better reason."

"You don't dismiss your servants because you have some sympathy for them. If they end up here on your doorstep it is because your mother has sent them to apply for a post. If you don't take them in and give them work until the next role comes along, some of them—particularly the women—will end up on the street. And some will not survive at all."

"I'm a charity house for unemployed theater people?" He winced. "Is that what you're saying?"

"That seems to be the case. As charities go, it seems a fine one. It is certainly one of the reasons I agreed to take the position with you back at the start of this arrangement."

He pinned her with a look.

"And then you quit," he said very softly.

"Yes, well, it was not my intention. And I did hope to return."

"Did you?"

"May I ask what sort of . . . eccentricities you possess that you feel would likely put off potential applicants for posts here in this house?"

He released the chair, widening his hands. "Do you have any idea how hard it is to find a cook who will serve vegetarian fare at every meal?"

Ursula blinked, caught entirely off guard. She tried to stifle a giggle but failed.

"Good heavens," she said in mock horror. "You're one of those? A vegetarian?"

He seemed disgruntled by her teasing, as though not quite certain what to make of it. He took off his glasses, whipped out a pristine white handkerchief and began to polish the lenses.

"Is that really so strange?" he demanded. "There is no need to look at me as though I had grown a second head or turned green."

She smiled. "Sorry. Your answer was not quite what I was expecting, that's all."

He paused in the act of polishing the spectacles. His startling eyes locked with hers. Once again she wondered why he bothered with eyeglasses.

"What sort of eccentricity were you expecting me to admit to?" he asked.

She waved a hand in an airy manner, aware that she was starting to enjoy herself.

"There have been some rather bizarre speculations in the press," she said. "I was inclined to dismiss them, of course, but when you mentioned that potential staff might be put off by your eccentricities, I did wonder precisely what you meant. Rest assured that vegetarianism was not the first thing that came to mind."

He started to put on his spectacles. Then, very deliberately, he set them on the desk. For the first time there was a glint of amusement in his eyes.

"Why don't you take a seat, Mrs. Kern, and tell me exactly what sort of eccentricities popped into your mind?" he said.

She had known that it would be a mistake to tease him about the vegetarianism. She did not know what had come over her. For whatever reason, making the small, lighthearted comment had been irresistible. But she should have heeded her intuition, which had warned her that any conversation of a personal nature was a high-risk venture with this man.

She sat down on a chair and tweaked the folds of her skirts, aware that she was a bit flushed. "I think perhaps we should change the subject."

"This may come as a shock to you, but I also read the press," Slater said. "I believe there is some concern in certain quarters that I have a secret chamber here in my house and that I have forbidden the servants to enter it."

"Oh, dear. You know about that nonsense, do you? I assure you I put no credence in the story."

"Evidently there are some who are convinced that I lure unsuspecting females into my secret chamber and practice the odd exotic ritual upon their persons."

"The definition of an exotic ritual is in the eye of the beholder, isn't it?"

"Do you think so?" Slater asked.

"As far as I'm concerned, the necessity of wearing fashionable gowns that feel like a suit of armor and weigh approximately the same, with skirts so heavy and voluminous that they make the simple act of walking a difficult endeavor, is an exotic ritual. Yet ladies here in London do it every day." Ursula paused for emphasis. "Including me."

She felt quite daring, she realized. Perhaps even a bit reckless. Something about being alone with Slater had that effect on her.

Slater looked startled by her response for about two seconds and then he laughed his short, rusty laugh.

"It is good to know that you take such a worldly view of exotic rituals," he said.

She opened her mouth, determined to use the opening to urge him back to safer ground, but an ominous knock stopped her. Webster opened the door as though it were the entryway of a crypt, allowing Mrs. Webster to sweep in with the tray of tea things. She set the tray on the one table near Ursula's chair and stood back.

"Shall I pour?" she asked with a hopeful air.

"No, thank you," Slater said. "We can manage."

Mrs. Webster did not bother to conceal her disappointment. "I'll be off, then. Ring if you need me."

"I'll do that," Slater said.

He waited until the door closed behind her and then he looked at Ursula. The brief moment of sensual amusement that had charged the interior of the library dissipated. She reached for the pot and filled two cups.

Slater came out from behind the desk and crossed the room to accept the cup and saucer she held out to him. He returned to the desk and stood in front of it.

"I'm aware that, in addition to the rather annoying speculation about exotic rituals carried out in a secret chamber, the press has also suggested that the experience on Fever Island may have affected my mind," he said. "And, in truth, perhaps it did. It certainly changed me in ways that are difficult to explain."

"That is hardly surprising," she said.

She spoke quietly and calmly, trying to let him know that he was free to tell the story in his own way. She was a woman with secrets. She understood that if they were confided, they needed to be confided carefully.

"Torrence and I were friends." Slater set the cup and saucer on the desk, the coffee untouched. "We had a mutual interest in antiquities. Early on we became intrigued by the legend of Fever Island. At some point the search for the island became an obsession for both of us. It took us two years of research before we finally got the first clue to the actual location of the damned place."

He broke off, gathering his thoughts. Ursula waited, making no effort to hurry him along.

"The charts that I discovered were buried deep in an old sea captain's journal and they were vague, to say the least," he said. "Torrence was half afraid that they were the product of a deranged mind but he agreed to make an attempt to find the island. In the end the captain of the ship we chartered discovered the place more by accident and good luck than because of the charts."

Slater went to stand at one of the windows. He looked out into the garden.

"From what we could tell, Fever Island was uninhabited," he said. "Torrence and I found the entrance to an ancient temple and what appeared to be an endless maze of burial chambers and treasure rooms all carved into the base of a volcano. We called the complex the City of Tombs." Slater paused and then shook his head slightly. "It was quite . . . astonishing."

Ursula sat very still and watched his hard profile. She knew that it was the temple tombs of Fever Island that he saw now, not the fogbound garden.

"It must have been a wondrous discovery," she said.

"Unlike anything I had ever seen in my life. It was as if we had stepped into a dream world."

Slater fell quiet again. She drank some of her coffee and waited.

"We had brought a small crew of men with us to assist in the excavation work," he said. "The entrance to the tomb complex was a long corridor of stone that led deep into the mountain. At the end of the tunnel was a vast chamber. The walls and floor were painted in dazzling colors. Statues of fantastic beasts were everywhere—large birds and reptiles unlike anything Torrence and I had ever seen. Each was studded with incredible gemstones."

"I saw the statue of the Jeweled Bird that Lord Torrence exhibited in the British Museum in the months following his return," Ursula said. "It was extraordinary. There was a great sensation when it was reported stolen."

"There were so many artifacts crammed into the temple chamber that we could only assume they had been collected over a long period of time—several centuries, perhaps."

"Do you think they were of Egyptian or Greek origin?"

"Neither," he said. "I'm quite certain of it, although there were similarities to both of those ancient civilizations. But I am convinced that we discovered the tombs of an unknown culture that was so old, so rich and so powerful that it may have left its influence on the great civilizations that rose after it was gone."

A sense of wonder came over her. "Good heavens, sir, do you think you and Lord Torrence discovered the royal tombs of *Atlantis*?"

He shook his head. "Atlantis is a legend."

She smiled at that. "I would point out that you are reputed to be something of a legend yourself. Such tales are not woven out of thin air. There is usually a grain of truth in them."

He shrugged. "It is unlikely we will ever discover the truth about Fever Island, at least not in our lifetime. The island volcano erupted years ago, burying the tomb complex beneath rivers of lava and mountains of ash. All I can tell you is that there were indications that the science and literature of the people was well developed, certainly the equal of ancient Greece or Rome or Egypt."

"You must have been thrilled when you first walked into those tomb caves."

Slater glanced at her over his shoulder, one brow slightly elevated. "I was thrilled—right up to the moment when the trap was triggered, sealing me inside the main tomb chamber."

Ursula's sense of wonder and excitement congealed. The cup trembled a little in her hand. Hastily she set it down.

"I cannot even begin to imagine what it must have been like," she said. "You no doubt believed that you had been buried alive."

"That was my first conclusion," he admitted. "I knew immediately that there was no hope that Torrence and the others would be able to rescue me."

"Why not?"

"I realized that they almost surely had to believe that I had been buried beneath countless tons of rock.

But even if they had held out some faint hope, they had no practical way to dig through the boulders that clogged the tunnel that led to the main chamber."

"How did you survive?"

"The trap that closed the exit tunnel was designed to protect the treasure and the sarcophagi in the burial vaults. The only part of the City of Tombs that was destroyed was the passageway that led to the outside world."

"How did you escape?"

"There were three passageways off of the burial chamber in which I found myself. The walls were covered with spectacular paintings. Each passageway told a different story. One was an epic history of endless wars. The second corridor told a story of vengeance. By luck and intuition, I chose the third legend. It led me into a passage that proved to be a labyrinth, not a maze."

"You mean it led to a central point?"

"Yes," Slater said. "Another exit, to be precise."

"Thank heavens. But when you emerged you discovered that you were alone on the island. You had no way of knowing when another ship would arrive. The loneliness must have been . . . unnerving."

He smiled and turned around to face her. "The press got that bit wrong. I was not alone on the island."

She was stunned. "There was no mention of that."

"No. I certainly never told anyone. As for Torrence and the others on the expedition, they had no way of knowing that there was a small group of people living on the island."

"The descendants of the people who built the tombs?"

"No," Slater said. "The people I met come from various corners of the world to form a monastery of sorts—a place of refuge and reflection. They called their community the Order of the Three Paths. Some who found their way to Fever Island stayed for only a short span of time. The teachings and the discipline of the Order did not suit them. Others thrived on the instruction and took what they learned back out into the world. Some remained on the island and became teachers."

"This is astonishing," Ursula said. "There has been nothing in the press about a religious order on Fever Island."

"It was not a religious order. It could best be described as a philosophical community. The physical and mental exercises would strike most people here as esoteric or exceedingly eccentric."

"I see." She paused. "I assume that you became a vegetarian during your stay on the island?"

He smiled briefly. "I'm afraid so. In any event, a ship arrived a year after I emerged from the tombs. By then I had become a full initiate of the Order."

"Well, it doesn't sound as if there was a great deal to do on the island except study the ways of this Order."

Slater's eyes gleamed with amusement "True. But

I found that the ways of the Order suited me. The teachers told me that I was a natural student."

"These teachers—they spoke English?"

"Some did. As I told you, they came from various parts of the world. The Far East, Europe. There was even an American at the monastery—a ship's captain who found his way to the island and decided to stay."

"But you chose to leave when the opportunity presented itself."

"I returned to London long enough to assure my parents that I was alive and well but I discovered that London no longer felt like home. I told my father that I intended to go abroad to find my own true path. He promptly cut me off without a penny." Slater chuckled. "A perfectly logical parental response under the circumstances."

"Perhaps, but it must have put quite a crimp in your archaeological explorations. Financing such expeditions is very expensive."

Slater looked out the window. "I found other ways to make my living."

"Did you discover this true path that you sought?" she asked. But she had already sensed that the answer would be no.

Slater smiled faintly and shook his head. "A year into my quest, I returned to Fever Island because I felt the need for more instruction and training. I had questions. But in the time I had been away, the volcano had erupted. The destruction was complete. There was nothing left to indicate that the monastery had ever existed."

"So you went back to your search until family obligations summoned you home."

"Where I will be obliged to stay, at least for the foreseeable future. Managing my father's estate is not something that can be done from a distance."

"Evidently at some point along the way you and your father reconciled," Ursula said.

"I think he developed a grudging respect for the fact that I had chosen to go my own way."

"More than a grudging respect, I'd say. According to what I've heard he entrusted the entire estate to you."

Slater shrugged. "There was no one else."

"There are always other ways to handle vast sums of money," Ursula said. "Your father obviously trusted you."

Slater did not respond but he did not argue.

"Are you going to tell me how you made your living during the years when you were wandering the world without the financial backing of the family fortune?" she asked. "That is why you brought me here today, isn't it?"

He glanced at her. "Sometimes you see me too clearly, Ursula."

"Does that offend you?"

"It is unsettling but, no, it does not offend me. Just takes a bit of getting used to, that's all. In answer to your question, I made a living recovering lost and stolen artifacts."

"How . . . unusual. There is a living to be made in that business?"

"A very good living, as it happens. Collectors are an eccentric, obsessive lot. They will pay almost anything to possess the objects of their desire. The business sent me to the far corners of the earth. I dealt with some rather difficult people at times."

She watched him. "What is your definition of 'difficult' in this case?"

"Dangerous."

She caught her breath. "I see."

"Collectors and those who move in the underground world of antiquities often employ violent people to steal the objects of their desire. They employ dangerous people to guard their relics. They build vaults and safes and lock them with complicated mechanisms. Some are willing to commit murder to obtain certain artifacts. In short, my clients were obsessed with chasing legends."

"They hired you to chase those legends for them."

"And things sometimes became violent." Slater turned around. His fierce eyes locked with hers. "The reason I brought you here today, Ursula, is to explain that, for a time in my life, I found the unwholesome excitement of my work, even the occasional violence, gratifying. There is no other word for it. And that is the truth about my eccentric nature."

"Am I supposed to be shocked?"

"Aren't you?"

"Not nearly as shocked as I probably ought to be. But here's the thing, Slater. My life has taken a few odd twists and turns and I find that the experience has made me more tolerant of the odd twists and turns in other people's lives."

"That is a very broad-minded point of view," he said rather dryly.

"Do you believe that Lord Torrence deliberately triggered the trap so that he could escape alone with the Jeweled Bird?"

"No. What I believe is that removing the Bird from the pedestal is what triggered the trap. But because the mechanism was so ancient it was not in good working order. It moved slowly and ponderously. That is why Torrence and the others had time to get to the entrance."

She thought about the expression she had seen on Lady Torrence's face. "Perhaps you should make it clear to Lord Torrence that you do not blame him."

Slater was grimly amused. "I think he knows how I feel about the matter. He is not interested in having a personal conversation about Fever Island."

"Why not?"

"I think it is very likely that he suspects that I know what really became of the Jeweled Bird."

"What are you talking about? It was stolen."

"I was in the business of searching for lost and stolen artifacts, remember?"

A small shock of understanding struck her. "Good heavens. Yes, of course. You must have heard about the theft at the time."

"It was a sensation throughout the world of collectors and museums. A number of clients offered to pay me handsomely to find it. But I went looking for it on my own."

"You found it, didn't you?"

There was a short silence.

"I know what happened to it," Slater admitted.

"According to the press, the Jeweled Bird has become a legend. They say it is the source of the animosity between you and Lord Torrence."

Slater watched her very steadily. "I don't give a damn about the Jeweled Bird."

She studied him for a moment. He was telling her the truth, she decided.

"Yes, I can see that the fate of the Bird doesn't matter to you," she said. "Your experience on the island is more important to you than the treasure."

"My time at the monastery changed me, Ursula."

"What are you trying to tell me, Slater?"

He walked slowly, deliberately, toward her and came to a halt in front of her, inches away.

"I'm trying to tell you that meeting you changed me yet again. I do not feel as if I am watching you from offstage. When I am close to you as I am now, I feel you in every fiber of my being."

She was speechless. Her mouth opened but she could not find words.

"There is something I must ask you," he continued.

She went very still, half afraid that he would ask her for the truth about her past. The thrilling heat of the moment was instantly transmuted into an icy dread. She could not imagine that he had guessed her secret but she had to acknowledge that someone—the blackmailer—certainly had. There was no knowing now who else might be aware of her past.

"The question I must ask you has been keeping me awake nights ever since I met you," Slater said.

She braced herself. "What is it?"

"You wear deep mourning. But I have been told that your husband died a few years ago. Do you think it will be possible to move past your state of grief and find it within yourself to form an attachment to another man?"

She was so stunned that for a moment she could only stare at him in shocked silence. Something dark and haunted moved in his eyes, drawing her out of her trance.

"Good heavens, Slater, I'm not locked in deep mourning," she said, the words sharpened with relief. "Quite the opposite. I was married for less than two years. By the time my husband broke his neck falling down a staircase at a brothel, he had destroyed any love that I had once felt for him. I know I should be ashamed to admit it but frankly, even after discovering that he had gambled away every penny we possessed, I was relieved to have him out of my life. Does that answer your question?"

"Yes," he said. "I believe it does."

She could see the heat in his eyes. It robbed her of breath. Her pulse skittered and she was oddly shaky. She raised her gloved fingertips to touch the edge of his mouth.

He framed her face with his powerful hands and drew her closer.

His mouth closed over hers and everything she thought she knew of passion went out the window.

Matty's words of warning floated through her mind. *"They say Roxton practices exotic sexual rites upon unsuspecting females."*

Evidently not all of the legends about Slater Roxton were false.

FIFTEEN

Her mouth was incredibly warm, soft and sensual. It was the stuff of a lonely man's dreams. He was half afraid that he would awake to discover that he was hallucinating. But her response acted like a catalyst, ripping him out of the remote dimension from where he watched the world. It plunged him into the hot storms of passion.

He heard a harsh, reverberating groan and realized with a sense of shock that it came from somewhere deep inside him. Kissing Ursula was like opening a door in a maze, like walking out of a dark place into the sunlight. He was alive. He was free. Sensations cascaded through him so quickly and so intensely that he could hardly catch his breath. His blood roared in his veins.

He released her face and slid his hands down her elegant, tightly laced rib cage to the gentle curve of her hip. Layers of fabric and the stiff stays of the gown's bodice kept him from the intimate contact he longed for but he was nevertheless thrilled just to know that he was so close, just to know that he was touching her, holding her at last—thrilled to know that she seemed to want him.

He was afraid of pushing too far, too fast but when she put her hands around his neck he got a little light-headed.

The next thing he knew she was up against a bookcase and he had one booted foot between her legs. The ankle-length skirts and petticoats of her dress rode up over his knee.

He caged her there, his hands planted on either side of her head, and wrenched his mouth away from hers with an effort. She gripped his shoulders as though afraid she might collapse beneath the onslaught. He found the sweet, silken skin of her throat. Her womanly scent aroused his senses and tightened every muscle. He was so hard he ached.

"Slater." Ursula spoke into his ear, her voice softer and huskier than ever. "I was not expecting this."

"Is that so?" He raised his head and looked into her sultry, rather dazed eyes. "How odd. I have been waiting for this to happen since the day I met you."

"I understand." She was breathless and flustered. "Do you?"

"You said that during your time on Fever Island you lived a monastic existence, and if the gossip is correct you have not formed a romantic liaison with anyone here in London. That is not a normal condition for a man of your obviously virile nature."

Reality washed over him in an icy wave.

"Let me be sure I comprehend you," he said evenly. "You think this is happening because I've been without a woman for too long?"

She flinched, obviously alarmed, and tried to retreat but she was already up against the barrier of the bookcase.

"It is just that I want you to be certain that your feelings for me are not inspired by your somewhat extended periods of, uh, celibacy."

He stared at her for a long moment, unable to tell if she was joking.

"You're forgetting the exotic sexual rituals in the forbidden chamber," he said finally. "The rites I practice on unsuspecting females."

She narrowed her eyes. "You're teasing me."

"Am I?"

She made a visible effort to compose herself. "I don't place any credence in those outlandish stories in the press."

"Perhaps you should," he said, making his tone deliberately ominous.

"Nonsense."

Her stylish little black cap had fallen down over one eye. He took his hands away from the wall, freeing her. Straightening, he angled the cap into its proper position. The process gave him a chance to touch her coppery hair.

She nipped smartly away from the bookcase and turned to face him.

"I am not rebuffing your advances," she said quickly.

"Thank you for clarifying the matter. So, as a matter of curiosity, how do you act when you actually do rebuff a man's advances?"

"That is not amusing. I am trying to explain things here."

"Excellent," he said. "While we're on the subject, please do me the courtesy of telling me whether or not you will welcome further advances of an intimate nature from me. Because if you are not interested in that sort of connection I'd rather know now."

"I am not entirely averse to the possibility of a romantic connection with you, sir," she said.

He was starting to become amused by her flustered condition and her contradictory statements. He was still as frustrated as hell; nevertheless, there was something rather charming about Ursula unnerved.

"You give me hope," he said gravely.

"It is just that I want both of us to be very sure of what we are about," Ursula said, more earnest than ever.

He held up one hand, palm out. "Don't say another word, I beg you. You'll ruin the moment. Small as it was, I wish to treasure it."

She angled her chin. "You call that embrace we just shared a *small moment*, sir?"

"I'm assuming you want the truth?"

"Of course."

"Very well, then, that kiss was not nearly enough to satisfy me, madam. Indeed, it merely whetted my appetite. But apparently it will have to suffice for now."

"I see." She looked as if she wanted to say something more but could not summon the words.

"Your turn, Ursula," he said quietly. "Will a few stolen kisses be enough for you or do you think you will want more at some point in the future?"

To his astonishment her air of alarm increased dramatically.

"Mr. Roxton," she sputtered. "Must you be so . . . so direct?"

"Forgive me. I believe I explained that in my time away from London I lost some of my conversational skills."

"I doubt that you forgot anything at all, sir," she shot back. "You are simply impatient with the polite ways of Society."

He nodded soberly. "Very true. The thing is, Ursula, you were a married woman. I assumed you understood the nature of intimate relations between two people."

"Of course I do," she snapped. "I understand that sort of thing very well. But you are obviously a man of strong passions, sir. If you are sincerely interested in an *intimate* connection with me—"

"Oh, I am," he said softly. "I am most definitely interested."

She cleared her throat. "Then you deserve to know that my own temperament does not run to the extremes."

He went blank. "The extremes?"

She waved one hand. "I refer to the sort of extreme passions that your mother writes about in her plays."

"Nobody in his or her right mind acts the way the characters do in my mother's melodramas. I'm afraid you have gone too deeply into the weeds of polite euphemisms. I am lost. I have no idea what you are talking about."

She shot him an irritated look.

"I am merely trying to tell you that I may not be the right woman for a man of your passionate nature, sir," she said. "I'm trying to warn you, as it were."

He was most certainly enjoying himself now, he decided.

"Ah," he said. "We are back to your concerns about those exotic sexual rites in the forbidden chamber, is that it? Never fear, I won't expose you to that sort of thing unless you request me to do so."

"Damn it, Slater, you are deliberately mocking me."

He grinned. "I do believe I am. I think I rather enjoy teasing you. It's only fair, given your remarkably ridiculous concerns about your own temperament."

She sighed. "You are not going to take my warnings seriously, are you?"

"I suggest we examine this situation from my point of view."

She gave him a wary look. "What do you mean?"

"Given my periods of extended celibacy it seems likely that I am out of practice when it comes to matters of sexual rituals. I have no doubt grown clumsy, or possibly quite inept."

"Inept?"

"At the very least I'm sure my timing will be off," he said.

"Timing?"

"If memory serves—and after my experience on Fever Island I cannot be at all certain that it does serve—I believe timing is critical in acts of physical intimacy. Clearly I have moved too quickly today, for example."

"It is not that you moved too swiftly," she assured him. "It is just that I was taken somewhat by surprise."

"My fault, entirely," he said.

"Well, not exactly."

"Given my ineptitude, bad timing and lack of practice, it is clear that I need a woman who will be patient with me," he said. "One who will be understanding. Considerate. Gentle."

"You are impossible, Mr. Roxton." She glared. "What's more, I have had quite enough of your deliberately provocative conversation. I strongly suggest that you do not say another word on the subject of your poor timing and inept ways or exotic sexual rites and rituals. If you do I will terminate our partnership and continue with the investigation on my own. Do you understand me, sir?"

A knock on the door made both of them pause. Slater stifled a groan.

He fished his spectacles out of his pocket and put them on. "Come in."

The door opened. Webster loomed in the opening. "Lady Roxton is here, sir. She is asking to see you.

Insists that it's very important." There was a slight hesitation before he added in his darkest tones, "She brought the children, sir."

"In that case, whatever you do, don't send them in here," Slater said. "The last time the boys were in my library they made every attempt to destroy my collection." He glanced out the window and saw that the fog had dispersed. "Send them out into the garden and show Lady Roxton to the terrace. I'll join her there."

Webster was visibly relieved. "Very good, sir."

He left, closing the door.

Ursula turned to Slater. "You have guests. You'll want privacy. I should return to the office."

"You may as well stay and meet the rest of the family," Slater said.

Ursula glanced at him with a flash of curiosity and then concentrated on opening her satchel.

"I would not wish to interfere in your private affairs," she said, taking out a small hand mirror. She frowned at the glass and raised one hand to remove a long, steel hatpin. She adjusted the cap and anchored it with the pin. "I understand that your relationship with your father's widow and her children is complicated."

"My entire life has become complicated of late," he said. He watched her close the satchel. "But it has also become more interesting."

SIXTEEN

～

It is a pleasure to make your acquaintance, Mrs.
Kern," Judith Roxton said. "I'm sorry to interrupt
your work with Slater. Since his return he has been
so busy dealing with matters relating to his father's
estate that he has not had time to devote himself to
his collection of artifacts. I know he is relieved to be
able to get back to the cataloging."

"You didn't interrupt anything important," Ursula
said. That was a blatant falsehood but she could
hardly explain that she and Slater had been in the
midst of a heated discussion of their odd relationship
when Judith and the children had arrived. "We were
finished with the day's business."

Judith was not at all what Ursula had expected.
Blond, blue eyed and dressed in the height of fashion,
Judith was more than pretty. There was a ravishing
fragility about her. She did not appear conscious of

her extraordinary appeal. Nor did she seem like the sort of female who relied on her beauty to manipulate others. Quite the opposite, Ursula thought. This was a woman who looked as if she needed rescuing. And that quality, too, no doubt drew the male of the species.

Judith also appeared to be a devoted mother to the two young boys who were playing in the garden. Slater was with them, alternately catching and tossing the ball. Crawford and Daniel were eight and nine years old, respectively. Dark haired with cognac-colored eyes, they bore a striking resemblance to their much older half brother.

It was obvious that they adored Slater. They had come running up to him the moment he appeared on the terrace, demanding that he play a game with them. It occurred to Ursula that Slater seemed to be enjoying himself. He looked younger and more carefree than she had ever seen him.

So much for the gossip of a family feud, she thought.

Judith smiled at the sight of the three males engaged in vigorous play.

"Crawford and Daniel are very fond of Slater," she said. "When I said that I was going to come here today they begged to accompany me. I could not refuse. Slater is very generous with his time. Not every man in his position would be so kind to two half brothers who stand to inherit most of the family fortune."

"Mr. Roxton is unique," Ursula said, trying to sound noncommittal.

"I know what the gossips say about our family," Judith said. "And, as is the case with most legends, there is some truth to the rumors. Slater's mother and I do not move in the same circles, nor do we go out of our way to do so. But I respect Mrs. Lafontaine and she has never been cruel or unkind to me or the boys, even though she knows that they will inherit what should, by right of blood, have been her son's inheritance."

"Lilly Lafontaine is a very pragmatic woman and I can assure you that she is well situated financially."

Judith did not take her attention off Slater and the boys. "My husband loved her. My marriage was the usual business arrangement, but Edward was very kind to me and I think he was fond of me in his own fashion. Don't believe everything you read in the papers. I can tell you with absolute certainty that Edward was enormously proud of all three of his sons. He made the mistake of trying to control Slater by cutting him off but when that effort failed it only served to make Edward respect Slater all the more."

Slater tossed the ball one last time and then sent the boys off to play in the far corner of the garden. He walked along the graveled path and climbed the three stone steps to the broad terrace. He lowered himself onto a wrought-iron bench with easy grace and reached for the glass of lemonade that Mrs. Webster had provided.

"I wasn't expecting you, Judith," he said. "I assume a problem has arisen?"

Judith looked stricken. "I'm sorry," she said. "I

should have sent a message asking if it would be convenient for me to speak with you."

"It's all right," Slater said patiently. "Tell me what this is about."

Judith seemed to crumple in on herself. "I'm afraid it is the usual."

"Hurley." Slater said the name as though weary of it.

Judith bowed her head. "He came around early today. Stormed into the morning room at breakfast."

"I told you not to allow him into the house."

Ursula realized the conversation was becoming extremely personal. She rose and started to pull down her veil.

"Gracious, look at the time," she said. "I must be off. Don't worry, Webster will see me out the door."

"No." Slater got to his feet. "You may as well stay for this."

Ursula glanced at Judith. "I really don't think that's a good idea."

Judith did not seem to notice that there was a bystander. She gave Slater a helpless, imploring look.

"Mrs. Brody allowed him in without asking my permission," she said. "He threatened her."

Ursula made to step around Judith and move toward the house. Without a word, Slater caught her hand, chaining her. He did not speak but the look he gave her said it all. He wanted her to stay. She sank back into her chair and sat quietly.

"Hurley cannot be allowed to intimidate your

housekeeper," he said to Judith. "You will have to let her go. You need someone stronger at the door."

"My stepfather will simply bribe or threaten the next housekeeper. He has become increasingly aggressive of late. It was bad enough when he threatened me. This morning he dared to imply that if I did not give him money, something dreadful might happen to the children. That is why I came here to see you. I'm frightened, Slater."

Slater went very still. "He threatened the children?"

"It was a veiled threat but it was a threat." Judith clasped her hands together in her lap. "I am terrified, Slater."

"He has gone too far," Slater said calmly. "I will deal with him. In the meantime, you and the boys will go to the country house and you will stay there until I have dealt with the problem of Hurley."

Tears of relief glittered in Judith's eyes. "I am more grateful than I can say, Slater. But when Hurley realizes you are the one standing in his way, I fear he will turn his attention toward you."

"I told you, I will take care of him," Slater said. He looked toward the house. "Here comes Mrs. Webster with sandwiches and cakes. Feed the boys while I see Mrs. Kern on her way."

For the first time Judith seemed to remember Ursula's presence. She turned quickly. She looked quite horrified and embarrassed.

"I do apologize, Mrs. Kern," she said. "This is such

an unpleasant family matter. I should not have exposed you to my problems with my stepfather."

"No need to apologize," Ursula said. She touched Judith's arm. "This is none of my business but it is obvious that you and the boys are in danger. You were right to come here."

Judith gave her a shaky smile. "I'm afraid that my husband quite deliberately dumped the problem of my stepfather onto Slater's shoulders. I know the gossips say that Slater somehow cheated me out of my inheritance but the truth is that my husband knew full well that I could not protect the boys from Hurley. If Edward had left me in control of the fortune, Hurley would have done something terrible to force me to give him what he wants."

"I understand." Ursula watched Slater unfold neatly to his feet. "Mr. Roxton appears to be balancing a number of complicated problems these days."

"Enough," Slater said. He reached down to take Ursula's hand. "Mrs. Kern has a business to mind. I will see her out and return in a moment."

He took Ursula's arm and steered her back toward the house. Once inside, they continued along the corridor to the front hall. Webster opened the door.

Slater guided Ursula down the steps toward the carriage where Griffith stood deep in friendly conversation with Lady Roxton's coachman. Ursula glanced at the expensive carriage that had brought Judith and the boys to Slater's house.

"Can I assume that Judith married your father in part to escape a brutal stepfather?"

"I think Judith would have married anyone to escape Hurley's clutches," Slater said. "And as it happened, my father needed a legitimate heir for the title and the estate. The situation worked well for both of them. While my father was alive, Hurley was careful to keep his distance. But he has grown bolder now that I am in control of the money."

"He sounds dreadful. What will you do to keep him away from Judith and the boys?"

"There is only one thing that a man of Hurley's low nature comprehends."

"What is that?"

"Fear."

She stopped short, rounding on him.

"What are you talking about?" she whispered, conscious of the possibility of being overheard by Griffith and the coachman.

Slater was obliged to halt, too. He smiled in what he no doubt believed to be a reassuring manner.

"Hurley will be made to understand that remaining in London would not be good for his health. I shall offer to assist him in his travel plans. The choice will be his."

He sounded as if he were discussing the weather or a train schedule—a matter of fact, not a subject that could be debated.

For a moment Ursula was utterly bewildered. And then with a cold shock, understanding dawned. She was amazed by the sheer audacity of the threat.

"Do you think he will believe your threat?" she asked.

Slater handed her up into the cab, his eyes chillingly calm behind the lenses of his spectacles.

"It won't be a threat," he said.

"Slater, Judith says he is a violent man."

To her amazement Slater smiled. "Are you worried about me?"

"Well, yes, as a matter of fact, I am."

"I'm touched. Truly."

"I hope you know what you are doing."

"I admit my social skills are limited, Ursula; nevertheless, I am capable of communicating with men like Hurley. Now, don't forget, we are to have dinner with my mother tonight. Seven-thirty."

Slater stepped back, closed the door of the carriage and waved to Griffith, who was up on the box. The vehicle rumbled forward.

Through the window Ursula watched Slater go up the front steps and disappear into the big house. There was something different about him this afternoon, she concluded. He appeared younger and his spirits seemed brighter. It was as if the darkness around him had dissipated a little.

Probably just her imagination, she decided.

SEVENTEEN

"O f course I would be delighted to try to arrange a meeting with the proprietor of the Pavilion of Pleasure." Lilly smiled across the table at Ursula. "I cannot say that Mrs. Wyatt and I are close but years ago we shared some mutual gentlemen acquaintances. That was before I met Slater's father, of course. Nan Wyatt was an actress in her day. Rather good, actually. We appeared in *A Twist of Fate* together."

"Do you think Mrs. Wyatt will be willing to speak with us about her business association with the Olympus Club?" Ursula asked.

"From what I recall about Nan, she is strongly motivated by money." Lilly looked at Slater, who was seated at the far end of the long table. "As long as she is well paid for her information and assured of confidentiality, I think that she will be happy to discuss her connections to the Olympus Club. But she will be expensive."

Dinner with Slater's mother was proving to be a surprisingly comfortable affair, Ursula thought. She was not quite certain what she had expected—Lilly was nothing if not unpredictable. But Lilly's love of all things theatrical and dramatic was on full display tonight. She was taking great delight in contributing to the investigation.

The meal offered both fish and chicken. There was also a surprisingly wide variety of mushy, overcooked vegetables and a solid-looking nut loaf that could have served as a doorstop—the cook's grudging concession to the one guest who was a declared vegetarian.

"I have no objection to paying for information," Slater said around a bite of nut loaf. "In my experience, that is usually the cheapest way to obtain it. Mrs. Wyatt can be assured that we will keep her secrets. But time is of the essence."

"I will contact her first thing in the morning," Lilly said. She paused. "No, I will send a message tonight. The nature of Mrs. Wyatt's business requires her to work nights. I very much doubt that she rises until noon."

"Thank you for your assistance," Ursula said. "I am very grateful."

"I'm delighted to be able to aid you in your investigation," Lilly said. She picked up her wineglass. "It is quite the most exciting thing I've done in ages. It has inspired me with all sorts of ideas for my next play."

Slater gave her a repressive look. "I don't want to see any of this in your next script. We are venturing into some dangerous territory with this inquiry."

"Don't fret," Lilly said airily. "I assure you that you won't recognize any of the characters or events by the time I have finished writing the play."

Slater aimed a fork at her. His eyes were a little tight at the corners. "I want your word that you will allow me to read the script before you show it to anyone else."

"Yes, of course," Lilly said in soothing tones. "Discretion in all things is my motto."

"Is that right?" Slater said. "I hadn't noticed."

"I'll dash off a note to Mrs. Wyatt as soon as we finish dinner. Have some more nut loaf, Slater. If you don't finish it I shall be forced to feed it to the squirrels. No one else in this household eats nut loaf."

Slater eyed the brick on the platter. "I think I know why. Tell your cook that she need not bother sending the recipe to my housekeeper."

SHE HAD BEEN BOTH ANXIOUS and thrilled about the prospect of being alone with Slater in a darkened cab late at night. But in the end Ursula was chagrined to discover that she had nothing to worry about. Nothing at all.

Absolutely nothing.

Slater barely spoke to her on the way back to her house. He was not unfriendly, she concluded, merely preoccupied. He watched the street through the window for most of the journey and when they finally arrived, he walked her to her front door and saw her safely into the hall with barely a word.

"Good night, Ursula," he said. "I will speak with you tomorrow."

"Right," she said, trying for an equally casual farewell.

She stepped back into the hall and closed the door. It was only then that it dawned on her that Slater had other plans for the evening. Intuition warned her about the nature of those plans.

She drew a sharp breath, whirled around and yanked open the door.

"Slater," she hissed.

He was at the foot of the steps, heading toward the carriage. He stopped and half turned back.

"What is it?" he asked patiently.

"For heaven's sake, promise me that you will be careful."

In the light of the streetlamp she could see that he was smiling. He looked pleased.

"You really are concerned about me," he said. "But there is no need. I have had some experience in this sort of thing. I have not spent the past few years working on my knitting."

"Just . . . be careful. And when it's over let me know that you are safe."

"You'll be in bed."

"No," she said. "I will be watching from my bed-room window. I expect you to stop in the street at least long enough to let me know that all is well."

She closed the door before he could say anything else.

EIGHTEEN

⌁

Roxton had cheated him out of everything that should have come to him and now he had lost what little he had left.

Hurley stared at the cards on the table. He was ruined.

"I'll have the money for you by the end of the week," he said.

Thurston smiled his thin, humorless smile. He watched Hurley through a haze of smoke.

"That's what you said the last time we played, Hurley. I'm not sure I can rely upon your word. So, as a convenience to us both, I'll send a man around in the morning to collect my winnings."

He sounded bored.

Hurley lurched to his feet. "I said the end of the week, damn you. I have to make arrangements."

"You mean you have to find a way to convince

your stepdaughter to get the money from the trustee of her children's fortune." Thurston scooped up the cards with a practiced movement of one long-fingered hand. "I suggest you get busy. From what I hear, Roxton is not inclined to indulge you. Takes after his father in that regard."

"Damn you, I told you I'd get the money. Give me at least two days."

Thurston appeared to consider that closely for a moment. Then he shrugged.

"Very well, you've got two days," he said. "But just to be clear—if you don't come up with the money that you owe me, my men will pay you a visit."

Hurley's heart pounded. His palms went cold. A visit from Thurston's enforcers meant a severe beating. Everyone in the room knew it.

Hurley turned without a word and crossed the card room, heading for the door.

Outside in the chill night air he stopped, trying to think. He would have to go to Judith's house and make her get him the money. She cared about her sons. If he grabbed one of them she would make Roxton pay whatever it took to get him back.

The only problem with the plan was that Roxton was a mystery. There were rumors about him. He might be deranged. One never knew what a madman would do.

Thurston, however, was not a mystery. He was a dangerous man with a reputation in the hells.

When a man found himself caught between two devils, he had no choice but to go with the one he knew and understood—the one most certain to be an immediate threat. In this case that was Thurston.

He started along the street, hoping to find a hansom. Two men approached out of the fog. The first one wore a long black coat that swept out like dark wings around his boots. The collar was pulled up high around his face. When he moved through the glare of the streetlamp the light glinted on his spectacles. His companion was a giant of a man.

Hurley dismissed the man with the glasses immediately. It was the giant who worried him. He started to move to the side of the walkway, giving the big man and his associate some room.

The one with the spectacles spoke.

"Good evening, Hurley. I was told I might find you outside this hell tonight. I don't believe we've met. Slater Roxton."

Hurley froze. He'd been drinking for most of the night and his mind was somewhat fuzzy. It took him a moment to realize what was happening. So this was Roxton.

Hurley experienced a surge of relief. The bastard did not appear either mad or dangerous. He looked like a scholar. Nothing like his father at all. The big man was evidently a servant.

"What the devil do you want, Roxton?" Hurley asked.

"I came here tonight to say farewell to you," Slater said.

"I'm not going anywhere."

"You will be leaving on a ship bound for Australia

early tomorrow morning. Your passage is paid. One way. You will not be returning. Mr. Griffith, here, has your ticket. He will see you safely to your lodgings tonight and assist you with your packing. Once I receive word that you are actually in Australia, I will send you a small financial stake to help you get started in your new life. After that you will be on your own."

"You really are mad," Hurley said. "I'm not leaving London."

"The choice to go or stay is yours, of course."

"Damned right it is."

"I would point out that, while your creditors have some interest in keeping you alive, at least as long as they believe that you might be able to get some money out of the Roxton estate, I have no such interest. Indeed, I find you a great inconvenience."

"Are you threatening me?"

"No, Hurley, I am giving you my solemn promise that if you are not on that ship to Australia tomorrow morning you will not have to concern yourself with the payment of your outstanding debts. You will have . . . other problems."

"You bastard. That money should have been mine. I'm Judith's father. I have every right to control the income from the Roxton estate."

"My father left strict instructions in his will. You are not to receive a penny from the estate. Therefore, I am using my own money to finance your passage to Australia. One way or another you will disappear from all our lives tomorrow, Hurley. If you do not board that ship in the morning they will pull your body out of the river tomorrow night."

Hurley struggled for words. "No. *No.*"

Slater looked at the giant. "Mr. Griffith, please see Mr. Hurley to his residence and stay with him until he boards the ship."

"Yes, sir," Griffith said.

"You can't do this," Hurley yelped. "You really are mad."

Slater removed his glasses with a world-weary motion of one hand and looked at Hurley. He did not speak. There was no need. In that moment Hurley knew that of the two devils, this was the one he feared the most.

Slater put on his glasses, turned and walked away into the night.

NINETEEN

～～

He took a hansom back to Ursula's house because Griffith needed the carriage to transport Hurley and his trunks to the docks.

She was where she had promised to be, watching the street from an upstairs window. A candle set on the windowsill burned low. There was just enough light to show him that Ursula was wearing a wrapper. Her hair was in a single braid that hung down over one shoulder.

At the sight of her the remnants of the cold, battle-ready tension inside him were instantly transformed into another kind of readiness—the sort that burned. The fierce need caught him by surprise.

He got down from the cab, intending to go up the front steps. She would open the door for him and he would carry her upstairs to bed.

But Ursula opened the window and leaned out.

"You are all right?" she demanded.

"I'm fine," he assured her.

"Excellent. In that case, good night, sir."

She closed the window with a bang and drew the blinds shut.

The message could not have been more clear.

Stifling a groan, Slater got back into the hansom.

TWENTY

~

The following morning Ursula got out of a cab, paid the driver and walked briskly through the fog. From time to time she glanced down at the address she had transcribed from Anne's stenography notes. The cab driver had been very helpful but she was starting to wonder if he had made a mistake. Stiggs Lane appeared to be fronted by largely abandoned, boarded-up buildings. The livery stable one street away was the only active business in the vicinity.

But just as she was about to turn around she saw the sign over Number 5. *Rosemont's Perfumes and Soaps.*

The shop was hardly inviting. In spite of the shadows and the damp fog, there was no welcoming light behind the dark, grimy windows. The adjacent buildings were empty. The unmistakable scents of the livery stable in the next street drifted on the damp air. All in all, it was an odd location for a perfume and soap business, Ursula thought.

She stopped in front of the door and checked the address she had deciphered in Anne's notebook. There was no mistake. She took a closer look at the handful of items on display in the front window. There was a small scattering of porcelain and glass perfume bottles, each one decorated with roses. The design was identical to the one on the empty perfume bottle that she had found in Anne's house. Everything in the window was shrouded with a thick film of dust.

Tentatively she tried the doorknob and was somewhat surprised when it turned in her hand. A bell shivered and chimed when she entered the shop. She was assaulted by an unpleasant mix of chemical fumes strong enough to make her breath catch in her throat. Hastily she covered her nose and mouth with one gloved hand and looked around. There was no one behind the sales counter.

"Who's there?"

The voice—thin, high, and tight with anxiety—emanated from behind a partially closed door. The speaker could have been either male or female.

"I've come to inquire about your perfumes," Ursula said, intuitively trying to reassure the person behind the door. "A friend of mine has some that she said she obtained from this shop. I am interested in purchasing a bottle for myself."

There was a great deal of nervous dithering on the

other side of the door before a man edged nervously out of the back room. He was as thin as his voice, small and jittery. A few wisps of graying brown hair were plastered across the top of his head. A pair of spectacles framed his pale eyes. He wore a stained leather apron and leather gloves.

He regarded Ursula with a mix of suspicion and anxiety.

"Mr. Rosemont?" She employed the calm, confident, you-can-trust-me voice she usually reserved for clients who wished to hire a secretary for the purpose of taking down confidential information.

"I'm Rosemont," he said. He removed his gloves and shoved them into one of the pockets of his apron. "You say a friend sent you?"

"That is correct." Ursula crossed the room to the counter. "Miss Clifton."

For the moment she wanted Rosemont to think that Anne was still alive. There was no reason that he would be aware that was not true. There had been no notice in the press. Women who lacked family or connections died every day in London, leaving behind very little evidence of their existence.

"I don't remember a customer by that name," Rosemont said quickly—too quickly, perhaps.

"Are you quite certain?" Ursula pressed.

"Positive." Rosemont started to retreat behind the door. "If you don't mind, I'm rather busy."

Ursula opened her satchel and took out the perfume bottle that had belonged to Anne. She placed it on the counter.

Rosemont stared at the bottle. He looked horrified. "Where did you get that?" he demanded.

"In my friend's house. Miss Clifton has disappeared. I am trying to find her."

"Disappeared? *Disappeared?*" Rosemont's voice rose to a squeak. "See here, that's no business of mine. I can't possibly help you."

"I am trying to reconstruct her comings and goings in the days just before she vanished. According to her appointment calendar she called in at this shop on a number of occasions during the past year—including last week."

"I told you, I don't remember a Miss Clifton."

This was not going well, Ursula thought. She had come here for information but it was starting to look as if she would leave no wiser than when she had entered the shop.

She could not afford a significant bribe and something told her that Rosemont would not be persuaded by a small offering—assuming he could be convinced to talk in the first place.

"How odd that you would not remember such a loyal customer," she said.

Rosemont stiffened. "I beg your pardon."

"Allow me to refresh your memory."

Ursula reached back into her satchel and took out the paper on which she had transcribed several brief passages from Anne's notebook. Rosemont watched in mounting panic as she unfolded the paper and smoothed it flat on the counter with one gloved hand.

"What is that?" he yelped.

"A record of some of her recent visits to your shop. They began about eight months ago and continued on a twice-monthly basis right up until last Wednesday. Oh, wait, I do believe that if we examine the dates more closely we see that in recent months she began stopping in more frequently." Ursula shook her head, seemingly mystified. "It's very odd, isn't it?"

Rosemont glared at her. "I see nothing odd about it."

"I do. You see, I happen to know that Anne earned a respectable living from her secretarial work. Nevertheless, I cannot imagine that she was able to purchase so much expensive perfume. And such a great quantity of it. I wonder what she did with all that fragrance. She certainly did not give any to me or her colleagues at the agency."

Rosemont stared at the damning sheet of paper. Then he collected himself.

"Let me check my journal of receipts and transactions," he said brusquely. "Wait here, I'll be right back."

She had won. Rosemont was backing down.

Cheered by the success, she gave him a cool, benign smile. "I'll come with you, if you don't mind. I wouldn't want you slipping out the back door before you tell me what you and Anne were about with all those perfume sales."

Rosemont drew himself up, momentarily projecting an air of defiance. Then his shoulders collapsed and he gave a heavy sigh.

"Very well, come with me if you must," he said. "I

will show you my records. But I must tell you that I have absolutely no idea why Miss Clifton purchased such a great quantity of perfume."

He turned and disappeared into the back room.

Ursula whisked up her skirts. Satchel in hand, she hurried around the end of the counter.

"Did she come to your shop so frequently because she was in the habit of meeting someone here, Mr. Rosemont?" she asked. "If that is the case it is very important that you tell me the name of the individual. Perhaps you were bribed to remain silent or perhaps you simply feel you owe her some loyalty. But as her employer and her friend, I can assure you that there is no longer any reason to protect Anne."

She stopped short just inside the doorway. The front of the shop was steeped in gloom but the back room was drenched in even deeper shadows. The chemical odors were stronger in that room.

There were none of the things one expected to see in the back of a perfume shop. No bundles of dried herbs and flowers dangling from the ceiling. No jars of fragrant oils. No containers of orange peels or bottles of cinnamon and vanilla beans.

Instead, there was a shipping crate.

The lid was open, revealing a number of neatly packaged bags inside. Beneath the thick chemical fumes she detected a dark, slightly acrid, strongly herbal note. The odor was coming from the wooden crate.

When her eyes adjusted to the low light she noticed two bookcases against one wall. They were crammed with leather-bound volumes. Herbals and other books of botanical lore, she concluded.

She looked around, searching for Rosemont. He had vanished through a door set between the book-cases. Alarmed that he was trying to escape, she hurried to follow him.

"Mr. Rosemont?"

"In here," he called from the next room. "Come along, I've got my journal ready for you to examine. Kindly be quick about it. The sooner you vacate the premises, the better, as far as I'm concerned."

She went to the doorway between the bookcases and found herself looking into a shuttered room lit by gas lamps. The windows were covered with thick boards that had been nailed to the walls. She could see two workbenches littered with chemistry apparatus—glass beakers, flasks, scales and a burner. An exceptionally well-equipped stillroom, she thought. Rosemont evidently took a very modern, very scientific approach to the ancient art of perfume making.

"Welcome to my laboratory, madam," Rosemont said. He stood near a small writing desk where a large notebook was open. He still sounded nervous but his voice was steadier now—the tone of a man who has made a decision and is determined to see it through. "This journal contains a record of the transactions that interest you."

She walked across the room and looked down at the book. The pages were covered with dates, amounts and quantities. She leaned over a little, trying to decipher the cramped handwriting.

"Can you please point out the entry that shows Miss Clifton's most recent visit to your shop?" she asked. "I don't have time to read through all of your notes."

"You're wrong, madam. I don't know who you are but rest assured you have all the time in the world to read that journal."

She straightened and turned quickly, intending to bolt toward the door. She stopped when she saw the gun in Rosemont's hand.

"What on earth do you think you're doing?" she said. "Have you gone mad?"

"Stay where you are." Rosemont edged back toward the door. "Don't move. I swear I will kill you where you stand. You very likely noticed that I do not have many neighbors, certainly none that will pay any attention to a gunshot. A guarantee of privacy was the reason I established my business here."

The gun was shaking in his hand. That was probably not a good sign. Rosemont was a desperate, unnerved man. He was so jittery now that it was possible he would pull the trigger accidentally.

"Very well," she said, trying for a calm tone. "I will do as you say." The only practical strategy that came to mind was to keep Rosemont talking. "Are you aware that Anne Clifton is dead?"

"I assumed that was quite likely when you said you wanted to know about her visits to this shop."

"Did you kill her?"

"*What?* No. Why would I murder her? Things were going quite well. But I feared the arrangement would not last forever. Bargains with devils and all that. That is why I made plans for an eventuality such as this."

"What plans would those be, Mr. Rosemont?" she asked.

He ignored the question. "Who are you?"

"My name is Mrs. Kern. I was Anne's employer."

"I see. Well, you were a fool to get involved in this affair, madam."

"What affair? What is going on, Mr. Rosemont? I think you owe me some explanation."

"I owe you nothing but I will tell you this much—I rue the day I agreed to make that damned ambrosia drug. The money was excellent but it did not compensate me for the risks I have taken."

Rosemont stepped quickly back into the adjoining room and slammed the door shut. She heard the clank of a heavy, old-fashioned iron key in the lock.

"Scream for help if you like," Rosemont called through the door. His muffled voice was barely audible. "No one will hear you. Not that you'll be screaming for long. This will all be over quite soon, I assure you."

TWENTY-ONE

For a moment she stood very still, her heart pounding in a drumbeat of near panic. The squeak and groan of the floorboards told her that Rosemont was moving around in the shop. There was no way to know what he planned to do next. Perhaps he meant to starve her to death. That didn't make sense, though. He had told her that it would all be over quite soon.

She shivered, drew a deep breath, collected her nerve and took stock of her surroundings.

There was a second door that probably opened onto an alley. Not surprisingly, it was locked. There was no key in the lock. Next she checked the window. The boards that covered the glass panes were securely attached to the walls but she thought she might be able to loosen them given time and an object that could serve as a pry bar.

She began to search the room for a useful tool. Large ceramic containers were lined up against one wall. She lifted the lid of one of the pots very carefully—and quickly replaced it when choking fumes wafted out.

She spotted a long iron rod standing in one corner and decided it would work. But Rosemont was still moving around in the outer rooms of the shop. Prying the boards off the windows would be a noisy and time-consuming process. She did not want to attract his attention. He had indicated that he would soon be leaving. She decided to wait to tackle the boarded-up windows until he left the premises.

She looked at the sacks in the corner. Judging by the odor, they contained the same herbs that were in the packages stacked in the shipping crate.

One of the sacks was open. Reaching inside, she plucked out a handful of dried plant material. She took a hankie out of her satchel, wrapped up a sample and secured it with a knot.

The floorboards groaned again. She thought she heard the faint thud of an outer door closing. A great silence descended. She was quite certain that she was now alone.

She dropped the little bundle of dried herbs into her satchel and rushed to the door that opened onto the back room. With luck Rosemont had left the key in the lock out of sheer force of habit. He had, after all, been very nervous. In her other life she had learned a thing or two about keys. A woman on her own could not be too careful.

She heard a muffled whoosh just as she knelt in

front of the doorknob. The faint scent of smoke
wafted under the door.

A fresh dose of fear iced her spine. She had assumed that once Rosemont left the shop she would
have time to work out an escape. She was wrong. The
perfume maker had set fire to the premises on his
way out the door.

The shock stole her breath and threatened to par-
alyze her. The building was going to burn down
around her.

The smoke wafting under the door was stronger
now. It carried a strong herbal odor. Rosemont had
ignited the fire in the crate of dried plant materials.
The stuff was no doubt highly flammable. The wall
and the thick door that stood between the laboratory and the back room would buy her some time but
not much.

She peered into the keyhole. Relief jittered through
her when she saw that the key was, indeed, still in
the lock.

She rose and rushed back to where her satchel
stood on the workbench. She grabbed her stenography notebook, opened it and tore out two pages.
Rushing back to the door, she crouched and pushed
the pages under the bottom edge. She could only
hope that the fire would not reach them before she
finished what she intended to do.

Stripping off one glove, she removed a stout hatpin
and eased it into the lock. She manipulated the length
of metal carefully, pushing the key out of the lock.

She heard it clatter when it fell to the floor on the other side of the door.

She bent down to peer under the door to see if the key had landed on the paper—and got a strong dose of herb-scented smoke for her trouble.

Her head swam. It was as if she were floating in midair. A strange, terrifying excitement roared through her. The sensation was so disorienting that if she had been standing she would have lost her balance altogether.

She straightened to her knees, automatically covering her nose and mouth with one hand. When the terrible feeling eased somewhat, she raised her skirts and tore a strip off her petticoats. She tied the fabric around the lower half of her face to serve as a mask. She took a breath and leaned down again to see if she had been successful.

A relief that was even more powerful than the disorienting sensations swept through her when she saw that the iron key had landed on one of the notebook pages.

Gingerly she tugged the paper with the key on it under the edge of the door.

Her heart sank when she discovered the key was warm to the touch. If the heat was already so intense in the back room it might be too late to make it to safety.

She peered through the keyhole and saw that her worst fears were confirmed. The other room was an inferno of dark smoke. She had no idea how long the thick wooden door would hold out against the flames.

She looked across the laboratory at the locked door that opened onto the alley and then she looked down at the key she had just retrieved.

No shopkeeper would bother to install two different locks requiring different keys for doors that locked the same room.

She hurried to the alley door and inserted the key. It turned readily in the lock. The door opened and she was free. She was about to rush to safety when she remembered her satchel.

Whirling, she dashed back across the laboratory and grabbed the bag. Then she hurried through the doorway into the narrow fog-choked alley.

A man in a sweeping black greatcoat raced down the lane toward her.

"Ursula," Slater shouted.

He wrapped one arm around her and hauled her toward the far end of the alley. Behind them the old building gave one last groan and started to collapse in on itself.

The explosion occurred a short time later, just as Slater got Ursula into the hansom. The horse bolted. Griffith swore and fought to control the animal.

Slater made it into the cab. "Get us out of here," he ordered.

Griffith did not argue. The hansom took off at a great rate of speed.

Slater looked at Ursula. "What the devil?"

"Chemicals," she managed. She took great, deep breaths. "The laboratory was full of them. The fire must have set them off."

TWENTY-TWO

~⌒

I do wish that you would sit down, Slater," Ursula said. "Watching you pace back and forth like a caged lion is making me nervous. I have already sustained a fair amount of stress today."

They were in her study. She was seated on a stool in front of the fire, drying her hair and drinking the medicinal dose of brandy that Mrs. Dunstan had poured for her.

There had been very few words spoken in the hansom. Slater had locked one arm around her and virtually imprisoned her. For the most part he had simply repeated her name and asked her over and over again if she was all right. She had assured him each time that she was fine while secretly taking comfort in his strength and the warmth and the scent of him.

She was accustomed to being alone but in the

aftermath of the near disaster she had to admit to
herself that she was very glad of Slater's company.
The sense of intimacy would not last but at the moment it was a blessing like no other.

The moment they walked into the front hall of her
town house, Mrs. Dunstan had taken charge, usher-
ing her upstairs and into a warm bath. By the time
she emerged, the early dark of a winter night had
settled on the city.

She had put on a dressing gown and descended
the stairs to the study to dry her hair in front of the
fire. She had been shocked to discover that Slater was
waiting for her.

She had hesitated in the doorway. The comfortable, loose-fitting dressing gown with its long skirts
and full sleeves was quite modest. Indeed, the fashion journals considered such gowns suitable attire
for ladies to wear downstairs to breakfast. But there
was no escaping the fact that there was a suggestion
of intimacy about a dressing gown. The style, after
all, had been inspired by the French.

She had walked into the study, thrilled not only
by Slater's presence but by her own daring. The burning look that Slater had given her had warmed her
as nothing else could have done. She had unwrapped
the towel that bound her wet hair and sat down on
the stool in front of the hearth.

Mrs. Dunstan had brought in a tray with a light
supper of hot vegetable soup, hard-boiled eggs,
cheese and bread. Slater had spoken little during the
meal. He had helped himself to some of the cheese

and bread and devoted himself to prowling the small space while Ursula dined.

It was not until Mrs. Dunstan had removed the tray that Ursula realized that the expression in Slater's eyes was the heat of controlled anger, not desire. He was in a dangerous mood.

"I'm making you nervous?" he asked. "How the devil do you think I felt when I realized Rosemont's shop was on fire and there was no sign of you anywhere?"

Ursula adjusted the towel around her shoulders and reached for the brandy glass.

"Very well," she said, trying to acknowledge his point with grace. She swallowed some brandy and set the glass aside. "I do comprehend that you may have been somewhat startled by the fire."

"Startled?" Slater closed the distance between them with two long strides, reached down and hauled her up off the stool. "*Startled?* Madam, I was teetering on the brink of madness when I saw you emerge from the alley door. It's a wonder I'm not being fitted for a straitjacket and booking a room in an asylum at this very moment."

Her own temper flashed like lightning. "I am very sorry you are so overset by recent events, Mr. Roxton, but I would remind you that I am the one who nearly died today."

"Good Lord, woman, don't you think I realize that? You scared the hell out of me. Don't ever do anything like that again, do you understand?"

"It's not as if I intended to end up in a house fire."

"You should never have gone to that shop alone. If you hadn't mentioned your destination to your housekeeper—" He broke off, jaw tightening.

"It was a perfume shop, for heaven's sake, a place that Anne had evidently visited any number of times."

"Exactly. And I would remind you that Anne Clifton is dead. What were you thinking?"

She opened her mouth to answer him but she never got the chance. He yanked her hard against his chest and kissed her with a fierceness that stole her breath.

The kiss was not meant to summon her response, nor was it an exploratory kiss intended to woo her and invite her into greater intimacy. This was a lightning strike of a kiss, meant to lay waste to any thought of resistance. It was a claiming, conquering kiss, a kiss fueled by a wildfire of desire and demand. Slater branded her with the kiss as though he were intent on marking her as his and his alone.

The kiss ignited her senses.

After a stunned few seconds, an electrifying thrill arced through her. She was consumed with a deep, aching urgency, a need that matched the primal forces she sensed in Slater.

She wrapped her arms around him and threw herself into the sensual battle. He responded with a shuddering groan that reverberated through every fiber of her being. The towel around her shoulders fell to the floor.

Without warning, Slater broke off the kiss and set her a few inches away, his hands locked around her forearms.

"Don't move," he said.

His low, husky command sent another wave of shivery excitement through her.

He released her, crossed the room to the door and turned the key in the lock. The ominous clink of iron-on-iron rang like a distant thunder in the small space. When he paced back toward her, yanking at the knot of his black tie, the dark promise in his eyes sent a delicious shiver of anticipation through her.

By the time he reached her the strip of silk dangled around his neck. He stood still, not touching her. She knew that he was waiting for some sign.

Fingers trembling, she reached up and undid the first button of his shirt.

That was all he needed. He clamped his hands around her waist, lifted her up off the ground and sat her on the edge of her desk. Before she realized his intention, he pushed the skirts of the dressing gown up over her knees and moved between her legs.

"Slater."

She did not say anything else. Torn between shock and a rush of feverish excitement, she could not find any more words.

He anchored her with one hand wrapped around the back of her neck and kissed her again. She arched into the embrace, tightening her legs around his thighs. She savored the exotic drug that was his scent, a mix of sweat, soap and the unique essence that was Slater. No other man had ever clouded her senses in such a way.

And then he was undoing the fastenings at the front of the dressing gown. The layers of velvet and lace fell apart at his touch as though made of clouds and mist. There was no corset or camisole to bar his way. When his palm covered her breast she closed her eyes and turned her head into his shoulder to suppress a small cry.

"Half of London wonders why I have not shown any interest in forming a liaison with a woman," Slater said. His thumb and forefinger tightened gently around one nipple. "I have asked myself the same question from time to time. But now I have the answer."

She looked up at him through half-closed eyes and kissed his throat.

"What is the answer?" she asked, astonished by the sultry sound of her own voice.

He moved his hand from her breast to her knee. Deliberately he eased his palm up under the skirts of the gown, along the sensitive skin of her inner thigh and found the hot, wet place between her legs. She took a sharp breath, shivering in response to the intimacy.

"I was waiting for you," he said. "I just didn't know it until I met you."

"Slater."

This time she said his name in an aching whisper because she could barely speak at all now.

She slipped her hand inside his partially open

shirt and flattened her palm on his chest. She could feel the hard, sleek muscle beneath his warm skin.

He stroked her, drawing forth a response that took her by storm. His touch had a shattering effect on her senses. An unfamiliar tension built inside her. When he tugged on the sensitive bud at the top of her sex, her nails turned into small claws on his chest.

He slipped two fingers gently inside her. She caught her breath, instinctively tightening herself against the sensual invasion. The clenching action only served to ratchet up the tension.

In the early days of her marriage, before she had discovered the weaknesses in Jeremy's character, she had enjoyed his kisses and thought herself content with the physical side of marriage. Jeremy had been nothing if not charming and he had accounted himself an expert lover. But even at the dawn of their relationship, when she had still been in the giddy, hopeful phase of love, she had never experienced the level of excitement that gripped her now.

Perhaps it was the result of having very nearly perished in the fire. Perhaps the doctors were correct—maybe widowhood took a toll on a woman's nerves. Whatever the reason, her reaction to Slater stunned her.

"I cannot take any more of this torment," he said against her throat. "I need to be inside you. I need it more than I have ever needed anything in my life."

He opened the front of his trousers, freeing his heavy erection. She was shocked anew when she looked down and saw the size of the man.

But before she could decide what to do next, he pushed her knees wider apart, gripped her hips with both hands and thrust hard and deep into her wet heat.

Instinctively she clenched herself around him but he withdrew and plunged back into her, again and again until she was breathless and desperate.

Without warning the coiled tension that had tightened her lower body was released in a series of deep waves.

She was not sure what was happening. She tumbled helplessly over a seemingly endless waterfall. She clutched Slater's shoulders and hung on for dear life.

Slater gave a muffled roar. He thrust deep one last time. But instead of pouring himself into her, he pulled free. In the next instant his climax ripped through him. She felt the hot stream spill across her bare thigh, heard his ragged breathing and sensed the shuddering tremors that pounded through him.

When it was over he braced himself with both hands on the desk on either side of her body and leaned over her, his eyes tightly closed. Perspiration gleamed on his forehead and dampened his chest.

"Ursula," he said. "Ursula."

An eerie hush descended on the study. Ursula knew that when reality returned, nothing would ever be the same—not for her.

TWENTY-THREE

⁓

Rosemont lurched awkwardly along the fog-and-night-darkened street, a heavy suitcase in each hand.

He was no fool, he thought. He had known from the start of the affair that there were risks—only to be expected in a situation where there was a great deal of money and some very ruthless people involved. He had made preparations for precisely the sort of emergency that had struck today.

He had not breathed easily until he had heard the explosion. He had been several streets away at the time, cowering in a doorway. The muffled rumble had given him some comfort and reassurance. No one could have survived such a conflagration. Mrs. Kern was dead, and everyone connected with the Olympus Club would assume that he, too, had died in the fire that had destroyed the shop.

One final transaction and he would be out of the dangerous business he had entered a year ago.

Concocting the drug had made him a wealthy man but no amount of money could calm his nerves. He had been in a perpetual state of anxiety for months now. He looked forward to retiring to a quiet seaside village. If he got bored, he would go back into the perfume and soap business. But never again would he distill the damned drug. His nerves could not take the strain.

True, for years he had done a brisk little side business peddling his own uniquely powerful laudanum products and cleverly disguised arsenic "tonics." But it had all been quite discreet. His customers had consisted primarily of wives who were desperate to rid themselves of difficult husbands and heirs who wished to speed the passing of a relative who had the misfortune to be standing in the way of an inheritance. He had always been careful to accept only clients who came to him by referral.

But his life had changed after he had agreed to take on the business of concocting the ambrosia. In addition to the dangerous people involved, the chemicals required to craft the drug were highly volatile. He could not wait to put it all behind him.

The clatter of hooves on paving stones behind him made him stop. He turned and watched a dark carriage roll toward him out of the fog. The vehicle looked anonymous, just one of many such hired conveyances on the street. But there was a small white handkerchief fluttering from the whip. That was the signal.

He set down one of the suitcases, yanked a white handkerchief out of his pocket and hailed the carriage somewhat hesitantly. It rumbled to a halt in front of him. The door opened. An intimidatingly large man in a heavy greatcoat, his features shadowed by the brim of a stylish hat, looked out from the dimly lit interior of the cab. He carried an ebony walking stick trimmed in gold. A gold ring set with onyx and diamonds glittered on one hand. He appeared to be in his early forties and not ill-favored. There were likely women who would notice such a man but in Rosemont's opinion there was something about Damian Cobb that put one in mind of a great beast of prey.

"You must be Rosemont. Allow me to introduce myself. Cobb, at your service. It's about time we met. We have, after all, been business associates for several months now."

Rosemont had known all along that Cobb was an American and that he lived in New York so the accent did not come as a surprise. But the harsh, whispery quality was unnerving. One could dress a villain in fine clothes and polish his manners but that did not make him any less dangerous. Quite the opposite, Rosemont thought.

"I'm Rosemont," he said, making a fierce effort to sound confident and assured.

"Please join us. This is my valet, Hubbard. We will

complete our business and set you down wherever you wish."

For the first time Rosemont saw that there was another man sitting in the shadows across from Cobb. Slight of build, with thinning hair and possessed of a face so gaunt one could almost see the skull beneath the skin, he appeared a mere shadow of a man. Hubbard was the perfect valet, Rosemont concluded, remarkably unremarkable in every aspect except for the subtle perfection of his sartorial style. From his elegantly knotted four-in-hand tie and turnover collar to the cut of his coat and his elegant walking stick, Hubbard was a model of refined fashion. Not that anyone would ever take much notice of him, Rosemont thought. He could almost bring himself to have some sympathy for the valet. He knew what it was like to be easily overlooked.

Hubbard inclined his head a fraction of an inch, acknowledging the introduction, and examined Rosemont with eyes so lacking in warmth they appeared reptilian.

"Allow me to take your bags, sir," Hubbard said. There was an oddly strained quality to the words, as though he were endeavoring to put a dignified polish on an accent that had obviously come from the American streets.

Rosemont handed both suitcases up into the carriage and climbed in after them. He sat down next to Hubbard, putting as much distance as possible between them.

"You may convey me to the railway station," Rosemont said. "I'm leaving London tonight."

"I understand," Cobb said. He raised his walking
stick and tapped the roof of the cab twice. The vehicle rolled forward. "I think we had best close the
curtains while we complete our business. I have been
assured that London is a far more civilized city than
New York; nevertheless, I have always found it best
to err on the side of caution. Hubbard?"

Without a word Hubbard responded. Deftly he
closed the curtains with a minimum of quick, efficient movements. Rosemont found himself mesmer-
ized by the valet's leather-gloved hands.

"Thank you, Hubbard." Cobb looked at Rosemont.
"I got your message. Why the sudden panic?"

Rosemont tore his eyes away from Hubbard's
hands, which were now folded quietly on top of his
walking stick. The valet was as motionless as a spider
waiting in a web.

Compose yourself, man, Rosemont thought. *This will
soon be over and you will be safely away from this dreadful business.* He drew a shaky breath.

"A very fashionable widow c-came to see me today," he said. He tried to steady his voice. "She was
asking after Miss Clifton."

Cobb inclined his head in a sorrowful manner.
"Who, I understand, recently took her own life."

Rosemont knew a small measure of relief.

"So it was a suicide?" he said. "Mrs. Kern seemed
to suspect that the death was a case of murder."

"Or an accidental overdose," Cobb said. "The newer version of the drug has unpredictable effects on some people. I understand Miss Clifton used the ambrosia."

"Yes, yes, she did. I tried to warn her but . . . Well. A suicide or an accident. I suppose that explains things. For a time I wondered . . . Never mind."

"What concerns you, Mr. Rosemont?" Cobb asked. "Were you fond of Miss Clifton?"

"She was a very attractive woman and always quite pleasant to me." Rosemont sighed. "I was just startled to learn that she was dead. I had not heard the news until the widow showed up at my shop today."

"Such a small death in such a large city is hardly the sort of tragedy that finds its way into the press." Cobb tapped one gloved finger against the top of his walking stick. "And now you tell me that you wish to conduct one more transaction and then retire from the business?"

"That is correct." Rosemont straightened his shoulders. He had committed murder that afternoon and set fire to his own shop. He was made of sterner stuff than he had ever imagined. "There is a large quantity of the drug crated and ready for shipment sitting in the warehouse. It should be enough to satisfy your customers in New York until you can find a new chemist to replace me."

"I see. You really do wish to get out of the business."

"Very much so. I could not endure another day like today." Rosemont leaned down and opened one of the suitcases. He took out the notebook that sat atop the neatly folded clothes. "I have written down the instructions required to prepare the formula from the raw leaves and flowers of the plant straight through the various preparations—powder, liquid or gas. Any good chemist can produce whatever you wish provided he has a supply of the plant and access to certain chemicals."

"I see." Cobb took the notebook. He flipped it open and glanced casually at the formulas and instructions inside. He nodded, satisfied, and closed the notebook. He set it on the cushion. "Who was this woman—this widow—who came around to your shop inquiring about Anne Clifton?"

"She called herself Mrs. Kern. She said she was Miss Clifton's employer. At first she tried to tell me that Miss Clifton had recommended my perfumes. I knew at once that was a lie, of course. As soon as she showed me the perfume bottle that I had given to Miss Clifton, I realized something terrible had happened. I only use those bottles for the liquid form of the drug."

"Why do you suppose this widow was making inquiries into Miss Clifton's death?"

"I have no idea. But I soon realized she was in possession of some rather dangerous information."

The beast came and went in Cobb's eyes. "What sort of information?"

"She had a list of the dates on which Miss Clifton had come by the shop to deliver the dried plant material," Rosemont said.

"I see. That is, indeed, rather disturbing. Miss Clifton must have kept a record of her appointments."

Rosemont widened his hands. "She was a trained secretary, after all. I'm sure she kept very accurate records of a great many things."

"An even more unsettling thought." Cobb pondered for a moment and then fixed Rosemont with another piercing look. "I assume you did not divulge any information regarding our business arrangements to Mrs. Kern?"

"Of course not." Rosemont paused. "Not that it matters. I had made preparations just in case I was overtaken with such a disaster. I locked her in the laboratory and set off an explosion which caused a great fire. She died in the blaze."

"You are quite certain of that?"

"Positive." Rosemont longed to raise the curtains to see if they were in the vicinity of the railway station. He glanced at Hubbard's gracefully folded hands and resisted the impulse to open the shades.

The driver rapped twice on the roof of the cab. The vehicle drew to a halt.

"I believe we have arrived," Cobb said.

"Thank goodness." Rosemont gathered his nerve. "As I told you, the final shipment is in the warehouse. I would like my payment now, if you don't mind."

"I'm afraid I do mind." Cobb reached inside his coat.

Rosemont froze. Sweat broke out on his brow. He started to shiver.

Cobb smiled a faint, derisive smile. Very deliberately he removed a gold cigarette holder from an inside pocket. "Really, Mr. Rosemont. You British have such a low opinion of your former colonials. We are not all western outlaws who go about armed to the teeth. Hubbard, please see our guest to his destination."

Hubbard unfolded his hands and opened the door. Dank fog carrying the odor of the river swirled through the opening. Rosemont had just taken a relieved breath. Now another wave of panic hit him.

"This isn't the railway station," he said.

"Isn't it?" Cobb shrugged. "You must forgive me. I'm new in town. I find that the streets of London are a maze. Get out, Rosemont. As we are no longer business partners I do not owe you any favors. I'm sure you will eventually find a cab."

Hubbard kicked down the steps and descended to the ground. He held the door open.

Rosemont scooted across the seat, edging toward the door. He was terrified now, but not of the neighborhood.

"What of my fee?" he managed.

Cobb seemed bored. "Hubbard will see to it that you receive payment in full. Be so good as to get out of my carriage. I have other business to attend to this evening."

Rosemont scrambled through the doorway and reached back inside to collect his suitcases. He took one last look at the big man in the cab and knew for certain that he was very fortunate to be escaping with his life tonight.

He turned and started walking very quickly. The fog glowed with just enough moonlight to show him that he was in the middle of an unlit street lined with darkened warehouses.

After a moment it dawned on him that Cobb's carriage had not moved off. A dark, primal terror rose within him. The sense that some terrible beast was closing in on him struck with such force that he stopped and whirled around.

The interior lights of the cab were turned down low but Cobb was visible inside. He was smoking a cigarette, as though he had no urgent appointments. There was no sign of the little spider of a valet.

Rosemont hurried toward the corner. He heard faint footsteps behind him and started to swing around again but by then it was too late. Pain exploded for only an instant when the stiletto sank deep into the back of his neck.

And then there was nothing.

TWENTY-FOUR

~~~~~

Slater sprawled in the wingback chair, contemplating the pleasant torpor and the deep sense of satisfaction that warmed him. He had been cold for a long time, he realized. But he had grown so accustomed to the sensation that he had come to think of it as a normal condition. He had been wrong. Ursula had brought him enlightenment on that particular matter and she had done so in a spectacular fashion.

He watched her do up the front of the dressing gown. He would be content to watch her dress anytime, he concluded. It would be even more gratifying to watch her take off her clothes.

"There is no question in my mind but that Anne was involved in some dangerous affair linked to Rosemont and his laboratory," Ursula said. She started to pace the room. "But I cannot imagine how that could have come about."

"Before we discuss Rosemont and his very interesting laboratory, I would like to ask you a question," Slater said.

Ursula stopped and looked at him, a stern frown knitting her brows. "What is that?"

He gestured at the crumpled towel on the floor. Ursula had used it to wipe all traces of him off her thighs.

"Are we going to talk about what just happened here in this room?" he asked.

A visible jolt went through her. But she quickly composed herself.

"What is there to discuss?" she asked warily.

His spirits, which had been in fine form a moment ago, were suddenly plunged into the depths. He exhaled deeply. What had he expected from her? A declaration of undying passion? She'd been through hell that afternoon. Her nerves were no doubt in a fragile state and he had taken advantage of her while she was vulnerable. He should have consoled her, not engaged in an intense bout of heated intercourse.

He rose slowly. She flushed and quickly turned away when he set about the business of refastening the front of his trousers and his shirt. So much for the air of intimacy he thought existed between them. He braced himself for the apology he knew he owed her.

"I'm sorry, Ursula," he said.

She turned back to face him, startled. "What?"

"I know an apology is hardly sufficient under the circumstances but there is nothing else I can offer."

She narrowed her eyes. "What, exactly, are you apologizing for, sir?"

He glanced at the towel and then met her eyes. "For what happened between us. It was my fault."

"Was it, indeed?"

He wasn't sure what to make of her tone. She sounded angry. He probably deserved that.

"You were very nearly murdered this afternoon," he said. He flexed the fingers of one hand, thinking about Rosemont. "Your nerves are still in a delicate state. I should have realized you were not yourself. I took advantage of your fragile condition—"

"Bloody hell, sir, how dare you apologize to me?"

She *was* furious. He looked at her, uncertain how to deal with the situation.

"Ursula, I'm trying to explain—"

"Yes, I know." She watched him with fierce eyes. "You wish to explain that you think I'm such a silly goose that I did not understand what I was doing when we . . . when we . . ." She broke off, waving a hand at the chair and the towel.

"Your nerves—"

"There is nothing wrong with my nerves. It's my temper that should concern you. Are you implying that I don't know my own mind?"

"No, absolutely not," he said. He was starting to feel cornered. That, too, was an unfamiliar experience.

"Then what are you trying to say? That you regret our recent encounter?"

"No, damn it." His own temper started to surface. "I found the experience quite satisfying."

She folded her arms very tightly beneath her breasts. "Then there is nothing more to be said."

Something was inciting her outrage but damned if he could reason out what the problem was.

"Do you regret it?" He watched her, trying to read her eyes. "Because if so, I'd rather you told me now so that I can ensure it doesn't happen again."

"For the last time, I knew what I was doing and I do not regret it. Is that enough for you to be certain that my nerves have not been completely shattered?"

"Thank you," he said.

She drummed her fingers on her forearms. "Well? You appear to be waiting for me to say something else."

He cleared his throat. "This might be an appropriate time to tell me that you found our encounter at least mildly pleasurable if not entirely satisfactory."

Her eyes widened in shock. "Oh. Yes. Well, as to that, I am not sure."

He winced. "On second thought, it might be best if we moved on to another topic. At this rate you will completely unman me."

"The thing is, something did happen—something that was . . . unfamiliar to me."

"Generally speaking it's not the sort of thing that is easily confused with other activities."

She started pacing again. "I believe I experienced what the doctors refer to as a paroxysm. A cathartic paroxysm."

"I'm not sure I could even spell *paroxysm*. What the devil is that?"

She paused to glare at him. "You know what I mean. A physical . . . release."

"Are you trying to tell me that you experienced a climax?"

She raised her chin. "The medical profession calls it a paroxysm when it happens in women. I suppose they don't think it's possible that women are capable of actually experiencing pleasure in the way that men do so they give it a label that makes it sound more like a case of shattered nerves."

A relief so great that it equaled the pleasure he had experienced a short time ago nearly overwhelmed him. He started to smile, caught himself and quickly suppressed it.

"Ah," he said. "I see."

She shot him a suspicious look. "What do you see?"

He could no longer suppress the smile. Crossing the short distance that separated them he cupped her face in his hands.

"I realize that you have been a widow for many years now. Perhaps it has been some time since you enjoyed that sort of thing."

She wrinkled her nose. "I never enjoyed one of *those*. I expect that is why I did not recognize the sensation at first."

"Your marriage was not a happy one? Not even in the beginning?"

"I told myself I was content—at least, I did until I discovered Jeremy's gambling habit and his taste for brothels. I understood belatedly that he had married me to get his hands on the small inheritance my father left me. I did not realize that there was something missing in our physical relationship. I suspect it is that way for many other women, as well. It certainly explains why so many of them are making appointments with their doctors for the treatment of congestion and hysteria."

"Are you telling me there is a treatment for, uh—"

"I believe a medical instrument called a vibrator is involved."

"You're serious, aren't you?"

She was bright pink now. "Yes, as a matter of fact, I am. My assistant, Matty, booked an appointment for a treatment with a doctor last month. She was practically glowing when she returned to the office. She says she plans to schedule another appointment soon. She recommended the therapy. Highly."

Slater was stunned. And then he started to smile again. The smile turned into a grin and then a chuckle. Without warning he was suddenly roaring with laughter. Ursula watched him, bemused.

Eventually he regained his composure. When he did he realized he felt uncharacteristically light-hearted.

He brushed his mouth lightly across her lips. "Promise me that you will consult with me before you make any appointments with a doctor."

She blushed a deeper shade of red and then she smiled. It was a brilliant, dazzling smile. Sensual laughter lit her eyes.

"I will do that," she said.

He realized he was getting hard again. He wanted to pick her up in his arms and carry her back to the chair to demonstrate to her that what she had experienced was not a one-time event.

He groaned and pulled her to him. "I would like very much to make love to you again but I regret to say we have more pressing issues."

"Rosemont and his laboratory." Ursula raised her head. "And Anne's connection to the drug trade, which appears to have been going on for several months. I just do not understand it."

"Neither do I, not yet. But her involvement may have led to her death."

"That reminds me." Ursula stepped out of his arms and went to the satchel sitting on top of her desk. "I have something to show you. I collected a sample of the dried herbs that I found in Rosemont's laboratory. I think he used them to concoct the drug. I saw no other plant specimens on the premises. And he said something about ruing the day he agreed to make the ambrosia."

"He admitted that he was concocting the drug?"

"Yes."

Slater watched her open the satchel and remove a small bundle created from a knotted handkerchief. When she untied the square of linen he saw a handful of dried leaves and flowers.

"I don't recognize that plant," he said. "It's nothing like the opium poppy."

"I have never encountered it, either."

"One way or another, we must consider the stuff

to be dangerous. Rosemont was willing to commit murder and destroy his own laboratory to protect his secrets. If you don't mind, I'll take the sample to a botanist I know. He was a friend of my father's. Perhaps he will recognize the leaves."

"I suppose I could ask Lady Fulbrook about the herb."

"No," Slater said. "We don't know what is going on in the Fulbrook household. You must not tell Lady Fulbrook or anyone else what happened to you today. Above all, you must not let on that you discovered these leaves."

"Very well."

"We need more information," Slater said.

"About the plant, do you mean?"

"That, too. But I want details of the goings-on at the Olympus Club."

"I thought that was why we were trying to arrange an interview with the brothel madam, Mrs. Wyatt."

"I don't think that we can count on obtaining a great deal of information from her—not if she is involved in this drug business. She will have her own interests to protect."

"Will you talk to one of the members of the club?" Ursula asked.

"That would be the best approach. Unfortunately, there is a problem. I am not a member of the club, and due to the fact that I have been out of the country for the greater part of the past decade, I lack the social connections I need to convince a member to confide in me. But there are other ways to gather information."

Ursula was silent for a little too long.

"What are you thinking?" he asked.

"I'm thinking that your partner, Lord Torrence, might be able to assist you," Ursula said.

"You refer to my *former* partner, who evidently detests the sight of me."

"I told you, I don't think Torrence hates you. I believe he is afraid of you."

"I think you're wrong but even if you're correct, it comes to the same thing. He won't help me."

"It will be your task to convince him to change his mind. Meanwhile, it occurs to me that whoever was supplying the herbs to Rosemont must be a very expert gardener. It might be interesting to take a closer look at the contents of Lady Fulbrook's conservatory tomorrow."

Ghostly fingers touched Slater's neck. "I don't think you should return to that house."

"There's nothing to worry about." Ursula smiled reassuringly. "After all, Griffith will be out front in the street the whole time I am inside."

TWENTY-FIVE

Matty looked up from her typing when Ursula opened the door of the office.

"Good morning," Matty said. "You're late. I was starting to wonder if you were not feeling well."

Ursula unpinned her hat and tossed it onto a table. "Once and for all, I am not ill." She flung her gloves after the hat.

Matty blinked a few times and then she smiled. "No, you are not. In fact, you are positively glowing with good health this morning."

"What's that supposed to mean?"

"Nothing," Matty said. "Just that I have the impression that you will not need to make an appointment with Dr. Ludlow for the treatment of congestion and hysteria."

Ursula sighed and sank down into her chair. "Is it that obvious?"

"That you and Mr. Roxton have become very, very good friends?" Matty chuckled. "Yes, it is, and I congratulate you."

"I'm not sure congratulations are in order."

"Nonsense. We are both well past the age when we need concern ourselves with our reputations. So long as we are discreet, there is no reason why we should not enjoy the few benefits available to widows and spinsters."

Ursula had been about to open a desk drawer. She paused.

"We?" she repeated.

Matty smiled serenely and looked at the flowers on her desk.

"Mr. Griffith stopped in to see me first thing this morning," she said.

"Griffith brought you flowers?"

"Pretty, aren't they?"

It was Ursula's turn to smile. "Yes, they are."

"Mr. Griffith is a very impressive man," Matty said. "He spent years touring the country and America with a theatrical group."

"I had heard that." Ursula paused. "He is a very large man."

"Yes, he is." Matty looked pleased. "I believe it is all muscle."

"No doubt." Ursula clasped her hands on her desk. "Do you remember Anne's satchel?"

"Yes, of course. Why?"

"I woke up during the night and remembered that it was not among her things. If you will recall, we packed all of her possessions and clothes into two trunks. I went through both this morning. Her satchel was not in either trunk."

Matty raised her brows. "It was a very nice satchel. Remember how she showed it off to us the day she bought it? I wonder if her landlady pinched it."

"I found Anne's jewelry behind the water closet but there wasn't room to conceal a large leather satchel there." Ursula surveyed the office. "Where would you hide a satchel?"

Matty reflected briefly. "I don't know. I've never considered the problem."

"If I wanted to hide something as big as a satchel and if I didn't have a safe or some other secure place, I might keep it in a location where a burglar was unlikely to look."

"Where would that be in a house?"

"Not in a house, Matty." Ursula jumped to her feet. "In an office."

She started opening drawers. Matty joined her.

In the end, Ursula discovered the satchel at the back of a filing cabinet drawer.

"She must have been very anxious about the possibility that someone would steal her lovely new bag," Matty said. "Wonder what's inside?"

Ursula set the satchel on a desk and unlatched it.

There was a small bundle of letters inside. Ursula selected one at random.

"It's from Mr. Paladin," she said. "Editor and publisher of the *Paladin Quarterly* in New York."

"Who is Mr. Paladin?" Matty asked.

"Lady Fulbrook's publisher." Ursula removed the letter from the envelope and read it quickly.

Dear Miss Clifton:

I have received your short story, "A Proposal from a Lady." It is clever and intriguing, just the sort of thing that would be of interest to our subscribers. If you have any other stories of a similar style and content I would be happy to consider them for publication in our literary quarterly.

Sincerely,
D. Paladin

"Well, no wonder Anne was careful to hide those letters," Matty said. "I'll wager Lady Fulbrook would be furious if she knew that her secretary was secretly selling short stories to the *Paladin Quarterly*."

"Do you think so?" Ursula asked.

"Certainly. Very likely she would have viewed Anne as competition."

TWENTY-SIX

"Your suggestion that we go into my conservatory to work is excellent, Mrs. Kern." Valerie rose slowly from her chair, as though burdened by a weariness of the spirit so heavy she could scarcely bring herself to move. She rang a bell and drifted slowly toward the door of the library. "I can always count on inspiration from my plants and flowers."

Ursula collected her stenography notebook and her satchel and got to her feet.

"It was just a thought," she said lightly. "I'm glad you believe that it might have a beneficial effect on your poetry."

"Very little lightens my spirits, Mrs. Kern. But I do find some peace in my conservatory."

The plan, such as it was, could only be described as simplistic, Ursula thought. She was no botanist but she had done a careful sketch of the dried leaves and small flowers of the herb that she had salvaged from Rosemont's laboratory. She thought she would recognize the plant in its growing state if she saw it in the conservatory.

Valerie led the way down a long hallway and out into the lush garden. A maid followed at a discreet distance. They crossed a small brick courtyard and went along an ornamental path.

The big mastiff staked to a heavy chain lumbered to his paws and watched them with a wolf's unblinking stare. Ursula kept a wary eye on him. On the previous trip to the conservatory Valerie had explained that the dog was turned loose at night to guard the grounds. The animal looked as if it would cheerfully rip out one's throat.

At one point Valerie glanced briefly over her shoulder at the maid.

"I hate them all, you know," she confided in low tones.

"The servants?" Ursula asked, keeping her voice equally low.

"They watch me day and night. I cannot leave the house unless my husband is with me. He and that witch of a housekeeper hire each and every member of the staff. They serve as his spies and prison guards. I cannot trust any of them."

When they reached the large, gracefully arched, glass-walled hothouse, Valerie took a key out of the pocket of her day gown and handed it to the cold-faced maid, who used it to open the door.

A soft rush of warm, humid air freighted with the

scents of rich soil and growing things wafted through the opening. Valerie breathed deeply of the lush fragrance. Some of her tension and anxiety visibly lessened, just as it had the last time Ursula had accompanied her into the glasshouse.

"That will be all for now, Beth," she said. She took the key from the maid and made it disappear into her pocket. "Mrs. Kern and I are not to be disturbed."

"Yes, ma'am." The maid gave Ursula a disapproving look that bordered on suspicious, bobbed a curtsy and hurried back toward the house.

"Bitch," Valerie whispered.

Ursula studied her surroundings. The first time she had accompanied Valerie to the conservatory she'd taken only a cursory look around. The glasshouse was huge, the largest facility of its kind that she had ever seen. Ferns, palms, orchids and a myriad assortment of towering, leafy plants filled the glass chamber. The foliage was so abundant that in many places it formed a canopy that was thick enough to block the daylight.

Ursula looked at Valerie. "I hope you don't mind if I tell you how much I admire your conservatory. It's nothing short of magnificent."

"Thank you. I have always been interested in horticulture and botanical science. But after my marriage this conservatory became my passion." Valerie walked slowly down an aisle formed by rows of broad-leafed plants that arched over her head in a natural green tunnel. "It is the one place where I know I can find privacy and peace. No one comes in here without my permission, not even my husband."

"Lord Fulbrook does not share your passion for gardening?" Ursula asked, trying to make the question sound as innocent as possible.

Valerie paused at the far end of the leafy tunnel and smiled. For the first time since they had met, Ursula got the impression that she was amused.

"My husband avoids this place as if it were filled with poisonous substances—which it is, at least for him."

Ursula was halfway through the green tunnel. She stopped, eyeing some tropical flowers with a bit of trepidation.

"You grow poisonous plants?" she asked.

"Calm yourself, Mrs. Kern. I doubt that there is anything in here that could harm you. If you were as unpleasantly affected by the atmosphere as Fulbrook is, I'm sure you would be aware of it by now. After all, you were here on a prior occasion."

"I see." Ursula relaxed and resumed making her way through the tunnel. "Your husband is one of those who suffers from the symptoms of a head cold when he is near certain plants and trees?"

Valerie chuckled. "His nose becomes so congested that he is forced to breathe through his mouth. His eyes turn red. He sneezes and coughs and is generally quite miserable."

"No wonder he does not like to enter your

conservatory," Ursula said. She hesitated, knowing she had to tread carefully. "You are fortunate."

The amusement faded from Valerie's eyes. "In what conceivable way, Mrs. Kern?"

"Some husbands would have insisted that a conservatory that induced symptoms of a head cold be removed."

Valerie surveyed her green realm. "My husband sees some small value in my conservatory. Like my poetry, it keeps me entertained and therefore makes me less of a nuisance to him."

"I see."

"Do you take an interest in gardening and horticultural matters, Mrs. Kern?"

"Oh my, yes," Ursula said. She did not have to pretend enthusiasm for the subject. "Indeed, I would be thrilled if I could ever afford such a place as this."

"That is not likely, is it?" Valerie's smile was cold and crushing. "Considering your circumstances."

I suppose that puts me firmly in my place, Ursula thought.

"No, Lady Fulbrook," she said, "it's not likely."

"You appear to be prosperous in a middle-class sort of way, but a fine conservatory such as this one will always be beyond the reach of a woman in your position."

The cool edge of the words iced Ursula's nerves.

"You are quite correct, Lady Fulbrook. Only a woman possessed of great wealth could afford this place or your lovely mansion."

"Very true. The only possible solution for you would be marriage to a man far above your station."

"I suppose so."

"But such dreams are merely illusions for a woman like you, Mrs. Kern."

Ursula tightened her grip on her satchel. "Are you trying to tell me something, madam?"

"I am trying to warn you, Mrs. Kern. I have been informed that you have been seen in the company of Mr. Slater Roxton. Yes, I'm aware that it is his carriage that delivered you here today and that the same carriage will be waiting for you when you leave, just as it was on the previous occasion. There was also some chatter in the newspapers about you and Roxton putting in an appearance at a certain museum exhibition. I will be blunt. It is obvious that you are Roxton's mistress."

Ursula smiled a steely smile. "For a while there, you had me concerned, Lady Fulbrook. I was afraid you were about to accuse me of trying to seduce your husband, which would have been quite silly."

Lady Fulbrook flinched as if she had been struck. Astonishment flashed in her eyes. It was followed by rage. She was not accustomed to taking return fire from someone who occupied a much lower rung on the social ladder.

"How dare you talk to me of such things?" she snapped.

"I would remind you that you were the one who raised the subject by saying that it was obvious that I was Mr. Roxton's mistress."

"I was trying to give you some sound advice," Lady Fulbrook said tightly. "A man of Roxton's wealth and connections will never consider marriage to a woman of your sort. Even though he's a bastard son and his mother was an actress, he can nevertheless afford to look much higher—and mark my words, he will—when he decides it's time to marry. But I doubt that you will take my warning seriously. Just as Anne Clifton failed to abide by my advice."

Curiosity overcame Ursula's temper. "You gave Miss Clifton similar advice?"

"The foolish woman thought she was so clever seducing a man who is far above her reach." Valerie started drifting along the aisle formed between two workbenches. "That's what killed her in the end, you know."

Ursula followed at a cautious distance. "No, I didn't know. Please enlighten me."

"She must have concluded that her dreams could never become reality." Valerie reached out and snapped the bloom off a flower stalk. "I'm sure that's why she took her own life."

"You seem to know a great deal about Anne's state of mind at the time of her death."

"Miss Clifton and I spent a great deal of time in each other's company during the past several months. We often spoke of love and passion because my poetry deals with such matters. She got in the habit of confiding in me."

That was hard to believe, Ursula thought. Anne

had been clever, resourceful and ambitious—a determined survivor who had learned the hard way not to trust anyone who held power over her. She had once confided that at the age of seventeen, while working as a governess, she had been raped by the husband of her employer.

The wife had blamed Anne and turned her off immediately. That outcome was only to be expected in such situations. What had enraged Anne and made her forever wary of all future clients was that her employer had refused to pay the quarterly wages Anne was owed and also refused to provide a reference. That had made it impossible to find another post for a time. Anne had come very close to selling herself on the street in order to eat.

No, Ursula thought, it would have been very unlike Anne to confide in Valerie.

"Are you certain that Anne was involved in a love affair?" Ursula asked.

"I didn't say it was a love affair." Valerie snapped off another bloom and continued along the aisle. "It was a seduction or, rather, an attempted seduction. The object of her desire was barely aware of her existence. She was no more than a servant to him. I will not say that I sympathized with her but I understood her."

"In what way?"

"I know exactly how she felt." Valerie picked up a pair of shears and cut off the drooping frond of a palm tree. "I am no more than a servant in my husband's eyes."

A bell chimed somewhere behind Ursula. She was so intent on the conversation that she started at the unexpected sound.

"I told Beth that we were not to be interrupted," Valerie said, annoyed. She looked down the length of the green tunnel toward the door, frowning. "It's the housekeeper. Excuse me, I'll be back in a moment."

She went back through the green tunnel, heading for the door of the greenhouse.

Ursula waited until she heard the door open and then she whisked up her skirts and went quickly along the aisle formed by the plant beds, potted trees and workbenches. In the distance she could hear Valerie speaking in sharp tones to the housekeeper but she could not tell what was being said.

She did not see any leaves or flowers that resembled the dried ones she had brought out of Rosemont's laboratory. When she reached the end of the aisle, she turned to the right and went along a narrow gravel path.

"Mrs. Kern?" Valerie called. "Where are you? I can't see you."

"I was just enjoying some of the specimens," Ursula sang out. "This is an extraordinary collection. I would be honored if you would give me a proper tour."

"Come here at once. You must leave now. I won't be needing your services any longer."

Damnation. Valerie was going to let her go. She would never be able to get back into the conservatory.

"Coming," Ursula said. "Rather difficult to find

one's way around in here, isn't it? I can't even see the front door."

"Stay right where you are, Mrs. Kern. I will find you and escort you out."

Ursula kept moving, trying not to betray her location with the sound of her footsteps. She continued to scan the foliage but none of it resembled the dried herb material.

"Mrs. Kern, where are you?"

It struck Ursula that there was a new and surprising vigor in Valerie's voice. It wasn't just impatience. There was another kind of energy vibrating just beneath the surface. Excitement.

"Really, Mrs. Kern, I do not have time for this. You must leave at once."

"I understand, madam. But I cannot see anything except greenery. It is all quite disorienting."

"Stand still. I will find you. Do you understand?"

Ursula obeyed, not because of the command but because she had just come face-to-face with a wall of glass and a locked door. For the first time she realized that the greenhouse was divided into two distinct sections. The inner portion behind the door was smaller than the main chamber. A profusion of radiant green foliage studded with golden flowers filled the room. She was quite certain she was looking at a great mass of the herb that Rosemont used to concoct the ambrosia.

Valerie appeared from a cluster of palms. Her face was flushed and her eyes were fever-bright. She had fistfuls of her skirts in both hands, hoisting the heavy fabric of her gown above her knees so that she could move more quickly.

The light glinted briefly on a small object attached to her petticoats. A button or some other bit of decoration, Ursula thought. Most women used lace and ribbons to add a whimsical touch to their underclothes.

"There you are," Valerie said. She let her skirts fall back into place. "Do come with me and don't dawdle."

Ursula obediently fell into step beside her. "May I inquire why you are letting me go?"

"It is none of your affair but as it happens I have just received word that a houseguest from America will be arriving the day after tomorrow. I—we—were not expecting him until next month."

"I understand."

"There is so much to be done. He will be staying with us, of course." Valerie gave a laugh that was very nearly a giggle. "My husband will not be pleased. He does not care for the company of Americans. He finds them lacking in the social graces. But Mr. Cobb is a business associate. He must be treated with the proper degree of respect."

"Perhaps your husband will suggest that Mr. Cobb book a room in a hotel."

"A hotel is out of the question. Mr. Cobb entertained us quite lavishly in his mansion when we visited New York a few months ago so we must repay the favor. My husband will have to take comfort in knowing that our houseguest will not be staying very long—only a few days, in fact."

"A remarkably brief visit considering how far Mr. Cobb will have traveled."

"Mr. Cobb is a very busy man," Valerie said. "As I was saying, I will no longer require your stenography services, Mrs. Kern."

"Would you like a typed copy of your latest poem sent to you?"

"That won't be necessary."

The housekeeper hovered just outside the entrance of the glasshouse. Her middle-aged features were stamped with the impassive expression of a woman who had long ago learned that the secret to keeping her post was to keep her employers' secrets.

"Show Mrs. Kern to the door," Valerie instructed.

TWENTY-SEVEN

⁓

Griffith was lounging against the trunk of a tree in the small park across the street from the Fulbrook mansion. When he spotted Ursula he straightened and moved to open the door of the carriage.

He glanced at the house with a speculative expression. "You're finished early, Mrs. Kern. Everything all right? I know Mr. Roxton was concerned about your plans to come here today."

"Lady Fulbrook just let me go." Ursula collected her skirts and went up the steps into the carriage. She sat down and looked at Griffith. "With no notice and without a reference, mind you."

"Not that you need one from her."

"No, thank goodness. But I have some news, Griffith. I persuaded Lady Fulbrook to take me into the conservatory again and I saw a great quantity of the ambrosia plant growing in a special chamber."

Griffith's eyes tightened. "You're certain?"

"As certain as I can be without a closer examination."

"So Fulbrook is growing the plant?"

Ursula shook her head. "I don't think so. Evidently Fulbrook cannot tolerate the atmosphere of the greenhouse. It gives him all the symptoms of a bad cold. I believe that Lady Fulbrook is the one cultivating the plant for him. I must get word to Slater immediately."

"After I take you to your office I'll track him down and give him the information," Griffith said.

"Please take me home, instead. There is something I want to do there."

"Aye, ma'am." Griffith started to close the door.

Ursula put out a hand to stop him. "Speaking of Slater, where is he today, do you know?"

"He went to see his father's botanist friend."

Griffith closed the door, vaulted up onto the box and loosened the reins. Ursula watched the front of the Fulbrook mansion until it disappeared from sight.

Lady Fulbrook had been more than flustered about the prospect of the visitor from America. She had looked thrilled. Evidently she had no problem tolerating the rude American manners of her husband's business associate.

MRS. DUNSTAN OPENED the door of the town house with an air of concern.

"You're home early today, Mrs. Kern. Is everything

all right? Still feeling a bit rattled by your dreadful experience yesterday? Perfectly natural, if you ask me. I told you that you ought not to go to work today."

"I appreciate your concern, Mrs. Dunstan, but I am quite fit, thank you." Ursula removed her hat and stripped off her gloves. "I'm home early because my client let me go. She got word that a houseguest from America is arriving the day after tomorrow. She was in quite a flap over the whole thing. I would have had Griffith take me to the office but I remembered some business that I want to take care of here."

"I see." Mrs. Dunstan waved farewell to Griffith and closed the door. "A note arrived for you while you were out. I set it on your desk in your study."

"A note?" Ursula dropped the hat and gloves into Mrs. Dunstan's capable hands and hurried down the hall to the study. "From Mr. Roxton, perhaps?"

"If it is from him, he neglected to put his name on the outside of the envelope," Mrs. Dunstan called after her.

Ursula swept through the door of the study. She had returned to her house to take a closer look at Anne's private correspondence with Paladin, the editor of the literary quarterly. But when she saw the note on her desk she recognized the handwriting at once. Her insides went cold. She forgot about the correspondence.

She opened the envelope slowly, dreading what she knew she would find inside. She reminded herself that she had a plan. Her hand steadied.

She scanned the contents of the note. The black-mailer had, indeed, named his price.

> . . . *As you can see, a trivial amount. An excellent bargain. Leave the money in the weeping angel crypt in the cemetery in Wickford Lane. Make sure the payment is there by four o'clock today or the press will be notified of your true identity.*

IT WAS NOT THE AMOUNT of money involved that caused rage to splash through her veins. The price of the extortionist's silence was not nearly as high as she had expected. It was the knowledge that the payment was destined to be the first of an endless string of demands that infuriated her.

She refolded the note.

She had a plan. It was time to implement it.

She went to the gilded floor safe in the corner, crouched and opened the combination lock. She pushed aside a handful of mementos from her other life—a photograph of her parents, the last letters her father had written to her before perishing of a fever in South America, and her mother's wedding ring.

Storing the latest message from the blackmailer alongside the small velvet pouch that contained Anne's few pieces of jewelry and the Paladin corre-spondence, she took out the small, dainty pistol her father had given her. He had taught her how to use the gun before he set out on his last trip abroad. "*A*

lady never knows when she might have to defend herself."
She had been eighteen at the time.

She made certain the pistol was loaded and then she closed and relocked the safe.

Rising to her feet, she put the gun inside her satchel and searched the room, looking for something suitable to use as fake bank notes. A copy of yesterday's edition of the newspaper was on the table. She tore it into several sheets, stuffed them into an envelope and dropped the envelope into the satchel.

Hoisting the bag, she hurried out into the front hall. She was taking her gray cloak off the peg when Mrs. Dunstan appeared from the kitchen, wiping her hands on her apron.

"Going out again, madam?" she asked. She peered through the sidelight window. "The fog is coming in."

"I just remembered that I have an appointment with a new client this afternoon. I almost forgot."

"Bit late for a meeting with a client, isn't it?"

"Clients can be very demanding."

Mrs. Dunstan opened the door with obvious reluctance. "Shall I summon a cab?"

"That won't be necessary. It will be faster if I walk through the park."

"Where does this client live?" Mrs. Dunstan asked, increasingly uneasy. "After what happened yesterday—"

"Don't worry about me, Mrs. Dunstan. The client resides in a very quiet neighborhood. Wickford Lane."

TWENTY-EIGHT

The old church and the cemetery on Wickford Lane were both in a state of deep neglect. The small chapel was locked and shuttered. The nearby graveyard was overgrown with weeds. The gates stood open, sagging on their hinges. There were no fresh flowers on the graves. The monuments and crypts looming in the fog were badly weathered and, in many cases, cracked and broken.

Ursula made her way slowly through the stone garden of grave markers, searching for a weeping angel. She gripped her satchel in one hand. The pistol was in her other hand, concealed beneath the folds of her gray cloak. The mist was thickening rapidly. She could no longer see the iron fencing that surrounded the cemetery.

The fog was a good thing, she told herself. It gave her ample cover for what she intended to do.

For a few unnerving minutes she worried that she might not be able to locate the weeping angel. In the end, she nearly collided with one broken wing.

She stepped back quickly and looked at the figure guarding the entrance to a crypt. It was a large, stone angel in a weeping pose.

The wrought-iron gate that had once secured the opening to the burial vault stood open.

The muffled sound of a footstep somewhere in the fog sent a shock of icy fear through her. The blackmailer was somewhere nearby, watching her. She resisted the temptation to turn around and search for him. She told herself she must give no indication that she was aware that she had heard him.

She moved through the doorway of the crypt. It took a moment for her eyes to adjust to the low light. Between the windowless interior and the gray glow from the entrance she could barely make out the stone bench that had been designed as a place to sit and contemplate mortality.

She took the envelope out of her satchel and set it on the bench.

The task accomplished, she moved out of the crypt and walked steadily toward the front gates. She listened closely and thought she heard the soft thud of footsteps in the fog. They seemed to be moving toward the burial vault but she could not be certain.

She hurried out of the cemetery trusting that, with her gray cloak, she would soon vanish into the mist. She made certain her footsteps echoed on the pavement for a time, hoping to give the impression that she had left the scene. Then, walking as quietly as possible, she ducked into the arched doorway of the church.

From where she stood, she could just barely make out the posts of the iron gates at the entrance to the fogbound graveyard. As far as she had been able to discern, it was the only exit from the cemetery.

She waited, her heart pounding at the prospect of what she intended to do.

For a time nothing moved in the mist. She began to fear that her plan had gone awry, that the blackmailer had eluded her. Perhaps she had been wrong about the footsteps in the cemetery. But surely he had been waiting and watching for her, she thought. He would want to seize his payment quickly before some vagrant searching for shelter happened upon it by accident.

She was in the middle of trying to concoct a new plan in the event the first one failed when she saw a shadowy figure moving in the dense fog that pooled inside the cemetery. She stilled, hardly daring to hope that her scheme had worked and not wanting to consider too closely what she intended to do next. She had made up her mind. She must not lose her nerve.

The figure in the mist proved to be a man in a shabby greatcoat. The collar was pulled up around his neck and a low-crowned hat concealed his features. He paused at the gate, searching the vicinity. Ursula knew he could see very little in the fog.

The time had come to implement her plan. The

goal was to trap him inside the cemetery. If she waited until he exited, he might take off running. It was highly unlikely that she would be able to outrun him—not burdened as she was with several pounds of clothing—and the small pistol was not accurate at any great distance. It was meant for the close confines of a gaming hell or a carriage or a bedroom.

She gripped both her nerve and the handle of the gun very tightly, steeling herself, and then she stepped out of the vestibule and went swiftly toward the cemetery gates. The blackmailer did not see her at first.

When he heard her light, rapid footsteps he swung around, alarmed. But by then she was only steps away.

"Stop or I will shoot," she said.

Her fierce anger and determination must have been evident in her tone because the blackmailer let out a startled squeak of fear and retreated deeper into the cemetery. He ducked behind a nearby stone marker.

"Don't shoot," he yelled in a voice freighted with panic.

It was not the response she had anticipated. She had just assumed that when confronted by a dangerous weapon, the blackmailer would freeze and obey her every command. It was certainly what she had done when Rosemont had held her at gunpoint. Evidently not everyone behaved the same in a crisis.

It dawned on her that her only option was to stalk the blackmailer through the fogbound cemetery. She moved uneasily through the entrance, heading toward the gravestone that shielded the villain.

"Come out," she ordered. "I won't shoot unless you make it necessary."

"No, please, it's all a terrible mistake."

The blackmailer leaped to his feet like a startled rabbit and dashed deeper into the cemetery.

"Bloody hell," Ursula whispered.

Monuments and grave markers loomed everywhere. She began a methodical search. There was more scurrying and harsh breathing. She knew her target had changed positions yet again.

It occurred to her that the mad game of hide-and-seek could go on indefinitely.

The plan was not working as intended. Perhaps the best option was to retreat to the entrance and outwait the extortionist. He could not remain inside the cemetery grounds indefinitely.

She was edging cautiously toward the gates when she heard pounding footsteps in the fog—not hers and not the blackmailer's, she realized. At least two more people had arrived on the scene.

"Damn," Slater said. He came up behind Ursula and seized her forearm, yanking her to a halt. "What the devil?" He broke off, glancing down at the pistol. "You've got a gun?"

He snapped the weapon out of her fingers before she realized his intent.

"Give that back to me," she said. A fierce desperation surged through her. "He'll get away."

"No," Slater said. He raised his voice a little to call out into the fog. "Griffith?"

"I've got him," Griffith shouted.

He appeared from behind a crypt holding the blackmailer by the collar of the greatcoat. The extortionist's feet kicked wildly a few inches above the ground.

"Among his many tasks with the traveling theatrical group, Griffith was the one who guarded the day's receipts and made certain no one got in to see the performance without paying the price of admission," Slater explained.

"Put me down," the blackmailer yelped. "I'm an innocent citizen. The crazy woman pulled a gun on me. What else could I do but run?"

Griffith looked at Slater. "What do you want me to do with him, Mr. Roxton?"

"Bring him here, Griffith. We're all going to have a short chat and sort this out."

Griffith plopped the extortionist down on both feet.

"Who are you?" Slater asked.

But for the first time Ursula got a good look at the blackmailer. Fresh outrage slammed through her.

"His name is Otford," she announced. "Gilbert Otford. He works for that gutter rag, the *Flying Intelligencer.*"

TWENTY-NINE

This dreadful creature is trying to blackmail me,"
Ursula said. She gave Otford a disgusted look.
"I came here today to stop him."

"You were going to shoot me." Otford stared at
her in shocked disbelief. "In cold blood. How could
you do such a thing?"

Otford was in his late thirties. He had pale blue
eyes, lank, reddish-blond hair and a ruddy complex-
ion. His clothes had seen better days. The sleeves of
his coat and the cuffs of his trousers were frayed. His
shirt had once been white but it was now a dingy
shade of yellow. Threads dangled from his limp tie.

Otford was not a career criminal, Slater concluded;
rather, a desperate man. Such individuals might be
inept but that did not make them any less dangerous.

"I wasn't going to shoot you—well, not unless I was

left with no alternative," Ursula said. "I merely wished to discover your identity."

Otford eyed her with grim suspicion. "Why did you want to learn my name unless you intended to kill me?"

"So that I could go to the police, of course," Ursula said. She gave Otford a steely smile. "I'm quite certain that a man who would stoop so low as to blackmail a lady would have a few secrets of his own he'd want to keep hidden."

Slater looked at Griffith, who was watching Ursula with undisguised admiration. Slater was not entirely certain how he, himself, felt about the situation. He was still trying to cope with the knowledge that Ursula had found it necessary to own a gun. He had never met a lady who carried one. Granted, it was a very small handgun but at close range it was a potentially deadly weapon. And to think that he had begun to believe that he knew Ursula well enough not to be surprised by anything she did. He had been very much mistaken.

"Well, I've got news for you, Mrs. Kern, I don't have any secrets to conceal." Otford straightened his thin shoulders. "I'm a journalist."

Ursula ignored that. "You recognized me from the trial, didn't you? I remember your face in the crowd. You sat right in front every single day like a vulture waiting to tear apart dead meat."

"I covered the Picton divorce trial, yes." Otford raised his chin. "It was my duty as a journalist."

"Rubbish. You were one of the so-called gentlemen of the press who ruined my good name and made it necessary for me to adopt a new identity. I very nearly ended up in the workhouse or on the street because of you, Mr. Otford. And now you have the nerve to try to blackmail me?"

"I asked for only a couple of pounds," Otford shot back. He waved a hand at her gown and hat. "It looks like you've done quite well for yourself, madam. Whereas I am the one in danger of starving. I'm going to be thrown out of my lodgings at the end of the week if I don't come up with the rent. I've been eating at a charity kitchen for the past month."

"But you've got a job." Ursula narrowed her eyes. "Have you become a gambler, sir? Is that why you are going hungry?"

Otford exhaled deeply. His shoulders collapsed. "No, I haven't fallen prey to the vice of gambling. My editor let me go. He said I hadn't brought in anything the public actually wanted to read in months. Not earning my keep, he told me. I'm working on a plan to publish a weekly magazine that covers the news of the criminal class and the police, but setting up in that business takes money."

"So you decided to try to extort money from me," Ursula said. "Who else are you blackmailing, Mr. Otford?"

Otford was clearly offended. "I don't intend to make a career out of extortion, madam. It was just a little something to tide me over."

"It's been two years since the Picton trial," Ursula said. "I took great pains to disappear. How did you find me?"

A flash of intuition crackled through Slater.

"That," he said, "is a very good question." He took Ursula's arm and nodded to Griffith, who clamped a hand around Otford's shoulder. "I suggest we retire to another location to discuss the answer. There's no reason to stand out here in the street."

THIRTY

Slater took them all back to his house, sat them down in the library and then asked Mrs. Webster to bring in a tea tray. She had sized up the situation immediately. A tray piled high with sandwiches and small cakes sat on a table in the center of the room.

Otford had very nearly come to tears when he saw the sandwiches. He had fallen upon them with the appetite of a man who had not eaten well in days. Griffith had not been shy, either. He had loaded up a small plate with several sandwiches and a couple of lemon tarts.

Slater leaned back against his desk, folded his arms and watched Ursula. He was starting to worry about her. She showed no interest in the food and very little in the strong, fortifying tea. She had been in a fine fury a short time ago but now she sat tensely in her chair. He got the feeling that she was bracing herself for complete disaster.

"Ursula," he said gently, "it's going to be all right."

She looked up with a slightly dazed expression. Her thoughts had clearly been elsewhere. But abruptly she focused on him.

"How did you know where I was this afternoon?" she asked, clearly suspicious.

"I went to your house to see you. I had some news to share with you. Mrs. Dunstan told me that you had gone haring off to Wickford Lane to see a new client. She seemed to think it was unlikely that anyone in that neighborhood would be in the market for a fashionable stenographer."

"I see."

"Ursula, she was worried about you."

Ursula ignored that. "What was this news you had for me?"

"They found Rosemont's body in an alley near the docks this morning."

"What?" Ursula had been about to take another sip of tea. She set the cup down so quickly that some of the contents splashed into the saucer. "He's dead?"

"And not by accident," Slater said. "He was murdered."

"Good heavens," Ursula said.

"Murder?" Otford asked around a mouthful of sandwich. His eyes widened. "What's this? Who is Rosemont?"

"A recently deceased purveyor of perfumes," Slater said.

"Oh." Otford lost interest and selected another sandwich. "No one of note then."

Slater turned back to Ursula. "I talked to the police. The detective in charge of the case was kind enough to give me some information."

"Well, of course the police would pay attention to you," Ursula said grimly. "You're Slater Roxton."

Slater pretended not to hear that. "I'm told Rosemont's death looks like the work of a professional assassin. Stiletto in the back of the neck."

She blinked and then a speculative look appeared in her eyes. She was not the only one paying attention. Otford actually stopped munching again.

"What's this about a professional assassin?" Otford gulped down a bite of sandwich and wiped his mouth with the back of his sleeve. He whipped out a small notebook and a pencil. "Stiletto, you say? Makes all the difference if there's a professional villain involved, you see, not your average run-of-the-mill member of the criminal class. My editor might be interested. I can see the headline now, *Assassin Stalks London Streets*."

Slater held up a hand. "You are not going to your editor, Otford, not yet at any rate. There is an even bigger story here and you can have an exclusive report if you do what I tell you."

Otford stopped writing. "A bigger story? Any chance of a whiff of scandal? Readers prefer thrilling news, you see."

"You cater to such a discerning audience, Mr. Otford." Ursula gave him a chilly smile. "You must be very proud."

Otford glared. "I have a responsibility to the public, madam."

"What about a responsibility to the truth, Mr. Otford?"

"Now, see here, that little incident in the cemetery does not make me a villain, madam."

"I disagree," Ursula snapped.

Slater decided to step in before the situation deteriorated further.

"Let's try to stay on topic," he said. "I think there is a strong probability that the assassin will attempt to murder someone else and quite soon."

"Indeed?" Otford brightened.

"Mr. Otford, I think I can safely promise you a story that will help you launch a career as a publisher of one of the most popular weekly crime-reporting magazines in London." Slater paused a beat before adding softly, "What is more, if you assist us in this investigation, I will help you finance your project."

Otford looked dazzled. "You would back me financially, sir?"

"Yes, because I think you can be helpful to us."

"I will do my best, sir. Count on me, Mr. Roxton."

Ursula raised her eyes to the ceiling and drank some tea.

"In exchange for your assistance in the investigation that Mrs. Kern and I are conducting," Slater continued,

"I will pay your rent this week and provide you with some visible means of support until you are ready to publish your first penny dreadful. But I must have your solemn promise that you will keep your mouth shut until I give you permission to print the story."

"Absolutely, sir. You have my word as a man of honor."

Ursula sniffed. "You're an extortionist, Mr. Otford. That rather undercuts your claim to being a man of honor, don't you think?"

He contrived to look hurt. "My life has become quite complicated lately, Mrs. Grant."

"The name is now Mrs. Kern, thanks in large measure to you and your nasty reporting of the Picton divorce trial. And for your information, my life has become complicated, as well."

Slater held up one hand. "Enough. I think it is time that we all agree to set some priorities and move forward in an effective, efficient manner. First things first. Otford, how did you discover Mrs. Kern's identity?"

Otford cast an uneasy glance at Ursula and cleared his throat. "As to that, sir, I'm afraid I cannot say."

"I understand that your journalistic ethics may be of more importance to you than your desire to cooperate in this investigation," Slater said. "However, if that is the case, I'm afraid our financial arrangements must be canceled."

Otford was panic-stricken. He waved both hands wildly. "No, no, you misunderstood, sir. I didn't mean

I *won't* tell you who informed me—I meant that I can't tell you. I don't know the identity of the person who gave me the information."

Ursula pinned him with a dangerous look. "Then kindly explain how you discovered me."

"An envelope was pushed under my door earlier this week." Otford sighed. "Monday afternoon, quite late in the day, to be exact. Someone evidently knew that I had covered the Picton trial and that I would likely recognize you if I saw you again. The note supplied your home address and the address of your secretarial agency. I went around to your office immediately and got a look at you through the window as you were closing up for the day. I knew at once that you were the woman who had testified at the trial. You've changed the style of your hair and you wear mourning now; nevertheless, there is something singularly peculiar about you, Mrs. Grant—I mean, Mrs. Kern."

"Peculiar?" Ursula sounded as if she had her teeth clenched.

"It's not your looks," Otford assured her hastily. "They are not particularly memorable but there is something about your character that leaves what I can only describe as a lasting impression."

Slater thought it wise to distract Ursula before she could counterattack.

"You said you received the message concerning Mrs. Kern on Monday?" he asked.

"That's right," Otford said.

Slater looked at Ursula. "That was the same day that you met with Lady Fulbrook for the first time."

"You did say that someone watched me leave in your carriage that first day," Ursula said.

Griffith reached for the coffeepot. "Sounds like someone wanted Mrs. Kern out of the way."

"In that case, why not simply dismiss me?" Ursula said. "That's what Lady Fulbrook did today."

"Terminating the arrangement with your secretarial agency might have kept you out of the Fulbrook house," Slater said, "but it would not have kept you from investigating Miss Clifton's death."

"But I didn't tell anyone that I was investigating," Ursula said.

Slater raised his brows. "You summoned the police the day you found the body. When that did not do any good, you insisted on taking Miss Clifton's place as Lady Fulbrook's secretary. And you were seen leaving that day in my carriage. All in all, I think it's safe to say that you made someone quite nervous. And the fact that you were seen in my company meant that it would have been risky to simply murder you outright."

Ursula swallowed hard. "Because you would no doubt demand—and get—a full-scale police investigation."

"Which is the last thing Fulbrook wants," Slater concluded.

Otford perked up again. "I say, do you think Lord Fulbrook is the one who put the message about Mrs. Grant—Mrs. Kern—under my door?"

"More likely he sent a servant to perform the task but, yes, I think it is a distinct possibility that Fulbrook alerted you to Mrs. Kern's identity."

Ursula's eyes glittered with unshed tears. "But that means that Anne must have told him my real identity. Why would she do that? I trusted her."

Slater wanted to comfort her but he knew that it was not the time. "What Fulbrook could not know was that Otford would try to blackmail you instead of exposing you in the sensation press."

Otford smiled benignly at Ursula. "There now, I did you a favor, Mrs. Kern. It all worked out well in the end, did it not?"

Ursula did not bother to respond. She grabbed a hankie from her satchel and blotted her eyes.

Slater looked at her. "Today when Griffith came to pick me up at the botanist's house he told me that Lady Fulbrook had sent you away immediately after she received a message about a houseguest who is due to arrive from America the day after tomorrow."

"That's right." Ursula had herself back under control. She swallowed some tea and lowered the cup. "Lady Fulbrook was visibly cheered by the news. She was excited—said something about not having expected Mr. Cobb until next month. She made it clear that her husband did not think highly of the American but that he was forced to treat Cobb politely because they were business associates. Evidently Cobb is a wealthy, powerful man in New York. Several months ago he entertained Lord and Lady Fulbrook when they visited there."

"Interesting," Slater said. Absently he removed his spectacles, took out a handkerchief and began to polish the lenses. "Let us consider what we have here.

Two people who have a connection to the ambrosia drug trade are now dead—Anne Clifton and Rosemont. And a wealthy American business associate of Fulbrook's is on his way to London."

"There's something else, as well," Ursula said. "I saw the ambrosia plants today."

Slater went still. "Did you?"

"Lady Fulbrook has a hothouse dedicated to cultivating them."

A sense of knowing whispered through Slater. "That is even more interesting. Another step on the path. The pattern is finally becoming more visible."

He realized the others had fallen silent and were gazing at him with curious expressions. He put on the spectacles.

"The botanist I consulted this morning informed me that what we are calling the ambrosia plant—it has a rather long and complicated Latin name—is something of a legend in the botanical community," he said. "All the references to it come from the Far East and most of those are mere hearsay. He knew of no specimens that had been successfully cultivated in Great Britain. According to the few notes he found, the plant can produce a powerful euphoria and induce visions."

Otford had been scribbling madly. He paused and looked up, face scrunched into a frown. "What makes this particular drug so special? It is not as though there is not a wide variety of opium-based drugs available for sale everywhere. Most housewives have their own family recipes for laudanum."

"At the moment ambrosia has the distinction of being unique because, as far as we can tell, it is only available from one source," Slater said. "The Olympus Club appears to have a monopoly. Monopolies can be quite profitable."

"Huh." Otford tapped his pencil against his notebook. "The name of that club rings a bell. Can't quite remember why."

"In that case I would like you to see what you can find out about the Olympus," Slater said. "Talk to some of the people who work there but I advise you to be discreet. People are getting killed in this affair."

Otford brightened. "Right. Murdered. Assassin running around."

"So it seems," Slater said. "I think we need to find out whatever we can about Cobb."

"But he isn't even in London yet," Ursula said.

She was not challenging him, Slater realized, merely curious about his reasoning.

"The fact that Cobb's ship has not yet docked doesn't mean he is not involved in this affair," he explained. He went behind his desk, sat down and reached for a sheet of paper. "Griffith, I am going to give you a telegram addressed to a former client of mine in New York. I want you to take it to the nearest telegraph office immediately."

Griffith polished off one last tart and dusted his hands. "Aye, sir."

Slater wrote out the message. Griffith took it and glanced at the address. "Your client is a director of a museum?"

"I occasionally tracked down stolen artifacts for him and I helped him avoid some of the frauds that were offered to him. One case, in particular, had the potential to ruin the museum's reputation. But as it happens, things worked out well and now the director owes me a favor. He may not know anything about Cobb, personally, but he will have connections among the city's wealthy elite. If Cobb has money, which seems to be the case, people will know about him."

"Right, then." Griffith folded the paper and tucked it into his pocket. "I'll be off."

Otford waited until the door closed behind Griffith. Then he cleared his throat.

"I believe I see where you are headed here, sir," he said. "Do you really think that a high-ranking gentleman like Lord Fulbrook may be involved in these murders?"

"I don't know," Slater said. "I am still collecting information. The sooner you conduct your interviews, the sooner we will have some notion of what is going on."

"Understood, sir." Otford bounced to his feet and grabbed the last sandwich off the tray. "I know exactly how to go about gaining information from servants. My parents were in service. But I can tell you right now that no one will talk to me unless I make it worth their while."

"I will instruct my butler to supply you with some bribe money." Slater tugged on the velvet bellpull. "Webster will also take care of your rent."

Otford chuckled and headed toward the door. "Very kind of you, sir. Look forward to working with you on this project. With a story this big and your financial backing, I will be able to launch my magazine."

He disappeared out into the hall.

Ursula looked at Slater. A deep curiosity burned in her eyes.

"You did a favor for the director of a museum in New York?" she asked without inflection.

"I warned you that I had a checkered past, Ursula."

She smiled ruefully. "As do I."

"Perhaps that is an indication that we are well suited to each other."

"Some pasts are more checkered than others. But given what has happened, I suppose you are due an explanation."

"You are entitled to your privacy," he said. "Everyone has secrets."

"Unfortunately, it appears that mine are no longer hidden."

THIRTY-ONE

Ursula drank a little more tea and set the cup aside. She got to her feet and went to stand at the window, looking out into the garden.

"I suppose I should thank you for following me to the cemetery this afternoon," she said.

"That's not necessary," Slater said.

She was not certain what to make of his quiet patience. Most men would have been aghast to discover that they were conducting a liaison with a woman who was being blackmailed; one who had been involved in a notorious divorce scandal; a woman who carried a pistol to a meeting with an extortionist.

"I wasn't going to kill him, you know," she said after a moment. "Otford wasn't worth getting myself arrested and hung for murder. But I thought that I might be able to frighten him into leaving me alone."

"It was a perfectly reasonable plan."

She glanced at him over her shoulder. "Do you think so?"

"It suffered from the usual problems associated with a spur-of-the-moment strategy but, yes, overall, not a bad plan. It might have worked."

She found his approval quite cheering.

"I must say you handled him very well," she said. "A plate of sandwiches and a little money and suddenly he is working for you."

"He believes that he's working in his own best interests and that is true in some respects. I have learned that most people are amenable to projects in which they see a personal benefit."

She smiled. "Do I detect a note of cynicism?"

"I consider myself a realist, Ursula."

She was almost amused now. "Yet you are the ultimate romantic, Mr. Roxton."

He appeared to be blindsided by that remark. When he recovered his expression went hard.

"What the devil makes you say that?"

"I am very much afraid that you had the grave misfortune to be born with the spirit of one of the old chivalric heroes, Slater. You employ a ragtag household staff that no one else would hire. You returned to London to guard the inheritance of your two half brothers even though the title and the money should have come to you by right of blood. You do not feel at home here but you stay because of the responsibilities that were thrust upon you. And you insisted on getting involved in what most would call a foolish, utterly ridiculous scheme to investigate a murder because you were afraid I might be in danger."

He shook his head. "Ursula."

He stopped, evidently out of words.

"Yes, Slater, I'm afraid you are doomed to play the hero."

"That's nonsense." He got to his feet and crossed the room to stand beside her. "What matters is finding out who slipped the note containing the information about your real identity and your address under Otford's door."

"The only person who knew the truth about me—at least as far as I am aware—was Anne Clifton. She must have confided the information to someone in the Fulbrook household. But why would she do that?" Ursula blinked tears out of her eyes. "I trusted her. I thought she was my friend."

Slater put his arm around her and hugged her close. "Not everyone is worthy of your trust."

"Don't you think I know that?" Ursula freed herself from his grasp and hurried across the room to her satchel. She took out a handkerchief and wiped her eyes. "I knew Anne was reckless in some ways but we had so much in common. And it's difficult to go through life without having at least one other person know the truth about oneself."

"You were alone and lonely. You took a risk. Things didn't work out. It's not the end of the world."

She gave him a misty smile. "No, it's not, is it?"

"The real question here is, who did Anne Clifton

tell?" Slater began to prowl the room. "Lady Fulbrook, who, in turn, might have confided in her husband?"

Ursula tried to make herself concentrate. "Remember I mentioned that I thought Anne might have been involved in a romantic liaison?"

Slater stopped at the far end of the room and looked at her. "Yes."

"Perhaps she became Lord Fulbrook's mistress. Lady Fulbrook said she tried to warn Anne not to get involved with a man who was far above her on the social ladder. If Anne was having an affair with Fulbrook it might explain why she got involved in his drug business." Ursula paused. "And perhaps it would also explain why she told him the truth about me. She might have felt it safe to confide in a lover."

"We don't have all the answers yet," Slater said. "We are still on the path."

"What path?"

"Just an expression," he said rather absently. He crossed the room to where she stood, caught her hand in his and kissed her palm. He met her eyes. "Never fear, we will find our way out of this labyrinth."

A hush fell on the room.

"About the Picton divorce trial," Ursula said after a moment.

"It doesn't matter."

"Yes, it does matter." She freed her hand and went to the window. "You deserve to know the truth."

"I can tell you now that none of it will make any difference."

"There is not much to the tale," she said, determined to get through the business. "The difficulty was that no one believed my version of events." She took a breath and composed herself to get through the sordid tale as quickly as possible. "After my husband's death I was left penniless. I took a post as a paid companion to Lady Picton. It was obvious from the start that Lord Picton lived a very debauched life. The housekeeper advised me to lock my door at night and I made certain to do so."

Slater said nothing. He waited as if he had all the time in the world.

"One night Picton came home quite drunk," Ursula continued. "He tried the door of my bedroom. It was not the first time he had done so but in the past he had always gone away when he discovered that the door was locked. That night, however, he had the key. I realized later that Lady Picton had given it to him."

"She sent him to your room that night because she wanted grounds for divorce," Slater said. "Proof of adultery."

"She reasoned that adultery, together with charges of cruelty, would be sufficient grounds. Picton intended to rape me that night. That never happened. I fought him and started screaming. The next thing I know Lady Picton and half the household staff are standing in the doorway. Lady Picton had a pistol. Picton turned on her in a drunken fury. She shot him in the leg. I think she intended to kill him and pretend to have mistaken him for a burglar who had attacked her companion. But she was a poor shot. It was all very messy. The trial was worse."

"You were the star witness, I take it?" Slater said.

"Yes. Picton fought the divorce because he had married Lady Picton for her money. He did not want to lose access to her family's fortune. In the end, Lady Picton got her freedom but my reputation was in ruins."

"You created a new life for yourself," Slater said. "That is a remarkable accomplishment, Ursula. Few people would have been able to summon the courage and the will to do that. I am in awe of you, madam."

Her eyes were watery again. She hurried to her satchel and took out the sodden handkerchief. Feeling quite awkward, she blotted her eyes for the third time.

"My apologies," she said. "It has been some time since I lost my composure like that. All I can say is that it has been a rather trying day."

He smiled. "I would never have guessed that was the case."

She dropped the damp linen square back into her satchel. She was about to fasten the bag when she noticed her stenography notebook. The sight of it reminded her of the possibility that had occurred to her earlier, before she had read Otford's blackmail demand and set out for the cemetery.

She closed the satchel and turned to look at Slater.

"This afternoon, after Lady Fulbrook dismissed me, I intended to go home to reread some of the entries in Anne's notebook—lines that did not make much sense as poetry."

"What has occurred to you?"

"I wondered if perhaps Lady Fulbrook was dictating love letters to Anne, not love poems."

Comprehension heated Slater's eyes. "Love letters to a Mr. Cobb in New York, perhaps?"

"Who concealed his identity by posing as Mr. Paladin, the editor of a small literary magazine. Would that be so far-fetched? Lady Fulbrook is very unhappy in her marriage. If she and Cobb had an affair several months ago during that visit to New York she might have continued the relationship through love letters. But she could not risk having her husband discover what was going on beneath his nose so she used Anne as a go-between."

"That would shed a very interesting light on the investigation."

"If Lady Fulbrook believes herself to be in love with Cobb, it would explain her giddy delight this morning when she discovered that he was due to arrive much earlier than expected. But there is something else. I believe that Anne may have established her own private correspondence with Paladin. I haven't had a chance to read all the letters that she received from him but in the first few he acknowledges having received a short story from her. He indicates he's interested in publishing it."

Slater's brows rose. "Did Miss Clifton write short stories?"

"Not to my knowledge. If she had attracted the attention of a publisher I'm certain she would have mentioned it. Another thing—I suspect Lady Fulbrook is the one who came up with the pen name Paladin."

"Why do you say that?"

"Well, she is the one with the vivid imagination." Ursula smiled sadly. "And if you will recall, the word *paladin* refers to a chivalrous knight."

The knock on the door stopped Slater before he could react to that observation.

"Come in, Mrs. Webster," he said.

The door opened. With a flourish, Mrs. Webster held out an envelope. "This just arrived for you, sir. It's from your mother."

"Thank you."

Slater ripped open the envelope and unfolded the note.

Ursula watched him, sensing the subtle whisper of anticipation that shivered in the atmosphere around him.

"Is it something important?" she asked.

"Perhaps," he said. "Mrs. Wyatt, the proprietor of the Pavilion of Pleasure, has agreed to meet with us. She will await us this evening at the folly in Lantern Park."

"She does not want us to be seen at her establishment."

"She is taking precautions," Slater said. "She notes there will be a price for any information that she provides."

Ursula did not bother to conceal her excitement. "Your mother did warn us that Mrs. Wyatt was very much a businesswoman."

THIRTY-TWO

~~~~~

The folly in Lantern Park was cloaked in the shadows of a rainy evening. The light of a nearby streetlamp illuminated the fanciful gazebo.

Ursula stood in the shelter of the umbrella that Slater held aloft. Together they surveyed the octagonal structure. There was no sign of Mrs. Wyatt or anyone else.

"Damn," Slater said. "I was hoping she would not change her mind at the last minute. Perhaps she lost her nerve."

"Why send the message agreeing to meet with us if she hadn't concluded that the money you were prepared to offer was enough to make her take the risk?" Ursula asked.

Slater studied the wet landscape with close attention. His jaw was set in a grim line. He put one hand inside his greatcoat. She knew that he had just

wrapped his fingers around the handle of his revolver. She had seen him take it from a locked drawer
in his desk just before they set out.

"It's possible that she was delayed by the weather
or traffic," Slater said. But he did not sound convinced. "We'll give her a little time. Let's wait inside
the gazebo, out of the rain."

Ursula looked at him. "You are uneasy about this
meeting?"

"I'm uneasy about this entire affair. Would you
mind taking the umbrella?"

"No, of course not."

He wanted to keep his hands free, she realized.
There was an air of prowling alertness about him, as
if he were prepared for something—anything—to go
wrong. He was definitely having qualms about the
meeting with Mrs. Wyatt.

They walked around the gazebo and found the
steps that led up into the sheltered sitting area. They
were not the first to arrive.

Ursula stopped on the second step, her shocked
mind searching for a reasonable explanation for what
she was looking at.

Her first thought was that a vagrant had sought
shelter from the rain and decided to take a nap. But
even as she tried to make herself believe that, she
knew the truth. The figure on the floor of the gazebo
was no transient. The quality of the cloak that covered most of the unnaturally still body was very fine.
The feathers in the fashionable hat must have cost a
small fortune.

"Bloody hell," Slater said very softly.

Ursula saw that he had taken the revolver out from beneath his coat. He crossed the gazebo floor and crouched beside the body. She watched him turn the body slightly to examine the back of the woman's neck. Ursula shuddered at the sight of the dark ribbon of blood.

"The assassin struck before we could speak to her," Slater said. He moved back toward the steps with long, quick strides. He did not look at Ursula. His attention was on the wooded parkland that surrounded the gazebo. "We must get away from this place. The killer may be watching us."

Ursula collected her skirts and went quickly down the steps. "Will you notify the police?"

"Yes, although I doubt if it will do much good. I want to go to Mrs. Wyatt's establishment immediately, before her death becomes common knowledge. I do not have time to take you home. Do you mind stopping at a brothel? We can enter through the alley. You have your cloak and your veil to conceal your face."

"I most certainly want to accompany you," Ursula said. "What do you hope to accomplish?"

"It might be useful to take a quick look around Mrs. Wyatt's private quarters before the police become involved in this matter."

"I see. What makes you think we will be allowed inside the establishment?"

"It's a brothel, Ursula. Money can buy anything in such a place."

"I take your point." She glanced back at the gazebo. "None of this makes any sense. Why would someone murder Mrs. Wyatt?"

"I can't say for certain yet but the path through the labyrinth is rapidly becoming clear. First, Anne Clifton, the courier, is murdered. Then Rosemont, the drug maker, is dispatched. And now a woman who supplied prostitutes to the club where the drug is dispensed is found dead."

"I understand," Ursula said. "But what is this pattern that you see?"

"Someone appears to be closing down the ambrosia business."

THIRTY-THREE

Hubbard watched from the shadows of the hansom as Roxton and the woman emerged from the park. He could tell from the swift manner in which Roxton bundled the female into a closed cab that they had discovered the body. It was possible they would go to the police but that was of little concern. The death of a brothel madam might interest the gutter press but it was doubtful that the authorities would conduct a serious investigation.

Even if they bothered to look into the death it would do them little good. Back home in New York, where his work had not gone unnoticed and where he enjoyed a bit of a reputation—the press had labeled him "The Needle"—he was still free to go about unrecognized on the streets. He prided himself on being neat and tidy in his work. He rather suspected that the reason the police did not search very hard for him was because, as a rule, he specialized in removing some of the very same people they were paid to take off the streets.

His employer's business interests were extensive, crossing all the murky boundaries that were supposed to separate legitimate enterprises from those that operated deep in the criminal underworld.

Damian Cobb employed an army of lawyers, accountants and sharp managers to deal with the competition in the respectable side of his affairs. When it came to his less respectable businesses, he used different types of experts. It was a competitive environment, to be sure. There was ample work for a professional who carried out tasks cleanly and skillfully while avoiding detection.

Hubbard watched the closed carriage pull away into traffic. Then he spoke to the driver through the opening in the roof of the hansom.

"The Stokely Hotel," he said.

"Aye, guv."

The driver shook the whip over the horse's rump. The hansom rolled forward.

Hubbard wondered if the driver intended to cheat him when it came time to pay the fare. The problem with being a visitor in town was that for the most part he had no idea of where he was at any given moment. He knew New York well. He had grown up in the city. But London was a sprawling maze that defeated his sense of direction. He hated the place. Here he was totally reliant upon the cab drivers, who all seemed remarkably well versed in the mysteries of the streets.

Fortunately, Cobb did not intend to remain in London for long. The loose ends were almost all completely snipped off. When the business was concluded they would sail home to New York.

Hubbard looked down at his gloved hands. He was impatient to return to his room at the hotel. His technique ensured that very little blood was spilled. Nevertheless, he always washed his hands afterward.

THIRTY-FOUR

⟡

M rs. Wyatt is dead?" Evangeline glanced at Ursula's veiled face and then turned back to Slater. "Are you certain?"

"Trust me, there is no mistake," Slater said. "We had an appointment to meet with her a short time ago. When we arrived at the location we found her body. The police will soon be making inquiries. My associate and I would like to conduct a brief investigation of our own before the authorities descend on this house and trample over every possible clue."

"Your associate?"

Evangeline looked at Ursula with a politely neutral expression. But her eyes said it all. Respectable women did not have dealings with the women in Evangeline's world.

Ursula raised the net veil and crumpled the delicate web up onto the brim of her hat, revealing her face. She smiled.

"I'm Mrs. Kern," she said. "It is a pleasure to meet you, Evangeline. Thank you for assisting us tonight."

Evangeline hesitated and then she inclined her head. Some of her wariness faded.

Slater gave no indication that he had noticed the moment of social tension.

"Evangeline was the lady who was kind enough to answer a few questions for me the other evening when I toured the grounds of the Olympus Club," he said.

"I did not see your face clearly that night," Evangeline said. "But I remember your voice. You were . . . quite helpful to me. Indeed, I am in your debt."

They were standing in the hallway outside the kitchen. The Pavilion of Pleasure was not busy yet. The customers would no doubt show up much later in the evening. Ursula occasionally heard footsteps on the stairs and muffled voices but Evangeline had explained that most of the women were in their rooms, dressing. The only place where there was significant activity was the kitchen. Through the open door a sweating cook and several assistants could be seen laboring over trays of canapés.

Ursula had not known what to expect inside a brothel. Nevertheless, she was mildly astonished by how normal it all appeared. She might as well have been in the hall outside the kitchen of any fashionable mansion preparing for a reception or a party.

A few minutes ago they had arrived at the back door of the Pavilion. Slater had handed some coins to the housekeeper and asked to see Evangeline, who had soon appeared. When she saw Slater, her expression had turned wary.

"The thing is, I'm not sure I should let you into Mrs. Wyatt's rooms," Evangeline said, glancing over her shoulder. She lowered her voice. "Charlotte's in charge when Mrs. Wyatt isn't around."

"Then please ask Charlotte to come downstairs," Slater said. "Make certain she knows that there will be a night's pay in this if she manages to remain discreet."

Evangeline hesitated. "I know I owe you a favor, sir, but I never thought you'd ask to settle accounts this way."

Slater slipped more coins into her hand. "For your trouble, Evangeline. Please hurry."

Evangeline did not argue. She disappeared. When she was gone, Ursula lowered the veil.

"You did not have to reveal yourself to her," Slater said without inflection.

"Of course I did."

Slater smiled slightly but he did not say anything else on the subject.

Evangeline returned with an older woman. Charlotte was suspicious at first and genuinely shocked by the news of her employer's death. But when Slater produced still more money a great transformation came over her. She led the way to a suite of private rooms.

"Why would anyone murder Mrs. Wyatt?" she asked, fitting a key into the lock of a door.

"We don't know." Slater ushered Ursula ahead of him into a lavishly decorated parlor. "We were rather hoping you might be able to tell us."

Charlotte eyed him and then looked at Ursula. "Why would the likes of you two care about the death of a brothel madam?"

"Because Mrs. Wyatt is not the first person to die in this case," Ursula said. "A woman who worked for me was also murdered. She was a friend of mine. I want to find out who killed her."

"There is one other fact you may wish to consider," Slater added.

"What's that?" Charlotte asked.

"It's quite possible that your colleague who supposedly jumped into the river was murdered either because her client was dangerously intoxicated or because, like Mrs. Wyatt and the others, she knew too much about the ambrosia trade," Slater said.

"Nicole," Charlotte said, her voice very grim. "We all know she did not jump off that bridge, at least not willingly." She gestured toward the parlor. "I will wait in the hall while you have your look around. Be quick about it. I don't think it is a good idea for you to be here."

"Thank you," Ursula said. She looked at Slater. "I will examine the bedroom while you investigate this room."

Slater nodded and went swiftly to the desk near the window. Ursula hurried into the adjoining room.

Mrs. Wyatt's bedroom was another surprise. Like the other parts of the big house that Ursula had viewed, the décor was a tasteful mix of yellow and peacock blue. The four-poster bed was draped with white netting and decorated with an attractive yellow quilt. The carpet featured gold flowers against an azure background. The wallpaper was set off with yellow and blue stripes.

There was, Ursula thought, no hint that the former occupant had been involved in the brothel business. Perhaps that was the intent.

She went to the wardrobe first. Ignoring the array of fashionable gowns, she opened the drawers at the bottom and worked her way through the neat pile of freshly laundered and crisply ironed underclothes.

Finding nothing of note, she crossed to the dressing table.

She discovered the perfume bottle tucked away in the back of a drawer. The little porcelain jar looked almost identical to the one she had found among Anne's things. Unlike that one, however, Mrs. Wyatt's bottle was not quite empty. There were a few drops at the bottom.

Cautiously, Ursula removed the stopper. The scent that wafted out held the familiar taint of a dark herb.

"Find something?" Slater asked from the doorway.

Ursula turned quickly and saw that he had a leather-bound volume in one hand.

"A perfume bottle," she said. "Just like the one I found at Anne's house. There are a few drops left and they smell like the dried herbs at Rosemont's shop."

"Both Mrs. Wyatt and Anne were using the drug."

"Evidently."

Slater moved, radiating impatience. "Come, we must leave."

She glanced at the notebook he held. "What did you find?"

"Wyatt's journal of accounts."

"What can that tell you?"

"Possibly nothing. But I have found that money is rather like blood. It leaves a stain."

THIRTY-FIVE

~⁓~

Brice Torrence descended the front steps of his club shortly before midnight. He was dressed in the black-and-white formal attire he had worn to a ball that evening. He raised a silver-handled walking stick to signal the first cab in the line of vehicles that waited in the street.

Slater moved out of the deep shadows cast by a nearby doorway vestibule.

"I'd like a word with you, Brice," Slater said.

Brice tensed and turned halfway around. His initial start of surprise was transmuted into anger.

"Roxton," he said. "What in blazes do you want?"

"Some brief conversation. You owe me that much, don't you agree?"

"Do you want me to apologize for what happened on Fever Island? To tell you that I'm sorry I left you for dead in those damned temple caves? How was I to know that you were still alive? Hell and damnation, man, *I thought you were dead.*"

Slater was stunned by the way the words spilled out of Brice. It was not the response he had expected. For a moment he was not sure how to handle it.

"I know you thought that I had been killed by that fall of rock," he said. "I don't hold you responsible."

"I left you to die while I sailed home with a priceless artifact. Some things are unforgivable in a friendship."

"This is not the conversation I want to have," Slater said.

"What do you want to discuss? Restitution? How am I supposed to make things right between us? How do I change the past?"

"This is not about the past, at least not those aspects of it. I want to talk about the Olympus Club."

Brice stared at him. "What the devil?"

Slater heard the door of the club open again. He glanced over his shoulder and saw two very drunk men come down the steps. Their laughter was too loud as they debated where to spend the rest of the night.

There was another man on the street, as well. He came quickly along the walkway as though late for an appointment. When he moved through the glary light of the streetlamps, Slater caught a glimpse of him. He was small in stature but he cut a fashionable figure in an excellently tailored suit. He carried a walking stick in one hand.

Slater did not recognize him but he knew the

sort—a clubman, making his nightly rounds of the most exclusive gentlemen's haunts.

Slater turned back to Brice and lowered his voice.

"Will you come to my house with me?" he said. "We can discuss this over some very good brandy."

"You can say whatever it is you think needs saying right here."

"If you insist," Slater said. "But perhaps we could put some distance between ourselves and the front door of your club?"

Brice looked wary but he accompanied Slater a short distance away from the light of the gas lamps that illuminated the front steps.

Slater glanced back to make certain that no one was close enough to overhear the conversation. He saw that the dapper little man with the walking stick was nearing the steps of the club. In another moment he would disappear through the doorway.

Slater shook off the uneasy feeling and focused on Brice.

"I warned her this was probably not a good idea," Slater said.

"Warned who? You're not making sense."

Slater was about to respond but it occurred to him that he had not heard the small man's shoes on the front steps of the club. Instead, the brisk footsteps were continuing along the walkway, coming closer.

The cab line was across the street, Slater thought. The little man was not headed in that direction, either.

The footsteps echoed in the fog, moving more quickly now and in a purposeful manner.

"Brice, do you know the man coming up behind me?" Slater asked. "The small fellow with the walking stick?"

"What?" Distracted, Brice peered past Slater. "No. Why do you ask?"

"Because you know just about everyone in Society. If you don't recognize him, that is not a good sign."

"Have you been drinking?" Brice demanded.

The footsteps were closing rapidly now. Slater glanced over his shoulder again. The little man had one hand clenched around the handle of the walking stick. He grasped the lower end of the stick in his opposite hand.

He looked very much like a man who was preparing to unsheathe a dagger.

Or a stiletto, Slater thought.

He took off his spectacles, dropped them into the pocket of his coat and turned back to Brice, who was speaking impatiently. Something about getting on with it. Slater fixed his attention on him, as though paying attention. But he listened, instead, to the footsteps closing the distance behind him.

And there it was, the slight shortening of the small man's stride. Like a jumper collecting power to take the fence, the assassin was readying himself for the kill.

Slater shoved Brice into the bushes at the border of the pavement, simultaneously twisting away from the attack.

Brice yelped, outraged.

Slater whirled around to confront the assassin.

A needle of steel gleamed in the luminous fog.

Suddenly aware that he was going to miss his target, the little man tried frantically to change direction.

Slater took advantage of the opening. He made one hand into a straight edge and brought it down in a hard, chopping blow that caught the assassin on the forearm close to the wrist. Bone cracked. The stiletto and its walking stick sheath clattered on the ground.

It had all happened very quickly—a matter of seconds—but the commotion was starting to attract attention from the cab line.

"Footpad."

"Send for a constable."

Slater started toward the assassin.

"You crazy son of a bitch," the little man hissed. "You'll pay for this, I swear you will."

He turned again and ran off into the fog.

"Damn." Brice got to his feet, brushing off his clothes. "He got away. He'll disappear into the stews."

"Not likely," Slater said. "You heard the accent. He's an American criminal trying to escape in our fair city. I doubt that he'll get far."

"What do you mean? It's a very big city, in case you haven't noticed."

"He'll stand out on the streets," Slater said. "After all, he can barely speak the language."

THIRTY-SIX

D amian was waiting for her in the conservatory. The moment she opened the door and moved into her private Eden, Valerie knew he was there. It was as if she were so attuned to him she could sense him on the metaphysical plane. Her pulse skittered in delight. A euphoria that was more intense than what the ambrosia could induce swept through her.

"I got your message, Damian," she whispered into the darkness.

The indoor jungle was drenched in shadows and moonlight. She had not dared to bring a lantern or a candle. She had been afraid that one of the servants would notice. She could not trust any of them.

The faint scent of cigarette smoke floated lightly on the fragrant air. A dark figure stirred near a bed of towering ferns.

"Valerie," he said. "I have missed you so much

these past months. I could not wait any longer to be with you."

She flew toward him, her chest so tight with the force of her emotions that she could scarcely breathe.

"Damian," she said. "Damian, Damian, my beloved. I have been in torment waiting for you to come to me. Every day without you has been an eternity."

He opened his arms and she flung herself into the safety and the rapture of his embrace. He extinguished his cigarette in the fern bed and then his mouth closed over hers.

His kisses thrilled her senses, just as they had all those months ago in New York when they had become lovers. Two lost souls, he said, who had found each other at last. He had vowed to find a way for them to be together. All that was required was time and careful planning.

She looked up at him, savoring the sheer size of the man. Like a gallant knight of old, he had come to rescue her from the cruel tyrant she had been forced to marry.

"It was so clever of you to come to London before you were expected," she said. "As far as Fulbrook is concerned your ship will not dock until the day after tomorrow. How long have you been in town?"

"A few days. I'm staying at a hotel under another name. I have been afraid to let you know I was here for fear the secret might slip out. But tonight I could not wait any longer. I had to see you."

"I will keep your secrets. You can trust me."

"I know."

He kissed her again and then he caught her hands in his.

"I cannot stay long tonight," he said. "I will not let you take the risk of being discovered, not now when we are so close to the fulfillment of our plans."

"Don't worry, we are safe," she said.

"It is imperative that your husband believes that I am still on board ship. He must not suspect that I arranged to arrive a few days ahead of schedule."

She touched his hair, hardly daring to believe that he was real, that this was not a dream.

"How much longer until we can be together?" she asked.

"Not long, my love." He touched her mouth with one gloved finger. "Not long at all. The last shipment is in the warehouse. We will take it with us when we sail to New York. There are a few more matters that must be dealt with and then it will all be over."

"You must promise me that you will be careful. Fulbrook is not strong like you but he is powerful in his own way and quite ruthless."

"Do not fear, my sweet. In a very short time he will no longer be a problem for either of us. But now I must go. I should not have come here tonight but I had to see you. It has been agony, exchanging secret letters and thinking about you here with Fulbrook."

"My husband spends his time with his whores and at his clubs, not with me. I have been alone—so very alone. At night I dream of you. During the day I cannot stop thinking about you."

"Soon you will be safe with me in New York."

"Safe." She breathed the word with a sense of wonder. "Safe at last."

He kissed her again and her heart soared.

THIRTY-SEVEN

～

"Yºu want me to pack a bag and move to your house now?" Ursula clutched the lapels of her wrapper at her throat. "It's the middle of the night, Slater. I don't understand."

They were standing in the front hall of her house. Slater's greatcoat dripped rain on the black-and-white floor. At the foot of the steps a carriage waited, the interior lamps turned down.

"The assassin came for me less than forty minutes ago," Slater said. "At this point I cannot be certain who he will go after next, assuming he is still capable of murdering anyone. I think I broke his wrist. But that is not enough of a guarantee. I want you in my house. It is much more secure. My locks are excellent. There are more people around to keep an eye on things."

Ursula stared at him, trying to get past the first

shock. "Are you telling me that someone tried to murder you tonight?"

"Yes," Slater said. He did not bother to conceal his impatience. "You need only bring what you need for tonight. Your housekeeper can pack the rest of your things tomorrow."

"You were nearly murdered tonight?"

Slater frowned. "It's all right, Ursula. I'm fine. Thank you for your concern."

"Is that all you can say?" Her voice was rising. "You were nearly killed. Because of me. Because of my investigation."

"Don't be ridiculous. Pack a bag. I'd appreciate it if you would not dither about."

"I'm not dithering, damn it. I have just sustained a great shock to my nerves. There's a difference."

"Really?" The edge of his mouth curved faintly. "I hadn't noticed."

"Bloody hell." She swung around and marched up the staircase. "I shall be down in fifteen minutes."

"Don't worry," Slater said, "I'll wait. Oh, and you needn't concern yourself with the proprieties."

She stopped halfway up the stairs. "And why is that?"

"Webster has been dispatched to collect my mother. She will act as a chaperone."

"Lilly Lafontaine. Playing the role of chaperone. Something tells me she will find that endlessly amusing."

THIRTY-EIGHT

~~~~~

It was nearly one-thirty in the morning when they finally gathered in Slater's library.

Ursula sat on the sofa with Lilly. Brice was sprawled in a wingback chair, brandy glass in hand. Slater was the only one on his feet. He was clearly energized by the events of the night. He gripped the mantel and contemplated the fire with a fierceness that sent little frissons of electricity through the room.

She, on the other hand, was dealing with an entirely different kind of tension. Slater had very nearly been murdered tonight—because of her.

"Do you really think the police will find that man who tried to kill you?" she asked.

"Eventually." Slater looked up from the leaping flames. "I think that they will certainly look very hard because the assault occurred right in front of one of the most exclusive clubs in London and because Brice and I both have some notoriety attached to our names. Between the two of us we were able to give the constable a fairly decent description."

"Our old archaeological training came in handy," Brice said. He spoke from the depths of the wingback chair, where he drank brandy in a very methodical manner. "Between the two of us, Slater and I noticed a number of small details. But Slater is right, even without a decent description it would be impossible for a well-dressed killer who speaks with an American accent and who is sporting a broken wrist to conceal himself on the streets for long."

Lilly brightened. "I see what you mean. In the end, his accent will give him away. He won't be able to go to ground. He will have no colleagues who will feel an obligation to protect him. In fact, I expect there will be any number of members of the criminal class who will be only too happy to do the police a favor."

"What was that about?" Brice demanded. He swallowed another dose of brandy, loosened his tie and glared uncertainly at Slater. "Why did the American try to murder you?"

"It all goes back to the Olympus Club," Slater said. "That is why I wanted to talk to you tonight."

"But I am not a member. I don't see how I can help you."

"You may not be a member but your social world is a small one. You no doubt know some men who do belong to the club. I've been away from London too long. I don't have the connections I need to get answers."

Brice reflected. "I've heard one or two mentions of the Olympus. Very secretive."

"We believe that the management of the club makes a certain drug called ambrosia available to the members," Slater said. "The killings appear to be linked to the trade in the drug. Lady Fulbrook is evidently growing the plant from which the stuff is derived."

"Lady Fulbrook?" Brice shook his head. "That makes no sense."

"It does if one considers that the ambrosia business is apparently quite lucrative—so much so, in fact, that we believe Fulbrook may be in business with an American businessman named Damian Cobb. Thus far three people are dead—a courier, a drug maker and a certain Mrs. Wyatt, the proprietor of a brothel named the Pavilion of Pleasure."

Brice's expression tightened in a troubled frown. "I've heard talk of that house. Supposed to be very exclusive."

"When you're talking about brothels the word *exclusive* can have a great many different meanings," Slater said.

"True," Brice agreed. "But I seem to recall overhearing someone say that the Pavilion accepts clients by referral only."

"Whatever the case, Mrs. Wyatt and the other two murdered people all had one thing in common,"

Ursula said. "All three were involved in the ambrosia trade."

Understanding settled on Brice. He switched his attention to Slater. "You believe that little man who attacked you tonight killed those three people?"

"I'm quite certain he murdered Wyatt and Rosemont," Slater said. "I'm not entirely sure that he killed Anne Clifton. It's possible she died accidentally from an overdose of the drug."

Ursula clasped her hands very tightly together. "I am certain Anne was murdered."

Slater let that go without argument.

"Why would anyone commit murder because of a drug?" Brice asked. "It's not as if drugs are illegal."

"Opium is legal, but for centuries wars have been fought over it and fortunes founded on the trade," Slater said.

Brice grimaced. "I take your point. The opium business has a very violent history. A damned pity, given the great medical benefits of the drug."

"There's another factor involved here that may explain the violence we are seeing," Slater continued. "In the past few years the attempts to regulate opium and the products derived from it have started to gain momentum on both sides of the Atlantic. There is talk now of making such drugs illegal altogether. If that happens, the business will be driven underground."

"Where men like Fulbrook and Cobb stand to make huge profits," Ursula said. "Assuming they can control the trade."

Lilly swirled the brandy in her glass. "Viewed from that perspective, the ambrosia offers an unusual business opportunity. Opium is widely available from many sources. It will be impossible for anyone to establish a total monopoly. But as far as we know the ambrosia plant is still quite rare and hard to cultivate. If a strong, ruthless individual can establish control of all ends of the trade, he might be able to establish a very lucrative empire."

They all looked at her. Lilly smiled sweetly.

"Slater's father always said that I had a head for business," she said. "Edward wasn't all that interested in such matters. He always took my advice when it came to investing the Roxton fortune."

There was a short silence.

Ursula cleared her throat. "Evidently you did very well when it came to that sort of thing."

"Yes," Lilly said. She swallowed some brandy and set the glass down. "I did very well by the Roxton money. Which is, of course, why Edward was always so generous to me."

Ursula smiled. "He paid bonuses and commissions, didn't he?"

Lilly raised her brows. "I assure you I earned every penny."

"If we might return to the matter at hand," Slater said.

"Yes, of course," Lilly murmured.

"I am now convinced that Cobb is planning to emerge as the sole winner in this affair," Slater said. "Evidently he is due to arrive the day after tomorrow.

My first assumption was that he sent his assassin ahead to get rid of certain people in the business who were no longer of any use to him—those who knew too much about the trade. Taking care of that end of things before he even set foot on shore would ensure that he never became a suspect in the deaths."

Ursula set her brandy glass down very slowly. "But tonight the assassin came after you. I understand that Cobb might have sent a man ahead to murder people like Mrs. Wyatt and Anne Clifton and Rosemont. Cobb must have been aware of their roles in the ambrosia business for months. But you are new on the scene. How would he know about you?"

"An excellent question," Slater said quietly. "I could envision some complicated scenarios, all of which would involve coded telegrams sent to and from Cobb's ship, but I think it makes sense to go with the simplest and most likely explanation. I suspect that Damian Cobb is already in London."

"But that telegram he sent to Lady Fulbrook announcing his arrival the day after tomorrow—" Ursula paused. "Right. It could have been sent by someone on Cobb's staff in New York."

Brice frowned. "Do you really believe that Lady Fulbrook is romantically involved with Cobb?"

"Yes." Ursula looked at him. "She is desperately unhappy in her marriage."

"I understand, but still, from the sound of things, Cobb is an American criminal."

"From the sound of things," Ursula said evenly, "Fulbrook is a British criminal."

Brice flushed. "I take your point, madam."

Lilly reached for the brandy decanter. "I did a little research of my own. Fulbrook and his wife were married a few years ago. One cannot help but notice that there has been no offspring from the union."

"Hmm," Ursula said.

Slater looked at Lilly. "What are you getting at?"

"The most important thing a man in Fulbrook's position wants and needs from a wife is an heir," Lilly said.

A small hush fell on the scene. Ursula noticed that everyone in the room with the sole exception of Slater appeared to be somewhat uncomfortable. Slater, naturally, was amused.

Ursula rushed to fill the vacuum. "Lilly is right. Fulbrook might have his own reasons to be dissatisfied with his marriage."

"What does that have to do with this situation?" Slater asked.

"Fulbrook has a reputation for being prone to outbursts of violence," Lilly said. "If he blames his wife for the failure to produce an heir, she might fear for her life."

"A woman in that situation would have a powerful motive for making herself indispensable, wouldn't she?" Ursula suggested. "If Lady Fulbrook stumbled onto the properties of the ambrosia plant, she may have given her husband the notion of going into the drug trade. In the process she purchased some degree of safety for herself."

"Because Fulbrook needs her to cultivate the

plant," Slater said. "Yes, I like the logic in that. But if our speculations are correct, Lady Fulbrook may feel she is living on borrowed time. If chemists like Rosemont can produce the drug in large quantities, sooner or later Fulbrook might decide to employ botanists and gardeners to cultivate the plant."

"At which point," Lilly said, "he will no longer need his wife. I suspect Lady Fulbrook has already reasoned that out for herself. She is quite probably a terrified woman."

Brice looked at Slater. "If there was a plan to close down the British side of the ambrosia trade, as you believe, it has been badly disrupted tonight. Cobb's assassin will even now be struggling to survive on London's most inhospitable streets. There will be a great sensation in the press tomorrow because two well-known men were attacked by an American criminal outside an exclusive gentlemen's club. Cobb may well conclude that the situation is on the brink of disaster. What do you think he will do next?"

"Logically, he should cut his losses," Slater said. "If he is in town, as I believe, he should buy a ticket on the first ship bound for New York. But in my experience, people rarely behave rationally when there is a lot of money at stake."

"What, exactly, do you want from me?" Brice asked.

"Anything and everything you might have heard about the Olympus Club and its members."

"That does not amount to much," Brice warned.

"But now that I consider the matter there is something that may or may not have some significance."

"What is that?" Slater said.

"In the past couple of months, two high-ranking men died. In Mayhew's case the death was reputed to have been a hunting accident but no one believed that. Davies jumped off a bridge."

"I remember the reports in the press," Lilly said. "There were rumors of suicide in both cases."

"For what it's worth, I heard that both men were members of the Olympus Club," Brice said.

A SHORT TIME LATER Slater escorted Brice outside to the waiting carriage. The rain had stopped but the fog was prowling back into the streets of London. Brice climbed into the cab and sat down. When he did not speak, Slater stepped back and started to close the door.

"Thank you," he said.

Brice put out a hand to stop the door from swinging shut.

"Did you mean it earlier when you said that you do not blame me for what happened on Fever Island?" he asked.

"None of it was your fault," Slater said.

"Some people believe I deliberately triggered that trap."

"I never believed it," Slater said. "Not for a moment."

"About the Jeweled Bird," Brice said.

Slater smiled. "I know it was not stolen. It no longer exists, does it? You took it apart, stone by stone, and sold the gems off very quietly."

Brice's expression hardened. "The family was bankrupt. I did the only thing I could think of to do in that situation."

"You did what you had to do for the sake of the family. I understand."

"Do you?"

"It is what I would have done in the same circumstances," Slater said.

Brice was quiet for a time.

"I thought it possible that you might not hold me responsible for the disaster on the island," he said at last. "But I was certain you would never forgive me for destroying what turned out to be the only surviving artifact of an unknown civilization."

"My perspective on some things changed during that year on Fever Island."

Brice looked at him. "If I hear anything else about the Olympus Club I will contact you."

"I appreciate that. But be careful, Brice. This affair has become dangerous."

"Yes, I saw that for myself tonight. What have you been doing all these years while you were away from London? It was common knowledge that your father cut you off in an attempt to bring you home. How did you make a living?"

"I did what you and I used to do together—I traced lost artifacts. But I did it for the money, not the thrill of discovery."

"And is there a lot of money in that line?"

"Enough."

Brice snorted softly. "No wonder you knew the Jeweled Bird no longer existed. You went looking for it and couldn't find it."

"It would have been hard for something like that to disappear altogether into the underground market."

"And now you're stuck here in London because your father saddled you with the responsibility for the family fortune. Hard to envision you settling down to city life. You were never interested in Society. Do you think you'll become bored?"

"I worried about that for a time. But no longer. I have a hobby."

"Hobby?"

"Haven't you heard? I practice exotic sexual rites on unsuspecting ladies in my basement."

Brice laughed.

Slater smiled and closed the door. He watched from the front step until the cab disappeared into the fog.

THIRTY-NINE

The dream of the City of Tombs pulled him out of a restless sleep. He opened his eyes, giving himself a moment to cross the murky boundary between sleep and wakefulness.

He threw aside the covers and sat up on the edge of the bed. Mrs. Wyatt's journal of accounts was on the nightstand along with the page of notes he had made.

He got to his feet and picked up the notes. It was a list of payments from clients who were identified only by their initials in the journal. There was something about the figures that did not look right.

He needed to think. He needed to walk the labyrinth. Tossing aside the notes, he pulled on his trousers and took the black silk dressing gown off the hook.

He opened the door and went out into the hall. The

lamps were turned down low for the night but there was enough light to illuminate the corridor and the stairs. The Websters knew that one of their priorities was to make certain that the house was never enveloped in complete darkness. He had survived the experience of the Fever Island labyrinth but that did not mean that it had not left him with a few eccentricities.

He was quite capable of making his way silently down the hall. He knew every board that squeaked or groaned. He could avoid all of them. That was exactly what he intended to do until he found himself a step away from the door of Ursula's bedroom.

He paused, examining his motives and desires. And then, very deliberately, he put a little weight on the spot in front of her door that he knew would betray his presence—assuming she was awake.

He did not stop again. He moved on toward the staircase, wondering if Ursula had heard the faint groan of the floorboard. If she had, would she bother to open the door to see who was up and around at that hour? Would she care? And even if she did go so far as to peek out into the hall, what would she do if she saw him on the stairs? She might simply close the door and go back to bed.

He was on the third step when he heard her door open. A thrill of anticipation excited his senses. He stopped and turned to look back along the hallway.

Ursula emerged from the room, one hand tight on the lapels of the chintz wrapper. Her hair was loose around her shoulders. Her eyes were dark with mystery and anxiety.

"Is something wrong?" she whispered.

"No," he said. "I'm not in a mood to sleep so I decided to take a walk."

"Outside?" Her eyes widened. "In the garden? At this hour?"

"No, downstairs in my basement—where I conduct those exotic rituals on assorted unsuspecting females."

She relaxed, smiling a little. "Now you are teasing me." She started to edge back into the bedroom. "I understand that you wish to be alone."

"No," he said. He held out his hand the way he had once reached for the climbing rope that brought him up out of the temple caves. "Come with me."

She hesitated. "This is something two people can do together?"

"We will no doubt arrive at different truths but there is no reason that we can't make the journey in harmony."

She walked toward him, smiling. "Did you talk in such a philosophical fashion before you went to Fever Island?"

"I've been told that I have always been difficult to understand. The experience on Fever Island probably did not improve my conversational talents."

She came down the stairs.

"As it happens, I have had some experience transcribing and interpreting coded language," she said.

His spirits lightened as if by magic. He gripped her hand very tightly.

At the bottom of the stairs they turned and went

along the corridor to the basement door. He inserted the key into the lock and opened the door to his private realm. At the top of the stone steps he paused to light the lantern. Without a word he gave it to her. She held it aloft.

He started down the steps, drawing her with him.

"I would be very grateful if you would refrain from making any remarks about Hades leading Persephone into the darkness," he said.

"Never crossed my mind," she assured him.

"It certainly crossed mine."

"There are times, sir, when I suspect that you take satisfaction in your reputation for eccentricity. I expect you get your melodramatic tendencies from your mother."

He smiled. "Now there's an unnerving thought."

He stopped in front of the door of the labyrinth chamber and selected the key on the iron ring. When he got the door open, he stood back to allow her to enter the room.

She walked a few steps into the chamber and set the lantern on the small table. He watched her study the intricate pattern of blue tiles on the floor.

"It's an elaborate labyrinth," she said after a moment. "Not a maze."

"Walking the path helps me clarify my thoughts. I find that if I begin with a question, the answer is sometimes waiting at the end."

"This is what you learned on Fever Island?" she asked.

"An aspect of what I learned, yes."

"How do you perform this walking meditation?"

"There's no trick to it," he said. "You compose a question and then you just start walking. Concentrate on each step. Don't think too far ahead and don't think about where you have been. But consider closely how one step leads to another. Contemplate connections and links. Immerse yourself in the pattern."

She took a tentative step forward and stopped on the first blue tile. "You said something about starting with a question."

"Do you have one?"

She thought about that, a faint, secretive smile edging her lips. "Yes, I do have a question."

"Are you going to tell me?"

She glanced at him, tilted her head slightly as though contemplating her answer. "No," she said finally. "I don't think so. Not yet."

"Will you tell me if you find the answer at the other end of the path?"

"Perhaps." She started walking the labyrinth, concentrating intently. "One step at a time, correct?"

"Yes."

He was so fascinated by her aura of seriousness that it was a moment or two before he realized that he was still standing at the entrance—just standing there, watching her. He could watch her all night. Forever, if necessary.

A question whispered through his mind.

He followed Ursula into the labyrinth.

They walked the path in silence. He was careful

to keep a few paces behind. If he got any closer he would be able to touch her and that would shatter the meditative trance. If he touched her again he would kiss her and if he kissed her he would want to sweep her out of the pattern and take her upstairs to bed.

Usually he never noticed the time once he started the journey. The ritual was so familiar and his mind was so in tune with the technique required to navigate the path that he was able to forget the factor of time. But tonight, walking behind Ursula, the dragon claws of impatience tore ragged holes in his control. Indeed, he wondered if he might go a little mad before they arrived at the center of the labyrinth.

With one last step, she entered the circle of knowing. She closed her eyes and went very still. He waited, centering himself as he did before starting the martial arts exercises that were the physical extension of the mental exercises.

She opened her eyes. He could not abide the suspense.

"Will you tell me your question now?" he asked.

She glanced briefly back at the entrance to the labyrinth and then she fixed her attention on him once more.

"I'm afraid my question was not particularly philosophical or intellectual in nature," she said. "It was, in fact, a rather simple, mundane question."

"Did you find the answer?"

The secretive smile danced in her eyes. "As to that, I'm still waiting."

He moved into the circle and caught her chin on the edge of his hand. "Is this your way of informing me that I can answer your question?"

"How very perceptive of you, sir. At the start of the journey—which, for me, began upstairs when I heard you pass my bedroom door, not here in this chamber—my question was, will you kiss me tonight?"

The smoldering fires of sexual anticipation that had been burning deep inside him exploded in a conflagration that incinerated his plans to carry her upstairs to bed. He could see the sultry heat in her eyes. The knowledge that she wanted him was all it took to erase most of what was left of his self-control.

"Before I answer your question, you must answer mine," he said. "Do you want me to kiss you tonight?"

She put her hands on his shoulders and tightened her fingers. "Yes, Slater. I want you to kiss me. I want that very, very much."

With a husky groan, he pulled her hard against him and covered her mouth with his own. When he felt her arms go around his waist his blood roared in his veins. This was what he needed. Now. Tonight.

He could feel the shivery excitement coursing through her sweetly rounded frame. Her mouth softened under his in both surrender and seduction and he was lost.

He lowered his hands to her waist, found the sash of the wrapper and fumbled with the knot. By the time he got it undone, he was desperate and feverish.

He pulled the garment off her shoulders, freeing

her arms. The wrapper slipped to the floor at her feet, leaving her clad in a prim cotton nightgown. For a few heartbeats the exquisite intimacy of the experience dazzled him. And then he realized that she was loosening the sash of his dressing gown with trembling fingers.

He took a step back, stripped off the garment and unfurled it across the floor like a battle flag. The heavy black silk covered the heart of the labyrinth where all the answers waited.

When he turned back to Ursula he saw that she was watching him with a strangely intent expression. He was suddenly very conscious of his erection beneath the fabric of his trousers. A new and different kind of heat scalded him. He was rushing her, just as he had the first time. He had promised himself that if he got another chance he would show her that he could be a thoughtful, considerate lover—the kind who could take his time.

He willed himself to woo and seduce. Wrapping one hand around the back of her neck, he drew her gently to him. He brushed his mouth lightly across hers and then he kissed the curve of her neck. Her scent clouded his mind and tightened every fiber of his being. It was a wonder he did not shatter, he thought.

"I will do whatever it takes to make you remember this night," he vowed. "To remember me."

She trailed her fingertips across his bare shoulder. "As if I could ever forget you, Slater."

When he stripped off his trousers he heard her

sharp, indrawn breath. He saw that she was gazing at his erection, transfixed. "I promise you that I will not do anything you don't want me to do," he said. He threaded his fingers through her flowing hair. "I would never hurt you, Ursula. Please believe me."

She raised her eyes to meet his. "I know that. I trust you. It is why I am here with you tonight." Her mouth curved in a quick, mischievous smile. She braced her hands on his shoulders. "Well, that and the fact that I find you very attractive, sir."

Waves of excitement swept through him. He drew her down onto the makeshift blanket and leaned over her, bracing his hands on the black silk beneath her.

Deliberately he began to kiss her, working his way down her body. When the nightgown got in his way, he opened the garment, unwrapping her as he would a precious gift.

She drew a sharp breath when he took her breast into his mouth. Her fingers tightened on his shoulders.

He moved lower, glorying in the sweet, hot intimacy of the moment. The scent of her arousal stormed his senses.

He found the hot, damp place between her thighs. She froze when she belatedly realized his intention. Her fingers locked in his hair.

"*Slater.*"

He gripped her thighs and anchored her.

"What are you—?" She broke off, torn between shock and desire. The combination effectively immobilized her.

He kissed her deeply, drinking of her essence. She

was wet and she tasted of tropical seas and sunshine and moonlight. No drug could ever come close to intoxicating him the way Ursula did. He would never be able to get enough of her.

Her knees lifted and her fingers clenched even more tightly in his hair. When her release shuddered through her, she gave a breathless cry.

He moved up her body, thrusting into her before the small tremors had ceased. He caught the waves and rode them to his own crashing climax.

Somewhere in the darkness of the City of Tombs, a man gave an exultant roar that echoed off ancient stone walls. And then he climbed the staircase out of darkness into the sunlight.

FORTY

~~~

Hubbard stumbled out of the hansom. He was exhausted and panicky and in great pain. He was certain that his wrist was broken.

He had concluded early on that he did not like London but tonight he had come to truly loathe the hellish place. His mad flight into hiding in the wake of the failed commission had proven disastrous. It had taken him into a dark maze of terrifying lanes and alleys. One narrow passage, in particular, had nearly been the end of him. Two men armed with knives had cornered him in a dark doorway. He had feared for his life.

He had been saved by the miraculous arrival of a hansom that had disgorged two very drunk gentlemen bound for a nearby brothel. The would-be thieves had disappeared into an alley. Hubbard had leaped into the hansom.

When the driver inquired about a destination he had to stop and think for a moment. He dared not go back to the hotel. Cobb would be furious. Roxton and his companion had both gotten a good look at him. Without a doubt they had recognized his accent. Worst of all, Roxton had managed to seize the stiletto walking stick. The staff at the hotel would most assuredly remember it if questioned.

There was only one safe place for him at that moment—the warehouse. He needed to rest and collect his nerve, and then he needed to find a doctor.

He needed Cobb's assistance.

He paused beneath a streetlamp and tried to get his bearings. It was nearly hopeless. In the moon-infused fog all of the warehouses looked alike. He had been in the vicinity on only one other occasion—the night that he and Cobb had brought the perfume maker here.

Cobb had pointed out the warehouse at the end of the street and given him precise instructions and a key. *"Make a note of the address. If problems arise that make it dangerous for us to meet at the hotel, you are to let yourself into that building and wait for me. If I conclude that something has gone wrong I will know to look for you there."*

Hubbard left the eerie glow cast by the single streetlamp on the corner and trudged nervously along the pavement. Abandoned warehouses loomed on either side. He listened for the smallest sounds in the mist, terrified that he would hear footsteps coming up behind him.

He knew that at least some of his victims had sensed him in the instant before the kill. He had seen the unnatural stillness that had come over them just before he drove the stiletto into their necks. A few had even glanced over their shoulders as he approached—only to dismiss him immediately. The relief he had glimpsed in their eyes had always amused him. His stock-in-trade was the fact that he did not appear the least bit threatening. Indeed, most people looked straight through him, as if he did not exist. That had been the case with the brothel madam.

But tonight the target had heard him or sensed him in some primal way. Roxton had not only registered the threat immediately, he had acted.

In that brief encounter, Hubbard had glimpsed the icy awareness in the other man's eyes and known that Roxton was not just another commission.

Hubbard had known true fear for the first time in a very long while. The panic and terror had only grown stronger during the time it had taken him to find his way to the warehouse. He told himself that his shattered nerves would recover once he got home to New York. In time his wrist would heal, provided he could get it properly set by a doctor. He would survive.

Not much longer now, according to Cobb. Soon they would both be free of this nightmarish city.

He had to strike a light to locate the door of the warehouse. It took two or three attempts to get the key into the lock and for a few seconds he almost despaired. But in the end he got the door open.

He sucked in a shaky gasp of relief when he saw the shielded lantern that someone had left on top of an empty crate. He got the device lit and held it aloft to survey his surroundings.

At first glance the warehouse appeared to have been abandoned. There were a number of empty crates and barrels scattered about. Frayed hoisting ropes dangled from the loft. Bits of moldy straw covered much of the floor.

When he looked more closely, however, he saw a trail of muddled footsteps. Rosemont's, he concluded. The perfumer must have come here frequently during the past several months, delivering the crates filled with the drug and preparing them for shipment to New York.

He followed the prints to the crates. When he reached them he stumbled to a halt and sank down onto one of the wooden containers. He took off his coat, folded it neatly and set it aside. His tie seemed to be restricting his breathing so he removed it and loosened the collar of his shirt. Gingerly he examined his aching wrist.

It was, he reflected, going to be a very long night.

But in the end, the night proved remarkably short.

Hubbard was stretched out on top of the crate, trying in vain to rest, when he heard the door open. A sharp jolt of panic stabbed through him. His heart pounded. He sat up abruptly and fumbled with the lantern.

"Who's there?" he called out. "Show yourself."

The newcomer held his own shielded lantern aloft.

"Calm down," Cobb said.

"Oh, it's you, sir." Hubbard pulled himself together. It was not a good idea to let the client sense nervousness or anxiety. "For a moment there— Never mind."

"Are you injured?" Cobb asked with some concern.

"The bastard broke my wrist."

"When you failed to return to the hotel I assumed something had gone wrong with the plan. What happened?"

"Unfortunate turn of events." Out of long habit, Hubbard adopted his most assured, most professional tone. "These things happen. I'll take care of the matter within twenty-four hours."

"What, precisely, occurred?"

Cobb sounded as if he were inquiring about a minor carriage accident or some equally mild mishap. *As well he should*, Hubbard thought. Missing the target tonight was not a major catastrophe. Considering his spotless record, it was only right that Cobb ought to overlook a small error, one that could easily be corrected.

"The son of a bitch noticed me," he said, maintaining his authoritative tone of voice. "That sort of thing doesn't usually affect the outcome but Roxton reacted more swiftly than the average person in such circumstances."

"In other words, you missed your target."

"As I said, I'll take care of the problem soon enough."

"Where is your stiletto stick?"

Hubbard flushed. "Lost it along the way. No matter. I've got a spare in my trunk."

"Which is at the hotel."

"Yes, well, if you would be good enough to deliver it to me, I'll take care of Roxton." Hubbard looked down at his creased shirt and trousers. "I would be grateful if you would bring a change of clothes, as well."

"You lost the stiletto at the scene, I assume?"

"Roxton chopped it right out of my hand. Never seen anything like it."

"Did you speak to Roxton?" Cobb asked.

"What? No. Why would I do that?"

"Did you say anything at all? Did you swear?"

Hubbard suddenly sensed where the questions were going.

"No," he said quickly. "Never said a word. Just took off running. Someone was shouting for a constable."

"I think you're lying, Hubbard. I must assume that the police are now aware that a killer with an American accent attacked a man in front of a gentlemen's club and is now loose on the streets of London. I expect the press will have a field day tomorrow."

"No," Hubbard said. "Roxton never got a good look at me."

"He didn't need a close look in order to provide the police with a fairly accurate description. You won't require a change of clothes or your spare stiletto, Hubbard. You are no longer of any use to me."

Belatedly sensing disaster, Hubbard looked up very swiftly. But he was too late. Cobb had taken a revolver out from under his coat.

"No." Hubbard stared in disbelief. "I'm the best there is."

"I have news for you, Hubbard. There are plenty more where you came from."

Hubbard froze, just as so many of his victims had, in that last instant.

Cobb pulled the trigger twice. The first shot struck Hubbard in the chest with such force that he was thrown backward onto the crate. He was still trying to comprehend what had happened to him when the second bullet entered his brain.

COBB STOOD OVER THE BODY for a moment, making absolutely certain of death. He did not want any more complications. The plan had been simple and straight-forward. He would gain exclusive control of the drug and use it to build an empire that would rival the kingdoms founded by Rockefeller, Carnegie, J. P. Morgan and the other men the press labeled robber barons. What's more, he would adopt their business tactics to achieve his objective—he would establish a monopoly on a product that a great many people would pay dearly to obtain.

It was unfortunate that a woman had been the key from the start. In his experience females were diffi-cult, demanding and unpredictable. But a man had to work with what he had. He could only be grateful that Valerie was not only quite beautiful but also unhappy in her marriage. That had made her seduction much less of a chore than would have been the case had she been a dowdy, middle-aged hag.

He had worked for months to construct the foundation of his business in New York. Eventually the network of greenhouses, laboratories and distributors would reach across the continent. He had come to London to implement the final stages of his strategy. Everything should have gone smoothly but there had been one complication after another.

It all came down to women. One had been the key to his empire but now another female, Ursula Kern, had become a serious problem. Because of her, a wealthy, powerful man had taken an interest in the death of the courier. One thing had led to another and now disaster loomed.

The strategy had appeared obvious—remove Roxton, whose murder would cause a great uproar in the press. While the focus of attention was on that spectacular homicide, it would be possible to quietly dispatch Kern. In the end Hubbard would be found dead and the police would be satisfied that the American killer was no longer haunting the streets of London.

Hubbard had been useful but even the best employees could be replaced. The real question, as always in such situations, was how to dispose of the body. In New York he relied on the river for that sort of thing. There was a river here in London and evidently bodies turned up all the time. But tonight he was faced with the task of dragging Hubbard out of the warehouse and along the street for some distance. He did not want to take the risk of being seen.

He heaved Hubbard's body into an empty crate and closed the lid.

The disposal completed, he collected the lantern and went outside into the fog. He had told the driver of the hansom to wait two streets away.

Revolver in hand, he started walking.

The city of London considered itself to be socially more polished than New York, culturally superior in every way that mattered. But he failed to see the appeal. He detested the fog, the filthy, dangerous streets and the damned accents that made it next to impossible to comprehend cab drivers, shopkeepers, servants and upper-class snobs alike.

His ship could not sail soon enough, as far as he was concerned. He would be very happy to see the last of London.

FORTY-ONE

~~~~~~~

N ext time we really ought to find a bed," Slater
said.

Next time. Like the bubbles in a glass of champagne, the simple words lightened Ursula's spirits.
She watched Slater lever himself up to a sitting
position on the black silk dressing gown. He moved
with the lazy masculine grace that did interesting
things to the muscles of his chest and her insides.

Next time implied a future together, she thought.
She tied the sash of her wrapper while she considered
the implications of the delicious words. Realistically,
she had to accept that it might be a very limited future. Lady Fulbrook had tried to warn her about the
dangers of falling in love with a man who was far
above her on the social ladder.

But Slater was very different from any other man
she had ever met, and the obstacles to an extended

future with him were also very different. Nevertheless, for the first time she dared to hope that those obstacles might not be insurmountable.

Slater eyed her as he got to his feet. "The thought of a bed amuses you?" He scooped up the dressing gown. "Perhaps you prefer desks and cold stone floors? If so, I'm willing to oblige."

She made a face, aware that she was blushing furiously. "I have nothing against the notion of using a bed for this . . . sort of thing." She waved a hand at the dressing gown.

He studied the damp spot on the black silk with a thoughtful expression. "I find *this sort of thing*, when done with you, invariably interesting."

She turned away to find her slippers. "I'm surprised that the type of physical exercise we just engaged in doesn't have a confounding effect on your well-ordered thoughts."

"It most certainly does," he said very softly. "It dazzles my mind utterly. Indeed, when we are engaged in this type of *exercise* I cannot think of anything else except you."

The sensual humor in his words made her turn quickly. He was smiling his rare, wicked smile—the smile that never failed to make her catch her breath.

"Oh," she whispered. She fell silent, at a loss for words.

"The fascinating thing is that afterward I find I have moments of great clarity," he continued. There was an edge on his voice now. The cold fire of knowing lit his eyes. He dropped the dressing gown on the floor and reached for his trousers. "I think I know what those numbers in the journal mean. You are brilliant, Ursula."

He seized her by the shoulders and gave her a fast, triumphant kiss.

"Absolutely brilliant," he said.

He released her and headed for the door. "Hurry. I've got to get back to Mrs. Wyatt's journal."

She suppressed a little sigh. He was no longer talking about her or their relationship. The champagne bubbles dissipated. She followed him to the door.

"What is it that you believe has been clarified, sir?"

He opened the door, evidently unaware of her dry tone. "I attempted to read the journal before I slept tonight but my mind was not entirely clear."

"Hardly surprising, given that you were nearly murdered tonight."

"I knew I was looking at something important. I should have seen it right from the start."

She followed him out into the hall. "Kindly explain yourself, sir."

"There are some odd figures in the income column. The entries are cryptic but they don't appear to be fees for the usual brothel services. There are also some mysterious items listed under expenses. I think I understand now. Mrs. Wyatt was buying a quantity of the drug from Rosemont and selling it to some of her own, personal clients."

"She was dealing the ambrosia on the side?"

"I think so—which may explain why Cobb had

her killed. Well, that and the fact that she knew too much about the British end of the business."

"Cobb saw her as competition?"

"In a small way." Slater opened the door at the top of the stairs. "But Cobb's real problem is Fulbrook. I can see so much more of the pattern now. And it's all because of you."

"Me or the exercise?" she asked very politely.

"You."

At her bedroom door he stopped long enough to hoist her off her feet and gave her another jubilant kiss.

He set her back down just as abruptly and went down the hall, heading for his own room.

"By morning, I should have this mostly sorted out," he said over his shoulder.

"How very nice for you, sir. Perhaps you would be so good as to reveal your deductions to those of us who are still muddling through the fog."

But she was speaking to an empty hallway. Slater had vanished into the bedroom.

She shook her head, smiled to herself and started to go into her own room. The door on the other side of the hall opened.

"Oh, there you are, dear," Lilly said. She sounded much too cheerful. "I thought I heard someone up and about. Everything all right?"

"Everything is fine." Ursula moved through the doorway of her bedroom and turned to look at Lilly. "You can go back to sleep."

Lilly smiled a very satisfied smile. "You're good for him, you know."

"Am I?"

"Yes, indeed. He is a changed man these days and it's all because of you."

"I am, of course, delighted to know that I am useful."

Lilly blinked, taken aback. "Now, dear, I never meant—"

"The question I must ask myself is whether or not Mr. Roxton is good for me."

She closed the door before Lilly could say another word. Halfway back to her bed she turned around and went back to the door. Very deliberately she turned the key in the lock.

If Slater needed any more inspiration before morning he would have to find it elsewhere.

She snuggled into bed, pleasantly exhausted. Her last thought before drifting off to sleep was that one question about Slater Roxton had certainly been answered. He did, indeed, practice exotic sexual rituals on unsuspecting females in his basement.

SHORTLY BEFORE DAWN she thought she heard the faint sound of someone trying the doorknob. She waited to see if Slater would knock when he discovered that the door was locked. But there was only silence out in the hall.

She lay awake for a time, telling herself that she

had done the right thing by locking the door. If she was to continue in the affair with Slater, it was important for him to realize that she was not merely a convenience or an aid to creative thinking.

Unfortunately, the small victory was somewhat obscured by the weight of regret.

FORTY-TWO

~~~~~

I told you I believe that Cobb is intent on creating a monopoly to control the drug," Slater said. "Furthermore, I'm sure he plans to operate his business from New York, not London. And he doesn't want any competition on this side of the Atlantic."

They were gathered at the breakfast table. Lilly reigned at one end, nibbling delicately on a piece of kippered salmon. Slater sat at the other end, plowing through an enormous mound of eggs and toast while he explained his conclusions. Ursula, seated in the middle, thought he looked remarkably vigorous for a man who could not have gotten more than a few hours of sleep. There was nothing wrong with his appetite, either.

He had said nothing about the locked door of her bedroom. If he had been disappointed, he certainly concealed the fact well. She found his enthusiasm and energy extremely irritating.

"You say you think Lady Fulbrook intends to take some specimens of the ambrosia plant when she runs off to New York with Cobb?" Lilly asked.

"Right." Slater ate some more eggs. "Specimens or seeds, at least. Regardless, she will no doubt arrange to destroy the rest of the plants in the conservatory. Cobb will want to make certain that no one else can continue in the ambrosia business after he and Lady Fulbrook are gone."

Ursula put down her fork quite suddenly. "Seeds."

Lilly and Slater looked at her.

"What is it?" Slater asked.

"When I found Anne Clifton's stenography notebook and jewelry I also found some packets of seeds," Ursula said. "I think the odds are good that they were from the ambrosia plant."

Lilly's artfully drawn brows crinkled a little. "Perhaps she intended to cultivate the plant in her own garden."

"Or sell the seeds to the highest bidder," Slater said. "Someone like Mrs. Wyatt would have paid well for them."

A cold chill feathered Ursula's spine. "I think that Anne planned to use them to buy her way into Damian Cobb's side of the business."

Slater contemplated that possibility. "Huh."

"It would have been a very bold thing for her to do," Lilly said quietly. "Cobb is a dangerous man."

"Anne was a very bold woman," Ursula said. "And

remember, she had been acting as a go-between for
Lady Fulbrook and Cobb for months. She may have
felt she knew Cobb in a sense—that she understood
him. She was not particularly fond of men but she
was confident of her ability to manipulate them. She
was, after all, a very attractive woman. Lady Fulbrook may have been writing love letters to Cobb but
I think Anne was trying to seduce him."

Slater frowned. "What makes you say that?"

"I haven't had a chance to read through all of the
letters from Cobb. They are written under the pen
name he used when corresponding with Lady Fulbrook, Mr. Paladin. But I can tell that there was some
sort of delicate negotiation going on between the two
of them. On the surface Paladin is showing an interest in her short stories but I'm quite sure that is not
what they were actually discussing."

"Anne spent a great deal of time in Lady Fulbrook's
company in the conservatory," Slater said. "She might
have learned how to cultivate the ambrosia plant."

"That would certainly explain some of the oddities
in the poems that she wrote down in her notebook,"
Ursula said. "There are several references to quantities and times. I remember one line in particular, the
*flower is delicate and potent. Three parts in ten bring on
visions that thrill. Seven will kill.*"

"Your friend was playing a very dangerous game,
indeed," Slater said softly.

"I know," Ursula said. "I can tell you one thing. If
Cobb intends to destroy all those herbs in Lady Fulbrook's special greenhouse before going back to New

York, he's going to have to do something drastic. That room in the conservatory is crammed with those bloody damned ambrosia plants."

There was a short silence. Ursula continued to munch toast for a few seconds until she realized that both Lilly and Slater were watching her.

"What?" she said around a bite of toast. "Did I say something?"

Lilly chuckled and went back to her salmon.

Slater cleared his throat. "I believe it was the phrase *bloody damned ambrosia plants* that stopped us for a moment. You sounded somewhat annoyed."

"I am annoyed." Ursula swallowed the last of the toast and reached for her coffee cup. "With the slow pace of our investigation."

Lilly raised her brows. "I thought you and Slater were making excellent progress."

"Depends on one's point of view," Ursula said. She looked at Slater. "As I recall, you were describing what you discovered in Mrs. Wyatt's financial records. But how does that lead us to the proof we will need to have someone arrested for Anne's murder?"

Mrs. Webster appeared in the doorway before Slater could respond. She carried a silver salver. A single envelope sat on the tray.

"This telegram was just delivered, sir," she announced in her carrying voice.

Slater winced a little and took the envelope.

Mrs. Webster departed, stage left, to return to the kitchen.

Ursula and Lilly watched Slater open the envelope. He read it quickly and looked up.

"It's from the director of the New York museum. I was right, Damian Cobb is known in philanthropic circles. The director says there has been some speculation regarding the source of Cobb's fortune but no one asks too many questions. That is not the most interesting thing in the telegram, however."

"For pity's sake," Ursula snapped, "don't keep us in suspense. This is not a melodrama. What is the point of the damned telegram?"

Slater raised a brow at her sharp tones but he did not comment.

"According to the museum director, the staff at Cobb's New York mansion claim that he left on a business trip ten days ago."

"The Atlantic crossing takes about a week," Ursula said. "Sometimes less. You were right, Slater. Cobb has been in London for at least a few days."

Mrs. Webster reappeared in the doorway.

"Mr. Otford is here to see you, sir," she said. "Shall I tell him to wait until you've finished breakfast?"

"No," Slater said. "If he's here at this hour, he must have something interesting for us. Send him in, please."

"Yes, sir." Mrs. Webster started to move back out into the hall.

"You'd better set another place for breakfast, Mrs. Webster," Slater added. "I have a feeling he will be hungry."

"Yes, sir."

Mrs. Webster disappeared. Less than a moment later Gilbert Otford scurried into the room. He stopped short and gazed at the heavily laden sideboard with a worshipful expression.

"Good morning, ladies," he said. He did not take his attention off the array of serving platters. "Mr. Roxton."

"Good morning, Otford," Slater said. "Please join us."

"Delighted, sir. Thank you."

There was a flutter of activity before Otford sat down across from Ursula. His plate was heaped high with sausages, toast and eggs. He fell to the meal with enthusiasm.

Slater seemed content to wait until Otford had made some inroads on his breakfast before questioning him but Ursula was not in a patient mood.

"Well, Mr. Otford?" She fixed him with a look. "What have you to tell us?"

"Cost me a small fortune to get one of the housemaids and a footman to chat," Otford said around a mouthful of sausage. "Those who work at the club have been told to keep quiet about what goes on there. Anyone caught gossiping will be turned off without a reference. No one wants to lose a post at the club because the pay and the gratuities are excellent."

"That's all you got for Mr. Roxton's money?" Ursula asked. "The information that the servants are well paid?"

Otford looked at Slater, perplexed. "Is she upset about something?"

Slater was suddenly occupied drinking his coffee.

"*Mr. Otford*," Ursula said. "I asked you a question."

"No, Mrs. Grant—uh—Mrs. Kern," Otford said hastily. "That was not all I learned. I was just coming to the interesting bits."

"About time," Ursula said.

Slater drank a little more coffee and then looked at Otford.

"You were saying?" Slater prompted in a manner that was almost gentle.

"Right." Otford flipped a page in his notebook. "Here's the information that made my ears prick up. Evidently there are two levels of membership—the general level and the inside elite known as the Vision Chamber members. Those who belong to the Chamber are provided with more intense forms of the drug and some very exclusive services."

"Exclusive services?" Ursula said. "What are those?"

Otford squirmed in his chair. This time he looked to Lilly for help. She gave him a benign smile and turned to Ursula.

"I believe Mr. Otford is referring to the sorts of exclusive services that only a very expensive brothel such as the Pavilion of Pleasure might be able to provide," she said.

"Oh." Ursula sat back in her chair, flushing. She was careful not to let her gaze snag with Slater's. She was quite certain he was amused by her naïveté. "Go on, Mr. Otford."

He cleared his throat and concentrated on his notes. "Services available only to the members of the Vision Chamber include a choice of partners of either sex and various ages, the use of certain implements and, ah, equipment, designed to enhance physical pleasure—"

"I told you to continue with your report, Mr. Otford, not provide a detailed list of the brothel services offered to the members of the Chamber," Ursula hissed.

Otford swallowed hard. "Sorry. I beg your pardon. Got confused."

"You aren't the only one," Slater said in low tones.

Ursula glared at him. Slater pretended not to notice.

"Carry on, Otford," he said. "Were you able to find out how the drug is delivered to the Olympus?"

"An excellent question," Ursula said.

"Thank you," Slater said in very humble tones.

Otford plunged ahead, speaking rapidly. "One of the footmen said that the ambrosia was delivered by a man with a horse and cart. On the days the drug was scheduled to arrive Fulbrook was always on hand to supervise the unloading of the bags. The drug is stored under lock and key in the basement, along with the spirits and cigars, but it's kept apart in a special room."

Slater thought about that. "I assume that Fulbrook is the only one with the key to that room?"

"Yes, according to the footman." Otford winked. "Doesn't mean that a little bit of the drug doesn't go

missing from time to time, mind you. In my experience, gentlemen like Fulbrook stop noticing servants
after a while. I got the impression from the footman
that he and his friends have helped themselves to a
little of the drug as well as the brandy and cigars
from time to time."

"You've done some excellent work, Otford," Slater
said.

Otford beamed. "Thank you, sir. It's all quite fascinating, I must say. This story could be huge—
absolutely huge."

Ursula narrowed her eyes. "Perhaps it would be
more entertaining if there were fewer murders."

Otford flushed and grabbed his napkin to stifle a
cough.

Slater sat back in his chair. "The next step is to find
the deliveryman."

Otford grunted. "There must be thousands of
horses and carts in London."

Ursula straightened abruptly. "The livery stable
near Rosemont's Perfumes."

Slater gave her an approving smile. "It makes
sense that Rosemont would have rented a horse and
cart and very likely a driver as well from the nearest
establishment that offered such services."

"Good heavens, why would anyone situate a per-
fumery near a livery stable?" Lilly asked of no one
in particular.

"Because Rosemont was not blending delicate perfumes," Slater said. "He was brewing a dangerous
drug and producing large quantities of it—enough

to satisfy not just the requirements of the Olympus Club and Mrs. Wyatt's little side business, but the American market, as well. He needed a way to transport his product across town and to the docks for shipment to New York."

"Well," Ursula said very softly.

They all looked at her, waiting for her to say something brilliant.

"Well, what?" Slater asked.

"It just occurs to me that I may have a bit of a flare for this investigation business," she said, trying for an air of modesty.

"I don't recommend it," Slater said. "Stick with the stenography profession."

"Why?" Ursula said, annoyed again.

"In case it has escaped your notice, the income from the private investigation business appears to be somewhat limited. In addition, the price of doing business can be high. I've already lost track of how much money I've had to dispense in the form of bribes, fees and other expenses on this case."

"Hmm." Some of Ursula's enthusiasm evaporated. "I hadn't considered the financial angle."

FORTY-THREE

ye, sir, Rosemont was in the habit of hiring a horse and cart from my establishment," Jake Townsend said. "Employed my son, Ned, to load the bags of incense and deliver the goods."

Slater stood with Ursula at the wide entrance of the livery stable. J. Townsend Livery Services advertised private carriages, wagons and carts for hire. Judging by the size of the stable, however, it appeared to be a small business—he could see only three stalls inside the building and a single, aged, badly sprung carriage. Nevertheless, a stable was a stable and the scent of horses and all things related to them was heavy in the atmosphere.

Townsend was middle aged, with a weather-beaten face and the tough, wiry build of a man who had spent a lifetime around stables. But he was eager to chat once Slater had made it clear to him that he would be paid for his time and cooperation.

Townsend was easy enough to deal with, Slater concluded, but Ursula was a complete mystery to him this morning. She was once again concealed behind her stylish widow's veil. It was impossible to read her expression—not that he had been able to read it earlier at breakfast.

She had been in an odd mood when she descended the stairs that morning and her temper hadn't improved with Mrs. Webster's excellent coffee, at least not as far as he could discern. Initially he had assured himself that the problem was that she had not slept well but now he was starting to wonder—not without some dread—if she regretted last night's passionate encounter in the labyrinth chamber. Perhaps she regretted the first one in her study, as well.

He was convinced now that the fact that she had locked her door last night was a very bad omen.

He forced himself to focus on the task at hand.

"So, Rosemont was a regular customer?" he asked.

"That he was," Townsend said. He shook his head in a mournful way. "Going to miss his business. He sold a great quantity of incense and the French stuff he called potpourri. But I have to say, I'm bloody damned grateful that my establishment was in the next street when his shop went up in flames. The explosion not only destroyed his building, it did a fair amount of damage to the ones on either side, as well. Luckily, they were empty. Gave us quite a scare, I can tell you. Horses went mad for a bit."

"I can imagine," Ursula said.

Slater heard the icy impatience that edged her words but she had the sense not to rush Townsend.

"According to the press, the authorities believe the fire was caused by a gas explosion," Slater said.

"Aye, maybe." Townsend's face creased in disapproval. "But if you ask me, it was all those bags of dried leaves he kept stored in his workshop that fed the flames. And between you and me, there's no telling what chemicals he was using to make that incense and the potpourri. The smell hung over the neighborhood for hours."

"Thank you for your cooperation, Mr. Townsend." Slater took some money out of his pocket. "Just one more question and then we'll leave you to your work."

"What is it ye want to know, sir?"

"You said that Rosemont hired your son and a cart to make deliveries on a regular basis. I'd very much like to know the locations of those routine deliveries."

"There were only two addresses. One was a mansion that housed some sort of private club. The other was a warehouse near the docks. Rosemont shipped a lot of his goods to New York, ye see."

FORTY-FOUR

I understand now why you insisted on going back to your house to fetch a pry bar," Ursula said. "You knew the warehouse would probably be locked. Excellent thinking, sir."

Slater was in the process of wedging the iron bar into the narrow crack between the edge of the door and the frame. He paused long enough to shoot her an unreadable glance.

"I find it makes a pleasant change of pace." He leaned heavily on the pry bar. "Thinking, that is."

She blinked, not certain how to take the remark. "Change of pace?"

"Wouldn't want to overindulge, of course. Might get in the habit."

"Quite right," she said coolly. "Nasty habit, thinking too much."

"I agree."

"I must say, you are in a rather sour mood this morning, Slater."

"The odd thing is that I awoke in a very fine mood. Don't know what happened to change the situation."

She narrowed her eyes. "The weather, perhaps. It does appear as if we're in for a storm."

"Right. The weather."

He leaned once more on the pry bar. The lock groaned and then gave way with a protesting shriek of metal and wood. The door popped open. The musty smell of old, slowly rotting timber and damp air wafted out. There were other odors, as well; a whiff of an acrid, herbal scent caught Ursula's attention.

She stood beside Slater and looked into the shadowy gloom. There was just enough light slanting through the grimy windows to reveal the crates and barrels that littered the floor. Frayed ropes and hoists dangled from the loft.

"We have come to the right place," Slater said. He studied the trail of footprints on the floor. "There have been visitors here quite recently."

He followed the path toward a closed crate. Ursula fell into step beside him. She sniffed delicately and wrinkled her nose.

"I smelled that same odor inside Rosemont's shop," she said. "There is a large quantity of the drug stored in this place. But there is something else here, as well. A dead rat, perhaps."

Slater stopped in front of the first of three crates. "These are locked and ready for shipment."

He applied the pry bar to the lid of one of the

wooden crates. When it popped open Ursula saw a number of canvas sacks stacked neatly inside. The smell of the drug grew stronger.

"Don't move," Slater said quietly.

She froze at the soft command. When she followed his glance she saw the dark stains on the floor. A chill swept through her.

"Blood?" she whispered.

"Yes," Slater said. "And not very old."

He followed the trail to a nearby crate. It was not locked. He raised the lid and looked inside.

"Well, this answers one question," Slater said.

"Who—?" Ursula asked.

"The former owner of the walking stick stiletto."

Ursula remained where she was. She had no desire to go any closer. She watched Slater lean over the crate and methodically rummage through the dead man's clothes.

"How was he killed?" she asked.

"Shot. Twice. All very professional-looking."

"Professional?"

"It's safe to say that whoever murdered this man has had some experience in the business." Slater paused, reaching deeper into the crate. "But he was somewhat out of practice."

"Why do you say that?"

"He did not do a thorough job of stripping the body."

Slater straightened and turned around. She saw a small white business card in his gloved hand.

"What is it?" she asked.

"The address of the Stokely Hotel. I found it tucked safely inside his shoe. I have the impression that our visitor from out of town was terrified of getting lost in our fair city. He kept the address of his hotel in a place where he could be certain he would not lose it."

"What is our next step?"

"We've got a professional killer who has now become a murder victim," Slater said. "We do what any concerned citizen would do. We contact Scotland Yard."

FORTY-FIVE

Lilly picked up the teapot and poured tea into the two delicate porcelain cups that sat on the tray. "I must say, I have not seen Slater this interested in life since he returned to London."

"He does seem to have become quite fixed on the problem of Anne Clifton's murder," Ursula said.

She was acutely aware of the quiet *tick-tick-tick* of the tall clock in the corner of the library. Every time she glanced at the face it seemed that the hands had not moved.

Immediately after the discovery of the body in the warehouse, Slater had brought her back to his house and left her there with Lilly, the Websters and Griffith. He had then gone off to talk to someone at Scotland Yard. Upon returning from that venture, he had announced that he needed to spend some time in the labyrinth chamber. He was presently in his basement retreat. He had been downstairs for nearly an hour.

"I'm quite certain that it is not the murder of poor Miss Clifton that has brought him out of the shadows," Lilly said. "You are the reason he is showing more enthusiasm for life."

"Well, I am the one who brought the case to his notice," Ursula said.

"No, my dear, you had his full attention before you told him of the murder."

"How on earth could you tell?"

Lilly smiled serenely. "A mother knows."

"He certainly had me fooled."

"Now, dear, there's no need for sarcasm. I'm quite sure that Slater took a strong, personal interest in you the day I introduced the two of you."

"May I remind you that, before he returned to London, your son spent a year in a monastery of some sort. Following that, he passed the next several years knocking around the world pursuing lost and stolen artifacts. All in all, one can see that he has probably not had much opportunity to form a romantic attachment with anyone." Ursula cleared her throat. "And he is endowed with a healthy, vigorous temperament."

Lilly looked pleased. "You noticed his healthy, vigorous temperament, did you?"

"My point is that I'm quite certain that he would have taken a *strong, personal interest* in any unattached female who intruded into his life at the time I did."

"Trust me, my dear, Slater is more than capable of finding female companionship when he chooses to do so."

That was no doubt true, Ursula thought. The notion was dispiriting.

"The press noted that a young lady in whom he had a romantic interest got engaged and married to another man while he was stranded on Fever Island," she said in a subdued tone.

"The facts are correct but I can assure you that Slater's association with Isabella was a mild flirtation, at best. She used him to attract the attention of the gentleman who eventually offered for her. Slater was well aware that she had set her sights on someone else. He did not mind because he was focused on the Fever Island expedition. Marriage was the last thing on his mind in those days."

"You're certain?"

"Positive. Slater's heart was not broken at the time. But in the years since he left Fever Island I have become increasingly concerned about him. I had begun to wonder if he had no heart left to break."

Ursula looked up from her tea. "Why do you say that?"

"I feared those strange monks at that monastery had destroyed the part of him that was capable of passion."

"No," Ursula said quickly. "I'm sure that's not the case. Only consider that he is quite passionate—there is no other word for it—about solving the murder of my secretary."

"There are murders every week in London. I have not seen Slater take an interest in any of them. It is you who intrigues my son, Ursula, and for that I am more grateful than I can say. It is as if you have flung open a cell door and allowed him to emerge back into the daylight."

"Nonsense," Ursula said. She gripped the saucer very tightly. "You are overdramatizing the situation. The reality is that Slater simply needed some time to readjust to life here in London."

The door opened before Lilly could respond. Slater entered the room, icy determination electrifying the atmosphere.

"I have devised a plan," he said.

He explained quickly.

Ursula was horrified.

"You mustn't," Lilly said.

"Are you mad?" Ursula demanded.

"I understand that theory has been put forward in the press from time to time," Slater allowed.

FORTY-SIX

The vast gardens at the rear of the Fulbrook mansion were choked with moonlit fog. Slater paused for a moment on the top of the wall. A low growl emanated from somewhere in the shadows.

"Ah, there you are," he whispered. "Good dog."

He unwrapped the large chunk of beef that he had brought with him and dropped it. There was a soft thud when it hit the ground. A moment later a large, furry body rushed through the mist. The mastiff pounced on the meat.

Slater tied off the rope and repelled lightly down the brick wall. The dog stood, front legs braced over the beef, and growled a warning.

"The meal is all yours, my friend. Take your time."

The dog went to work on the large snack. Slater turned his attention to the job at hand.

The thick foliage combined with heavy mist provided ample cover. In fact, Slater concluded, it would have been all too easy to get lost. Fortunately, he had a decent sense of direction.

He also had Ursula's detailed description of what she had seen of the ground floor and the gardens. She had been alarmed upon hearing that he intended to let himself into the mansion and had tried to dissuade him. But eventually logic had won out. She had conceded that the information they needed was most likely concealed inside the house. There was no other way to search for it.

It took some time and a couple of close encounters with assorted garden statues but he managed to make his way to the back wall of the house. He found the French doors that marked the garden entrance to the library exactly where Ursula had said they would be.

Turning, he paced along the wall, counting the casement windows until he came to the third set. If Ursula was right, he had located Fulbrook's study.

There was only a crack and a ping when he used the pry bar to snap the lock and open the windows. He was inside within seconds. A surge of energy spiked with amusement heated his blood. Now that he was back in London he had not expected to find himself using the skills he had perfected recovering lost, strayed and stolen artifacts.

He paused in the darkened room, listening intently. There were no shouts of alarm, no pounding footsteps on the stairs. No rumblings from the servants' quarters.

He definitely had a talent for this sort of thing. And there was no denying that he got a bit of a thrill out of it. It occurred to him that he had missed the work.

The gas lamps had been turned down very low but there was enough light for him to make out the big desk and the heavy floor safe. He decided that if there was anything of great interest to be found, the odds were excellent that it would be in the safe.

He crossed the room to the door and was reassured to discover that it was locked. He would have at least a few seconds' warning in the event someone heard him and came to investigate.

He went to the safe, crouched and took the stethoscope out of his pocket. He fixed the earpieces in place and planted the other end of the device near the combination lock. He listened to the tumblers click into place as he turned the dial.

He got the safe open and reached inside. His fingers brushed against a large envelope and a leather-bound volume. There was also a thickly stuffed packet.

He withdrew the book, the envelope and the packet, rose and went to the desk. He opened the packet first and found a large supply of banknotes. He stuck the money back into the safe and returned to the desk to open the envelope. Several photographs and the negatives fell onto the blotter. It was too dark to make out the images.

He waited a few seconds, listening carefully to the sleeping house. When he was satisfied that no one had been awakened he turned up the lamp suspended over the desk. He studied the photographs for a moment and then he opened the journal. It did not take long to understand what he had found.

He turned down the lamp, closed and locked the safe and went back through the window.

The dog trotted up to him with a hopeful air. He scratched the mastiff's ears and then he climbed the rope to the top of the garden wall and descended to the ground on the other side. He paused to retrieve the climbing equipment and then he faded into the night.

It was gratifying to be back in business. He had missed the exercise.

FORTY-SEVEN

lackmail," Slater said. "That answers one question
about Fulbrook. We knew he was supplying the
drug to the members of the club. Now we know why."

Ursula looked at the photographs spread across
Slater's desk. Outrage swept through her. The images
were of naked lovers entwined and asleep in bed.
What made them so potentially damaging was that
both people in the erotically themed photographs
were male.

"Fulbrook is despicable," she said. "No wonder
Valerie will go to such lengths to escape him."

Lilly picked up one of the photographs. "I recognize the bald man in this picture—Lord Mayhew."

"He was one of the members of the Olympus Club
who was reputed to have taken his own life in recent
months, according to Brice," Slater said.

"The men in these photographs all appear to be asleep," Ursula said.

"More likely unconscious," Slater said. "I think it's obvious that the men engaged in a sexual encounter and then were exposed to a dose of ambrosia that was strong enough to induce unconsciousness long enough for the photographs to be taken."

"Society's attitudes toward women are harsh enough," Lilly remarked. "But they are just as cruel when it comes to liaisons conducted between two male lovers. Furthermore, as far as the law is concerned, such relationships are illegal. Mind you, the reality is that most people turn a blind eye to this sort of thing but if those photographs were made public, they would destroy the gentlemen involved."

Ursula glanced at the journal and then looked at Slater. "What else did you find in that book?"

"More detailed blackmail material. Rumors of relationships that could jeopardize the marriage prospects of the daughters of certain highly placed men. Notes about the financial distress of other members that could ruin them socially."

"Blackmail is a risky undertaking," Lilly said.

"Only if the victims know the identity of the extortionist," Ursula pointed out. "I have had some experience in that regard if you will recall."

"I do believe that Mr. Otford is well aware that he is fortunate to be alive," Slater said.

Ursula sighed. "At least he had a reason to blackmail me. He was hungry and on the verge of becoming homeless. Fulbrook does not have any such excuse. He is a wealthy man. Why would he stoop to something so terrible?"

"I doubt very much that this is about money," Slater said, "although there was a good deal of it in the safe. But there is one commodity that is even more attractive to some men. Power. If you know a man's secrets you can control him."

Ursula took a breath. "Yes, of course. But surely these men—the victims—would know the identity of the blackmailer. They would take action."

"I agree that if even one of those highly placed men knew who was behind the blackmail scheme, Fulbrook's life would not be worth a penny," Slater said. He turned away from the desk and went to stand at the window. "Which is why I'm sure none of them know the truth. We must assume that Fulbrook is very careful about what he is doing. I'm sure that none of the men in those photographs has any clear memory of the events."

"I have certainly seen men suffer blackouts after drinking too much," Lilly said. "And the effects of opium can be so intoxicating that users can become quite . . . careless."

Ursula looked at Slater. "What do you intend to do with the information that you have discovered?"

Slater glanced at her. "I'm going to talk to Fulbrook."

"You plan to tell him that you know that he is blackmailing people?" Lilly asked sharply.

"I am going to give him a chance," Slater said.

"That is more than Anne Clifton, Rosemont and Mrs. Wyatt got."

"A chance to do what?" Ursula asked.

"To survive," Slater said.

"I don't understand," Lilly said.

But Ursula did. She searched Slater's face. "You believe that Fulbrook is next on Damian Cobb's list, don't you?"

"I'm sure of it."

"Then why warn him?" Ursula said. She waved a hand at the photographs and the journal. "He's a blackmailer who has been responsible for the suicides of at least two men. His threats have no doubt made life a living hell for the other people in that journal. And what about that woman—Nicole—who worked for the Pavilion of Pleasure? Fulbrook is directly responsible for her death because he introduced the drug to the Olympus Club."

"I'm aware of that," Slater said. He took off his spectacles and pulled a handkerchief out of his pocket.

"Slater, he doesn't deserve to be warned," Ursula said. "I say let Cobb get rid of him."

Slater polished the lenses of his eyeglasses. "You are very fierce tonight. I find the quality admirable in a lady."

She folded her arms tightly beneath her breasts. "Fulbrook may have a title and a fine pedigree but he is, in truth, a crime lord who has gotten away with his crimes because of his rank in Society. You know very well that it is unlikely we will ever be able to find the proof we would need to have him arrested. Even if we did, it's even less likely that he would be convicted and sent to prison."

Slater put his handkerchief back into his pocket and looked at the tall clock. "I know."

She unfolded her arms and spread her hands wide, exasperated. "Then why warn him that Cobb may be about to kill him?"

Slater put on his glasses and gathered up the photographs. "I'm going to warn him because it will make no difference in the end."

FORTY-EIGHT

~~~~~

Slater ignored the barely veiled stares and the sudden hush that had descended on the club room. It was nearly two o'clock in the morning. Most of the men lounging in the deep leather chairs were dressed in formal black and white. Bottles of claret and brandy sat on every side table. A haze of cigar smoke hung in the air.

One elderly man whom Slater recognized as a friend of his father's snorted in amusement and winked. Slater nodded in acknowledgment and continued on his way into the card room. He had refused to surrender his greatcoat and hat to the porter so he dripped rainwater on the carpet.

Fulbrook was seated at a table with three other men. He held a handful of cards and he was chuckling at a comment one of the other players had just made when the room went very quiet. Like everyone else, he turned toward the door to see who or what had caused the sudden stillness. When he saw Slater, he grunted and made a show of examining his cards.

"Evidently the management of this club is allowing just anyone in these days," he said to his companions, "including those who are rumored to be candidates for an asylum."

One man snickered uneasily. The rest of the players concentrated on their cards as though the stakes had suddenly become life or death.

Slater walked to the table. "My apologies for the interruption, Fulbrook, but I have a rather important message for you."

"I'm busy, Roxton. Some other time."

"If you would rather discuss the matter of a certain journal and some photographs at a future date—"

Fulbrook shot to his feet so quickly his chair tipped over backward and clattered on the floor.

"Your father may have been a gentleman but it's clear that your manners must have come from your mother's side," he said.

"Your insult to my mother has been noted," Slater said. "But I have certain priorities tonight. Shall we continue with this discussion here or outside, where we can be assured of some privacy?"

"Outside. I don't want to subject my friends and associates to your presence any longer than is necessary."

Slater turned and went to the door without a word. Fulbrook hesitated and then followed. In the front hall the porter handed him his coat and his hat, gloves and umbrella.

Slater led the way outside and down the steps into the rain. He stopped at the edge of the circle of light cast by the streetlamp.

"I have a cab waiting," he said. He nodded toward the carriage sitting across the street.

Fulbrook unfurled the umbrella and glanced warily at the cab.

"You really are mad if you think I'd get into a cab with you," he said.

"As you wish. I'll try to make this quick. I have the photographs and the blackmail journal that you stored in the safe in your study."

"You're lying." Fulbrook started to sputter. "How could you possibly . . . you hired someone to break into my house, you son of a bitch. How dare you?"

"I didn't hire someone. I did the work myself. Feel free to press charges but if you do I shall, of course, have to tell a jury what I discovered inside your safe."

"You bastard." Fulbrook sounded as if he were choking. "You stand there and admit that you are a burglar?"

"And you are a blackmailer—also an excellent bookkeeper. Your records are very precise. I noticed that you crossed out the names of two of your victims—the ones who chose suicide rather than provide you with whatever it was you demanded of them in exchange for keeping their secrets."

"The time you spent on that damned island addled

your wits, Roxton. You apparently have no idea who you are dealing with here."

"You are the one who fails to grasp the severity of the situation. I am aware that you have formed a partnership with an American named Damian Cobb."

"What of it? I admit I have done some business with Cobb. He might be vulgar but he's a successful businessman, not a crime lord."

"In this case, there's not much distinction between the two. While we're on the subject, there are two things you should know about Cobb. The first is that he has no intention of maintaining a long-term partnership. His goal is to set up a monopoly to control the drug and he plans to run his business from New York. That means he no longer needs your manufacturing, production and distribution network."

Rage tightened Fulbrook's face. "That's a lie."

"Why do you think he employed an assassin to murder Rosemont, the perfumer who prepared the drug for you, and your courier, Anne Clifton, and Mrs. Wyatt?"

"There was an explosion at Rosemont's laboratory. The authorities believe that he was buried in the rubble."

"You're not keeping up with the news, Fulbrook. Rosemont's body was discovered yesterday. Someone took a stiletto to the back of his neck. Mrs. Wyatt died as the result of a very similar accident with a stiletto."

Fulbrook stiffened. "I heard she was murdered by one of her clients."

"She was dealing quantities of the drug on the

side. I'm not sure if Cobb got rid of her because she went into business for herself or if he simply decided that she knew too much. I suspect that's the reason he had Anne Clifton killed."

"The Clifton woman was a suicide or an overdose."

"It doesn't matter now. What matters is that you are the one member of the British side of the business who is still standing."

"That's ridiculous. Cobb can't get rid of me. I'm the only one who can supply him with the drug. He knows that."

"I suggest you take up that matter with Cobb. He's in town."

Fulbrook snorted. "You're wrong. His ship does not dock until tomorrow."

"He deceived you, Fulbrook. Cobb and his pet assassin arrived a few days ago, right around the time of Anne Clifton's death."

"How can you possibly know that?"

"Because I found the assassin's body last night. It was in a crate at the warehouse. You know the place, I'm sure. It's where Rosemont delivered the ambrosia that was scheduled to be shipped to New York."

Slater started to turn away. He stopped when Fulbrook grabbed his arm.

"Take your hand off me," Slater said very softly.

Fulbrook flinched. He released Slater's sleeve as though the fabric were made of hellfire.

"You said Cobb is in London," Fulbrook hissed. "If that's true, prove it. Where is he staying?"

"I can't be absolutely certain," Slater said. "But I found a card from the Stokely Hotel on the dead assassin. I sent a man to take a look. Sure enough, there is an American businessman registered there under a different name. The assassin apparently masqueraded as his valet."

Fulbrook was dumbfounded. "You're lying. You must be lying."

"We'll soon find out, won't we? The news will be a great sensation in the press."

"What news?"

"Your death, of course. The murder of a gentleman who is as well known in social circles as you are is always news."

"Are you threatening me, you bloody madman?"

"No, I'm doing you the courtesy of giving you a warning," Slater said. "I suggest you go directly to the railway station and depart London on the first available train. It is your only hope."

"Cobb would not dare murder me. He needs me, I tell you."

"I suppose there is a slight possibility that he won't kill you."

"He would *hang*."

"If he got caught," Slater said. "But even if I'm wrong about Cobb's intentions, that still leaves all your other enemies, doesn't it?"

"Now what are you talking about?"

"I have made arrangements for the various pages of your journal and the photographs and negatives to be delivered to your respective victims tomorrow.

Notes will be included mentioning that the materials were discovered in your safe. How long do you think you will survive once the powerful men you are blackmailing discover that you are the extortionist? Perhaps, instead of a train ticket, you should consider booking passage to Australia."

Fulbrook stared at him, stunned. "You're a dead man. *A dead man.*"

Slater did not bother to respond. He walked across the street and climbed into the hansom. The cab set off at a brisk pace.

He glanced back just before the vehicle turned the corner. Fulbrook was still standing in front of his club looking as if he had just received a visitation by the devil.

FORTY-NINE

❧

The bastard was lying. Roxton had to be lying. Everyone said that his experiences on Fever Island had affected his mental balance.

But that did not explain how he had come to learn about the journal and the photographs and the business association with Cobb. There was only one explanation—Roxton had, indeed, gotten into the safe. The high walls, the fierce dog, the modern locks—all for naught.

Fulbrook was still shivering with rage when he climbed out of the cab and went up the steps of his house. He banged on the door several times and swore when no one responded. It was nearly three in the morning. The servants were in their beds but that was no excuse. Bloody hell. Someone should have come to the door. Lazy bastards. He would fire them all in the morning.

He fumbled with his key and finally got the door open. He moved into the dark, empty hall. He tossed the hat onto the polished table but he was in too much of a hurry to bother with his coat.

He rushed down the corridor to his study. At the door of the study he paused again to take out another key. He stabbed the damned lock three times before he finally gained access to the room.

He turned up the lamp. A flicker of relief went through him when he saw that the safe was still locked. Perhaps Roxton had been bluffing. Still, how could he have known about the photographs and the journal?

He crouched in front of the safe and spun the combination lock. Whatever small hope still flickered within him was snuffed out when he got the door open. The journal and the photographs were gone. In a subtle but exquisitely cruel taunt, the bastard had left the several thousand pounds' worth of banknotes behind.

He went to the desk and collapsed into the chair. He buried his face in his hands and tried to think. It was difficult to imagine that Cobb would dare attempt to murder him. The American needed him. But he had to get away from London before the blackmail victims discovered that he was the one who had extorted certain financial and social favors from them during the past year. Roxton was right about one thing—some of the men he had blackmailed were dangerous.

He had to think. He had to escape. He had to protect himself.

He raised his head and unlocked the top desk drawer. The pistol was still inside. At least the bastard had not taken it. Another insult, no doubt.

He checked to be certain the gun was loaded and then he slipped it into the pocket of his greatcoat.

Lurching to his feet, he went back to the safe and scooped out handfuls of banknotes. He stuffed the money into his pockets.

He considered waking a member of the staff to pack his clothes and then concluded that he did not want to waste even that much time.

He left the study and went upstairs to his room. Halfway down the hall he stopped in front of Valerie's door. It was closed.

An acidic rush of rage flooded through him. This was all her fault. She was the one who had explained the properties of the ambrosia plant and painted a beguiling vision of how it could be used to make a fortune and control powerful people. He wanted nothing more than to strangle her.

Rage briefly overcame his panic. He tried the doorknob. When he discovered that the door was locked he hammered the wooden panels with one fist.

"Valerie, you stupid bitch."

There was no response.

Sanity returned in a searing flash of urgency. He

did not have time to break down the door. He would deal with Valerie later.

He hurried down the hall to his own bedroom. It took some time to find a suitcase. Packing was servants' work. How was he to know where the travel necessities were stored?

He stuffed a few essentials into the case and slammed the lid shut. Hefting the bag, he went out into the hall and made his way down the stairs. Belatedly it occurred to him that he should have instructed the cab to wait. No matter. He would find another one soon.

He let himself outside and started walking quickly toward the far end of the street. He listened fearfully but the steady rain muffled the sounds of the night.

A man in a greatcoat and carrying an umbrella appeared in the glow of a streetlamp. The figure came toward him. Each step appeared chillingly deliberate.

Terror ripped through him. He fumbled with his pistol.

A moment later the figure in the greatcoat went up the steps of a large town house and disappeared through the front door.

The relief that swept over Fulbrook was so intense that he was not aware of the presence behind him until a gloved hand slapped across his mouth. The knife slashed open his throat before he could understand what had happened.

He crumpled slowly onto his back. Through glazing eyes he looked up at the face of the figure bending over him. He tried to speak but he could not get the words out.

"It was a pleasure doing business with you," Cobb said. "But a better financial opportunity has presented itself. I'm sure you understand."

FIFTY

The following morning Ursula was in the library with Slater going over their notes on the case in an effort to construct a proper timeline, when the door opened.

"The biggest unknown here is the exact timing of Cobb's arrival in London," Slater said.

He broke off as Gilbert Otford rushed into the room. The journalist was flushed with excitement.

"Fulbrook's body was discovered early this morning by a constable," he announced. "Throat cut by a footpad. *The Flying Intelligencer* is printing a special edition as we speak. My editor is going with the headline *Murder in Mapstone Square. Rumors of a Great Scandal.*"

An eerie shock lanced through Ursula. Her palms tingled and the back of her neck felt as if it had been touched by fingers from a grave. It was not the news of Fulbrook's death that provoked the disturbing sensation—it was the realization that Slater had anticipated the report of the murder.

She looked at him. He sat quietly behind his desk, pages of notes arranged in a neat row in front of him, and looked at Otford with an unreadable expression.

It was one thing to use logic to deduce that a man might be the next target of a killer, she thought. It was another matter altogether to have that reasoning proved accurate. The fact that Fulbrook deserved his fate was not important. It was the realization that one had predicted the outcome—and that the outcome was death—that chilled the spirit.

"Where was the body discovered?" Slater asked quietly.

Otford consulted his notes. "Not far from his front door. It's believed that Fulbrook was attacked either after he got out of a cab or while trying to summon one. None of the neighbors heard or saw anything."

"Of course not," Ursula said.

"Not that the lack of witnesses will stifle the scandal." Otford snapped his notebook shut. "The murder of a gentleman on his own doorstep in an exclusive neighborhood is always a sensation. Every reporter in town is covering the story but thanks to you, Mr. Roxton, I'm the only one with knowledge of Fulbrook's connection to the Olympus Club, where men of rank enjoy a strange drug and the services of the women of the Pavilion. Mrs. Wyatt's murder will now also become a sensation because I can link her business to the club and the club to Fulbrook."

"I take it you are once again working for the *Flying Intelligencer*?" Slater said.

"My editor rehired me this morning when he realized I had a close connection to the story. Meanwhile, I will prepare the first edition of my new magazine. I'm going to call it the *Illustrated News of Crime and Scandal.*"

"That should appeal to a wide readership," Ursula said with a small sniff.

"Yes, indeed," Otford said, unfazed.

Slater leaned forward and clasped his hands together on the desk. "What did you tell your editor about Cobb and the drug business?"

"Don't worry," Otford said. "I've kept mum about the American crime lord and the ambrosia drug."

"You're certain you did not mention Cobb to your editor?" Slater said.

Otford looked sly. "Never said a word to him. Between you and me, the Cobb connection is my ace in the hole, as the Americans say. I'm saving it for the first edition of my magazine, which will be ready to go to press the moment this affair is concluded."

"We are assuming that Cobb will make a wrong move and manage to implicate himself," Ursula said.

"He will make one more mistake," Slater said.

Otford and Ursula looked at him.

"How can you be so certain of that?" Otford demanded, fascinated.

Slater shrugged. "He is responsible for the murder of a number of people, including a high-ranking gentleman, and at this point he thinks that no one suspects him because his ship does not dock until today. He will very soon be sailing to New York with a beautiful woman who sees him as a knight in shining armor. He's a crime lord and he's in the process of building an empire. Trust me, at this moment, he believes he is invincible. That is why he will make his last mistake."

"If you say so." Otford slipped his notebook back into his pocket. "I'll take your word for it. You haven't been wrong so far. Now I must be off. The police have promised that they will have an announcement for the press at one o'clock at the Yard. There'll be the usual idle chatter about how much progress they're making in the search for Fulbrook's killer, et cetera, et cetera. Nonsense, of course, but my editor will want it for the paper."

Otford hurried away and disappeared down the hall. Ursula waited until she heard Webster usher him out of the house.

She rose, crossed the room and very quietly shut the door. Turning, she looked at Slater.

"You knew what was going to happen to Fulbrook, even though you warned him," she said.

Slater got to his feet and went to look out the window at the rain-dampened garden. "It was not a certainty that Fulbrook would end up dead but there was a very high probability that would be the outcome. The pattern was almost entirely clear."

"Almost?"

"The pattern of the labyrinth is never completely clear until one reaches the center and sees the answer.

It's impossible to factor in every single element of an equation. Logic can be warped or deflected by unpredictable emotions."

"But in this instance, your logic held."

Slater turned around to face her. "Because I assumed that Fulbrook would not behave rationally. I knew he would probably panic. I was almost positive that he would go straight home to grab the money that I told him I had left inside the safe."

"And you knew that Cobb would be watching from the shadows."

"Cobb does not know his way around London and he is on his own now that his assassin is dead. I very much doubt that he could follow Fulbrook through our busy, occasionally dangerous streets. But he was certain to have Fulbrook's address. All he had to do was hire a cab to take him to Mapstone Square and wait for Fulbrook to appear."

Ursula walked across the room and stopped directly in front of him. She raised her hands to his shoulders, stood on tiptoe and brushed her mouth across his.

"Fulbrook does not deserve our pity," she said. "But I am very sorry that you had to walk the labyrinth so far into the darkness to deal with him."

Slater framed her face with his hands. "Thank you."

"For what?"

"For understanding."

He folded his arms around her and held her close for a long time.

FIFTY-ONE

❧

I'll wait for ye here, sir." The driver looked down from the box. "My boy, Tom, will give ye a hand with the crate. I'll stay with the carriage. This neighborhood looks to be on the shady side."

Cobb glanced around uneasily. It was nearly midnight. The darkened warehouse loomed in the foggy moonlight. There was no one else in sight and no reason to suspect that anyone had gotten to the drugs. His business in London had been successful, he reminded himself. There had been only the one problem with Hubbard but in the end that had proven manageable. Everything else had gone according to plan.

"We'll need a lantern," Cobb said.

"Got one right 'ere, sir," Tom said.

He grabbed the lantern and vaulted down from the box. A wiry lad of about thirteen or fourteen, he looked strong enough to handle one end of the crate. He was eager to claim the extra tip that Cobb had promised to pay.

"This won't take long," Cobb said.

With Tom beside him, he started toward the warehouse entrance. Logic told him that everything was under control but he could not escape the uneasy sensation that had gripped him all day. But it would all be over soon. The *Atlantic* sailed for New York tomorrow. He and Valerie and the crates of drugs would be on board. One thing was certain, he was never going to pay another visit to London. He detested the damned place.

Tom stopped at the door. "All locked up nice and tight, I see. Reckon whatever you've got stored inside must be valuable."

The curiosity in the boy's voice sent another shiver of unease through Cobb. What if the boy and his father conspired to murder him and steal the drugs? It was something he would certainly consider if he were in their shoes.

He reminded himself that he had chosen the carriage at random from the long row of cabs waiting in front of the hotel. There was no possibility that Tom and his father knew who he was or what he intended.

"The crates we're picking up tonight contain some fabric samples that I'm taking back to New York," he said.

"Fabric, eh?" Tom's enthusiasm faded. "Probably just as well ye locked up the goods. There's people who'll steal anything, even fabric samples. My pa

says the world is a dangerous place for an honest
man."

"Your father is right."

Cobb took the key out of his pocket and unlocked
the door. Darkness and the scent of the drug spilled
out of the interior. He stood back.

"You go first," he said to Tom. "You've got the
lantern."

"Yes, sir."

Tom held the lantern high and moved through the
doorway. "It's bloody damned dark in here, ain't it?
Do ye suppose there's ghosts?"

Cobb reached into his pocket and closed his hand
around the gun. He glanced warily at the crate that
held Hubbard's remains. Had he been careful when
he checked the body to make certain there was nothing that could tie the dead man to him? He had been
in a hurry that night.

"No such thing as ghosts, boy," he said aloud.

"That's not what my ma says. She went to one of
those séances the other night and talked to the spirit
of her sister, Meg. Aunt Meg died a year ago. Never
told anyone where she hid her teapot. My ma looked
all over for it. But Meg's ghost couldn't remember
where she put it."

"I told you, there are no ghosts," Cobb snarled.

Tom flinched.

"Yes, sir," he whispered. He looked around.
"Smells bad, don't it? I'll wager there's a dead rat
around here somewhere."

And suddenly Cobb was very certain that he

ought to take a look inside the crate that held Hubbard's body. He needed to be sure that he had not made any mistakes. But he could not allow Tom to see the corpse.

"Give me the lantern," he ordered.

Tom handed him the lantern.

"Wait over there by that stack of empty crates," Cobb said.

"Yes, sir." Tom wrinkled his nose and hurried across the room. "Must have been a real big rat."

Cobb went to the crate that held Hubbard. He would just take a quick look, he assured himself. Make sure the body hadn't been disturbed.

He set the lantern on top of a nearby crate. He could feel the boy watching him. *Probably thinks I'm crazy.* But there was no help for it. He had to be sure.

He got the lid of the crate open. The odor of death abruptly got stronger but Cobb barely noticed. It was not the first time he had encountered it.

He stared down at Hubbard's body. It was just as he had left it, he concluded. Relief pulsed through him. He started to go through Hubbard's clothing. He heard the boy moving about behind him.

"I'll just be a moment," he said, not bothering to turn around. "Then we'll take the crates and leave."

"Your hired killer had a card from your hotel tucked into his shoe."

The voice came out of the shadows, startling Cobb so badly he dropped the lid of the crate. He yanked the gun out of his pocket and whirled around.

At first he thought his eyes were playing tricks on

him. The boy had vanished. Then he heard harsh, frightened breathing coming from behind a stack of crates. Tom was hiding. Not that the boy mattered now. It was the voice in the shadows on the far side of the warehouse that rattled Cobb's nerves.

"Who are you?" he grated. "Where are you? Show yourself."

"I trust you are not going to panic." The figure moved out of the darkness, pausing at the very edge of the glary light cast by the lantern. "I came here to discuss a business venture with you. Now that Fulbrook is no longer involved, I am hoping that you will be interested in a new partner."

Cobb struggled to make sense of what was happening. "Who are you?"

"Roxton."

"So you're the bastard Valerie told me about—the one who took an interest in the stenographer's death. What do you want?"

"Yours is a simple, straightforward business plan. You intend to build a monopoly based on the ambrosia plant drug. You came here to close down the British end of the business. You will return to New York with everything you need to cultivate, harvest and concoct the drug in all its various forms. All you required are some specimens or seeds and an expert gardener who knew how to obtain the drug from the plant. Lady Fulbrook."

"You seem to know a great deal about my business affairs."

"I did my research."

"How did you discover Hubbard's body?" Cobb demanded. "There were no witnesses that night. I'm certain of that."

"London is my city. I know my way around."

Cobb gave that some thought. "I notice that you did not go to the police with your discovery."

"Why would I risk losing what promises to be a golden business opportunity? I will admit that I'm curious about why you got rid of Hubbard. He was, after all, the only person you could trust in London."

"Hubbard became a liability after he failed to get rid of you," Cobb said.

"I thought that might have been the case. He was useful, though, at least for a time. He took care of the people who knew about Fulbrook's connection to you. But with Hubbard gone, you had to take care of Fulbrook yourself, last night."

"You know far too much about my private affairs," Cobb said. "Are you one of Fulbrook's associates from the club?"

"Fulbrook and I were not friends and we did not do business together. But, yes, I know a great deal about your affairs."

"And now you want to take his place as my British business partner."

"I don't see why we can't double our profits with greenhouses and distribution routes in both countries. I can handle the Continent and the Far East. You will have all of America under your control."

"Where are your enforcers?" Cobb asked. "I saw no sign of them outside and you seem to be alone in here. Except for the boy, of course."

"You're here on your own, are you not? You murdered the one enforcer who could have covered your back."

"So you came here alone." Cobb snorted softly. "You bloody English. So damned arrogant."

"You're the stranger in town, Cobb, not me. We both know that from this distance and in this poor light, there is very little chance that you could even nick me, let alone get off a killing shot."

Cobb tightened his grip on the gun. If only the bastard would step into the circle of light.

"Let's discuss this bargain you're suggesting," he said. "You do realize that you lack what you will need to cultivate the plants successfully?"

"A few packets of seeds and the horticultural knowledge of how to grow the plants and process them into drugs? You're wrong, Cobb. You see, Lady Fulbrook was not the only person who possessed that knowledge."

"Yes, I know. The Clifton woman contacted me, or should I say, Mr. Paladin. Told me that she had observed Valerie for months and acquired the skills needed to cultivate the plants. She claimed to have packets of ambrosia seeds. Wanted to establish a partnership of sorts. But she is dead and the information died with her."

"That is not true. Miss Clifton was a very fine stenographer. Do you know what that means?"

Cobb felt a cold sweat break out on his forehead. "She was just a secretary."

"Anne Clifton recorded every detail of how to grow and process the plants in her stenographer's notebook. You may be interested to know that notebook is now in my possession."

"Even if you're telling the truth, you'd need the seeds or several specimens to grow a large quantity of the herb."

"Ah, yes, the seeds. Presently they are in safekeeping along with the notebook."

Cobb thought of Valerie naïvely allowing her secretary to observe her in the greenhouse and the stillroom. He wanted to crush someone—preferably Valerie. But if he got out of this situation he would need her, at least until he had established the plant in his New York greenhouse and set up the laboratory.

"The stupid woman," he said. "I should have known better than to get involved in a business arrangement with a female."

"Your hotel kindly informed me that the American businessman staying with them intends to leave tomorrow. I knew that you would not be able to resist returning here tonight to check on the body and pick up the crates."

Cobb got a cold feeling in his stomach. "How could you know that?"

"You're a crime lord operating on unfamiliar territory. That makes your actions astonishingly simple to predict."

"You son of a bitch. You can't prove any of it."

"I don't have to prove a thing, remember? I'm not from Scotland Yard. I'm just a businessman."

The situation had deteriorated into a disaster, Cobb thought. He should have cut his losses yesterday. Coming here tonight for the crates of processed drugs had been a mistake. Roxton was right—he was operating on unfamiliar territory and that was dangerous. He had to get out of London. If he could just get on board the ship he would be safe.

He glanced toward the door. The carriage was waiting outside. He started making plans. The boy knew too much now. He would have to die. But meanwhile he would serve as a hostage long enough to force the father to drive him to a safe neighborhood.

Yes, that strategy would work. But first he had to get rid of Slater Roxton.

"You're serious about a partnership?" he said.

"Why else would I be here? I could have taken the crates of drugs. You would never have known the identity of the thief."

"Yet here you are, offering a partnership. I'm starting to believe that what Fulbrook said about you is true—you are a little mad. Something to do with having spent a year stranded on an island, they say."

"I've heard those rumors about me, as well. Might be something to them. After all, how does one know if one is mad? But when it comes to arrogance, you take the prize, Cobb."

"What are you talking about?"

Slater walked out of the shadows, moving a short

way into the light. His hands were empty. Cobb breathed a sigh of relief.

Very casually Slater reached out to grip one of the hoist ropes that dangled from the loft.

"Some would claim that murdering a high-ranking gentleman like Fulbrook requires a breath-taking degree of arrogance," he said.

Cobb smiled. "Killing Fulbrook was very easy."

"Was it?"

"I waited for him outside his house in Mapstone Square. When he came down the front steps I followed him and cut his throat."

"I see. Can I ask why you are telling me this now?"

"Because I am not looking for a business partner."

Cobb raised the gun and prepared to pull the trigger.

But Slater was already tugging hard on the length of rope that dangled from the loft.

Cobb was focused on the kill. He never saw the heavy rope net fall out of the loft until it landed on top of him. The weight of it took him off balance and off his feet.

He yelled, reflexively pulling the trigger. The revolver roared but the shot went wild. Cobb struggled in the snare. He succeeded only in becoming more entangled in the web of thick rope.

The warehouse was suddenly filled with constables who appeared from the interiors of several crates and descended from the loft. One man in a suit and tie walked toward Cobb.

"Did you hear enough, Detective Inspector?" Slater asked.

"More than enough," the detective said. He reached through the netting and collected the revolver. "Plenty of witnesses heard this man's confession, as well. Mr. Cobb, I am placing you under arrest for the murder of Lord Fulbrook and the American named Hubbard. There will be other charges, as well. Someone's got to answer for the deaths of Rosemont, Wyatt and Anne Clifton."

There was a sudden disturbance in the doorway. A light appeared.

"What's going on in here?" the cab driver shouted. "Tom. Tom, are you all right? Where are you, son?"

Slater went to where he had hidden Tom a few minutes earlier.

"You can come out from behind the crate, Tom," he said. "You're safe."

Tom jumped to his feet. He took in the scene with an awed expression. Then he ran to his father.

"That man, the one that was going to pay us so much to haul the crate to the ship, I heard him say he cut someone's throat," Tom said.

The driver pulled Tom close against his side. "There, there, son, looks like the police have him in hand."

Slater walked across the floor through the lantern light and stopped a short distance from Cobb.

"Bastard," Cobb hissed.

"Welcome to London," Slater said.

FIFTY-TWO

~

"Lady Fulbrook has gone into seclusion in the country." Otford checked his notes. "She is said to be distraught over the murder of her husband."

"I'll wager that's a bit of an exaggeration," Ursula said. "I'm quite certain that *vastly relieved to have him out of the way* would be a more accurate description of her feelings."

They were gathered once again in Slater's library, listening to the latest news from a very excited Otford. Ursula was seated on the sofa beside Lilly, who was pouring tea. Slater was behind his desk. Ursula thought he was strangely calm for a man who had faced down a violent crime lord a few hours earlier. For her part, she was not feeling nearly so cool and collected. But there was, she had to admit, a great deal of relief and satisfaction in knowing that Cobb had been arrested.

Otford flipped another page in his notebook. "I could find only one person at the Fulbrook house in Mapstone Square, a gardener. Managed to speak to him through the back gate. He said Lady Fulbrook had let the entire household staff go except for him. According to the gardener, Lady Fulbrook got into a hired carriage shortly before noon and departed for the country house."

Ursula picked up her teacup. "Lady Fulbrook hated all of the servants. She didn't trust them. She believed they spied on her."

"She was a prisoner in her own home." Lilly looked thoughtful. "And now she is free."

Ursula turned to Slater. "What will happen to Damian Cobb?"

"I'm told he has sent a telegram to his lawyers in America who will, no doubt, arrange for him to hire the best lawyer in London." Slater scooped up his notes. "There is, of course, the possibility that he will go free, in spite of the confession and the facts of the case. But if he is that fortunate, I predict that he will book passage to New York on the first available ship."

"He won't dare hang around London, that's certain," Otford said. "He'll be notorious after the trial. The press and the penny dreadfuls—especially the *Illustrated News of Crime and Scandal*—will be filled with stories about him for months. The court may find him not guilty, but public opinion will hold an entirely different view. You know how it is, Mrs. Kern."

"Yes." Ursula set her cup down with a loud clink

of china on china. "I know very well how it feels to be notorious."

Otford stiffened and then flushed a dull red. "Sorry to bring up the subject. Well, I'd best be off. Got a meeting with a printer. The first issue of the *Illustrated News* goes on sale tomorrow." He paused and glanced uneasily at Slater. "Our deal still stands, sir, does it not? I assured the printer that he would be paid because you were backing my magazine."

Slater leaned back in his chair and steepled his fingers. "I will instruct my man of business to issue you a check no later than this afternoon."

Otford radiated excitement. "Thank you, sir. I promise you that you'll have a free lifetime subscription to the *Illustrated News of Crime and Scandal*."

"I will look forward to every issue," Slater said.

"Right, then, I'll be on my way." Otford nodded at Ursula and Lilly. "Good day to you, ladies."

He scurried away through the door.

Lilly looked at Slater. "You've certainly made Mr. Otford's dreams come true."

Slater took off his spectacles and started to polish them. "Always nice to have the press on one's side."

"Even if one must pay for the positive publicity?" Ursula asked.

Slater put on his eyeglasses. "So long as I get my money's worth, I have no complaints."

Lilly put her cup and saucer down on the table. "You must excuse me. I am going shopping. News of the Fulbrook murder is spreading rapidly and I suddenly find myself in great demand because of my connection to the Kern Secretarial Agency. Everyone is aware that one of their secretaries was a victim of the American assassin. Invitations have been pouring in all morning. At this rate, my calendar will be completely full for the next month or so."

She whisked through the doorway. Ursula waited until she was gone and then she looked at Slater.

"I can scarcely believe that it's finished," she said. "Everyone is talking about Fulbrook's murder but all I ever cared about was Anne's death."

"I know." Slater watched her across the expanse of the big desk. "It's possible that Cobb will evade the hangman's noose and go home to New York. But even if that is the case, he will not be able to escape the stain on his reputation. He has been labeled a murderer in the press on both sides of the Atlantic. He will never be free of the repercussions. Will that be enough for you?"

"Yes," she said. "I wanted answers and you helped me obtain them. If the judge and jury fail, I am certainly not going to allow you to assume the responsibility of meting out justice. There has been too much darkness. It is time for a bit of sunlight."

"Agreed." Slater looked toward the window. "As it happens, the sun is shining at this moment. Would you care to walk out with me?"

She smiled and got to her feet. "I would be delighted to go walking in the sunlight with you, Slater. I'll run upstairs and get my bonnet." She paused, gathering her nerve. "When we return, I really must pack and move back to my own house."

He watched her go toward the door. "There is no need for you to rush back to your home. You are welcome to stay here for a few more days—or longer. It's about time we got back to work cataloging my collection. This investigation business has created a serious delay."

She froze. After what they had just been through, his chief concern was the cataloging of his artifacts?

"I will be happy to assist you in the work," she said grimly, "but I can do that just as well while living in my own house."

He studied the collection of relics. "This house will feel . . . empty when you are not here."

"We both know that I can't stay here indefinitely as your houseguest," she said. "I must go home. The sooner, the better, I think."

He looked stricken. She told herself she must be strong for both of them.

"I'll just be a moment," she said. She went to the doorway.

"Ursula?"

A giddy sense of hope made her pause in the doorway. She turned quickly.

"Yes, Slater?" She tried to inject encouragement into her voice.

He came out from behind his desk. "It occurs to me that, from a certain perspective, there is one person who has come out of this tangle in remarkably good condition."

Her heart sank. "You refer to Mr. Otford?"

"I am thinking of Lady Fulbrook."

"Oh, I see what you mean."

"She has it all now, doesn't she?" Slater folded his arms and lounged back against the desk. "The Fulbrook money, her freedom and a conservatory crammed with the ambrosia plant. If she were of a mind to do so, she could go into the drug business herself."

"Perhaps," Ursula said, "but I doubt that she will do that. She is a very wealthy woman now. I am glad for her sake that she is free of that dreadful marriage but she did not get what she wanted most. She truly loved Cobb, you see. It's all there in her letter poems. She dreamed of running off to New York with him. That dream has now been shattered."

"Perhaps not," Slater said. "As I've said, I am sure Cobb will have an excellent lawyer. He commands wealth and power back in New York. He may yet be able to make Lady Fulbrook's dreams come true."

"But it would never be the same as it was in her fantasies. She knows the truth about him now."

He nodded. "Fantasies are gossamer things, are they not? Reality invariably crushes them."

Ursula turned swiftly to face him, anger flashing through her. She would not let him crush her fantasies, she vowed. She would fight to preserve them.

"Goodness," she said. "Will you just look at the time? I don't believe I have time to walk out with you after all, Mr. Roxton. I must go upstairs and pack."

Slater unfolded his arms and straightened abruptly. "But you agreed . . ."

She gave him a steely smile. "You appear bewildered, perplexed, perhaps even a trifle disoriented. Why don't you go downstairs and walk your labyrinth. All the answers you seek are there, are they not? Don't bother seeing me to the door. I'll ask Webster to have the carriage brought around. I'll be out of your way within the hour."

She grasped fistfuls of her skirts and whipped out into the hall. Very deliberately she closed the door on a stunned Slater.

A woman could only do so much. Slater was on his own now. This was about emotions, not logic. He knew where to find her when he finally came to his senses.

. . . If he came to his senses.

FIFTY-THREE

She had not miscalculated. She walked through the front door of her town house less than an hour later.

As homecomings went, it was not much to speak of. She had forgotten to send word of her impending arrival to Mrs. Dunstan. The silence of the front hall reminded her that the housekeeper was still at her daughter's house.

The little town house was very still, shadowed and chilled.

"You can put the trunk in the first bedroom on the right, Griffith," she said.

"Yes, ma'am."

Shouldering the trunk, he climbed the stairs with a slow, heavy tread. Like the Websters, he insisted upon acting as if her departure from Slater's mansion had once again plunged the household into deep mourning.

She took off her bonnet and gloves. Griffith came back downstairs and hovered for a moment.

"Shall I light a fire for you, Mrs. Kern?" he asked. "The fog is getting thick outside."

"I can deal with the fire, Griffith. Thank you for taking the trunk upstairs."

"Yes, ma'am. Well, if there's nothing else, I'll be off. Got to find a barber."

She blinked. "A barber?"

Griffith turned a dull red but his eyes were very bright. "Mrs. Lafontaine gave me two tickets to her latest play. Miss Bingham has agreed to go with me and have a late supper afterward."

"You? And Matty? Good heavens, I hadn't realized." It dawned on her that she had been so caught up in her feelings for Slater and the mystery of Anne's death that she had not been paying attention. She smiled. "That's wonderful, Griffith. I know you will enjoy yourselves."

"Expect so." He looked around. "You're sure you're all right here alone?"

"I'll be fine, Griffith."

She closed the door behind him and stood in the hall for a moment, trying to decide if she had done the right thing. She had more or less given Slater an ultimatum. The question was whether he had gotten the message and, if he had, what he would do about it.

Now she was starting to wonder if perhaps she

had been too subtle. Slater could be a difficult man to read. What if she had misjudged his feelings for her entirely? Perhaps she believed that he loved her simply because she knew now that she was in love with him.

The possibility that she had created a fantasy for herself was unnerving. That was exactly what Valerie had done. She had constructed a fairy tale that featured a murderous crime lord in the role of the hero.

"Well, one thing is certain," Ursula said aloud to the empty house, "Slater is not a murderous crime lord."

Surely that indicated that she was not quite as foolish as Valerie.

She went down the hall to the study, where she turned up the lamp and set her satchel on the desk. She knelt to light the fire. The warm blaze on the hearth took the chill off the small room. She drew the curtains open, allowing the foggy afternoon light to enter.

Valerie's words of warning to Anne floated through her mind. *The foolish woman thought she was so clever seducing a man who is far above her reach. That's what killed her in the end, you know.*

Ursula thought about that for a moment. At the time Valerie had implied that Anne was a fool to try to seduce Lord Fulbrook. But what if Valerie had known the truth—that Damian Cobb was the object of Anne's attempt at seduction?

The question sent a shiver of alarm through Ursula. Impossible. Anne would never have been so foolish as to reveal that she had tried to seduce Cobb with packets of seeds and the secrets of cultivating the ambrosia plant. Anne was too smart. Too clever.

But Anne was dead. She had not been smart enough or clever enough to avoid a killer.

Ursula crossed the room. Crouching, she unlocked the safe and took out the packets of seeds, the small bundle of Mr. Paladin's letters and the velvet bag that contained Anne's small collection of jewelry. She carried the items back to her desk and sat down.

For a time she contemplated the collection of damning objects. Then she started to read the letters from Mr. Paladin.

FIFTY-FOUR

~~~~~

The lantern light gleamed on the blue tiles set in the floor but it did little to alleviate the shadows that filled the chamber.

Slater stood at the entrance of the labyrinth. It always came down to asking the right question. The problem was that he was not accustomed to asking questions about his own emotions. It was so much simpler to bury such powerful sensations as he had been taught at the monastery. Once unleashed, there was no predicting where they might lead. Anger could metamorphose into rage. Desire could compel a man to ignore logic in hopes of grasping the fleeting promise of passion. Fear could so easily ignite a destructive panic. Despair could induce a man to abandon his responsibilities.

Love was the most dangerous emotion of all. But it was also the most powerful.

He knew then that there was no need to walk the labyrinth. The question was crystal clear. And so was the answer.

FIFTY-FIVE

*I am delighted to know that you are pleased with
the small token of my appreciation. I hope you will
think of me when you wear it. I look forward to a
long and successful partnership . . .*

Ursula put the last letter from Mr. Paladin aside,
loosened the cord on the velvet jewelry sack and
turned it upside down. Anne's small collection of
baubles spilled out.

She picked up the blue pouch and opened it. The
elegant silver notebook-and-pencil chatelaine fell into
her hand. She turned it over and examined the maker's mark. The name of the store was engraved on the
back. The firm was located in New York.

Anne had not received the chatelaine from a grateful client. Damian Cobb had sent it to her as part of
a long-distance seduction.

FIFTY-SIX

~~~~~

The sudden hammering on the door of the chamber brought him out of his reverie.

"Regret to disturb you, sir." Webster's voice was muffled by the heavy wooden panel but the fact that it was audible at all indicated he was shouting. "Mr. Otford has just arrived with what he says is news of critical importance."

Slater crossed the room to open the door. Webster stood in the hall, one fist poised in midair. Otford, flushed and breathless, hovered behind him.

"What is it?" Slater asked.

"It's Cobb," Otford gasped.

"What about him?"

"He was found dead in his cell a short time ago. The rumor is that it was poison. Seems Cobb had a visitor earlier today, a woman dressed as a widow. Unbeknownst to the guards, she managed to slip him a small flask of what appeared to be brandy. He died shortly after she left. You don't think that Mrs. Kern decided to take the law into her own hands, do you?"

"No," Slater said. "I think Cobb's death is the work of a woman scorned. I've got to get to Ursula."

He went through the doorway, past Webster and Otford, and took the ancient stone steps two at a time.

FIFTY-SEVEN

Ursula stood suddenly and gathered up the letters from Paladin. She put them back in the safe and then went toward the door of the study. So much for her determination not to call on Slater until he came to his senses. She had to see him immediately to tell him that she had discovered the identity of Anne's killer. Not that there would be any proof, she thought. Valerie would very likely get away with murder.

She heard the kitchen door open just as she emerged from the study. She stopped and looked back down the hall.

"Mrs. Dunstan?" she said. "You're home early. I wasn't expecting you until tomorrow morning."

Valerie, dressed in mourning with a black veil that dripped from a stylish hat, walked out of the kitchen. There was a small gun clutched in one elegantly gloved hand.

"I, on the other hand, have been waiting for you," she said.

"You were the one who murdered Anne," Ursula said. She retreated slowly back toward the doorway of the study. "That was not Cobb's doing, nor was it the work of his assassin. You killed her because you discovered that she was attempting to seduce the man you wanted—the hero who was supposed to rescue you and sweep you away into a fairy-tale life."

"For months I assumed that Anne was involved in an affair with my husband. Fulbrook was using her as a courier so it was logical to think she might be sleeping with him," Valerie said. "I did not care. She was welcome to him. I did try to warn her that she was just one more whore as far as he was concerned, but she paid no attention."

"You and your husband were operating quite an extensive business enterprise."

"I didn't give a damn about the business, although I don't mind telling you that it was my idea from the beginning. I was the one who understood the implications of controlling such a powerful drug."

"Was it your idea to blackmail those members of the Olympus Club?" Ursula asked.

"Yes, it was. Fulbrook already had money. But I thought that if I showed him a way to exercise real power at the highest levels of Society and inside the government, he would be forced to treat me with respect. Instead, I became more of a prisoner than ever."

"He feared losing you because you were the source

of his newfound power," Ursula said. "I know this will sound like a strange question under the circumstances, but why didn't you simply poison him? You obviously have the botanical knowledge to do that. You poisoned Anne."

"I thought about killing Fulbrook often back at the start of my marriage. But I feared being arrested for murder. Furthermore, I knew the entire household staff would testify against me. Just as I began to despair, my bastard husband informed me that we were going to New York to meet with a certain businessman."

"You met Damian Cobb and you convinced yourself that he would save you."

"Damian loved me." The gun trembled in Valerie's hand. "I know he did. We had an affair in New York right beneath my husband's nose. He never guessed. It was such an exhilarating sensation. Fulbrook despised having to treat Damian as an equal. It never even occurred to him that I might find Damian attractive. It was all quite delicious."

"When you returned to London you hired a professional secretary and dictated your love letters to her. Anne sent the poems to Cobb, who posed as Paladin."

Valerie smiled a wistful smile. "When Damian wrote back to me, he was very careful to pretend that he was an editor who was enthusiastic about my poems."

"When did Anne realize that you were carrying on a secret correspondence with a lover?"

"Very early on, actually. Our Anne was quite bright and vivacious and I was so lonely. I made the mistake of trusting her. She was my only friend and she was so eager to bring me the latest letter from New York—so excited to be part of the secret. I'm the one who suggested to Fulbrook that she would make a useful courier, by the way. I thought she would be loyal to me. But I was wrong. She betrayed me, just as Damian betrayed me."

"You saw Damian Cobb as heroic but in truth he was manipulating you."

"I was a fool but I will never play that role again," Valerie said.

"It was the chatelaine, wasn't it? When Anne started wearing it you realized somehow that Cobb had sent it to her."

"She wore the chatelaine to my house." Valerie's voice rose. "She pretended that a grateful client had given it to her but I knew the truth."

"How?"

"I recognized the maker's mark." Tears of rage glittered in Valerie's eyes. The gun in her hand shook violently. "Damian bought it at the same New York jewelry store where he purchased the brooch that he gave me."

"Cobb gave you a gift of jewelry?"

Valerie reached into the pocket of her cloak and took out a small blue velvet pouch. She hurled it onto the desk.

"He told me to think of him whenever I wore it beneath my gowns," she hissed. "I pinned it to my petticoats every day. Look at the mark on the back. *Look at it.*"

Ursula took the opportunity to move behind her desk, putting it between herself and Valerie. It wasn't much in the way of a fortress but it was all that was available.

She picked up the velvet bag and turned it upside down. An exquisite little brooch tumbled out. She remembered the day that Valerie had come running toward her in the conservatory, skirts raised to her knees. There had been something small and glittery pinned to her petticoats.

Ursula examined the markings on the back of the brooch.

"You are correct," she said. "It appears both items came from the same store. However, if it's any consolation, I think we can safely say that your brooch cost considerably more than Anne's chatelaine. But, then, Cobb would have known that if Anne showed up at the office wearing a fabulously expensive piece of jewelry, her colleagues as well as her clients would have asked a great many awkward questions."

"I did not need to ask any questions," Valerie spit out. "She flaunted that damned chatelaine in front of me. When I asked to take a closer look, she was only too happy to allow me to examine it. She gave me the same story she gave you—told me it was a gift from a grateful client. But when I saw the markings I knew for certain that she had betrayed me."

"Did she know about your brooch?"

"No. I did not dare to wear it openly for fear that one of the servants would tell Fulbrook. He would know that he had not given me the brooch. But I wore it every day in secret."

"How did you murder Anne?" Ursula asked. "You were never allowed to leave the house. You said the servants were always watching."

"During the past few months I have become very expert with the drug. In some formulations, it can kill. I spent hours testing the poisonous version on mice and rats. I knew that Anne enjoyed the ambrosia and that she kept her supply in a perfume bottle that Rosemont gave her. She was a bit of an addict, I'm afraid. I instructed her to bring the bottle to me so that I could give her a sample of the latest version of the drug. I knew she would not be able to resist trying it."

"You told yourself that with Anne dead, things would go back to the way they had been between you and Cobb."

"He would realize that he needed me," Valerie wailed. "I was the only one left who could give him the secrets of the ambrosia. And then you showed up, insisting on taking Anne's place as my secretary."

"Why did you let me do that?"

"Because I realized that you might have ulterior motives. Anne had often talked about how smart you were, how you had reinvented yourself after a great scandal. She said she had left everything to you. I started to wonder if she had left the secrets of the ambrosia to you, as well."

"I made you nervous so you decided to contact the reporter who ruined my reputation two years ago."

"Anne told me about him and his newspaper. I explained to Fulbrook that you might be dangerous. He agreed we had to be cautious when it came to getting rid of you because if you turned up dead, Slater Roxton was bound to cause trouble. I gave my husband the idea of exposing you to the journalist, Otford. I was certain that he would smear your name in the gutter press. I thought that would be the end of you—that Roxton would not want anything to do with you after he found out that you were involved in a great scandal. Then you could quietly drown yourself in the river."

"Why did you come here to kill me? I had nothing to do with Anne's connection to Damian Cobb."

"You had *everything* to do with it." Valerie used both hands to grip the gun. "You are the one who sent that whore into my home."

"Anne and Cobb did not have a romantic connection. Anne wanted to become his business partner."

"I don't believe that, not for a moment. And even if it's true, it doesn't matter. They betrayed me. If it had not been for you, things would have ended the way they were supposed to end. I would be on my way to New York with Damian."

"Cobb wanted you, not Anne," Ursula said. "And I can prove it."

The lie came with astonishing ease. Perhaps that was because she had gotten rather good at the business in the wake of the Picton divorce scandal, she thought. Or perhaps the words came quickly because she was desperate to distract Valerie.

Whatever the case, it worked. Valerie was visibly stunned.

"What are you talking about?" she whispered.

"Anne held back his last letters to you. She never delivered them because she was still trying to convince Cobb to take her on as his partner. She wanted to destroy your relationship. She knew that if he had you, he wouldn't need her."

Valerie stared, transfixed with shock.

"No," she whispered.

"I stored his last letters in my safe. Would you care to see them? They are all addressed to you."

"I don't believe you. Show them to me."

"Certainly."

Ursula crouched in front of the safe, unlocked it with trembling fingers and reached into the dark interior for the gun. With her other hand she picked up the envelope that held the copy of the penny dreadful.

She rose slowly to her feet, holding the gun out of sight in the folds of her skirts.

"Perhaps it would be better for all concerned if we burned these letters," she said. "It could be embarrassing if the press were to get hold of them."

"*No!*" Valerie shrieked.

Ursula tossed the letters into the flames.

Valerie screamed and rushed across the room to the fireplace. In her desperation to save the letters she dropped the gun on the carpet so that she could grab a poker.

Ursula moved out from behind the desk. Very quietly she picked up the gun. Valerie seemed unaware of what was happening. She sobbed hysterically and stabbed at the flames with the poker.

A shadow moved in the doorway. Startled, Ursula turned quickly and saw Slater. He, too, had a gun in his hand.

He took in the situation in a glance and made his weapon vanish inside his greatcoat. He looked at Ursula.

"Are you all right?" he asked.

His voice was ice cold. His eyes burned.

"Yes," she said. She tried to sound just as cool and just as controlled as he did but she could hear the shaky edge in her own voice. "She's the one who murdered Anne."

"I know."

Valerie collapsed onto the carpet, distraught and hysterical.

Slater put one arm around Ursula and pulled her close. Together they watched Valerie cry herself into exhaustion.

FIFTY-EIGHT

~~~

Two days later Ursula was inspired to send an invitation to tea to the small group of investigators. Mrs. Dunstan bustled about excitedly all morning preparing the rarely used drawing room. Dust covers were swept away. Drapes were pulled back to allow the watery sunlight into the space. After the cleaning had been completed to her satisfaction, she retreated to the kitchen, where she prepared a veritable feast of small sandwiches, lemon tarts and little cakes.

The guests arrived unfashionably early. Lilly took up a position on the sofa, a formidable figure in a red gown trimmed with white lace. Otford, a hot-off-the-press copy of the *Illustrated News of Crime and Scandal* tucked under one arm, headed straight for the silver tray.

Slater was in his customary head-to-toe black. He

lounged gracefully against one wall and munched a sandwich.

"Lady Fulbrook won't hang, you can be sure of that," Otford announced. He popped a cake into his mouth. "Her sort never do. Mark my words, she will quietly disappear into a private asylum and spend the rest of her days there."

"I would not wager a great deal of money on that outcome if I were you," Lilly said. "In my opinion, the woman is a consummate actress. It wouldn't surprise me in the least to learn a few months from now that Lady Fulbrook has been miraculously cured by a practitioner of the modern theory of psychology."

"An alienist?" Ursula paused her teacup in midair while she pondered that. "Good heavens, I had not considered that possibility."

"We will keep an eye on her," Slater said. "But if she is set free, I do not think she will return to London. She certainly cannot go into Society. She is now a notorious woman, thanks to Mr. Otford and his colleagues."

"That she is," Otford said. He waved the copy of his magazine. "I must admit I am grateful to her. Nothing better than a woman on the cover to attract the attention of the public."

"Let me see that." Ursula got up, marched across the room and yanked the magazine out of Otford's hands. She sat down beside Lilly and examined the penny dreadful.

The cover was a melodramatic bedroom scene that depicted a beautiful woman in a diaphanous nightgown clinging to the arm of a villainous-looking American armed with a very large revolver. The body of a gentleman was sprawled on the floor, his throat slashed. The title said it all:

THE FULBROOK MURDER

**Lady Fulbrook Driven Mad by Illicit Tryst
with American Crime Lord! Conspiracy!
Poison! Scandal!**

Ursula paged quickly through the magazine, checking for other illustrations. "If I find my name or the name of my agency in this article, Mr. Otford, I vow—"

"Calm yourself, madam." Otford flapped a napkin in Ursula's direction and spoke around a mouthful of cake. "I assure you that you are not referenced anywhere in the magazine. Neither is anyone else in this room. Per Mr. Roxton's instructions, I gave full credit to Scotland Yard."

"If Lady Fulbrook is committed to an asylum, what will happen to the Fulbrook estate?" Lilly asked.

"I suspect that heirs and potential heirs on both sides of the family are currently marshaling their forces—specifically their lawyers—to do battle over the fortune," Slater said.

"What of the ambrosia plants?" Ursula asked.

Slater stirred and pushed himself away from the

wall. He wandered across the room to contemplate the items on the tea tray.

"As it happens, there was a fire in the Fulbrook conservatory last night. It started in the stillroom, where a number of chemicals were stored. Evidently everything, including the plants in the special chamber reserved for the ambrosia, was destroyed."

"Huh." Otford stopped eating and pulled out his notebook.

Ursula watched Slater. "There may be other ambrosia plants out there, somewhere. And packets of seeds, as well."

Slater shrugged and selected a sandwich. "Perhaps someone will discover something useful to do with the plant. It is not as if we do not need better medicines."

"Well, there is that, I suppose," Ursula said. "Now, then, no doubt you are all wondering why I asked you to tea today."

Everyone looked at her.

Lilly frowned. "There is a reason? Besides tea, that is?"

"Yes, there is a reason." Ursula picked up the silver card case on the coffee table. "I called you together to announce that Slater is about to embark on a new career."

Slater coughed and sputtered around a bite of sandwich. "What?"

"This tea is a celebration of his new profession, and I am delighted to make him a present of his first business cards." She selected one of the crisp white cards and held it up so that everyone could admire the elegant engraving.

"Let me see that." Slater crossed the room in two long strides and snapped the card out of Ursula's fingers. *"Slater Roxton, Private Inquiries. Discretion Assured."* He looked up. "What the devil?"

There were startled gasps from everyone else in the room. The gasps were followed by murmurs of approval.

"Yes, of course," Lilly said. She was suddenly radiant with enthusiasm. "It's the perfect career for you, Slater. I should have thought of it, myself."

Slater stared at Ursula with the expression of a man who had been shaken to the core. "Business cards?"

"Perhaps I can be of assistance to you in your new line," Otford suggested eagerly. "You'll need a man who knows how to dig up information. In exchange for exclusive stories like the Fulbrook murder, I offer my investigative services."

"People got killed," Slater said.

Otford cleared his throat. "Right. Murdered. Very unfortunate."

"The important thing to remember," Ursula said, "is that additional people would very likely have been murdered and others would have been forced to submit to the misery of blackmail if it had not been for Slater's inquiries."

Slater rounded the coffee table, leaned down,

wrapped his hands around Ursula's waist and lifted her off the sofa. He held her so that her satin slippers did not touch the carpet.

"What in blazes do you think you're doing, woman?" His voice reverberated dangerously around the room. "I'm not going into the private inquiry business."

"You need a career, Slater," she said. She braced her hands on his shoulders and looked down at him. "Your days of wandering the world chasing lost artifacts are concluded. You are home now and you must find something new to do with your life. It is time you put your skills to work."

"What skills?"

"You know how to look for answers. That is a surprisingly uncommon talent. Searching for answers is what private inquiry agents do. Really, it's what you've been doing for years. Now you've got the business cards to go with the business, so to speak."

He set her slowly on her feet. "Never thought of it as a profession."

"Furthermore, I may be able to assist you from time to time," she continued. "As a secretary, I can go into a great many places without arousing curiosity or suspicion—business establishments, private homes, almost anywhere, really. Who doesn't need a secretary from time to time?"

"No." Slater eyed her with steely determination. "Absolutely not. I forbid it."

"We can discuss the details later," she assured him.

"There will be nothing to discuss," he said.

She sat down quickly and picked up the pot. "More coffee?"

"Damn it, Ursula—"

"Perhaps another sandwich." She nudged the silver tray across the coffee table.

"Damn it, Ursula—"

"I believe you are repeating yourself. Try the chicken salad sandwiches. They're excellent. Oh, I do apologize. You're a vegetarian. The cucumber, perhaps? And by the way, I do love you, you know."

He looked at her as if he had never seen anything like her in his entire life, as if he were afraid to believe she was real.

"What did you say?" he got out.

"About the chicken salad sandwiches?"

They might as well have been alone in the room, she thought. No one else moved. No one spoke a word.

"About loving me," Slater said.

"You obviously heard me. You seem surprised. I would have thought that you would have learned that much from your labyrinth."

"I have been afraid to ask the question. Terrified, as a matter of fact. I was afraid the answer might not be the one I wanted to hear."

Ursula looked at Lilly and Otford. "Would you mind giving us a few minutes alone while we clear up some rather personal matters?"

Lilly shot to her feet. "Not at all, dear. Take your time."

She swept across the room to the door. Otford hurried after her.

Ursula faced Slater across the low coffee table.

"You, sir?" she said. "Afraid of answers? Forgive me, but I find that difficult to believe."

"Believe it."

"Perhaps it's just as well you did not seek the answer in your labyrinth," she said. "Some things must be done face-to-face."

He smiled. It was one of the rare smiles that banished the darkness from his eyes. He reached for her hand. She gave it to him. He drew her out from behind the coffee table.

"I knew the day I met you that you were the one I would love," he said.

It was her turn to be stunned. "Did you?"

"Why the devil do you think I employed you to assist me with cataloging those damned artifacts? I have no interest in them. As far as I'm concerned, the British Museum is welcome to haul away the whole lot. All I cared about was finding an excuse to keep you near me."

Joy rushed through her. She was suddenly weightless.

"You hired me because you were in love with me?" she whispered. "And to think that you tried to tell me that you were not a romantic man."

"Some answers are inescapable," he said. "You are one of them."

She smiled. "Do you think that will be a problem for you?"

"More in the nature of an amazing discovery. It occurs to me that in this case, one question leads to another."

"What is that?"

He smiled his slow, deep smile—the smile that revealed the truths and the passions that smoldered inside him. He framed her face in his powerful hands.

"Will you marry me, my love?"

"Are you quite sure you don't want to walk your labyrinth first with that one?"

"Your answer is the only one that matters," Slater said.

"The answer is yes."

She could have sworn that she glimpsed the glitter of tears in his eyes. Alarmed, she tried to step back.

"Slater?" she whispered.

"That was the answer I needed to hear," he said. He looked very satisfied. "So, once again I find myself taking the third path."

"What is that supposed to mean?"

"That day on Fever Island when I found myself entombed, I realized I had a choice of three paths. There was the Path of War and the Path of Vengeance. I chose the third path."

"What was it?" Ursula asked.

"The Path of the Lovers."

She smiled, gripped the lapels of his coat and stood on tiptoe to brush her mouth against his.

"What made you choose that Path of the Lovers?" she asked.

"It was," Slater said, "the only one that seemed to offer hope."

He wrapped her close. His mouth came down on hers and she gave herself up to his kiss and the future.

Keep reading for an excerpt from
the next book by Amanda Quick

'TIL DEATH DO US PART

Available now from Jove

S he belonged to him.

He was locked inside a cage the size and shape of a coffin. A dark thrill heated his blood like a powerful, intoxicating drug.

When the time came he would purify the woman and cleanse himself with her blood. But tonight was not the time. The ritual had to be followed correctly. It was a crucial part of the sacrament. She must be made to comprehend and acknowledge the great wrong that she had done. There was no finer instructor than fear.

He huddled inside the concealed lift, listening to the sounds of someone moving about in the bedroom on the other side of the wooden wall panel.

He peered through the narrow crack in the paneling. Excitement sparked when he caught a glimpse of the woman. She was at her dressing table, adjusting the pins in her deep brown hair. It was as if she knew he was watching and was deliberately taunting him.

She was passable in appearance but he had seen her on the street and had not been particularly impressed with her looks. She was overly tall for a woman and her forceful character was etched onto her face. She was dangerous. It was all there in her unnerving eyes.

No wonder he had been sent to purify her. He would save her from herself.

She was not the first woman he had saved. Perhaps this time he would finally be cleansed.

The lift had been installed inside the thick walls of the old mansion for the purpose of conveying an elderly, infirm lady from one floor to another. But the woman had died a few years ago, leaving the big house to her granddaughter and grandson. He had been told that neither of them made use of the device. Having been locked inside the cage for what felt like an eternity, he understood why. The air was close and still, and the darkness was almost as absolute as that of the grave.

The woman rose from the dressing table and moved out of sight.

He was free to descend in the lift at any time. It was operated by an arrangement of ropes and pulleys that could be controlled from either inside or outside the compartment.

He'd had a helpful chat with one of the many tradesmen who came and went from the mansion on the days when the woman held her salons. The man had informed him of the usefulness of the lift for conveying heavy items between floors. He had also mentioned that the woman and her brother never used the lift. Evidently the woman had a fear of being trapped inside the cage.

He heard the muffled sound of the bedroom door opening and closing. And then silence.

He slid the cage door aside and opened the wooden panel. The wall sconce had been turned down quite low but he could make out the bed, the dressing table and the wardrobe.

He moved out of the lift. The heady exhilaration he always experienced at such moments roared through him. With every step of the ritual he came closer to achieving his own purification.

For a precious few seconds he debated where to leave his gift. The bed or the dressing table?

The bed, he decided. So much more intimate.

He crossed the room, not concerned about the soft thud of his footsteps. The guests were gathering in the library on the ground floor. Voices were raised in conversation and someone was playing a piano to entertain the crowd. No one would hear him.

When he reached the bed he took the velvet pouch out of the pocket of his overcoat and removed the black jet ring. A fashionable item of memento mori jewelry, the stone was engraved with the image of a skull. The woman's initials were painted in gilt on the black enameled sides—C. L. When the time came a small twist of her hair would be tucked into the locket concealed beneath the skull stone.

He slipped the ring back into the pouch and placed the gift on the pillow where she could not fail to notice it.

He stood still for a moment, savoring the intense intimacy of the experience. He was in her most personal space: the room where she slept; the room where she believed herself to be alone; the room where she felt safe.

That sense of safety would soon be destroyed. She belonged to him. She simply did not know it; not yet.

He started to go back to the concealed lift but paused when he saw the framed photograph on the wall. It showed the woman as she had been some ten years earlier, a girl of sixteen or seventeen. She stood on the brink of womanhood, still innocent and unknowing, but already there was something disturbing about her eyes.

Her brother was also in the picture. He appeared to be about nine or ten years of age. The two adults in the photograph were no doubt the children's parents. He could see something of the man in the boy.

He took the picture down from the hook and hurried to the lift. Stepping inside, he closed the panel and then the cage door. Darkness as deep as the black jet stone in the ring enveloped him. He dared not light a candle.

He groped for the cables and breathed a sigh of relief when they worked. He lowered the lift to the ground floor.

When he emerged he found himself back in the small antechamber behind the rear stairs. There was no one about. The elderly housekeeper and her equally aged husband, the butler, were busy with the social gathering in the library.

In the old days, when the mansion had housed a large family and a dozen or more servants, it would have been nearly impossible to slip in and out of the place unseen. But now there was only the woman, her brother, and the old housekeeper and butler in residence.

He made his way out through the tradesmen's entrance. A moment later he was lost in the fog. Once he was safely in a hansom he allowed himself to sit back and reflect on the satisfaction of his night's work.

The woman with the unnerving eyes would soon understand that she belonged to him. It was her destiny to be the one to cleanse him. The connection between them was a bond that could be shattered only by death.

Ready to find
your next great read?

Let us help.

Visit prh.com/nextread

Penguin
Random
House